THE LO

Edited by S. T. Joshi   No. 13 (2019)

Contents

The Lovecraftian Solar System Fred S. Lubnow	3
"Hungry fer Victuals I Couldn't Raise nor Buy": Anthropophagy in Lovecraft Duncan Norris	27
The Rings of Cthulhu: Lovecraft, Dürer, Saturn, and Melancholy Andrew Paul Wood	53
"The Cats": An Environmental Ditty Cecelia Hopkins-Drewer	69
Lovecraft's Consolation Matthew Beach	75
"The Inability of the Human Mind": Lovecraft, Zunshine, and Theory of Mind Dylan Henderson	91
H. P. Lovecraft's "Sunset" H. P. Lovecraft and S. T. Joshi	102
The Pathos in the Mythos Ann McCarthy	111
"Now Will You Be Good?": Lovecraft, Teetotalism, and Philosophy Jan B. W. Pedersen	119
Lovecraft's Open Boat Michael D. Miller	145
Lovecraft Seeks the Garden of Eratosthenes Horace A. Smith	153
Diabolists and Decadents: H. P. Lovecraft as Purveyor, Indulger, and Appraiser of Puritan Horror Fiction Psychohistory Scott Meyer	175
Aquaman and Lovecraft: An Unlikely Mating Duncan Norris	189

How to Read Lovecraft 204
    A Column by Steven J. Mariconda
Reviews 215
Briefly Noted 101, 118

Abbreviations used in the text and notes:

AT	*The Ancient Track* (Hippocampus Press, 2013)
CE	*Collected Essays* (Hippocampus Press, 2004–06; 5 vols.)
CF	*Collected Fiction* (Hippocampus Press; 2015–17; 4 vols.)
IAP	*I Am Providence: The Life and Times of H. P. Lovecraft* (Hippocampus Press, 2010; 2013 [paper])
LL	*Lovecraft's Library: A Catalogue*, 4th rev. ed. (Hippocampus Press, 2017)
SL	*Selected Letters* (Arkham House, 1965–76; 5 vols.)

Copyright © 2019 by Hippocampus Press
Published by Hippocampus Press, P.O. Box 641, New York, NY 10156
www.hippocampuspress.com

Cover illustration by Allen Koszowski. Hippocampus Press logo designed by Anastasia Damianakos. Cover design by Barbara Briggs Silbert.

Lovecraft material is used by permission of The Estate of H. P. Lovecraft; Lovecraft Holdings, LLC.

Lovecraft Annual is published once a year, in Fall. Articles and letters should be sent to the editor, S. T. Joshi, % Hippocampus Press, and must be accompanied by a self-addressed stamped envelope if return is desired. All reviews are assigned. Literary rights for articles and reviews will reside with *Lovecraft Annual* for one year after publication, whereupon they will revert to their respective authors. Payment is in contributor's copies.

ISSN 1935-6102
ISBN 978-1-61498-284-5

The Lovecraftian Solar System

Fred S. Lubnow

"Such is the Solar System as it may be seen by all."—H. P. Lovecraft

H. P. Lovecraft had a lifelong love for science. As a boy, this love focused on chemistry but as a young teenager this love, almost obsession, shifted to the subject of astronomy. It was in the winter of 1902–03 that the universe first opened up to Lovecraft. What triggered this interest in astronomy was Lovecraft's finding of an old book on the subject in his grandmother's attic followed by the purchase of his first telescope (Joshi, *IAP* 84). Indeed, Lovecraft also vividly remembers the first new book on astronomy he purchased—Young's *Lessons in Astronomy* (Livesey 86). Additionally, Lovecraft confessed that his initial exploration of the cosmos largely "ignored the abysses of space" and that his interests largely focused on the solar system. More specifically, as S. T. Joshi notes in *Lovecraft and a World in Transition*, Lovecraft's early astronomical interests were mostly confined to the moon and Venus as well as the possible habitability of some of the other planets (233).

Lovecraft's discovery and subsequent appreciation of astronomy was so strong that he published a large number of articles on astronomy from 1906 to 1918. While the subject of each article varied considerably, a large number of them focused on the location of the various planets and constellations in the night sky in particular months. For example, from 2 August 1903 to 31 January 1904 he wrote weekly articles on astronomy for his periodical, the *Rhode Island Journal of Astronomy*. Each issue would include columns, features and astronomical charts, as well as a few advertisements.

In the 1 November 1903 issue of the *Journal*, Lovecraft documented his visit to the Ladd Observatory, operated by Brown

University, where a friend of the family, Professor Winslow Upton, gave him access to the telescope. During a subsequent visit to the Observatory on 31 October 1903 Lovecraft correctly found a problem with the telescope and stated: "The telescope is a 12 in. equatorial, but does not perform in the manner that a glass of its size should. Chromatic aberration is the principal defect. Every lunar crater and every bright object is surrounded by a violet halo" (Joshi, *IAP* 89).

Lovecraft made these observations when he was thirteen years old and was not attending school at the time. Thus, he clearly had a passionate interest in astronomy. However, astronomy did have its hazards for young Lovecraft. He noted that the perpetual craning of his neck to peer through the telescope was painful and "resulted in a permanent curvature perceptible today to a closer observer" (Joshi, *IAP* 88).

Some of Lovecraft's most detailed investigations and discussions on the solar system were generated as a series of articles for the *Asheville* [N.C.] *Gazette-News* from February to May 1915. In these articles Lovecraft systematically reviewed various aspects of astronomy, including discussions on the sun, the planets, comets and meteors, stars, clusters and nebulae, the constellations, and the use of telescopes. The majority of these articles can be found in *Collected Essays, Volume 3: Science*, edited by S. T. Joshi. As noted by Joshi, while these articles are "dry and undistinguished," Lovecraft would gradually introduce larger concepts such as the nebular hypothesis and entropy (*IAP* 194). It is quite obvious that many of these more cosmological concepts would eventually permeate into Lovecraft's weird fiction.

Arguably, one of Lovecraft's first "cosmic" tales was "Beyond the Wall of Sleep," written in 1919. Toward the end of that tale there is the discovery of a new star not very far from Algol, which becomes very bright and then fades in about one to two weeks. In the story, this documentation of a supernova is directly associated with a cosmic battle between the Daemon-Star Algol and an extraterrestrial entity that possesses a resident of the Catskill Mountains of New York by the name of Joe Slater. The identified supernova in the tale appears to originate from a textbook Lovecraft had in his library, *Astronomy with the Naked Eye* (1908) by

Garrett P. Serviss. Lovecraft's tale concludes with some cosmic concepts such as our entire solar system being swept away sometime in the distance future. This would not be the only instance where Lovecraft's pessimistic cosmic philosophy would see our entire world as well as our entire solar system in danger.

Indeed, Lovecraft's astronomical observations and subsequent articles were key components in the development of his philosophy of cosmic, mechanistic materialism. Lovecraft would tap into this philosophy in the evolution of his weird tales, which would go on to make him what Fritz Leiber would call a "literary Copernicus" of the early twentieth century. A key component of Lovecraft's interest in astronomy was associated with the solar system and, in turn, the possibility of the existence of life on the other planets. Some of his earliest observations of the heavens with a telescope focused on the moon and Venus, largely due to the potential for both our satellite and the second planet of the solar system to harbor life.

Life Beyond Earth in the Lovecraftian Solar System

While Lovecraft was interested and excited about the possibility of life on other planets or satellites, his perspective on the matter was very objective and scientific. Some brilliant examples of this are Lovecraft's articles on the moon. In his article "My Opinion as to the Lunar Canals," Lovecraft cites and largely discredits Harvard Professor W. H. Pickering's "theory" that the dark canals and bright rays radiating from principal craters may be streaks of vegetation. Lovecraft's conclusion is based on the fact that our moon does not have water or an atmosphere, "the two essentials for life either animal or vegetable" (CE 3.15).

Lovecraft's opinion of the possibility of life on the moon changed in 1906 when he wrote the article "Is There Life on the Moon?" While the absence of an atmosphere and the temperature extremes make the possibility of life on the moon unlikely, Lovecraft noted some more recent observations of bright "lunar rays" that may indicate the presence of snow, calling it a hoar frost. Additionally, as previously identified in *Collected Essays*, Professor Pickering identified small, dark streaks in some of the craters that change from time to time and concluded that this indicates the present of low forms of vegetation. Lovecraft concludes that based on this evidence, while the moon does not contain "high or animal life, [it] is yet not wholly dead" (*CE* 3.27). However, by 1915 Lovecraft described the moon as a dead world, and while he again cites Professor Pickering's hypothesis of the presence of low-lying vegetation on the moon, his enthusiasm for the possibility of life on the moon appears to be gone. Such changes in the opinion on scientific matters over the years by Lovecraft has been well documented in his writing on other subjects (e.g., Einstein's theory of relativity) and is always based on information available at the time. The ability to change or modify one's thoughts or ideas on a subject based on the available information is an important trait of an objective scientist, and Lovecraft certainly exhibited this, particularly in regard to the subject of possible life in the solar system.

Unlike his thoughts on the moon, Lovecraft never thought highly of the hypothesis of life on Mars. He stated, "As to animal life on Mars, we may say only that there is as yet no good proof either of its existence or of its absence" (*CE* 3.103). Lovecraft even states at one point that while Professor Percival Lowell's hypothesis of intelligent life on Mars is untenable, this should not tarnish Lowell's place in history as a competent observational astronomer. For Lovecraft, the bottom line of life on Mars is that it appeared to be a cold, dead world, particularly when compared to Venus. As he described in an April 1916 column in the Providence *Evening News*:

> Speculation concerning the inhabitants of other worlds is always fruitless, but in view of popular and extended discussions about possible intelligent life on Mars, it seems excusable to indulge in similar discussion regarding Venus, whose conditions are certainly better adapted to the maintenance of life than are those of the small and frigid Mars. (*CE* 3.180)

Lovecraft always thought our sister world was a better candidate for extraterrestrial life than Mars, given its size (similar to that of Earth) and cloud cover. Imagine Lovecraft's surprise if he knew what we know now regarding Venus and Mars. Venus, with crushing pressures, has some of the hottest temperatures found in the solar system. Astrophysicist Neil deGrasse Tyson, director of the Hayden Planetarium, is frequently quoted as stating that it would take nine seconds to cook a pepperoni pizza on the surface of Venus. In contrast, the presence of large deposits of water-ice as well as biomediated silica structures (stromatolites) on Mars provide some tantalizing evidence for the presence of at least microbial life at one point existing on the red planet.

While the golden age of science fiction populated every world in our solar system with humanlike aliens, science was just beginning to reveal the solar system as a dull, lifeless place full of rock and gas. However, as humans have sent probes, spacecraft, and robots throughout the solar system from the latter half of the twentieth century up to the present, we have learned much more about the planets and their satellites. The physical and chemical dynamics of these worlds are far more complex than just balls of rock and gas. The possibility of life on Mars (past or present), Europa (a moon of Jupiter), Titan or Enceladus (moons of Saturn), or even under the surface of the dwarf-planet of Pluto are real possibilities worth exploring. I am sure such information would have pleasantly surprised Lovecraft, who once said, "To us, and to all who may inhabit any of the planets of the solar system; light, heat, and vegetation, in short, life itself may be considered as emanating from but one tremendous source—the sun" (*CE* 3.280).

While light is critical for the majority of life on Earth, it may not be absolutely necessary for life on other worlds or moons, particularly if that life exists under the surface. The key to extraterrestrial life, at least in our solar system, is liquid water and possibly liquid hydrocarbons such as methane. This is the one required need for life on Earth that Lovecraft did not mention in the article just cited. However, in the early twentieth century no one would have thought of alien life living in a sub-surface sea on the moon of a gas giant.

While Lovecraft held a scientific and critical eye on any information presented on the possibility of extraterrestrial life, he never gave up the hope and possibility for the existence of life on other planets or moons. He also thought that this life might be far more complex and very different from us. In a letter dated August 1916 he stated: "Perhaps the most dominant creature—the most rational and God-like of all beings—is an invisible gas!" (cited Joshi, *IAP* 274). However, Lovecraft also thought that "[h]uman life and the solar system itself are the merest novelties in an eternal cosmos" (*IAP* 323).

In conclusion, the rest of this paper is a short "tour" of the planets (and one dwarf-planet) in the Lovecraftian solar system through the eyes of an early twenty-first-century observer. The various spacecraft, probes, robots, and telescopes the human species have used to date to understand our neighborhood of the universe are, in a sense, the brain jars of the Mi-Go, sailing through our part of the cosmos. These endeavors are accomplishing exactly what Albert N. Wilmarth pondered in Lovecraft's "The Whisperer in Darkness" when he considered the Mi-Go brain jar and said, "To shake off the maddening and wearying limitation of time and space and natural law—to be linked with the vast *outside*—" (*CF* 2.505). I would like to think that Lovecraft would have been absolutely amazed with what we know about the solar system to date—just imagine the tales he would have told!

Mercury

"In the early evening, whilst the twilight yet remains, we may often behold near the western horizon, just above the sunset points, a sparkling speck of ruddy or pinkish light, brilliant after a fashion, yet withal elusive to the untrained eye" (*CE* 3.282). This is how Lovecraft described Mercury, the smallest planet in the Lovecraftian solar system, which is only a little larger than our moon. Mercury is the closest planet to our sun, with an eccentric orbit that varies from 47 million kilometers (29 million miles) to 70 million kilometers (43 million miles) away from the sun. For reference, the Earth is 146 million kilometers (93 million miles) from the sun.

In Lovecraft's day, some thought that Mercury's time of rotation was similar to Earth's, so that one day would be equal to 24 hours. Others, including Lovecraft, hypothesized that Mercury rotated on its axis once during its revolution around the sun, resulting in half of the world facing the sun while the other half was in continuous darkness. In turn, Lovecraft thought that the range in temperature on Mercury must be extremely large and the potential for life on that world was very unlikely.

As identified numerous times in his articles on astronomy, the best time to see Mercury is in the early evening hours of the spring or the early morning hours of the fall. Originally, the ancients thought this planet was two distinct celestial bodies; the "morning star" was named Apollo while the "evening star" was named Mercury. Lovecraft also identified the difficulty in finding this planet in the heavens and noted that Copernicus was never able to observe this planet in his lifetime (*CE* 3.282).

While Lovecraft believed that it was very unlikely that life existed on Mercury, this did not stop him from incorporating Mercury as a "habitable" world in his stories. Specifically, in "The Shadow out of Time" it was mentioned that in our distant future, after human civilization, the Yithians would transfer their minds from the cone-shaped beings into an advanced race of beetles. Later, after the eventual destruction of Earth, the minds would then again migrate through time and space into the bodies of the bulbous vegetable entities of Mercury. Since the Yithians could travel both time and space, it is not known if the vegetable entities live in our distant past or distant future. More than likely they traveled into the distant past, since in the distant future our sun will only increase in size. Approximately 5 billion years in the future our sun will expand in size, turning into a red giant as it begins to burn helium instead of hydrogen. As our sun increases in size it will eventually consume Mercury, Venus, and Earth, so it would make more sense for the bulbous vegetable entities to exist sometime in the past rather than the distant future.

Other than their existence, very little is known about the bulbous vegetable entities (BVEs) of Mercury, at least in the writings of Lovecraft. For example, with a 1,000 degrees Fahrenheit (over 600 degrees Celsius) difference between night and day on Mercury, what form of "vegetable" life could have survived on this world, even in the past? One of two hypotheses are suggested. First, the BVEs may have existed underground, buried in the Mercurian soil, where such variations in temperature may not be as large. The second hypothesis is that, given the very slow rotation of the planet, perhaps the BVEs were in a perpetual mode of migration, continually moving to stay within the twilight of Mercury. Twilight is typically described, at least on Earth, as when the sun is 6 degrees below the horizon before sunrise (dawn) and after sunset (dusk). While no data are currently available on this, more than likely the temperature variation within the twilight zone would be substantially smaller than conditions of full day and night on Mercury.

Remaining within the twilight zone on Mercury may be possible if you can keep up with the rotational speed of the planet, which is not that fast. A full day on Mercury is about 58.6 Earth days, so its rotational speed at its equator is 10.9 km/hr or about 6.8 mph. For the sake of comparison, the rotational speed for Earth at its equator is about 1,600 km/hr or 1,000 miles per hour. If the BVEs' growth pattern is similar to that of a fungal mycelium, these creatures may have planet-wide filaments covering Mercury with actively growing tissues only found in the twilight zone, constantly migrating at a speed of a little under 7 mph.

There is another connection between Lovecraft and the planet Mercury. In March 2011 the NASA MESSENGER (which stands for Mercury Surface, Space Environment, Geochemistry and Ranging) robotic spacecraft arrived at Mercury, established an orbit, and initiated a planetary survey. On 26 March 2013, the Science Team working on the MESSENGER project received approval by the International Astronomical Union (IAU) to name nine craters on Mercury for a variety of renowned artists, musicians, and authors; and one of those was H. P. Lovecraft. At the August 2013 NecronomiCon Conference, Dr. Rachel Klima gave an informative presentation on the Lovecraft Crater and on Mercury in general. The Lovecraft Crater is a small, dark crater immediately adjacent to a larger, well-lit crater named after the Russian painter Nicholas Roerich. Naming these two craters after Lovecraft and Roerich seems very appropriate, since some of Roerich's artwork provided inspiration for Lovecraft's development of *At the Mountains of Madness*. More than likely Lovecraft would have been pleasantly surprised, stunned, appreciative, and a little embarrassed that such a unique and strange part of our solar system was named after him. The Lovecraft Crater is permanently shrouded in darkness and contains radar-bright material. Similar material has been identified at the north pole of Mercury and is typically associated with water ice and an unusual dark material. Is there something lurking in the darkness of Lovecraft's Crater? Perhaps someday robotic probes from Earth will land in Lovecraft Crater on Mercury and actually sample this unusual dark material. Then we may truly know what lurks in the darkness of the world closest to the sun.

Venus

"As a morning and evening star it [Venus] was thought by the ancients to be two distinct bodies; Phosphorus, the light bearer, as a morning star, and Hesperus in the evening" (*CE* 3.283). As described by Lovecraft, Venus has been an object of admiration throughout human history. Venus is the brightest starlike object in the heavens and can occasionally be glimpsed during the day and can even cast a shadow at night.

Venus is the second closest planet to our sun, being 106 million kilometers (66 million miles) from our local star. In addition, Venus comes closest to the Earth than any other planet; at its closest approach, it comes within 24 million miles to Earth (Sobel 51). In Lovecraft's time a Venusian day was thought to be very close to that of Earth—23 days and 21 minutes (*CE* 3.283). Instead, we now know that a Venusian day is approximately 243 Earth days, while a year for Venus (the time it takes that planet to revolve once around the sun) is estimated to be 224 Earth days. Thus, a Venusian day is a little longer than a Venusian year (Rothery 9). Another interesting fact on Venus is that it is the only planet in the inner Solar System that turns backwards, so the sun rises in the west and sets in the east.

In "The Shadow out of Time," when Nathaniel Wingate Peaslee's mind inhabits one of the cone-shaped beings (known as the Great Race), he learns of a number of entities that populate Earth and the solar system. In Peaslee's studies Lovecraft briefly mentions "a mind from the planet we know as Venus, which would live incalculable epochs to come" (*CF* 3.398). Nothing else is mentioned of Venus in "The Shadow out of Time" after this reference.

While previous stories include fairly brief references to Venus, the story "In the Walls of Eryx" (1936), which Lovecraft co-wrote with Kenneth Sterling, occurs entirely on Venus. Here Lovecraft and Sterling described and documented a completely alien ecosystem.

As described by Lovecraft and Sterling, Venus is a wet world covered in jungles, harboring leathery and tough vines as well as soft, rubbery vegetation. Although Venus is populated with large amounts of apparently photosynthetic organisms, there is still an insufficient amount of oxygen to sustain human life, which is why oxygen masks are required. While the Venusian plants may be producing oxygen, the atmospheric concentrations may be lower than those produced on Earth. However, this inability to breathe on Lovecraft's Venus may be primarily due to extremely high concentrations of carbon dioxide, which appear to be a result of the very high amounts of organic decomposition of the resident biomass as well as the extensive volcanic activity. Indeed, Venus is known to have more volcanos than any other planet in the solar system. It was noted that there are more than 1,000 volcanic structures, and the concentration of carbon dioxide in Venus's atmosphere is 90 times greater than on Earth (Sobel 60).

In addition to high concentrations of carbon dioxide, it is also mentioned that concentrations of cyanogen were high enough to kill a person on Lovecraftian Venus. Cyanogen is a colorless, toxic gas composed of two carbon atoms and two nitrogen atoms. As early as 1868 the astronomer William Huggins identified through spectroscopic analyses that the tail of Halley's Comet contains a variety of organic compounds included cyanogen. Since this compound is highly toxic, many people panicked as the comet approached the Earth in 1910, as our world was going to pass through the comet's tail. However, as documented in Carl Sagan's *Cosmos*, what many people did not understand at the time was that the tail of the comet contained such a diffuse amount of cyanogen that there was absolutely no health risk to the people of Earth (Sagan 80). In an article for the *Pawtuxet Valley Gleaner*, published on 16 November 1906, Lovecraft noted the upcoming return of Halley's Comet in 1910 (CE 3.299), and while there was no mention of cyanogen, Lovecraft and/or Sterling may have transferred the dangers of this toxic compound from the tail of Halley's Comet to the atmosphere of Venus.

To breathe on Venus, humans need to put chlorate cubes into their breathing masks. This technology is based on chemical oxygen generators, which were developed in the early twentieth century for firefighters and miners. Lovecraft and Sterling were certainly integrating cutting-edge 1930s technology into the tale. However, in contrast to the chemical oxygen generators, the origins of some of the other technology discussed in "In the Walls of Eryx" are more difficult to pinpoint, such as N-force barriers, lacol tablets (which function as a water substitute), and the weapons called D-radiation cylinders. Still, as with many of his other stories, Lovecraft made a serious effort to include the most up-to-date science and technology in this collaborated tale.

Mars

In an article Lovecraft wrote about the planet Mars, titled "The Truth about Mars" (1917), he concluded: "In these days, when our planet is so convulsed with the absurd hostilities of the insignificant denizens, it is calming to turn to the vast ethereal blue and behold other worlds, each with its unique and picturesque phenomena, where no echo of terrestrial strife or woe can resound" (*CE* 3.320).

Mars is about half (53%) the size of Earth. However, unlike the moonlike topography of Mercury or the cloud-shrouded mystery that is Venus, Mars in many respects is Earthlike. The Martian day is 24.6 hours (Rothery 9) and the planet itself is tilted on its axis by 25%, while Earth is tilted by 23.5%. This tilt is the reason why both planets experience seasons. Since the Martian year is 687 Earth days long, these seasons are considerably longer than Earth seasons. Mars is 227.9 kilometers (141.6 million miles) from the sun. Thus, if the Earth is 1.0 astronomical unit (AU) from the sun, then Mars is roughly 1.52 AU from the sun.

Percival Lawrence Lowell's suggestion that the canals transported water from the poles to an advance, yet dying, civilization was first proposed in 1896. Lovecraft responded to this incredible hypothesis in an article written in September 1906 called "Is Mars an Inhabited World?" with the subtitle "Startling Theories of Prof. Lowell on the Subject" (*CE* 3.24–25). In the article, Lovecraft reviews ideas of life on Mars prior to Lowell's hypothesis. He also critically and objectively reviews Lowell's hypothesis stating, "Lowell's theory when analysed, not only possible, but even probable. Still, we must not be too hasty in crediting it, as ignorance is better than false knowledge" (*CE* 3.25). Lovecraft also suggested that Martians would look very different from us due to the planet's lower temperature, thinner atmosphere, and lower gravity, about a third of the Earth's.

Lovecraft also mentioned Lowell and his ideas on Mars in a number of later essays, and in typical Lovecraftian fashion he continued to hold an objective view of them. For example, in a couple of essays titled "Mars and the Asteroids" and "The Truth about Mars," he mentioned that the true nature of the canals and spots on Mars is a matter of great dispute. In both articles, Lovecraft discusses Lowell's wild hypothesis on Mars and its "dying alien civilization"; however, in the later article he states, when referring to Lowell's idea of a Martian civilization:

> How baseless as most of these speculations may be, and probably are, it is nevertheless not impossible that LIVING BEINGS OF SOME SORT MAY DWELL UPON THE SURFACE OF MARS. It is, however, left to the imagination of the reader or of the ingenious novelist to portray their appearance, size, intelligence, and habits. (*CE* 3.293)

While Lovecraft mentions Mars numerous times in his astronomical essays, he only directly referred to the red planet once in his stories. Specifically, in "Through the Gates of the Silver Key" (co-written with E. Hoffmann Price), as Swami Chandraputra is describing Randolph Carter's travels through time and space, he says that Carter "gazed at the Cyclopean ruins that sprawl over Mars' ruddy disc" (*CF* 3.315).

The largest volcano on Mars, Olympus Mons, is also the solar system's tallest planetary mountain; it is 374 miles in diameter, which is about the size of Arizona. Olympus Mons is 15.5 miles tall, which is almost three times larger than Mount Everest. Olympus Mons was identified and known by astronomers since the nineteenth century. It was one of the few structures on Mars that could be seen during the planet-wide dust storms. Giovanni Schiaparelli first named it Nix Olympica, meaning the snows of Olympus. Later the name was changed to Olympus Mons when it was confirmed that it was a volcano. When Randolph Carter visited the Cyclopean ruins that sprawl over Mars, was Lovecraft referring to Nix Olympica, one of the few features that could be seen on Mars during its dust storms? Given Lovecraft's interest in both astronomy and detail in his stories, that may indeed be the case. However, we may never know the true answer to this question.

Jupiter

When describing Jupiter, Lovecraft stated that, "When at its best, shining resplendently in the eastern sky, it rivals even in Venus in brilliancy, sometimes casting a perceptible shadow" (*CE* 3.294). Jupiter is the first of the gas giants as one moves away from the sun and is the largest planet in our solar system. In fact, Jupiter is so large that it has more mass than all the other planets combined. More than a thousand Earths could "fit" into one Jupiter (Sagan 136). In fact, as more specifically stated by Lovecraft in an article on "The Outer Planets," dated March 1915, Jupiter is more than 1,300 times greater in size than the Earth (*CE* 3.294). Lovecraft frequently called the gas giants the "superior" planets, while he called the small, rocky worlds closer to the sun the "inferior" planets. Indeed, Lovecraft sketched Jupiter and its Great Spot, which can be found in *CE* 3.47.

Jupiter is one of the brightest planets in the sky, second only to Venus. A "Jovian" day is 10 hours long, while a Jovian year is 11.9 Earth years. As stated, the Earth is 1.0 AU away from the sun, while Mars is 1.52 AUs from the sun. In contrast, Jupiter is 5.2 AUs away from the sun, which is 778.6 kilometers (483.8 million miles).

In Lovecraft's day, it was recognized that Jupiter had "little or no solid matter, being a sort of plastic semi-sun" (*CE* 3.295). Indeed, it has been noted that if Jupiter had a little more matter, it could have ignited to become a sun, which would have made our solar system a twin star or binary star system. Thus, if the asteroid belt is a planet that failed to form, then Jupiter is a planet that failed to become a star.

In Lovecraft's time, there was a flurry of activity relative to the discovery of new Jovian moons. From Galileo's time till the late nineteenth century no new moons were discovered orbiting Jupiter. However, in 1892 E. E. Barnard discovered Amalthea. With the use of telescopic photography other moons were soon discovered. Lovecraft documented some of these discoveries in his astronomical articles. For example, in the *Providence Evening News* for 31 October 1914, Lovecraft mentions the discovery of a ninth moon orbiting Jupiter by Seth B. Nicholson earlier that same year (*CE* 3.129). As of 2019, the number of moons discovered orbiting Jupiter is 79.

Lovecraft has frequently cited both Jupiter and its moons in his astronomical writings; in his day beyond the four Galilean satellites, five additional moons were discovered between 1892 and 1914. Regarding the possibility of life existing on any of the Jovian moons, Lovecraft has stated that "Conclusions respecting the habitability of these orbs would be baseless. If they do possess inhabitants, a thing by no means impossible, their astronomers must be fortunate, indeed, for words cannot describe the grandeur with which Jupiter shines in their nocturnal skies" (*CE* 3. 198). However, if there are inhabitants on any of the Jovian moons, they are more than likely under the surface, living in an aquatic environment and would not have the opportunity to gaze into the Jovian skies.

Lovecraft mentions the planet Jupiter in "Through the Gates of the Silver Key." In the same passage where Swami Chandraputra is describing the travels of Randolph Carter and references Mars, he also talks about how he "learned an untellable secret from the close-glimpsed mists of Jupiter" (*CF* 3.315). What strange secrets do the mists of Jupiter hold? Was Randolph Carter talking about the Great Red Spot; is the Spot some vast entity feeding on the hydrogen and helium of Jupiter? Or is the Spot an entity slowly dying, which is why it is shrinking in size?

In "The Shadow out of Time," in the same passage where the protagonist Peaslee mentions a mind that will live on Venus in the distant future, he also talks about "one [mind] from an outer moon of Jupiter six million years in the past" (*CF* 3.398). The two outer moons of the Galilean four are Ganymede and Callisto. Is it possible one of these satellites was a way-station for the Yithians in the transfer of their minds eventually to Earth?

Probably the most intriguing citation of the Jovian system is in Lovecraft's story "Beyond the Wall of Sleep" (1919). In that tale, the entity or mind that possesses Joe Slater talks about his travels through time, space, and dimensions, which includes dwelling in "the bodies of the insect-philosophers that crawl proudly over the fourth moon of Jupiter" (*CF* 1.83). With the ranking of the major Galilean moons previously described, the fourth moon would be Callisto. Thus, do the insect-philosophers crawl over Callisto? Did Joe Slater's trip to the fourth moon of Jupiter to see the insect-philosophers occur millions or even billions of years in the past? Were the insect-philosophers the first sentient entities in our solar system or were they another experimental by-product of the Elder Things?

Whatever lives within the semi-plastic plasma of Jupiter or in the sub-surface oceans of its moons, Lovecraft had a strong affinity for our solar system's largest world. When reporting on what to observe in the night heavens in September 1915 Lovecraft stated, "For the amateur observer with an ordinary telescope the planet [Jupiter] is ever a source of delight, being perhaps the best seen of all celestial bodies save the sun and moon" (*CE* 3.157). As he has noted, if any inhabitant on any of the Jovian moons could look up into their sky, the view must be impressive to say the least.

Saturn

Regarding Saturn, Lovecraft wrote: "We now approach that which is without doubt the most impressive and unique object in the Solar System" (*CE* 3.296). Lovecraft went on to describe Saturn as a golden ball surrounded by three immense flat rings of light that nowhere touch the planet itself. Saturn is the furthest planet visible with the naked eye (Cox and Cohen 69). Given the beauty and mystery associated with Saturn, it is surprising that Lovecraft said very little about this ringed world in his tales.

In Lovecraft's time Saturn was thought to have ten moons, more than any other planet, with five of them being visible with an "ordinary telescope" (*CE* 3.297). Christiaan Huygens discovered Titan in 1655, which is larger than both the planet Mercury and the dwarf-planet Pluto. Giovanni Domenico Cassini discovered four moons between 1671 and 1684, and the astronomer William Herschel discovered two more in 1789. Currently, at least as of 2019, Saturn is known to have 62 moons, some of which actually help to create the rings of Saturn.

The one time where Saturn is explicitly mentioned by Lovecraft is in his novel *The Dream Quest of Unknown Kadath*. Specifically, there is a species of cats that originate from Saturn. The cats of Saturn are apparently substantially larger than Dreamland/Earth cats and are also their natural enemies. It is not known if the cats of Saturn originate from this gaseous world itself or from one of its moons. However, they do frequently visit the dark side of the Dreamlands moon and appear to be in league with the moonbeasts, which are the froglike, tentacle-faced residents of the Dreamlands moon. In addition, the cats of Saturn are one of the few species in the Dreamlands that Earth cats fear. Other than that, very little is known about these Saturnian felines. Given their amorphous and ambiguous nature, as well as their ability to travel from Saturn to the Dreamlands moon, the cats of Saturn may be composed of a sentient form of gas or plasma. If this is the case, then they may be the true residents of Saturn, living somewhere in the planet's large, gaseous atmosphere. However, this is only conjecture and the cats of Saturn may actually reside on one of the moons of Saturn or even originate from outside of our solar system, using Saturn as a temporary outpost in the Dreamlands universe.

Finally, this discussion of Saturn in the Lovecraftian solar system will briefly mention Tsathoggua, an entity that Lovecraft has mentioned frequently in "The Mound" (co-written with Zealia Bishop), "The Whisperer in Darkness," *At the Mountains of Madness*, "The Man of Stone" (co-written with Hazel Heald), "The Horror in the Museum" (co-written with Hazel Heald), "Through the Gates of the Silver Key," "Out of the Aeons" (co-written with Hazel Heald) and "The Shadow out of Time."

While frequently cited by Lovecraft, the entity Tsathoggua was invented by Clark Ashton Smith. According to Smith, Tsathoggua originates from Saturn, which to the inhabitants is called Cykranosh; eventually some unknown entities from the edge of our solar system brought Tsathoggua to ancient Earth (Harms 302). However, according to Smith's tale "The Door to Saturn," a sorcerer of ancient Earth, specifically living in the land of Hyperborea, by the name of Eibon escapes religious persecution by entering an interdimensional portal and going to the planet Cykranosh. This portal was provided to Eibon by Tsathoggua, known on Saturn as Zhothaqquah. The world of Cykranosh looks very different from the gas giant we know as Saturn. Thus, it is hypothesized that the interdimensional portal used by Eibon teleported him not just across space but across universes. The Cykranosh of this universe, possibly the Dreamlands universe, was very alien-looking relative to Earth but still had the appearance a rocky, interior world with rock, vegetation, and weather. Thus, it may be possible that in this alterative solar system Jupiter is not a "failed sun." Instead, in this alternative universe our solar system may be a binary star system of the sun and Jupiter, which may result in Saturn (or in this case Cykranosh) being a smaller rocky world rather than a large gas giant. In any event, according to Lovecraft Tsathoggua lives deep within the Earth; however, he does not explicitly state if this is our Earth or the Dreamlands Earth of another universe.

While Smith had a very clear description of Tsathoggua, Lovecraft's interpretation of this entity was more ambiguous and amorphous. Lovecraft called it "black and formless" or "black and plastic." In "Out of the Aeons," Lovecraft and Heald state that the black amorphous entity Tsathoggua was worshipped in ancient Hyperborea about 200,000 years ago, while in "The Shadow out of Time" a furry, pre-human species was known to worship Tsathoggua. However, Lovecraft makes no reference to Tsathoggua being originally from the planet Saturn or if it was from an entirely different solar system, galaxy, or universe.

Uranus

Regarding the planets Uranus and Neptune, Lovecraft wrote: "Both of these planets are visible as faint stars in opera glasses, yet their study seldom repays the observer" (CE 3.93). Such a statement is not surprising, since in Lovecraft's time very little was known about these two ice giants. Uranus was discovered by British astronomer William Herschel in 1781, who first misidentified it as a comet. It was the first planet identified with a telescope and not observed with the naked eye. As Lovecraft said, it "was the first planet discovered since the dawn of civilisation" (CE 3.191).

A day on Uranus is 17 hours, 14 minutes long, while a "Uranusian" year is 84 Earth years. As stated, the Earth is 1.0 astronomical unit (AU) away from the sun; Uranus is 19.1 AUs from the sun or 2.9 billion kilometers (1.784 billion miles) from the sun. Similar to Venus, Uranus rotates from east to west, which is the opposite direction from the other planets. What is particularly unique to Uranus is that it is tilted on its side, with its axis tilted at angle of 98 degrees. In contrast, the other planets have their axes tilted slightly off the vertical. For example, Earth is tilted by 23.5 degrees, which gives our world its seasons, while Jupiter's tilt is only 3 degrees, resulting in little to no seasonal differences. Tilted on its side, the rings of Uranus are in a vertical position instead of horizontal, like the rest of the outer planet's rings, and the poles are pointing either toward or directly away from the sun (Littmann 134).

Uranus is the third largest planet in the solar system and was discovered by the amateur astronomer William Herschel on 13 March 1781. At the time the idea that there was another planet beyond Saturn was unthinkable. In Lovecraft's time, very little was known about Uranus. Lovecraft mentioned the planet a few times in his astronomical articles. In addition to the quotation cited above, Lovecraft later stated that Uranus was more than likely "a hot and molten semi-sun" (CE 3.297).

Lovecraft made no specific reference to Uranus in any of his tales. There is only a brief mention of the Greek God Uranus (God of the sky) in "Poetry and the Gods," a story Lovecraft co-wrote with Anna Helen Crofts.

When Lovecraft peered through his telescope in the early twentieth century and observed Uranus he saw "a very small disc of greenish hue, destitute of all markings save possibly a faint suggestion of belts like those of Jupiter and Saturn" (CE 3.297). He did not see the 27 moons, the thin set of rings that surround the planet, or the dark and bright spots over the surface of the planet. When Lovecraft wrote his set of articles on the planets in March 1915, he knew of and listed the four major satellites of Uranus: Ariel, Umbriel, Titania, and Oberon. He did describe Uranus as more than likely being a hot and molten semi-sun; in a way, all the gas and ice giants can be described in that manner. Lovecraft also correctly stated that the atmosphere of Uranus was very dense.

In the Lovecraftian solar system who knows what the strange gaseous dark and light spots on Uranus represent? Given how Uranus is "tipped on its side," seasons would be more extreme on this world compared to Earth. The seasons on Earth are produced as a result of its having an axial tilt of 23.5 degrees; however, the tilt for Uranus is 98 degrees! Thus, the appearance and disappearance of the atmospheric spots are more than likely directly related to the seasons. Also, a "year" for Uranus is 84 Earth years, so a season would last decades. A planet tilted to its side means that only a thin strip of the planet experiences any night/day cycle, and the poles alternatively experience 42 years of continuous sunlight and 42 years of continuous darkness.

In the Lovecraftian solar system there may be large, sentient gaseous or plasma-based entities, feeding off the hydrogen, helium, and methane in the upper atmosphere of Uranus. Perhaps these large spots are failed (or successful?) experiments conducted by the Mi-Go or the Elder Things.

Neptune

In a letter Lovecraft wrote to the editor of *Scientific American* in July 1906 he stated, "In these days of large telescopes and modern astronomical methods, it seems strange that no vigorous efforts are being made to discover planets beyond the orbit of Neptune, which is now considered the outermost limit of the solar system" (*CE* 3.16). Lovecraft was elated when the letter was accepted and published in the 25 August 1906 issue of *Scientific American*.

Neptune is the outermost planet of our solar system and is one of the two ice giants (the other being Uranus). While Uranus is slightly larger, Neptune has a slightly greater mass (Littmann 147). It is 4.5 billion kilometers (2.8 billion miles) or 30.07 AU away from the sun. It takes Neptune 165 Earth years to make a complete orbit around the sun; in fact, since its discovery in 1846 Neptune made one complete orbit around the sun in 2011. Interestingly enough, a "day" on Neptune is approximately 16 hours. It is the only planet that can't be seen with the naked eye. Additionally, it is the windiest of all the planets, with storms as large as Earth and reaching speeds has high as 1,600 miles (2,575 kilometers) per hour.

Lovecraft called the discovery of Neptune "one of the most remarkable achievements of astronomical science, being no mere accident, but the result of long and extremely precise calculation" (*CE* 3.134), and he was correct. Before the planet was actually discovered, its existence was theoretically predicted by "reverse calculating" the irregularities in the motion of Uranus. Indeed, applying Newton's calculus and the universal law of gravitation resulted in the discovery of Neptune, simply with pen and paper in 1845, a full year before it was actually observed through a telescope (Sobel 198).

In Lovecraft's time Triton was the only moon identified for Neptune; it was discovered in 1846 by the British astronomer William Lassell, less than a month after Neptune was discovered by Johann Gottfried Galle. It was not until over a century later, in 1949, that a second moon, Nereid, was discovered orbiting Neptune. As of 2019 Neptune has 14 confirmed moons. Triton is the largest moon in the Neptunian system and is the only large moon in the solar system with a retrograde orbit; that is, it orbits Neptune in the opposite direction of its planetary rotation (Littmann 263). Many scientists hypothesize that this indicates that Triton did not form with Neptune but instead was captured by the planet's gravitational field millions of years ago. Additionally, Triton is thought to be a dwarf-planet that originated from the Kuiper Belt.

Unlike Uranus, Lovecraft did mention Neptune in his stories. This planet is cited a number of times in "The Whisperer in Darkness," specifically when he is referring to "the new planet beyond Neptune [that] had not been discovered" (*CF* 2.484). The new planet in the story was Yuggoth, which was then identified as Pluto. Later in the same story Henry Akeley is describing to Albert Wilmarth what beings are in the brain cylinders of the Mi-Go. At one point he states that the jars contain the minds of "Three humans, six fungoid beings who can't navigate space corporeally, and two beings from Neptune (God! if you could see the body this type has on its own planet!), and the rest entities from the central caverns of an especially interesting dark star beyond the galaxy" (*CF* 2.523). After that, the Neptunian beings are never mentioned again.

What does Lovecraft's Neptunian look like? A Neptunian would have to live in a nearly lightless world and frozen environment. As previously mentioned, the weather patterns of Neptune generate some of the highest wind speeds measured in the solar system. That's a lot of energy generated in addition to that generated by the heat and pressure of the world itself. Is it possible that

Neptunians are adapted to using the high winds as a source of energy or harvest material (hydrogen, helium, methane, and possibly ammonia) blown by the winds to live, grow, and/or reproduce?

Lovecraft also referenced Neptune in the story "Through the Gates of the Silver Key," where Swami Chandraputra is describing the travels of Randolph Carter through time and space. In one passage the Swami states that "He [Randolph Carter] saw Kynarth and Yuggoth on the rim, passed close to Neptune and glimpsed the hellish white fungi that spot it" (CF 3.315). What is interesting about this passage is that back in Lovecraft's time very few surface features or details could be observed on Neptune. Lovecraft stated in one of his astronomical articles that while Neptune was greenish in color like Uranus, it was not diversified by any visible markings. In spite of this, in 1932–33 he cited the presence of some white fungi that spotted the planet. During the *Voyager* 2 flyby of Neptune in 1989, a Great Dark Spot was observed in the southern hemisphere, and associated with this was a fast-moving bright feature or smudge called Scooter. Is it possible that Scooter is the white fungi that Lovecraft referred to?

Dwarf-Planet Pluto (also known as Yuggoth)

In the articles Lovecraft wrote on the planets for the *Asheville* [N.C.] *Gazette-News* in March 1915 he stated, "Whether or not there are unknown planets beyond Neptune, is a question still unsettled. In all probability such exist, but that we shall ever discover them is not likely, since the small amount of solar light received by them would scare be enough to make them visible to us" (CE 3.298). Obviously, Lovecraft did not think that technological developments and persistence would lead to the discovery of Pluto (known to many as Yuggoth). Imagine what Lovecraft would have thought of the photographs produced by the Hubble Telescope and the *New Horizons* spacecraft!

Of course, fifteen years after Lovecraft's *Gazette-News* articles, Pluto would be discovered. The minor-planet or dwarf-planet Pluto was discovered by Clyde W. Tombaugh on 18 February 1930. However, the official announcement of its discovery was not made until 14 March 1930 (Joshi and Schultz 320). "The Whisperer in Darkness" was written between 24 February and 26 September

1930, so while the discovery of Pluto did not inspire Lovecraft to begin writing "The Whisperer in Darkness," it obviously had a huge impact on the development of the story. Lovecraft wrote to his friend James F. Morton on 15 March 1930, "Whatcha thinka the NEW PLANET? HOT STUFF!!!" (Joshi, *IAP* 708). Thus, to Lovecraft Pluto became the Mi-Go's outpost called Yuggoth.

For Lovecraft, Yuggoth was originally described as "past the starry voids" in his sonnet series *Fungi from Yuggoth* (*AT* 80). However, it was in "The Whisperer in Darkness" that he identified newly discovered Pluto as Yuggoth, "rolling along in the back aether at the rim" (*CF* 2.487), and attributed this discovery to the mental influences of the Mi-Go. In fact, in "The Whisperer in Darkness" Lovecraft writes that the impostor of Henry W. Akeley states he "would not be surprised if astronomers become sufficiently sensitive to these thought-currents to discover Yuggoth when the Outer Ones wish them to do so" (*CF* 2.503).

Akeley's impostor goes on to describe Yuggoth in more detail, saying there are mighty cities composed of great tiers of terraced towers, built of black stone. So little light reaches Yuggoth from our sun that organisms living on this world cannot depend on light for an important sense such as vision. Indeed, the Mi-Go have other senses to perceive other portions of the EM spectrum. In fact, the impostor of Akeley states that light hurts and confuses the Mi-Go. Thus, even though the Mi-Go are not originally from Yuggoth, one can understand why they established an outpost there. More than likely there are other environmental conditions on Yuggoth, besides the extremely low light levels, that are similar to the Mi-Go home world or universe.

Since the Mi-Go are not dependent on the visible light portion of the EM spectrum for "sight," their great houses and temples on Yuggoth do not have windows. However, it must be emphasized that all the strange Cyclopean structures, buildings, and bridges on Yuggoth were constructed by "some elder race" that went extinct eons before the Mi-Go reached Yuggoth.

A natural topographic feature of Yuggoth specifically mentioned by the impostor of Akeley is the black rivers of pitch. Pitch is described as a viscoelastic polymer that could be natural (plant resin) or manufactured (petroleum or coal tar). Pitch is typically a black, thick tarlike material. Based on the survey conducted by *New Horizons* spacecraft in 2015, the surface of Yuggoth is covered with rocky material and a variety of ices (water ice, frozen nitrogen, frozen methane, and a small amount of frozen carbon monoxide). However, many of these ices are a complex mixture of ice, solid material, and complex organic chemicals, with much of this material having a dark or black appearance. While the dwarf-planet is covered in ice and rock, it also has ice volcanos that release methane ice under pressure that may temporarily melt, only to re-freeze once it reaches the surface. Are the black rivers of pitch described in "The Whisperer in Darkness" the temporary rivers of methane that are pushed to the surface through ice volcanos? Additionally, evidence also suggests that the frozen lakes and rivers on Yuggoth may have once been liquid nitrogen approximately 800 to 900 million years ago.

It takes about 248 years for Pluto to make one revolution around the sun. Thus, during a few years when the dwarf-planet is closest to the sun it actually gets warm enough for some of the methane to vaporize. Is there a point at which the frozen methane is in liquid form before it vaporizes, generating the black rivers of pitch? What else is released from the frozen surface of Pluto every 240 or so years? It is also interesting to note that data collected by *New Horizons* in July 2015 revealed that Charon, Yuggoth's largest moon, has a reddish material distributed over its northern polar region. This polar region, called Mordor Macula, is methane that escaped from Yuggoth's atmosphere only to end up on Charon. Is this stream of volatilized methane a source of energy for the Mi-Go? One can imagine large "flocks" of Mi-Go slowly migrating between Yuggoth and Charon, feeding on the methane as methanogenic bacteria feed on methane in the anoxic (no oxygen) zones of wetland soils.

In "Out of the Aeons" there was an ancient land or province on Earth called K'naa where the first people found monstrous ruins left by those who dwelt there long ago. The ruins were the bleak basalt cliffs of Mount Yaddith-Gho, and on top of those cliffs was "a gigantic fortress of Cyclopean stone, infinitely older than mankind and built by the alien spawn of the dark planet Yuggoth, which had colonized the earth before the birth of terrestrial life" (*CF* 4.412). Among the structures identified on Yuggoth when

New Horizon reached the dwarf-planet in the summer of 2015 were "polygonal features; a complex band of terrain stretching east-northeast across the planet, approximately 1,000 miles long . . ." Is the fortress of Cyclopean stone on top of Mouth Yaddith-Gho the same structure as those recently observed on Yuggoth?

It should be noted that a small vial of Tombaugh's ashes is on board of *New Horizons*—sort of our DNA-based ambassador to Pluto, the Kuiper belt and beyond. If the Mi-Go obtain this vial of Tombaugh's ashes, will they re-create the mind of this famous astronomer? Will the consciousness of Tombaugh be confronted with those whose world he revealed to humanity? Only Tombaugh will know. In conclusion, from a dark crater on Mercury to the Mi-Go's outpost on Yuggoth, our solar system is truly Lovecraftian in nature.

Works Cited

Cox, Brian, and Andrew Cohen. *Wonders of the Solar System*. Harper Collins e-books, 2010.

Harms, Daniel. *Encyclopedia Cthulhiana: A Guide to Lovecraftian Horror*. 2nd ed. Oakland, CA: Chaosium, 1998.

Joshi, S. T. *I Am Providence: The Life and Times of H. P. Lovecraft*. New York: Hippocampus Press, 2010. 2 vols.

———. *Lovecraft and a World in Transition: Collected Essays on H. P. Lovecraft*. New York: Hippocampus Press, 2014.

———, and David E. Schultz. *An H. P. Lovecraft Encyclopedia*. Westport, CT: Greenwood Press, 2001.

Leiber, Fritz, "A Literary Copernicus." 1949. In *Discovering H. P. Lovecraft*, ed. Darrell Schweitzer. Rev. ed. Holicong, PA: Wildside Press, 2001. 7–16.

Littmann, Mark. *Planets Beyond: Discovering the Outer Solar System*. New York: John Wiley, 1988.

Livesey, T. R. "Dispatches from the Providence Observatory: Astronomical Motifs and Sources in the Writings of H. P. Lovecraft." *Lovecraft Annual* No. 2 (2008): 3–87.

Rothery, David A. *Planets: A Very Short Introduction*. New York: Oxford University Press, 2010.

Sagan, Carl. *Cosmos*. New York: Random House, 1981.

Sobel, Dava. *The Planets*. New York: Penguin, 2006.

"Hungry fer Victuals I Couldn't Raise nor Buy": Anthropophagy in Lovecraft

Duncan Norris

Howard Phillips Lovecraft, a dedicated if amateur classicist, was intimately familiar with the myths of ancient Greece. If mythology can be understood as an insight into a cultural mindset, at first glance the repeated appearance of cannibalism in classical Greek legends holds disturbing implications. Yet a closer examination shows that while a relatively common motif in the Hellenic cultural landscape from Kronos onward, human, as opposed to divine, cannibalism is always transgressive, an act putting oneself out of the bounds of pardonable sin and inviting severe punishment. Tantalus' fate is well remembered enough to be proverbial, but the oft-forgotten reason for his endless punishment of unslaked hunger and thirst in a pool of water under fruit trees is the crime of feeding human flesh to the gods. His descendants, who were all in some way cursed by his action, include Thyestes, who was exiled in disgrace after being tricked into eating the flesh of his own murdered sons. As instructive mythology such behaviors lend themselves to easy interpretation. No community can possibly survive and advance that sees other members as potential food. Thus cannibalism, especially non-ritual endocannibalism (that is, inside one's community, such as the funerary eating of a dead relative), rather than exocannibalism (ingestion of those from outside the group, such as eating the heart of a warrior from an opposing tribe whom one has overcome), is a strong cultural taboo is most places the world over.

Yet exceptions most certainly exist. Lovecraft was indubitably familiar at least with the account of the mortuary cannibalism mentioned in Herodotus (*Histories* 1.216, 4.26), a copy of which he owned in the 1855 William Beloe translation (*LL* 446). As a materialist and atheist, Lovecraft understood the relative unimportance of the deed on a cosmic scale, but equally understood that it evoked for the reader of a weird tale ideas of savagery, decadence, and truly transgressive behaviour (*ES* 1.403–4). Thus it is curious that despite Lovecraft's expressed disdain for such commonplace gruesomeness as the eating of human (or at least sentient) flesh, exactly such behavior comes up in a surprisingly large number of his tales. This paradoxical situation creates a curious substratum of horror running as a thread throughout many of his works, yet in markedly evolving and often contrasting ways. The following study surveys the topic within his published fictional works, and an examination of the ideas evoked by his various uses.

It is important to understand that, while Lovecraft may have used the eating of human flesh to serious horror effect in his tales, in his letters he plays gleefully with the taboo. Two of his later missives contain extended passages in which he comically discusses his passion for cannibalism. In one letter to Willis Conover, after commenting that he prefers his human flesh well done, Lovecraft recommends "the canned brand sold by the Black Man of the Arkham witch-cult coven and prepared in the secret cannery at Innsmouth" (*SL* 5.308). Another letter, to Frank Utpatel, proclaims Lovecraft's "preferred diet is century-old vampire flesh . . . for they possess a mellow flavour not even approached by ordinary human carrion" (*SL* 5.411), and goes on to discuss the best methods of transhipment. This playful approach to a most grim topic also creeps marginally into some of the aspects of cannibalism in his tales, most notably the darkly comic "Herbert West—Reanimator," and to a lesser extent "The Lurking Fear" and *The Dream-Quest of Unknown Kadath*, although generally speaking in fictional writings Lovecraft does use the motif with all seriousness. In fact, S. T. Joshi categorizes cannibalism, along with inbreeding, psychological trauma, and miscegenation as one of the four common signposts of the dreaded horrors of devolution, which is such an important factor across the full corpus of Lovecraft's work (Joshi, "Time, Space and Natural Law" 203).

Before beginning the survey proper a brief note about terminology. According to the definitive authority on the English language, the *Oxford English Dictionary*, anthropophagy is defined as "man-eating," while a cannibal is a "man who eats human flesh," with the secondary meaning of "animal feeding on its own species." The classic American English language equivalent, Webster's Dictionary, of which Lovecraft owned several editions (*LL* 1021–24), directly defines anthropophagy as cannibalism, with anthropophagous having the additional expanded meaning of "eating human flesh," while cannibalism is almost identical to the Oxford definitions. Johnson's Dictionary, which Lovecraft greatly admired and took a great pride in owning a familial copy (*SL* 2.352, 3.408), defines anthropophagi ("it has no singular") as "man-eaters; cannibals; those that live upon human flesh," and cannibal as "an anthropophagite; a man-eater."

Cannibalism and anthropophagy are thus frequently used as a synonym for the other, yet there are a few important distinctions betwixt the terms that are important to our purposes. Cannibalism originally mean humans eating the flesh of other humans, but its definition has since broadened to any such intraspecies predation or devouring and other more metaphoric usages. By contrast, anthropophagy literally originates, after Latin deriving from Greek, in the term "man-eater," and, while implying human cannibalism, it can by extension refer to anything that preys upon man, being humanity in the poetic sense rather than the gender of male. Thus a crocodile eating its own offspring would certainly be cannibalism, while the same crocodile eating a human could, by some interpretations, be understood as anthropophagy. Such thinking resulted in the naming of huge predatory saurian whose teeth marks were found in *Homo habilis* remains in the Olduvai in Tanzania as *Crocodylus anthropophagus*, the human-eating crocodile (Blumenschine et al.).

This sort of distinction is important, as many creatures in horror tales generally, and in Lovecraft's tales in several particular instances, are not human in the commonly accepted sense and thus are more anthropophagous than cannibalistic. The word origins also carry various unspoken cultural baggage. The Androphagi (sometimes rendered as Anthropophagi)[1] were allegedly a race of

---

[1]. Literally "man-eaters" versus "people-eaters" and depending solely on how translation and interpretation is understood, but both holding the same meaning of cannibal.

cannibals first mentioned in Herodotus (4.106) and later cited by other ancient historians, including Pliny the Elder (*Natural History* 7.2) and Ammianus Marcellinus (*Res Gestae* 31.2.15). The word cannibal likewise derives from the designation of a New World tribe Europeans believed were in the practice of eating human flesh, the word coming from Spanish but ultimately having its origin in an Arawak language term concerning natives in the area. In fact, the name of the entire region today under the geographic designation of the Caribbean springs from the same root.

Yet despite similarities in origin, it is the word cannibal that has been most closely linked to ideas of cultural libel and as an excuse to exalt hegemonic supremacy over technologically inferior groups, and carries for some people a secondary emotional weight divested from the act itself. Nor is such ideology unspoken. Queen Isabella of Spain issued an order on 30 October 1503 concerning any people declared to be cannibals that "they may be captured and taken to these my Kingdoms and Domains and to other parts and be sold" (Sauer 161–62), providing a grim financial incentive to arbitrarily affix the label of man-eater to any New World group. Such underling notions concerning civilization and cannibalism are occasionally highly germane to our analysis in Lovecraft, but will be addressed as they arise. For the sake of opening the widest understanding of the theme involved in this monograph, I shall use the term cannibalism more broadly for the eating of sentient creatures by sentient creatures, placing such humanoid creatures as gugs and the inhabitants of Leng all into the broad category of human.

Cannibalism makes an early appearance in Lovecraft's canon, in the very short tale dealing with a man's ancestral memory of the fall of the land of Lomar and his failure therein, "Polaris" (1918). The mention is fleeting, but in context certainly promotes the ideas of cannibalism as marker of cultural and physical inferiority mentioned above for the migrating "men of Olathoë . . . valiantly and victoriously swept aside the hairy, long-armed, cannibal Gnophkehs that stood in their way" (*CF* 1.67–68).

No such undertones, or such clarity of explanation, exist in the next possible instance of anthropophagy in "The Cats of Ulthar" (1920). Although not explicitly stated, it seems clear in context that the eponymous cats, at the direction of either a spell of Menes or powers invoked by him, first executed, then ate, the old cotter and his wife in vengeance for the couple's vile ailurophobic killings—anthropophagy as poetic justice in the best Greek tragedic and fairy tale manner. Incidentally, while I could not find any forensically recorded cases of a cat or cats killing an adult human in an attack, such actions do occur occasionally in darker realms of fiction. Two of the more prominent examples include the ultimately fatal attacks of Mr. Wilde's sorely provoked cat in Robert W. Chambers's "The Repairer of Reputations" from *The King in Yellow* and the vengeful she-cat's precision strike causing a man's death in an iron maiden in Bram Stoker's "The Squaw," after which the purring puss "licked the blood which trickles through the gashed socket of his eyes" (Stoker 25). As to charges of feline anthropophagy, there are numerous substantiated instances of domestic felines eating portions of their deceased owners, normally after being faced with starvation in confinement with their owner's bodies (Chapman et al.).

"The Picture in the House" is the only one of Lovecraft's' tales that actually makes cannibalism a central aspect of the narrative, rather than an adjunct, motif, or small morsel of information to add atmosphere. The unnamed narrator takes refuge from a storm in the house of the antagonist, who it transpires has been unnaturally extending his allotted lifespan through the ingestion of human flesh. This particular trope of cannibalism as a source of longevity has since regularly appeared in a diverse variety of stories and media ranging from the western horror comedy film set about the time of the American Civil War, *Ravenous* (1999), to the Warhammer 40,000 novel *Ravenor vs Eisenhorn: Pariah*[2] (Abnett 94). Yet Lovecraft uses his example more traditionally. The setting, an old, remote, and unvisited house far from civilization, subtly evokes a fairy tale foreboding: cannibalism and anthropophagy are of course common motifs in such stories, "Little Red Riding Hood" and "Hansel and Gretel" being but two prominent examples of many. The story itself is filled with foreshadowing and the classic horror trope of the villain referring to his previous

---

2. Curiously, the Ravenor of the series title is not any reference to cannibalism, but purely coincidental.

victims in an oblique way. Yet Lovecraft very deftly never shows us any real-time horror directly in the tale. The cannibalism that is the central theme is all done at a remove by having it shown and extrapolated from the book in the old man's possession, and from the implications of the old man's ramblings.

In a typically Lovecraftian manner the mechanics of how cannibalism makes immortality, and even the absolute certainty that this is the case as presented expositionally, is never divulged other than the old man's theory that "they say meat makes blood an' flesh, an' gives ye new life, so I wondered ef 'twudn't make a man live longer an' longer ef *'twas more the same"* (*CF* 1.217). This is a clever juxtaposition, for it removes any overtly supernatural elements and by implication presents the idea that this is a plausible means to immortality, should anyone be decadent enough to try it. Yet the idea of the book driving him to commit the deeds of murder and forbidden consumption draws back to a possible hint of the ultramundane ("'tis a queer book"; "Queer haow picters kin set a body thinkin'" [*CF* 1.214]), especially to the average reader who would have no idea as to the actuality of the existence and contents of a book as obscure as *Regnum Congo*. In fact, the book's obscurity even today is such that an Internet search generally yields references to *Regnum Congo* in connection with this story before the book itself.

As a metatextual element concerning this exceedingly rare book in such an incongruous location Lovecraft is here probably making an extremely wry joke at his own expense. The narrator in the story, amazed by his find of such a singular book, comments that "he had often heard of this work," implying that he had not seen it firsthand. Lovecraft himself had not seen the actual book, and was working off information from an essay by Thomas Henry Huxley, as demonstrated by S. T. Joshi in "Lovecraft and the *Regnum Congo*." As such, Lovecraft gets certain details of the book incorrect, although they make no impact on the course or power of the story for all but the most erudite of readers.

For a cannibalism story without any overt cannibalism Lovecraft very carefully guides us to the horrific denouement and climax. In the first hints of what is the provender of the old man of the house the author, taking note of the book on the table, is disturbed by "the persistent way in which the volume tended to fall open of itself at Plate XII, which represented in gruesome detail a butcher's shop of the cannibal Anziques" (CF 1.210). We as readers of course never get to see this image, but are instead proffered the more effective personal mental picture of what such a sight might be. This personal mental image, whatever it may be for the individual reader, is then ameliorated by the expressed shame of the narrator in the following sentence at his being so affected by so slight a thing, potentially softening the possible conceptual picture formed. This false softening is then immediately discarded and the original image's potential grotesqueness is exacerbated and made more vivid by the gruesome implications of the line "especially in connexion with some adjacent passages descriptive of Anzique gastronomy" (CF 1.210). Inside two sentences we have an unknown image of cannibalism presented, imagined, softened, and then immediately made worse.

When we next address cannibalism it is almost a repetition of the original line that introduced the topic. "[T]he book fell open . . . to the repellent twelfth plate shewing a butcher's shop amongst the Anzique cannibals" (CF 1.215) restores whatever previous images that had created to the reader's mind, but with the additional details that the "Africans look like white men. The limb and quarters hanging about the wall of the shop . . . while the butcher with his axe was hideously incongruous" (CF 1.215). That the actual plates in the De Bry illustrations do not show the Africans as white men is immaterial to the effect produced. To the original reading audience whom Lovecraft undoubtedly envisioned, probably correctly, as white, this racial change takes the horror of cannibalism from the remote wilds of Africa, where they might conceive of such to occur, and brings it far closer to home. Likewise the small additional details, hanging limbs and the butcher's axe, force the reader to think about the brutal mechanics involved in the commercial butchery of a human being for meat, an intrinsically repellent image. Then the following line has the additional horrific punch of the host's enjoyment of this tableau.

Now follows a switch in perspective. Rather than the calm, reasoned, and steady voice of the narrator, who up to this point has given us all the information on cannibalism, we instead hear of it from the old man whom we as readers suspect of something nefarious. He describes the images again with greater detail: "thet feller bein' chopped up . . . see whar the butcher cut off his feet? Thar's his head on thet bench, with one arm side of it, an' t'other arm's on the graound side o' the meat block" (*CF* 1.215–16). He adds the crucial words "that feller," which has an effect of personalizing the entire scene. It is no longer an anonymous image, but is rather becoming more and more intimate. This idea is carried to a logical conclusion with the drop of fresh blood landing on the image to bring it from nightmare image to actuality, with the "large irregular spot of wet crimson" (*CF* 1.217) in direct association with the cannibal picture, leaving no doubt as to the intended fate of the narrator, save for the providential arrival of the lightning.

As an important aside at this juncture, Lovecraft is often criticized as a writer for lacking in the depth of his characterization. Given that such was not of interest to him as an author and thus not a focus of his work, focusing on a malignly indifferent cosmos, such a criticism is, as such, valid. Yet his insight and understanding about the human mind is often profound, as demonstrated for example in his prescient prediction of a forthcoming age of far greater promiscuity and, more importantly, the reasons why in a 1929 letter to Woodburn Harris (*SL* 3.68–70). The psychopathology of the old man in the tale as presented in only a few sentences has a distinct validity in modern psychological study of the serial killer mentality. The old man describes his interest in killing being awoken and then further stimulated as he read biblical passages about such events, and of overly enjoying the necessary slaughter of livestock and wanting more. His desire in obtaining the *Regnum Congo*, after chancing to discover that it contains the type of images of "slayin'" he already fantasizes about, starts him on the path that leads him ultimately to replicate the actions he saw.

This sort of progression, the escalation from daydreams to obtaining images and finally transformation into enacting such desires after obsessive focus upon them, is the most common model for the serial murderer as outlined in the FBI's seminal study *Sexual Homicide. Patterns and Motives*. Eerily, the real-life serial killer and cannibal Albert Fish, who was unknown and unsuspected but active during the period this story was written and not caught until 1934, strongly parallels the old man of the story. Albert Fish in physical appearance distinctly resembles a somewhat cleaner version of the character presented in the story: both were fond of violent biblical passages and various misquotings of Scripture, and the latter was only caught as he could not resist talking (or, in Fish's case, writing) of his deeds in a self-pleasuring and expositional manner that would lead to his exposure[3] (see Schechter).

There are several oblique references to anthropophagy in "The Outsider" (1921). Specifically, Lovecraft mentions ghouls twice and, in a line after the second mention, "the unnamed feasts of Nitokris" (CF 1.272). Ghouls may in this instance be a poetical term rather than a distinct designator of race or creature, and Lovecraft uses the adjective ghoulish earlier in the tale in the titular Outsider's unknowing self-description. Yet Lovecraft, having read much Arabian folklore and mythology as a child via the *Arabian Nights* (SL 1.122, 299), is certainly aware of the creature called a *ghul*. It from this word that English derives both the term and conception of the ghoul, whose most salient characteristic is as the eating of the human dead, and Lovecraft will certainly evoke this in later tales. Likewise, the cannibalistic implication derived from Dunsany of the Nitokrian feast are well established (Norris 20).

"Herbert West—Reanimator" (1921–22) sees Lovecraft draw upon cannibalism at its most bestial. The early specimens of West's experiments appear to be universally driven to anthropophagy, and such attacks are inspired as much by malice as other factors—there is no mention of them making any predation upon other creatures, and the known headlessness of at least one of those reanimated implies that there is not a need for such beings to eat. Indeed, this is specifically said of such other dead beings bought back to life by Joseph Curwen in *The Case of Charles Dexter Ward* (1927), who comments of the imperfect creatures raised of incomplete saltes: "Damn 'em, they *do* eat, but they *don't need to!*" (CF 2.352). Yet the Plague Demon that had been Dr. Halsey is noted specifically as having attacked and eaten three persons who had already died of the plague in its rampage. In his textual

---

3. In a morbid aside, HPL's correspondent and protégé Robert Bloch commented, when asked why the public was so interested in the Ed Gein case, that it was "because they haven't heard about Albert Fish."

repetition of the actions of Dr. Halsey it is not his seventeen murders that are given emphasis, but his cannibalism. Here cannibalism is used as the signpost of a creature completely unnatural and totally sundered from proper human behaviors, and this amoral horror is thus reflected back upon the creator of such that continues in the face of such actions by his creations.

"Reanimator" also gives in its eating of human flesh, arguably, one of the most vividly brutal and horrific scenes in the totality of Lovecraft's writings. After the dramas of a missing child the reanimated boxer who appears at a West's door is perceived to have "between its glistening teeth a snow-white, terrible, cylindrical object terminating in a tiny hand" (CF 1.308). While it is not overly dwelt upon in the tale, in complete book form it has lost somewhat of its intended effect as the cliffhanger-esque endpoint of a section in the unusual (for Lovecraft) serial format. Yet both the actual presented image and the deeper implications of this, of a high-spirited and adventurous young child attacked, killed, and eaten by a monster back from the grave, is a truly nightmarish conjuration.

"The Hound" (1922), rather than depicting the bestial cannibalism portrayed in "Reanimator," has a curiously restrained and deeply implicative type of anthropophagy. Despite the various renderings of people by the eponymous creature, there is no direct evidence that the titular Hound actually eats his victims. In fact, it seems unlikely that if St. John had been partially eaten he would be in any position to utter final words as happens in the tale. Yet the eating of the dead is referenced specifically in connection with the amulet, the theft of which sets the entire chain of events in motion. It is inscribed with "the ghastly soul-symbol of the corpse-eating cult of inaccessible Leng, in Central Asia. All too well did we trace the sinister lineaments ... drawn from some obscure supernatural manifestation of the souls of those who vexed and gnawed at the dead" (CF 1.343). Concerning this symbol the narrator speaks of reading in the *Necronomicon* of "its properties, and about the relation of ghouls' souls to the objects it symbolised" (CF 1.344). What exactly this means is open to the reader to interpret, and this passage has little in the way of other references to build upon in the wider body of Lovecraft's work. In fact, it is one of the few non-poetic references to souls in Lovecraft's fiction. Yet the term corpse-eating cult is unambiguous, and gnawing at the dead is not typically the provenance of the ghostly and immaterial. Ghouls likewise seem to imply a specific type of being rather than a descriptor as used earlier in the same, and many other, stories. In a tale replete with grave-robbing as "that hideous extremity of human outrage" (CF 1.340), it would seem that the limits of "abhorred practice" by the protagonists does not include cannibalism, and implies that such is the work of other orders of being.

Interestingly and as noted above, although Leng will make numerous appearances in Lovecraft's later work, the corpse-eating cult will not, at least directly. However, the inhabitants of Leng as presented in the Dreamlands are connected both with cannibalism, to be discussed below, and the prehistoric monastery solely inhabited by the high-priest not to be described. This may be an aspect, offshoot, or even genesis of the corpse-eating cult, but it cannot be confirmed textually. Intriguingly, the location of this corpse-eating cult in Asiatic Leng in "The Hound" raises some thought-provoking speculation as to Lovecraft's choice to place it there. The deliberately vague "mountains of China" (CF 2.38), it is to be remembered, is also the home of the undying masters of the Cthulhu cult as told by Castro in "The Call of Cthulhu" (1926). Speculation could thus be made that these masters gain their longevity through cannibalism as does the old man in "The Picture in the House," but again this tantalizing notion is unsubstantiated by the texts.

On more solid ground factually is that while mortuary cannibalism per se is not widely practiced by any large groups in this area, several practises are commonly mistaken for it. Sky burial in Tibet, in which the dead are ritually dismembered, still occurs today and was much more the cultural norm at the time Lovecraft was writing, prior to the annexation of Tibet by the Chinese, who discouraged the practise. In sky burial after excarnation the flesh is by custom frequently fed to waiting animals, commonly vultures and dogs. As animals refusing to eat of the deceased's body is considered a very baleful omen, such charnel remains are frequently added to other foodstuffs, such as various forms of dough, to encourage such feedings. Naturally this ceremony is easily mistaken for a cannibal feast by the casual onlooker. Indeed, given the practice of cleaning one's hands after such work by clapping them against each other, incidental cannibalism, albeit unintended and in minute quantities, is certainly a side effect of such observances.

Even in modern times the idea that the Tibetans eat their own dead has been widely believed to be true in certain areas. The religious practice in Buddhism, Tibet's dominant religion, of making ritual bowls and instruments out of human skulls and femurs is likewise easy to mistake as cannibalistic by the uninitiated. It is important to note that certain obscure Tantric practices involve the ritual ingestion of human flesh and tissue (as one of the forbidden five meats or five nectars, which are various bodily secretions and wastes), but these are largely historical practices and with medicinal connotations, much subject to debate about what such scriptures mean and whether they were actually implemented literally (Garrett 300–303). However, the small Indian Hindu sect of Aghori in the present day performs various cannibalistic practices such as eating from human skulls and ingesting and decorating in cremation ash; and while historically cannibalism was one of the Aghori's ascribed practices, its continuation today is deliberately obscured from the wider Hindu community and in generally not held to be a common practice (Barrett 77, 149, 155–56). Incidentally, these two practices are, in an admittedly highly simplistic explanation, often both medicinal and a form of ritual pollution of the body to achieve greater benefit for the soul, the latter vaguely analogous in theological terms to former Christian sects such as the Flagellants, mortifying the physical form for the soul's sake.

On a more practical bent, defleshing is a requirement after exhumation for burial in an ossuary, a ritual once common in European tradition but increasingly scarce in the modern Western world, with the notable exception of Greece (see Hadjimatheou). A similar practice in Thailand of the exhumation of unclaimed remains for proper cremation likewise requires defleshing, which can include boiling the remains in big cauldrons to prepare the bones. Akin to sky burial, this likewise can be easily mistaken for cannibalism. Indeed, graphic images of exactly such practices started rumors that caused problems in international relations between Nigeria and Thailand as recently as 2009 (Ewruje; Mikkelson). It is not coincidental that Nigeria so readily believed such an atrocity: tragically, murder and cannibalism remain a dark practice in traditional witchcraft in Nigeria (see BBC).

Passing beyond the merely physical body, it is also possible to see in the line about "souls who vex" shades of a dark mockery or shadow of Buddhist theology, or at least allusion to such for storytelling purposes. Finally, the creatures who would fall broadly into the modern category of zombie in the West are known as *Ro-Langs* in Tibetan mythology, and these include those raised by both necromantic ritual and possessive spirits (Wylie). Such creatures were not unknown to Lovecraft, and he will make a brief mention of a "Thibetan ROLANG" by name as part of an embryonic story idea in his commonplace book (item 192), although this was many years after writing "The Hound."

"The Lurking Fear" (1922) returns us again to the debased and uncivilized cannibals, this time being the degenerate scions of the Martense household who have become eaters of their own kind after the family's retrogression in their underground fastness. This idea of cannibalism as a marker of the truly savage is replete throughout the tale. The location of events is after "miles of primeval forest and hill" (*CF* 1.350), and phrases such as "gnawed dismemberment," "corpses ... horribly mangled, chewed, and clawed," and "on what remained of his chewed and gouged head" (*CF* 1.351, 352, 361) fill the story and leave no doubt as to the reason for the attacks by these troglodytic scions of inbreeding and possibly worse. Nor is their predation confined to the outer world; it is even practiced, in the most polymorphous perversion (here Lovecraft is clearly drawing on Freud's famous coinage of the phrase), upon their own kind, one of the creatures toward the end killing and making "a meal in accustomed fashion on a weaker companion" while "others snapped up what it left and ate with slavering relish" (*CF* 1.372).

Interestingly, while the narrator is digging in the grave of Jan Martense Lovecraft describes the scene as being one of "baleful primal trees of unholy size, age, and grotesqueness leered above me like the pillars of some hellish Druidic temple" (*CF* 1.362). Early in the tale he also describes the Martense mansion as an "antique, grove-circled stone house" (*CF* 1.351), which evokes both the known sacred spaces of the Druids and megalithic structures such as Stonehenge, which are popularly, although often incorrectly, associated with them. Druids, indeed most real-world religions, make no large imprint in Lovecraft's fiction. It seems likely that Lovecraft is using the association since classical times of human sacrifice and cannibalism in connection with the Celtic peoples and the Druids, whose priests were often accused cannibalism (Caesar, *Gallic Wars* 6.16, 7.77; Strabo, *Geography* 4.5.4).

Interestingly, Lovecraft does not actually use the term cannibalism (or variants thereof) until almost the end of the tale, then uses it twice in three paragraphs to emphasize the Martenses' degeneration. Yet overall "The Lurking Fear," like its contemporarily written companions "The Hound" and "Herbert West—Reanimator," is somewhat deliberately overwrought in its language and, while not the parodic piece of the former or with the darkly comedic tones of the latter, it certainly bears the marks of Lovecraft overplaying his literary hand in order to appeal to the imagined audience and editor for whom it was commissioned.

By contrast, Lovecraft's next tale, "The Rats in the Walls" (1923), is a genuine classic. As he often did with his stories, Lovecraft distills and refines the ideas of previous tales and creates a literary alchemical gold from the base metal of his foregoing attempts. In this tale the ideas of hereditary taint and underground cannibals become part of a far greater and more effective narrative. The passing atmospheric Druidic references of "The Lurking Fear" are returned to a reality and their proper context, while the bursting forth of a ravenous horde from the depths of the earth in the form of literal vermin becomes a more believable, less immediately central, yet vitally important motif. Rather than the frankly implausible mass murder of seventy-five people[4] by an all-devouring underground cannibal horde, several lone attacks, and one instance of the normalized familial cannibalism of one of the scions of the Martenses in the end of "The Lurking Fear," there is instead a throng of starved subterranean rats escaping to the sur-

---

4. For comparison, the worst roughly contemporary North American mass murder, the unprecedented tragedy of the 1927 Bath School massacre, resulted in forty-five fatalities.

face after their food source is removed, while under Exham Priory is a horrifically plausible system of human enslavement and breeding for consumption.

In a typically deft Lovecraftian manner, rather than talk endlessly of this cannibalism after making it clear that was what had been occurring here among other abominations, he leaves the details to readers' imagination with lines such as "Sir William, standing with his searchlight in the Roman ruin, translated aloud the most shocking ritual I have ever known; and told of the diet of the antediluvian cult which the priests of Cybele found and mingled with their own" (CF 1.394), while the luckless Norrys's wobbling legs after reading the graffiti in the butchers shop, where by now we would expect horrors, hammers home the vileness of the entire setting. Even the cannibalistic attack upon Norrys is explained by implication, as the narrator's caveat that "they accuse me of a hideous thing, but they must know that I did not do it" (CF 1.396) is undermined by his contextually damning constant descriptor of Norrys as "plump." In this way Lovecraft cleverly foreshadows the fate of Norrys, almost certainly descended of the folk who were the stock of the pens in the grotto, even as the narrator carries the taint of the de la Poers in his bloodlines. Lovecraft further juxtaposes this with repeated use of the "flabby" descriptor of the herd beasts of his dreams, then merges the two in the line about Norrys with "his plump face utterly white and flabby" (CF 1.392) before making the narrator's actions clear with his excessive protestation, "I am *not* that daemon swineherd in the twilit grotto! It was *not* Edward Norrys' fat face on that flabby, fungous thing" (CF 1.396). In a tale literally filled with "carrion black pits of sawed, picked bones and opened skulls" (CF 1.395) it is the final repetition of "plump" immediately before the succulently brutal "half-eaten body of Capt. Norrys" (CF 1.396) that conveys the truest frission of horror.

Yet concurrent with this idea of hereditary taint inclining to cannibalism is an allegorical usage of the same idea, giving the veneer of logical reasoning, albeit grossly distorted from a place of madness, to the narrator's actions. His final words, which he utters over the masticated body of Norrys, are filled with a justification of the validity of the actions: "Why shouldn't rats eat a de la Poer as a de la Poer eats forbidden things?... The war ate my boy, damn them all... and the Yanks ate Carfax with flames" (*CF* 1.396). The narrator's own heinous deeds are thus self-presented as part of an acceptable cycle of behavior given the cruel, predatory, and anthropophagic nature of the wider world, yet can clearly be seen simultaneously as a form of madness due to the loss of his son. For the reader this creates, in addition to the horrific emotions engendered by the death of the amiable Norrys, pathos for his killer, who is clearly distraught beyond sanity by the suffering and death of his only child. Thus cannibalism as metaphor, juxtaposed with the horrific actuality, creates a far deeper impact than either one might have allowed for singly.

Cannibalism, or at least the eating of human flesh of some type, seems likely be involved in "Under the Pyramids" (1924), but it is very much an off-stage or implied, depending on how literally the reader takes the usage of ghoul as a descriptor of Nitokris and whatever might have eaten the right side of her face. It does seem likely that the "unmentionable food" (*CF* 1.450) offerings being thrown to and devoured by the demonic Sphinx were of human origin, as few other potential foods would be worthy of such a title. This understanding is given further textual support as the descriptor "unmentionable" will be used again in connection with known habits of ghouls in *The Dream-Quest of Unknown Kadath*.

However, it does not take any imagination to connect cannibalism to the subject of the painting "Ghoul Feeding" in "Pickman's Model" (1926), while this is made almost explicit in the painting from the hidden studio "The Lesson," in which "a squatting circle of nameless dog-like things in a churchyard teaching a small child how to feed like themselves" (*CF* 2.65). Following the pattern established in "The Picture in the House," Lovecraft after two implications then becomes unambiguous concerning the foreshadowed horrors, with the unfinished image on the canvass that "held in bony claws a thing that had been a man, gnawing at the head as a child nibbles at a stick of candy" (*CF* 2.69); and he has Pickman offer the mocking comment, in archetypical villainous fashion, about the "rats" and "the deuce knows what they eat" (*CF* 2.71) after stating that the tunnels connect to the cemeteries.

The Dream Quest of Unknown Kadath (1926–27) has a number

of separate instances connected with cannibalism and the eating of at least semi-sentient creatures, and presents some curious differences and discrepancies of tone and attitude between each. In fact, cannibalism recurs with enough frequency and in different contexts to amount to one of the major leitmotifs of the novella. Yet in a typically Lovecraftian deftness of touch the word cannibal (or its derivatives) only appears once in the entire tale, and long before any such action or connection is described. In fact, initially we once again get only mention of "the hairy cannibal Gnophkehs" (CF 2.103) mentioned in "Polaris."

However, shortly thereafter we get the first such instance of cannibalism, as per the chosen understanding chosen above, in the eating of the trailing zoogs in Ulthar by the cats therein. Arguments could be made about the correctness of calling naturally carnivorous cats eating another creature cannibalism, but as the cats clearly have a language able to be understood by other sentient creatures and have a society functional enough to have army ranks, they are obviously far beyond the mere charming pets of our mundane waking world. Likewise, zoogs are patently intelligent, brewing alcoholic-style beverages, living in villages, and possessing their own language. Yet Carter openly pats the cats after they eat his unwanted following train. The justification of one zoog, especially as it is described as being young with all that that denotes, having evilly and hungrily eyed a black kitten, and the implications therein, would be a weak case in any court, yet Lovecraft presents the cats positively. However, it must be understood that this behavior is not apparently typical for the cats of Dreamland. In preemptively winning the war about to be sparked by their actions in eating the inquisitive and kitten-eyeing zoogs the cats neither decimate nor extirpate the zoogs, and explicit mention is made of "a large annual tribute of grouse, quail, and pheasants" (CF 2.146) that the zoogs will provide as provender for the victorious felines.

In contrast to the easy acceptance of the predatory actions of the cats of Ulthar, the folk of Leng who crew the ominous black galleys that trade at Dylath-Leen, and who are in turn the slaves of the even more terrible moonbeasts, are presented as indisputably evil. It is not their slave trading per se that is held to be an abomination, but that it is abundantly clear the slaves are literal livestock, to be fattened and eaten. There is no ambiguity to be found, either in disgust at the practice or of the practice itself, in the description of the merchants as having "never anything from the butchers and grocers, but only gold and the fat black men of Parg whom they bought by the pound" (CF 2.110). The absence of clear indicators of authorial intent is always potentially a slippery slope to analyze, but it is a certainty that Lovecraft, steeped as he was in the lore of his beloved New England, understood the role captains and ships from there played in the African slave trade, and this type of connection appears to be deliberately invoked here.

In choosing the unfortunate men of Parg as victims of predatory cannibalism, it is certainly possible Lovecraft is subconsciously trying to evoke ideas of the trope of cannibal tribes in a distant land, one that was very much alive and in full flourish in the pulp magazines, and elsewhere, of his era. But this is highly speculative. The merchants of the black galleys are incontrovertibly villains, and it is clear that the meat eaten by them on board the ship is almost certainly human in origin. Significantly, Carter does not partake of it. Later, on the unnamed island that serves as the moonbeasts' outpost, it is clear that the almost-men of Leng, as well as other undefined creatures, are equally subject to the fate of the men of Parg. The literal predation of the stronger upon the weaker is a frequent characteristic of the inhabitants of the Dreamlands. It is a nightmarish version of Darwinism as (mis)understood in the early part of the twentieth century. Yet by their purchasing or enslaving of sentient creatures for consumption, of creating an economic market and system for its continuance, not to mention the presumably even worse fates that such abhorrent creatures are prone to, these actions mark out the moonbeasts as a distinctly greater form of evil than other of the cannibal inhabitants of the Dreamlands, such as ghouls.

Ghouls are, by definition, eaters of the human dead, and although they play a large part in this tale and are patently connected with those mentioned in "Pickman's Model," they are not in any way presented as either deliberately or intrinsically evil. Only in Carter's initial encounter with them is there any hint of the truly predatory, and even this is mild, as "the ghouls were in general respectful, even if one did attempt to pinch him while several others eyed his leanness speculatively" (CF 2.134).[5] Their accustomed diet is wonderfully euphemized in the catch-all descriptor of "unmentionable idiosyncrasies" (CF 2.134), and their cannibalism is presented largely as a natural product of their natures, without accompanying judgment. It seems that Dreamland ghouls are largely necrophagous and scavenging by nature, rather than predacious, and it is noted that "a buried gug will feed a community for almost a year" (CF 2.137). This is not to paint ghouls as entirely beneficent eaters of the dead. Their former custom, noted as discouraged by Pickman, of eating their own wounded still indicates a certain degree of barbarity and lack of civilized mores, but they are clearly capable of adaptation and change within their natural limits.

This is in distinct contrast with the truly cannibalistic ghasts, who are significantly noted as being "very primitive, and eat one another" (CF 2.137) in addition to gugs and ghouls, and presumably any other unfortunate enough to encounter them. These creatures from the vaults of Zin, which are the prey of those higher in the abyssal structure of the Dreamlands, are described as both murderous and vindictive, the epitome of the savage cannibal aspect. Yet here in the underworld we have a third race of cannibals, or rather man-eaters, the gigantic gugs. They are clearly of a different type from the primal ghasts and the ghouls, who are carrion devourers by their nature. Gugs are unmistakably a somewhat more advanced race, living in a city surrounded by walls and filled with towers, and being organized enough to rear religious monuments and make offering and worship to the Other Gods and Nyarlathotep. Yet despite this veneer of civilization they have been banished under the earth for their blasphemies; "mortal dreamers were their former food, and they have legends of the toothsomeness of such" (CF 2.135–36), though now they are forced to subsist on the repulsive ghasts adjacent to their exile abode. Toothsome is an important adjective here. Having a meaning of "pleasant to eat," it also linguistically invokes the idea of the act of eating itself, of the mouth upon human flesh in this case. Thus the three different creatures with similar diets are presented very differently; the un-

---

5. Lucky they were not zoogs!

pleasant but amenable ghouls, the aggressive and feral ghasts, and the deliberately and evilly inclined gugs.

A side note here must be made of the web-footed wamps, who do "business in the graveyards of upper dreamland" (*CF* 2.135), as opposed to ghouls, who haunt the lower reaches. It is not explicitly stated what these creatures are, other than the wonderfully evocative descriptor that they are "spawned in dead cities" (*CF* 2.135), nor what they might be doing in graveyards. Yet it might be a reasonable assumption that they and ghouls share the same taste in provender, given that each allow the other a certain domain. However, the creature that steals a shiny object from Carter and exsanguinates his zebra on the slopes on the trip to Ngranek is specifically described as leaving webbed footprints, which implies, by the principle of literary conservation of details and Chekhov's Gun, that it may be a wamp. Yet Lovecraft was not in any way a keen adherent to these principles, and deliberately added ambiguities and unexplained aspects to his fiction to add greater depths and imaginative power. Notably, shortly after the incident at Carter's campsite, mention is made of the voonith as an "amphibious terror" (*CF* 2.126), which would likely also have webbed feet, although something so described seems unlikely to be satisfied with pilfering trinkets and zebra blood. All this confusion may be reflective of *Dream-Quest* being a draft rather than a finished manuscript, or of a deliberate attempt to instill a certain dreamlike ambiguity into the adventure, and all that may be said with certainty is that wamps may be cannibalistic, vampiric, or something else entirely.

Although, as noted earlier, those revived from imperfect saltes seem to have an indiscriminate appetite that would certainly have included any person whom misfortune cast into their grasp, *The Case of Charles Dexter Ward* (1927) certainly has a technical case of cannibalism. The reanimated Joseph Curwen was feeding upon the blood of humans, presumably a need generated as a result of his unnatural state, to judge by the associated words "must have it red for three months" (*CF* 2.298) connected with these sanguinary attacks. Blood is of course technically as much a tissue of the body as muscle is. However, the drinking of blood is rarely thought of as cannibalism in the same manner as the eating of human flesh, and in the story itself Lovecraft explicitly uses the term vampirism repeatedly in connection with Curwen's attacks. A claim of cannibalism could be made against the more paternally oriented brother of Wilbur Whateley in "The Dunwich Horror" (1928), given that the Elmer Frys, outside investigators, and the Bishop family all disappear, presumably digested or possibly absorbed by the titular horror. Yet not much emphasis is made of this aspect of this creature's attacks, and given its inhuman nature in the main, and its apparent willingness to eat any meat available, any cannibal implications are neither explored nor important as part of the horror of the tale.

"The Mound" (1929–30), while technically a ghostwritten piece yet widely understood as an almost wholly original Lovecraft work (*SL* 3.88), contains surprisingly modern ideas of posthumanism and genetic tempering concerning the nature of what is human: the livestock of K'n-yan are clearly generated from sentient creatures. The avaricious explorer Zamacona describes these unnatural kine as "the shocking morbidity of these great floundering white things, with black fur on their backs, a rudimentary horn in the centre of their foreheads, and an unmistakable trace of human or anthropoid blood in their flat-nosed, bulging-lipped faces" (*CF* 4.212–13). An entire paragraph is dedicated to speculations about the origins of these creatures, but in the final assessment the reality is a most brutal form of perpetual subjugation and cannibalism: "The flesh they ate was not that of intelligent people of the master-race, but merely that of a special slave-class which had for the most part ceased to be thoroughly human, and which indeed was the principal meat stock of K'n-yan" (*CF* 4.213).

Like the vile moonbeasts, the people who perpetuate such a system are shown to be saturated with evil, and the ultimate marker of the savage, the eating of one's own kind (or other sentient creatures, as the case may be), is juxtaposed against a high order of scientific development to show the truest debasement of the society in which these two disparate elements flourish. Interestingly, given this environment of decadent cannibalism, mention is made of the vaults of Zin, beneath the ruined city of Yoth, whose inhabitants had been quadrupedal. This may be an allusion to the fact that the inhabitants of Yoth became, possibly through deliberate or accidental genetic tampering, the primitive ghosts of *Dream-Quest*, whose faces are "so curiously human despite the absence of a nose, a forehead, and other important particulars" (*CF* 2.138), or perhaps that the ghosts are the remains of one of their experiments that survived them. After all, the waking world and the Dreamlands are definitively connected outside the medium of sleep: "the Pnakotic Manuscripts made by waking men [. . .] and borne into the land of dreams" (*CF* 2.103), while the enchanted wood of the zoogs "at two places touches the lands of men" (*CF* 2.101). Yet this possible connection between ghosts and "The Mound" is purely speculative. *The Dream-Quest of Unknown Kadath* was never even given a final draft nor submitted for publication, and "The Mound" was a revision work. Lovecraft may just have been merely cannibalizing earlier ideas and terms rather than creating them anew from whole cloth.

A mention should be made of the hidden cannibalism in tales connected with the sabbats and rituals perpetrated by cults and covens in tales such as "The Shadow over Innsmouth" (1931), "The Dreams in the Witch House" (1932), "The Thing on the Doorstep" (1933), and the aforementioned "The Dunwich Horror" and *The Case of Charles Dexter Ward*. In the letter to Conover noted earlier the canned human meat from the Innsmouth cannery "is prepared only from the plump, healthy bourgeois specimens (usually those sacrificed at the Sabbats and Estbats in the forest behind Arkham)." Although obviously very much in jest, this indicates that, in fiction, Lovecraft considers cannibalism to be a fixture, or at the very least a potential by-product, of such rituals, with all that that implies. This may be following either (or both) traditional European witch-lore or the practices of classical Greece, wherein once the sacrifice of the animal has been made to the gods and its essence/life/spirit given over, the remaining meat was then distributed to the worshippers. Thus while not textually supported internally in his fiction, this personal insight from a comical source paradoxically adds even darker undercurrents to the already grim events alluded to inside these tales.

The direct rendering of human remains as meat makes a grim and powerful final reappearance in *At the Mountains of Madness* (1931). The revived Old Ones, clearly perceiving that all earthly life, as their own creation, was meant for their own to use as they see fit, simply act in logical, almost clinical fashion with the bodies of those they have slain. The exact motives and sequence of events at the camp remain opaque. It is certain that there was a desperate fight, but whether this was initially defensive or aggressive by either side is deliberately unclear. Dyer posits sympathetically of the Old Ones an "awful awakening in the cold of an unknown epoch—perhaps an attack by the furry, frantically barking quadrupeds, and a dazed defence against them and the equally frantic white simians with the queer wrappings and paraphernalia" (CF 3.143), and this does seem a likely reading of events, although it is ultimately merely Dyer's supposition. Other speculation, admittedly without real textual grounds, might opine that the Old Ones were driven by the baser motivation of wanting fresh meat after their unprecedented torpor. Whatever the truth may be, the rescue party soon discovers "all the healthier, fatter bodies, quadrupedal or bipedal, had had their most solid masses of tissue cut out and removed, as by a careful butcher; and around them was a strange sprinkling of salt—taken from the ravaged provision-chests on the planes—which conjured up the most horrible associations" (CF 3.62). Lovecraft wanted it made abundantly clear to the reader that this excision is done with a view to later ingestion. Instead of the terms "man" and "dog" Lovecraft chooses biological descriptors to subconsciously connect each together while simultaneously bringing something of the alien in terms of the perspective in which humans normally view both themselves and their relation to animals. Lovecraft then deliberately uses the using term butcher, with its emotionally loaded connotations and alternative meanings, in place of possible substitutes like cutter, processor, surgeon, or dissector.

Mentioning the sprinkling of salt immediately makes the ordinary reader, especially of his time, think of the horrific connotations of preservation of human meat for later consumption. Such salting in the perpetual cold of the Antarctic is of course completely unnecessary, and while an argument could be made that the revived Old Ones are acting habitually or believe they will be heading into a balmier climate as they travel homeward, this is a spiral of pedantry that is both fruitless and unnecessary. The disturbing resonance of the literary effect far outweighs any latent illogic of the action, and I suspect few if any first-time readers ponder this potentiality.

The lack of differentiation between human and dog adds a particularly chilling element of the Old Ones' motives and understandings. There are no psychological or longevity motivations as in "The Picture in the House," no greedy desire for the "toothsomeness" of human flesh displayed by the gugs, or even the fulfillment of an order natural to a species such as ghouls. Clearly to the Old Ones, humanity is of no more import than cattle, but another source of protein, "used sometimes for food and sometimes as an amusing buffoon" (*CF* 3.100). This casual disdain for the entirety of humanity as a sentient species, seeing us rather as food upon the same level as any other mammal, is all the more disturbing for the later understanding gained that the Old Ones don't even require such sustenance as is derived from any living flesh. This is not to say that the Old Ones are entirely uninterested in the unusual simians and canines they have slaughtered. The body of Gedney and the missing dog taken by the Old Ones and later found in the abandoned city are certainly treated with "patent care to prevent further damage" (*CF* 3.130). Yet again Lovecraft conflates man and his domesticated beast as of an equal significance by having them given a like level of care. The Old Ones may have interest in other life, but it is the clinical interest of the archaeologist disturbing a sacred tomb or of doctors creating human anatomy specimens from living people in Auschwitz. Our possible intelligence and development is a matter of absolutely no intrinsic value, of no relevance other than perhaps as the scientific curiosity of the greater being for its subject. Thus even in the very humanocentric horror of anthropophagy Lovecraft is perfectly able to demonstrate the paradoxically malign cosmic indifference that underpins the entirety of his work and gives it so much of its unique power.

Works Cited

Abnett, Dan. *Ravenor vs Eisenhorn: Pariah.* Nottingham, UK: Games Workshop, 2012.

Ammianus Marcellinus. *Res Gestae*. Tr. John. C. Rolfe. Cambridge, MA: Harvard University Press, 1935–40.

BBC. "Nigerian Girl 'Killed for Witchcraft Rituals'." www.bbc.com/news/world-africa-41985115

Barrett, Ron. *Aghor Medicine: Pollution, Death, and Healing in Northern India*. Berkeley: University of California Press, 2008.

Bird, Antonia (director). *Ravenous*. Twentieth Century Fox, 1999.

Blumenschine, Robert J., Christopher A. Brochu, Llewellyn D. Densmore, and Jackson Njau. "A New Horned Crocodile from the Pilo-Pleistocene Hominid Sites at Olduvai Gorge, Tanzania." doi.org/10.1371/journal.pone.0009333, 24 February 2010.

Burgess, Ann W., John E. Douglas, and Robert K. Ressler. *Sexual Homicide: Patterns and Motives*. New York: Lexington Books, 1988.

Caesar, C. Julius. *Caesar's Gallic War*. Tr. W. A. McDevitte and W. H. Bohn. New York: Harper & Brothers, 1869.

Chapman, R. C., M. L. Rossi, A. W. Shahrom, and P. Vanezis. "Postmortem Injuries by Indoor Pets." *American Journal of Forensic Medicine and Pathology* (June 1994).

The Concise Oxford Dictionary of Current English, 5th ed. Oxford: Oxford University Press, 1964.

Ewruje, Henry Kester. "Cannibalism—Nigerians on the Run!!!" www.gatewaynigeria.tv/relocate/2009/11/cannibalism-nigerians-on-the-run/

Garrett, Frances. "Tapping the Body's Nectar: Gastronomy and Incorporation in Tibetan Literature." *History of Religions* 49, No. 3 (February 2010): 300–326.

Hadjimatheou, Chloe. "Why Greeks Are Exhuming Their Parents." *BBC Magazine*, www.bbc.com/news/magazine-34920068

Herodotus. *The Histories*. Tr. A. D. Godley. Cambridge, MA: Harvard University Press, 1920.

Igwe, Leo. "Ritual Killing and Pseudoscience in Nigeria." *Skeptical Briefs* 14, No. 2 (June 2004), www.csicop.org/sb/show/ritual_killing_and_pseudoscience_in_nigeria

Johnson, Samuel. *A Dictionary of the English Language*, 1755. 6th ed. London, 1785.

Joshi, S. T. "Time, Space and Natural Law: Science and Pseudo-Science in Lovecraft." In *Lovecraft and a World in Transition:*

Collected Essays on H. P. Lovecraft. New York: Hippocampus Press, 2014. 197–223.

———. "Lovecraft and the *Regnum Congo*." In *Lovecraft and a World in Transition: Collected Essays on H. P. Lovecraft.* New York: Hippocampus Press, 2014. 372–76.

Mikkelson, David. "Thai 'Cannibalism' Photographs." *Snopes* (11 July 2013), snopes.com/fact-check/marrow-escape/

Norris, Duncan. "Lovecraft and Egypt: A Closer Examination." *Lovecraft Annual* No. 10 (2016): 3–45.

Pliny the Elder. *The Natural History.* Tr. John Bostock and H. T. Riley. London: Taylor & Francis, 1855.

Robson, Steve. "Body of Woman, 56, Who Collapsed and Died in Her Home Is Gnawed and Eaten by Her Own Cats on Her Kitchen Floor." *Daily Mail* (13 August 2013), www.dailymail.co.uk/news/article-2391223/Janet-Veal-56-gnawed-eaten-CATS-kitchen-floor-died.html

Sauer, Carl Ortwin. *The Early Spanish Main.* Cambridge: Cambridge University Press, 1966.

Schechter, Harold. *Deranged: The Shocking True Story of America's Most Fiendish Killer.* New York: Pocket Books, 1990.

Stoker, Bram. "The Squaw." *"Holly Leaves": The Xmas Number of the Illustrated Sporting and Dramatic News* (2 December 1893).

Strabo. *The Geography of Strabo.* London: George Bell & Sons, 1903.

Webster's New World Dictionary of the American Language, Encyclopedic Edition. Cleveland: World Publishing Co., 1951.

Wylie, Turrell. "Ro-Langs: The Tibetan Zombie." *History of Religions* 4, No. 1 (Summer 1964): 69–80.

The Rings of Cthulhu: Lovecraft, Dürer, Saturn, and Melancholy

Andrew Paul Wood

As one of the most written-about works of Western art, Albrecht Dürer's engraving *Melencolia I* (1514) needs little introduction: an androgynous winged figure representing the melancholic humour sits, face resting on one hand, beside an assemblage of objects representing intellect and creative genius. In the background, over sea and beyond some partially flooded islands, a strange batlike creature bears the title as a banner across its wings, sharing the sky with a rainbow, and what is either an ominous comet or the planet Saturn, that baleful world being the astrological planet with influence over the melancholic humour. The engraving may be regarded as a kind of visual puzzle on the theme of melancholy. It is, as it turns out, a work that had a not inconsiderable influence on H. P. Lovecraft.

The doctrine of humours was a pseudoscientific concept that had significant influence over medicine and the theory of mind well into the nineteenth century, deriving from the belief amongst the Greeks and Romans that human temperament was a product of the interaction of four humours, yellow bile, black bile, phlegm, and blood, with one dominant. We still refer to people being sanguine, phlegmatic, and bilious today. The melancholic temperament (from the Greek μέλαινα χολή, *melaena chole*, or black bile) was associated with the element of earth, coldness, and, as stated above, astrologically associated with the influence of Saturn. The fullest account of Melancholia in English was encyclopedically compiled by Robert Burton (1577–1640) in *The Anatomy of Melancholy* (1621; frequently reprinted throughout the seventeenth century), a text that Lovecraft was familiar with.[1] C. S. Lewis in *The Discarded Image* describes the effect of Saturn thus:

> In the earth his influence produces lead; in men, the melancholy complexion; in history, disastrous events. In Dante his sphere is the Heaven of contemplatives. He is connected with sickness and old age. Our traditional picture of Father Time with the scythe is derived from earlier pictures of Saturn. A good account of his activities in promoting fatal accidents, pestilence, treacheries, and ill luck in general, occurs in [Chaucer's] *The Knight's Tale*. . . . He is the most terrible of the seven [planets] and is sometimes called The Greater Infortune, *Infortunata Major*. (105)

Lovecraft wrote mockingly of the astrological influence of Saturn in "The Science of Astrology" (1914) for the Providence *Evening News*, an essay rubbishing the superstition, describing it thus: "A Saturn person is of middle stature; small, black, leering eyes, thick nose and lips, large ears, dark hair and of melancholy expression. Tends to engage as a farmer, miner, brick maker, butcher, etc." (*CE* 3.341). The anti-Semitic tone is unquestionable and suggests a link in Lovecraft's mind between Saturn and the alien "other" that he was so notoriously paranoid about, but the irony is that Lovecraft himself typifies the classical description of the Melancholic or Saturnine type—gloomy, withdrawn, intellectual, artistic, witty, driven—something he shares with most of his protagonists, although it was not a characteristic he attributed to himself, writing, "I have never been able to cultivate a picturesque melancholy. Indeed, it has never even occurred to me to try" (*SL* 5.362).

Lovecraft was intensely interested in the psychology of mood and personality, making it central to his art, going so far as to say:

---

1. HPL possibly intimates a personal identification with Burton in his use of the pseudonym "Lewis Theobald, Jun." (as co-author with Winifred Jackson under the name "Elizabeth Berkeley") for their stories "The Crawling Chaos" (*United Cooperative*, April 1921) and "The Green Meadow" (*Vagrant*, Spring 1927). The unusual abbreviation "Jun." for "Junior," attached in homage to the name of the eighteenth-century Shakespeare scholar Lewis Theobald, recalls Burton's own nom de plume for *The Anatomy of Melancholy* as "Democritus Junior" after the Greek philosopher.

"In many sorts of literature—weird most of all—the *real* protagonists of the drama are *phenomena, and not people at all*" (*SL* 4.119; emphasis in original), and: "It must, if it is to be authentic art, form primarily *the crystallisation or symbolisation of a definite human mood*" (*SL* 5.128; emphasis in original). Some of these concepts might well have resurfaced in Lovecraft's awareness in researching his ancestor, the pre-Copernican Elizabethan astronomer John Field (1520/30–1587), of whom he learned around 1936 (*SL* 5.263ff.), though he had extensively researched the subject in 1926 (*SL* 4.153). Lovecraft would also have gleaned considerable information on the ritually occult aspects of Saturn from his copy of Lewis Spence's *Encyclopedia of Occultism*. Despite being a noted skeptic, Lovecraft, fascinated by the classical myths associated with the constellations since childhood (de Camp 34), was not one to throw the baby out with the bathwater if it provided his stories with picturesque texture, writing that though modern people might not "*believe* in centaurs & mermaids, we found all of these things of vital significance in art—as bearing on the life and beliefs of those ancestral ages which moulded & gave rise to ours" (*SL* 5.396; emphasis in original). Furthermore, as Will Murray has noted in his essay "On the Natures of Nug and Yeb," Lovecraft's genealogy for his pseudo-pantheon parallels that of the classical gods descending from Chaos (53). We might infer that a text like Hesiod's *Theogony* was a template.[2]

---

[2] Clark Ashton Smith, writing to August Derleth shortly after HPL's death in 1937, wondered if HPL's Mythos was deliberately vague, intended mostly for atmosphere and noting the "discrepant characters" assigned to the various alien deities. This is cited by David E. Schultz as evidence that the Mythos lacks any real premeditated structure and existed mainly as keeping manageable the utterly unknowable for narrative purposes (46). I suspect this may be overcompensating somewhat for Derleth's crude and overdetermined attempt to get HPL's cultic window-dressing to conform to his own mythopoesis, and HPL's attempts at, among other things, a genealogy for his entities suggests a more conceptual framework, even if only in fun, inspired by Dunsany's Pegāna pantheon, over whom presides Mānā-Yood-Sushāī, who made the world and the gods and now sleeps and when he awakens will destroy all. One might note a certain assonance between the names Cthulhu and Mānā-Yood-Sushāī. This sort of de-emphasis on the cosmic aspects of HPL's fiction ultimately ends up in the thin and salty gruel of Gavin Callaghan's *H. P. Lovecraft's Dark Arcadia: The Satire, Symbology and*

William Touponce notes that Lovecraft was deeply interested in the image of Dürer's *Melencolia I* (xviii), writing to Fritz Leiber in November 1936:

> My own temperament, I should say, is one of *scientific indifferentism* (the solar system is a meaningless drop in an unknown and purposeless cosmos, but what the hell of it?) rather than melancholy—though I suppose my constant interest in fantasy expresses a subconscious dissatisfaction with objective reality which is not far from certain phases of the genuine article. I've always been fascinated, by the way, by that engraving of Dürer's. (*SL* 5.343)

It is, perhaps, also Dürer, among others, whom Lovecraft had in mind when he wrote that his taste in visual art "run[s] overwhelmingly to the Greco-Roman (with, however, a parallel fondness for *fine* Gothic design and its Renaissance deviations" (*SL* 5.35; emphasis in original). "Albrecht Dürer" was also Lovecraft's pet name for Donald Wandrei's brother, the artist Howard Wandrei (*Letters with Donald and Howard Wandrei* 340n1).

Looking at what is popularly considered to be Dürer's personification of Melancholy itself, one is struck by the resemblance of the slumped figure to Lovecraft's sketch of an imaginary figurine of his most famous creation, Cthulhu, drawn in 1934 for his young correspondent and future anthropologist, R. H. Barlow.[3] One might also note that in both cases the wings are too small for the body, symbolically incapable of providing transcendent flight. Lovecraft may also have been familiar with Scottish poet James Thomson's use of Dürer's personification in his celebrated long poem *The City of Dreadful Night* (1880), which describes a bleak and hellish nocturnal metropolis (a version of London) over which looms Dürer's Melancholia as a colossal statue, "throned there / An Image sits, stupendous, superhuman, / The bronze colossus of a winged Woman, / Upon a graded granite base foursquare":

> Low-seated she leans forward massively,
>   With cheek on clenched left hand, the forearm's might
> Erect, its elbow on her rounded knee;

Contradiction (2013), and there we may safely leave it.
3. John Hay Library, Brown University, Providence, RI.

Across a clasped book in her lap the right
Upholds a pair of compasses; she gazes
With full set eyes, but wandering in thick mazes
Of sombre thought beholds no outward sight.
                            (Stanza XXI, ll. 4–14)

This makes interesting comparison to Lovecraft's description of Cthulhu (or what his protagonist thinks to be merely an idol of same) in "The Call of Cthulhu" (1926), "in the centre of which, revealed by occasional rifts in the curtain of flame, stood a great granite monolith some eight feet in height; on top of which, incongruous with its diminutiveness, rested the noxious carven statuette" (*CF* 2.36). It would not be too difficult to conceive Lovecraft's R'lyeh might be loosely influenced by Thomson's city, and it is intriguing to consider the possibility that Cthulhu might be Lovecraft's own embodiment of Melancholia (and, one speculates, his loathing of the cold and seafood). Lovecraft explicitly refers to the archetypal nature of his pantheon in a letter to the composer Harold S. Farnese in 1932:

> In my own efforts to crystallise this spaceward outreaching, I try to utilise as many as possible of the elements which have, under earlier mental and emotional conditions, given man a symbolic feeling of the unreal, the ethereal, & the mystical—choosing those least attacked by the realistic mental and emotional conditions of the present. Darkness—sunset—dreams—mists—fever—madness—the tomb—the hills—the sea—the sky—the wind—all these, & many other things have seemed to me to retain a certain imaginative potency despite our actual scientific analysis of them. Accordingly I have tried to weave them into a kind of shadowy phantasmagoria which may have the same sort of vague coherence as a cycle of traditional myth and legend—with nebulous backgrounds of Elder Forces & trans-galactic entities which lurk about this infinitesimal planet, (& of course others as well), establishing outposts thereon, & occasionally brushing up aside other accidental forms of life (like human beings) in order to take up full habitation. (*SL* 4.70)

The art historian Erwin Panofsky, in his analysis of Dürer's engraving, notes the characteristics of Melancholia as "awkward, miserly, spiteful, greedy, malicious, cowardly, faithless, irreverent and drowsy" (157–58), much of which would apply equally well to Cthulhu within the limits of anthropomorphism of such an alien sentience, but the notion of Melancholia as being cold and dry according to alchemy and the doctrine of humours only half fits: Cthulhu is, of course, cold and wet. However, as hinted at in the flooded islands in the engraving, Melancholia is ruled by Saturn—who, like Cthulhu, in some traditions sleeps in a hidden island until the stars are right (Plutarch 5.234)—and Saturn, in some aspects, is master of floods and tides (Klabansky et al. 314). Melancholy, like Cthulhu, was also thought to attract dreams of madness and ecstasy and inspire genius (Sohm). Certainly Lovecraft wasn't making the entity up on the fly, writing to August Derleth in 1928: "I spent enormous pains thinking out Cthulhu" (*SL* 1.154). The idea of old gods cyclically returning to reign anew applies to both Cthulhu in the Mythos and Saturn in classical mythology. In "Simplicity: A Poem" (1922), Lovecraft writes:

> And he, unspoil'd, may childlike bask again
> Beneath the beams of Saturn's golden reign. (*AT* 252)

This is an allusion to in Virgil's Fourth Eclogue, in which the Roman poet describes the Sibylline prophecy that Saturn and Astraea (the virgin goddess of justice) would return at some future point to usher in a new golden age.[4] Lovecraft alludes to the myth of the previous golden age of Saturn in one of his astronomy columns for the Providence *Evening News* (*CE* 3.205). In the medieval and Renaissance periods this was widely interpreted as a pagan prophecy of the birth of Christ. It is tempting to speculate that Lovecraft's reappearance of Cthulhu represents a nightmarish inversion of a coming golden age, with Saturn returning in his negative aspect as the *Infortuna Major* of classical astrology, come to purge the Earth of the people of the age of iron (i.e., modern civilization).

---

4. The great cycle of periods is born anew.
   Now returns the Maid, returns the reign of Saturn:
   Now from high heaven a new generation comes down.
   Yet do thou at that boy's birth,
   In whom the iron race shall begin to cease,
   And the golden to arise over all the world . . . (Mackail 275–76)

Saturnalia, the ancient Roman festival of Saturn, held on December 17 in the Julian calendar, also seems to have fascinated Lovecraft. A forbear of the Christmas holiday, Saturnalia was characterized by merrymaking and a temporary suspension of the usual social order—a return to the golden age reign of Saturn. Lovecraft wrote about the festival several times, in his astronomy articles (CE 3.131, 168, 205, 319), a poem ("Saturnalia"), and the "The Festival" (1923), which takes place at Yuletide, and we may assume that is also a dark reflection thereof.

Lovecraft would also have been familiar with Keats's fragmentary epic *The Fall of Hyperion: A Dream* (1819), which takes place after the Titans of Greek myth have fallen and been supplanted by the Olympian gods. The poem is narrated by the poet who, in a dream, is permitted to enter the ruined temple of Saturn to which the god, defeated by Jupiter, retreated. His priestess Moneta encourages the poet to ascend a stair upon which he experiences incredible torment and rebirth, and reveals to the dreaming poet that the purpose of poetry is to transcend dreams and embrace the burden of humanity's existential suffering:

> And saw, what first I thought an image huge,
> Like to the image pedestal'd so high
> In Saturn's temple. Then Moneta's voice
> Came brief upon mine ear "So Saturn sat
> When he had lost his realms" whereon there grew
> A power within me of enormous ken
> To see as a god sees, and take the depth
> Of things as nimbly as the outward eye
> Can size and shape pervade.
>   (Canto I, stanza iv)

This seems equally evocative of that which is promised to the worshippers of Cthulhu, and also the gift offered by the mysterious Shining Trapezohedron in Lovecraft's last major effort at fiction, "The Haunter of the Dark," as we shall see.

Lovecraft mentions Saturn the planet precisely twice in his fiction, once in "Pickman's Model" (1926), "There was none of the exotic technique you see in Sidney Sime, none of the trans-Saturnian landscapes and lunar fungi that Clark Ashton Smith uses to freeze the blood" (*CF* 2.63), alluding to the classical solar system where Saturn was the outermost world, and then in *The Dream-Quest of Unknown Kadath* (1926–27), where that planet is inhabited by alien cats who are the sworn enemies to the terrestrial variety. Of the mythological god, although not mentioned by name, as Donald R. Burleson notes in his *Lovecraft: Disturbing the Universe* (1990), the description of one of Pickman's paintings matches fairly closely to Goya's painting *Il Saturno* or *Saturn Devouring His Children*[5] (Burleson 92). On the whole this line of pursuit is less fruitful than consulting Lovecraft's astronomical writings, as will become apparent.

Don Webb suggests that the "horror" of Cthulhu "is that he is an accurate depiction of the human psyche, which has purposes larger than the here-and-now and is seldom awakened." This is true too of the powers attributed to Melancholia, and in Dante's *Paradiso* we are reminded that in the Heaven of Saturn, so close are they to the Empyrean and ultimately God, experiences are so intensified in pitch that the angelic chorus temporarily halts and the soul of his beloved Beatrice refrains from smiling lest it accidentally destroy the poet's mortal senses and blast his sanity (Dante 21.4–12, 21.58–63).

There is not room here for a full examination of the question of whether the Mythos might be interpreted as a fantastical reworking of classical astrology, that Cthulhu might be Lovecraft's version of Saturn, deity of the outermost Ptolemaic planetary sphere (with Nyarlathotep as Mercury, Shub-Niggurath as Venus, and so on, eschewing August Derleth's crude attempt to fit the Mythos to the cardinal elements), but it is diverting to speculate. There are other hints: in the Mythos, Father Dagon is closely associated with Cthulhu in "Dagon" (1917) and "The Shadow over Innsmouth" (1931), and Dagon in the context of the *interpretatio graeca* is identified with Cronus (the Greek name for Saturn) or is the brother of Cronus (Fontenrose). Robert M. Price makes a case for Dagon being an alias for Cthulhu based on contextual evidence in "The Shadow over Innsmouth" (49). Any links between the Dürer engraving and Cthulhu are mostly hypothetical on my

---

5. 1819–23, Museo Nacional Del Prado, Madrid.

part, but there seems to be a more concrete connection to Lovecraft's last story, "The Haunter of the Dark" (1935). Dürer would have once again been on Lovecraft's mind. In the winter and spring of that year, he attended public lectures at Brown University, including one on Dürer (de Camp 399).

The Danish scholar and critic Ib Johansen makes the link in relation to archetypal melancholia and Lovecraft's stock, knowledge-obsessed protagonists when he writes:

> The shape of the Shining Trapezohedron also reminds us of the polyhedron in Albrecht Dürer's graphic masterpiece, *Melencolia I* (1514), where a huge, oddly shaped stone-block (the polyhedron)—together with the magic square behind the allegorical representation of Melancholy herself—have been interpreted as "not just two iconographic elements, amongst many others, in the engraving, but perhaps even the *raison d'être* of the whole work. (320)

I would suggest the connection is actually much stronger than that. The term "trapezohedron" is an unusual one found in few contexts: geometry, crystallography (Lovecraft, being a keen reader in the sciences, could plausibly have encountered it that way), and in relation to the large irregular polygonal solid in *Melencolia I*. The so-called "Dürer's Solid" is a genuine truncated triangular trapezohedron as mathematically described. In 1900, the German art historian Paul Weber described this mysterious object in the engraving as crystalline and *"ein Rhomboëder mit abgestumpften Polen,"* a rhombohedron with truncated poles (76). The entry on "Crystallography" in the 1911 *Encyclopaedia Britannica* furnishes the synonym "trapezohedron" in relation to a diagram of a calcite crystal. Dürer's polyhedron also appears to incorporate a faint, shadowy image into one facet that has been variously interpreted as a skull (*memento mori*) or a self-portrait of the artist and is suggestive of visions or connections with some other entity (Sohm). To that we may add, as Steven J. Mariconda observes, Lewis Spence's description of contemporary scrying practice for the diabolical crystal's dimensions and setting:

> The crystal most in favor among modern crystal gazers is a spherical or oval globe about four inches in diameter, and preferably a genu-

ine crystal.... The crystal, as well as the stand on which it rests, must be inscribed with sacred characters. (Cited in Mariconda 206)

Is Dürer's Solid, therefore, the inspiration for the Shining Trapezohedron?[6] Conceivably it also supplies the model for the irregularly shaped and inscribed black stone from Yuggoth described in "The Whisperer in Darkness" (1930):

> The thing, as nearly as one might guess, had faced the camera vertically with a somewhat irregularly curved surface of one by two feet; but to say anything definite about that surface, or about the general shape of the whole mass, almost defies the power of language. What outlandish geometrical principles had guided its cutting—for artificially cut it was—I could not even begin to guess; and never before had I seen anything which struck me as so strangely and unmistakably alien to this world. (CF 3.482)

That, however, to return to "The Haunter of the Dark," is certainly not the only intriguing parallel. In the story, the titular Haunter is described as indistinct, smoky or cloudlike, but having wings: "the air trembled with a vibration as of flapping wings" (CF 3.474), and in the passage most directly based on Hanns Heinz Ewers's story "The Spider" (1915), "'I see it—coming here—hell-wind—titan blur—black wings—Yog-Sothoth save me—the three-lobed burning eye ...'" (CF 3.477). Is the batlike creature with the serpentine tail in Dürer's engraving the inspiration for

---

6. HPL was apparently tinkering with the idea by 1934, writing in a letter to James F. Morton the following imaginative passage: "[T]hink of the Eye of Tsathoggua, hinted at in the Livre d'Eibon, and of the carved primal monstrosity in lavender pyro-jadeite caught up in a Kanaka fisherman's hut of the coast of Ponape! God! Suppose the world knew why Curator Konbifhashi Taximeto of the Wiggiwaga Museum in Kyoto committed hara-kiri after examining the fluorescent emanations of this unholy blasphemy through the differential spectroheliograph!" (SL 4.394). Cf. the description of the Cthulhu figurine in "The Call of Cthulhu" (CF 2.23–24). The theme is a generic one that can be traced to various examples in weird fiction, especially H. G. Wells's 1897 story "The Crystal Egg," the folklore of magic mirrors and crystal balls, and of course, the historical example of Dr. John Dee, Edward Kelley, and their scrying crystal. Steven J. Mariconda investigates these in detail in his essay "Some Antecedents of the Shining Trapezohedron" (205–12), though he doesn't make a connection to Dürer.

the eponymous avatar of Nyarlathotep? Its form might have also inspired the "hybrid winged things ... not altogether crows, nor moles, nor buzzards, nor ants, nor vampire bats, nor decomposed human beings" of "The Festival" (*CF* 1.414). Thomson, in his poem, describes the creature as "a snaky imp, dog-headed" (Stanza XXII, ll. 39–40), which is certainly a more accurate description; it is a chimera of some kind. Conceivably it also brought to mind Lovecraft's childhood nightmares about being carried off by the demonic, batlike night-gaunts (Pearsall 301).[7] Note also that Dürer's demon bat appears to be fleeing the bright light in the heavens, much as the photophobic Haunter shuns and flees the light.

The nature of the "three-lobed burning eye" in "Haunter" escapes easy conjecture, being one of the most intractable enigmas of Lovecraft's fiction—though one might speculate a sympathetic relationship between it and the Shining Trapezohedron, and in the context of *Melencolia I*, when viewed from some angles when only three of the six pentagonal facets are visible, Dürer's Solid might reasonably be described as "three-lobed." The eyes of Dürer's bat creature are not detailed, nor terribly distinct, and it is possible that Lovecraft's imagination might have discerned them as "three-lobed" in some way, or perhaps Lovecraft interpreted the shadowy form in the Solid to this end. Another source altogether may have suggested the eye, such as Maurice Leblanc's *The Three Eyes* (1919; translated into English in 1921), in which a French scientist makes televisual contact with three-eyed Venusians.[8] However, to return to the link between Melancholia and seventh planet, we may recall Galileo's 1610 eyelike drawings of Saturn, made with the aid of his primitive telescope a century after Dürer created *Melencolia I*, wherein the astronomer interprets that planet's rings as enormous lateral lobes, writing to his Medici patron, Cosimo II:

> I discovered another very strange wonder, which I should like to make known to their Highnesses . . . , keeping it secret, however, until the time when my work is published . . . the star of Saturn is

---

7. HPL attributed these dreams to memories of Gustave Doré's 1866 illustrations of Milton's Paradise Lost.
8. HPL read it in 1927 and mentions it to Clark Ashton Smith in a letter dated 1 October of that year (*SL* 2.298).

not a single star, but is a composite of three, which almost touch each other, never change or move relative to each other, and are arranged in a row along the zodiac, the middle one being three times larger than the lateral ones, and they are situated in this form: oOo. (Cited in Van Helden 105)

Lovecraft was well aware of this passage of astronomical history and recounts it in some detail in one of his astronomy columns for the Providence *Evening News* (CE 3.130–31). Perhaps, therefore, the three-lobed eye isn't specifically the ocular organ of the Haunter, but rather an oblique reference to Saturn and, by extension, Melancholia. Steven J. Mariconda makes the connection between the visions of the Shining Trapezohedron and the eponymous casement in the Lovecraft fragment "The Rose Window" (elaborated by August Derleth into the novel-length pastiche *The Lurker at the Threshold*; the chiming with "The Haunter in the Dark" seems deliberate), and the pointed McGuffin above a bookcase of the carving of a strange octopuslike thing with round mirror capable of granting similar visions featuring as one large, Cyclopean eye (Mariconda 210), which also recalls to the reader's mind Cthulhu's octopus-like nature.

Elsewhere in his astronomical writings, Lovecraft describes the planet as "the bright yet strangely leaden-hued Saturn" (CE 3.296), suggesting an allusion to Saturn's alchemical association with lead, and melancholic temperament. Saturn rules the outermost planetary sphere before that of the fixed stars, a suitable interlocutor between a terrestrial "Church of Starry Wisdom" and the dark, post-classical planets beyond Saturn: Uranus, Neptune, Pluto (prior to the International Astronomical Union's decision to demote it in 2006) and/or Yuggoth, Shaggai (mentioned in "Haunter in the Dark"), and perhaps Kynarth (mentioned in the collaboration "Through the Gates of the Silver Key" [1933–34])—planets unknown to terrestrial science, as the epigraph for "The Haunter of the Dark," taken from the second stanza of Lovecraft's poem "Nemesis" (with substantial orthographical differences), would suggest:

> I have seen the dark universe yawning,
>   Where the black planets roll without aim—
> Where they roll in their horror unheeded,
>   Without knowledge or lustre or name. (CF 3.451)

The Shining Trapezohedron, as revealed by visions to the protagonist, was found or made on Pluto/Yuggoth by the fungal Mi-Go, and thus, in terms of classical astrology, fall somewhere between the influence of Saturn and the celestial sphere. There are also possible saturnine connections that might be made to Lovecraft's mysterious fictional pharaoh Nephren-Ka.[9] Confusingly though, the Haunter and/or the "three-lobed burning eye" are implied to be avatar(s) of Nyarlathotep, whose attributes most closely match those of Mercury—travel, commerce, communication between realms, fickleness, and service. C. S. Lewis writes of the difficulty in finding a unity in all conflicting aspects of the Mercurial essence because it is chaotic: "'Skilled eagerness' or 'bright alacrity' is the best I can do. But it is better just to take some real mercury [the metallic element] in a saucer and play with it for a few minutes. *That* is what mercurial means" (108). Likewise a fitting description of the Crawling Chaos, Nyarlathotep.

Lovecraft, self-declared materialist and noted astrological skeptic, presumably didn't feel a need to adhere too closely to any occult schema, not least one he largely invented himself. Nonetheless, according to William Lilly's *Christian Astrology* (1647), Mercury is a cool, dry planet and also has influence over the melancholy temperament, responsible for:

> a man of subtil and politick brain, intellect and cogitation; an excellent disputant or Logician, arguing with learning and discretion, and using much eloquence in his speech, a searcher into all types

---

9. The pharaoh Nephren-Ka, associated with the Shining Trapezohedron in "The Haunter of the Dark," appears to be based on HPL's reading of Diodorus and Herodotus on the historical pharaoh Khafra (Khaf-Ra, Khefren to the Greeks, reigning in the Fourth Dynasty of the Old Kingdom, who died 2480 B.C.E.). Herodotus describes Khafra as a tyrant and heretic who kept the temples closed after the previous pharaoh Khufu (Cheops), his father, had them sealed (Herodotus, *Histories* 2.124ff.), which might easily have inspired the lightless temple Nephren-Ka constructed for the Shining Trapezohedron. The name Nephren-Ka is probably a distortion of Khefren-Ra, from Khaf-Ra's pharaonic title as "like Ra" or "Son of Ra" the sun god. It is an outside possibility that HPL might have encountered the German philologist Franz Boll's *Sphaera* (1903), in which Boll makes reference to the Ptolemaic *interpretatio graeca* of the astrological planet Saturn as Mithras-Helios, and an ostrakon (potsherd) identifying Ra with Saturn (Boll 313–14n3).

of Mysteries and Learning ... a man of unwearied fancy, curious in the search of any occult knowledge; able by his own Genius to produce wonders; given to divination and the more secret knowledge ... (77)

The description of Nyarlathotep as diabolical scientist of the Nikola Tesla type in the 1920 prose poem of the same name, and as the "Black Man" in "The Dreams in the Witch House" (1932), however, suggest a distinctly saturnine appearance.

Lovecraft was an emphatic disbeliever in astrology, writing no less than five essays decrying and debunking the subject, and four pieces of Swiftian satire under the pseudonym Isaac Bickerstaff in his feud with Providence astrologer J. F. Hartmann in the pages of the *Evening News*.[10] Clearly, he did not take it seriously, and any use of it in his fiction is purely a literary device. It has become almost a cliché to suggest (however dubiously) that Lovecraft's *Necronomicon* was partially inspired by Manilius' *Astronomica*, a first-century treatise on astronomy and astrology in Latin hexameters.[11] Similarly, Lovecraft's fascination with Dürer's *Melencolia I* most likely provided a kind of catalyst or nucleus to which various dreams, experiences, snippets of weird lore, astrology, the doctrine of humours, astronomy, history, etc. from his vast breadth of reading and interest might adhere, from which Lovecraft was able to forge a synthesis that formed the basis for a significant part of the occult internal logic that gives the Mythos its aesthetically satisfying richness.

---

10. "Isaac Bickerstaff, Esq" was the pseudonym adopted by Jonathan Swift for his hoax letters (1708–09) satirizing and eventually predicting the death of his contemporary, the then-famous astrologer and maker of almanacs, John Partridge (1644–1714).

11. It is L. Sprague de Camp, following George T. Wetzel, who fingers Manilius (de Camp 167), but in a letter to Harry O. Fischer, HPL cites the *Almagest* or *Great Treatise* (Μεγάλη Σύνταξις) of Claudius Ptolemy (c. 100–170 C.E.), the Greek title of which HPL imaginatively extends to Μεγάλη Σύνταξις τῆς Αστρονομίας, which only adds to the confusion (*SL* 5.418).

Works Cited

Boll, F. *Sphaera: Neue griechische Texte und untersuchungen zur geschichte der Sternbilder.* Leipzig: B. G. Teubner, 1903.

Burleson, Donald R. *Lovecraft: Disturbing the Universe.* Lexington: University Press of Kentucky, 1990.

Dante Alighieri. *Paradiso* (*The Comedy of Dante Alighieri* III). Tr. Dorothy L. Sayers and Barbara Reynolds. Harmondsworth, UK: Penguin, 1962.

de Camp, L. Sprague. *Lovecraft: A Biography.* Garden City, NY: Doubleday, 1975.

Fontenrose, Joseph E. "Dagon and El." *Oriens* 10, No. 2 (December 1957): 277–79.

Johansen, Ib. *Walking Shadows: Reflections on the American Fantastic and the American Grotesque from Washington Irving to the Postmodern Era.* Leiden: Costerus New Series/Brill, 2015.

Keats, John. *The Complete Poems of John Keats.* London: Penguin, 1994.

Klibansky, Raymond; Panofsky, Erwin; and Saxl, Fritz. *Saturn and Melancholy: Studies in the History of Natural Philosophy, Religion and Art.* New York: Basic Books, 1964.

Leblanc, Maurice. *The Three Eyes.* Tr. Alexander Teixeira de Mattos. New York: Macaulay, 1921.

Lewis, C. S. *The Discarded Image.* Cambridge: Cambridge University Press, 1964.

Lilly, William. *Christian Astrology.* 3rd facsimile ed. London: Printed by Tho. Brudenell for John Partridge and Humph. Blunden, 1647. Regulus Publishing Co., 1985.

Lovecraft, H. P. *Letters with Donald and Howard Wandrei and to Emil Petaja.* Ed. S. T. Joshi and David E. Schultz. New York: Hippocampus Press, 2019.

Mackail, John William, tr. *Virgil's Works: The Aeneid, Eclogue and Georgics.* Whitefish, MT: Kessinger Publishing, 2003.

Mariconda, Steven J. *H. P. Lovecraft: Art, Artifact, and Reality.* New York: Hippocampus Press, 2013.

Murray, Will. "On the Natures of Nug and Yeb." *Lovecraft Studies* No. 9 (Fall 1984): 52–59.

Panofsky, Erwin. *The Life and Art of Albrecht Dürer*. 4th ed. Princeton: Princeton University Press, 1955.

Pearsall, Anthony B. *The Lovecraft Lexicon*. Tempe, AZ: New Falcon, 2005.

Plutarch, *Plutarch's Morals*. Translated from the Greek by Several Hands. Corrected and Revised by William W. Goodwin. Boston: Little, Brown, 1878. 5 vols.

Price, Robert M. "Mythos Names and How to Say Them." *Lovecraft Studies* No. 15 (Fall 1987): 47–53.

Schultz, David E. "Who Needs the 'Cthulhu Mythos'?" *Lovecraft Studies* No. 13 (Fall 1986): 43–53.

Sohm, Philip L. "Dürer's 'Melencolia I': The Limits of Knowledge." *Studies in the History of Art* 9 (1981): 13–32.

Spence, Lewis. *Encyclopedia of Occultism*. New York: Dodd, Mead, 1928.

Spencer, Leonard James. "Crystallography." *Encyclopaedia Britannica*. 11th ed.). 1911.

Thomson, James. *The City of Dreadful Night and Other Poems*. Edinburgh: Kennedy & Boyd/Zeticula Ltd, 2008.

Touponce, William F. *Lord Dunsany, H. P. Lovecraft, and Ray Bradbury: Spectral Journeys*. Lanham, MD: Scarecrow Press, 2013.

Van Helden, Albert. "Saturn and His Anses." *Journal for the History of Astronomy* 5 (1974): 105–21.

Webb, Don. "Why Lovecraft Still Matters: The Magical Power of Transformative Fiction." *NOVA Express* No. 14 (1997). www.epberglund.com/RGttCM/nightscapes/NS11/ns11nf2.htm Accessed 11 August 2018.

Weber, Paul, *Beiträge zu Dürers Weltanschauung: Eine Studie über die drei Stiche Ritter, Tod und Teufel, Melancholie und Hieronymus im Gehäus*. Strassburg, 1900.

"The Cats": An Environmental Ditty

Cecelia Hopkins-Drewer

At an initial reading, "The Cats" (1925; *AT* 72–73) appears to be a delightfully weird poem that combines images of the city at night with the nocturnal adventures of the cat community. A witchy, creepy city given completely over to the antics of cats at night is stimulating to the imagination and appeals to animal lovers. However, on further investigation the poem carries a legitimate environmental message. Moreover, the poem shares its imagery with two short stories written in the same year.

Lovecraft's poem is titled "The Cats," although the cats actually make their first appearance in verse four. The initial three verses appear to set the scene, which is "black" (l. 5), has "high" places for the cats to climb (l. 1) and tunnels of "catacomb deeps" for the cats to crawl through (l. 7). As we know, cats love to climb and explore. Cats also love smells, so the "live foetor" (l. 8) and "jumbles of odour" (l. 12) repugnant to a human would fascinate them.

In the beginning of the fourth verse the cats come out from the "alleys nocturnal" (l. 13) and yowl their territorial calls to the "moon" (l. 14). They are perceived as prophetic, as they are "screaming the future" (l. 15) amidst their challenges to their territorial rivals. Time is passing in verse five, as some of the "tow'rs and pyramids" (l. 17) are overgrown with ivy and beginning to crumble, and the streets are overgrown with weeds (l. 18). The once mighty bridges are "bleak" and "broken" (l. 18), and the "tide" of the sea is retreating (l. 19). The cats are joined by "bats" (l. 18), but the "belfries" of the towers the bats live in are tottering (l. 21), and only the "lean cats" (l. 24) live to answer "the wind and the water" (l. 23).

Poems about cats and their antics have a strong literary heritage. William Blake's "The Tyger" was published in 1798 and focuses on a member of the great cat family hunting at night; John Keats's "Sonnet to a Cat" was written around 1817, asking the cat what it has stolen and counting its war wounds. Charles Baudelaire's "Le Chat" was published in 1857 and associated the cat with the poet's mistress in a semi-erotic fashion. Baudelaire's poetry was cited by Lovecraft in a letter to his aunt, Lillian D. Clark, as part of his inspiration: "I wrote some verse involving cats—treating them in a somewhat Baudelairian way in connexion with the Babylonian decay of New York in the future."[1] Some of the features Baudelaire's poetry shares with Lovecraft's "The Cats" are attention to form and the vision of a decadent urban environment. It is interesting to note that Lovecraft's "The Cats," which was written in 1925, predates T. S. Eliot's delightful *Old Possum's Practical Book of Cats*, published in 1939, which delineates various cat personalities and adventures.

Another area of interest is the description of the urban environment. While inspired by Baudelaire, Lovecraft's images of New York are also reminiscent of Dickens's descriptions of London. According to Perdue, Charles Dickens was a great walker, traveling ten to twenty miles on foot at times. The London he saw in the mid-1800s was dirty and crowded, with the beginnings of factory-style production and a distinct lack of sanitation. Raw sewage flowed into gutters and the River Thames, which was also the source of drinking water for the population. Street sweepers were employed to clear the pavement of horse droppings and garbage using hand-brooms! Dickens incorporated the dirt of London into his writings, sometimes imaging the whole city as a filthy, heartless machine.

Like Dickens, Lovecraft was also a keen walker and his observations of environmental conditions in "The Cats" include "flames" from factories causing "poisonous" smoke and soot covering the bricks like "fungi" (ll. 2–3). The rivers, which should flow clean, are "oily" (l. 5), and the sewers are "catacomb deeps whose dank chaos delivers / Streams of live foetor" (ll. 7–8).

According to the New York City Department of Environmental Protection, the "upstate reservoir system" was not developed

---

1. 16 February 1925; ms., John Hay Library, Brown University.

until 1842, and until then New York had to depend upon wells for water. Waste-water treatment began in the late 1890s and early 1900s, with one plant at Brooklyn and another at Queens. Early waste-water treatment ponds would have been smelly, and this waste-water might have contained some of the rubbish that Lovecraft says "rots in the sun" (l. 8).

The early treatment plants would also have been overloaded by the time Lovecraft was writing in 1925. It is good to note that three more plants were constructed between 1935 and 1945 to serve the growing population. Before the treatment plants were built, the situation in New York had been almost as bad as London a century previous:

> With no system for disposing of sewage and garbage, human and animal waste polluted the water supply, causing frequent epidemics of contagious waterborne diseases, such as yellow fever and cholera. (New York City Department of Environmental Protection 5)

Certainly, if the pollution had been left unchecked, Lovecraft's prediction in "The Cats," that New York, a city of "colour and splendour, disease and decaying" (l. 9), would become fit for nothing but "weeds," "mosses," and the ever-hardly stray cats might have come true!

Another area of appeal in the poem is the sound patterning. "The cats" has an *abab* rhyming pattern, where the first line rhymes with the third and the second line rhymes with the fourth. This is consistent throughout, with the only technical hitch being the para-rhyme of "totter" (l. 21) and "water" (l. 23). The rhythm is also strict, as each line has between nine and eleven syllables, making approximately five stressed beats. To achieve this, the poet has sometimes used an apostrophe to guide pronunciation. For example, 'towering' is often lingered over by the tongue, but the poet wanted a sharp two-beat finish, so he spelt it "tow'ring" (l. 1). This also occurs with line 3 ("flow'ring"), line 18 ("weedcumber'd"), and line 22 ("effac'd").

Each line has internal sound patterning, the most common being alliteration or the close repetition of consonant sounds. Tight sound patterning does not work for all poetry and is less popular among modern poets; but for songs, nursery rhymes, and fantastic ditties about cats I would say it functions beautifully.

An additional area of interest is the way the imagery in the poem connects to the two short stories written several months later in August 1925 (according to Loucks's list of Lovecraft's writing, which follows Joshi's chronology). Lovecraft wrote three stories: "The Horror at Red Hook," "He," and "In the Vault," in 1925. He also wrote a few poems dedicated to his friends, and several notable weird poems, including "The Cats" and "Festival."

In "The Horror at Red Hook" the unnamed city of "The Cats" becomes the Red Hook area. The Red Hook region is described as "a babel of sound and filth" (*CF* 1.484), which echoes the "Babels of blocks" in line 1 of the poem. The "lapping of oily waves at its grimy piers" (*CF* 1.484) reflects the "oily rivers" described in line 5 of "The Cats." The "shrieking and ringing" of line 10 of the poem becomes the "monstrous organ litanies of the harbour whistles" and "hordes of prowlers . . . shouting and singing" in the story (*CF* 1.484).

The imagery of the poem flows into elements of plot in "The Horror at Red Hook." For example, in line 11 of "The Cats" the "rabbles exotic to stranger-gods praying" are undefined; and an image of cats howling under the moon to their cat-gods comes to mind. Alternately, commercialism is a "stranger-god" often associated with the city in urban literature, and comes to mind if the "rabbles" in the poem are interpreted as human beings. In "The Horror at Red Hook," however, the "rabbles" from the poem literally become people embroiled in "the polyglot abyss of New York's underworld" (*CF* 1.482), and the "stranger-gods" become ancient Babylonian gods, including Lilith (*CF* 1.495), who was the first wife of Adam according to Hebrew mythology (see Hefner).

"The Horror at Red Hook" is probably Lovecraft's most out-and-out rip-roaring horror tale. It is a detective story mixed with the supernatural and set in one of New York's major crime areas. According to *A&E Television Networks*, Johnny Torrio retreated to Red Hook after an injury and headed organized crime there, until he handed control of the Chicago operations to Al "Scarface" Capone later in 1925. The attempt on Johnny Torrio's life made headlines in newspapers on January 1925. The character of Robert Suydam, who attempts to achieve immortality, could be perceived as a metaphor for Johnny Torrio recovering from injury.

Red Hook has caught the imagination of many artists and is featured in Harlan Ellison's *Memos from Purgatory*, Thomas Wolfe's short story "Only the Dead Know Brooklyn," and the 1997 film *Cop Land*, among other works created since Lovecraft's tale. The area is also immortalized in popular culture as "East Hook" in in the cult video game *Grand Theft Auto*.

The imagery of the poem "The Cats" is further picked up in the short story "He," which was written a couple of weeks later. In line 1 of "The Cats," the "Babels of blocks" in a city such as New York would be the tall buildings, which like the tower of Babel in Genesis reach "to the high heavens." This image is echoed by "the Cyclopean modern towers and pinnacles that rise blackly Babylonian" in "He" (*CF* 1.506). The cats are "howling and lean in the glare of the moon" (l. 14), while in "He" the towers rise "under waning moons" (*CF* 1.506). The narrator in "He" has taken to walking at night (*CF* 1.507), and the cats are also "nocturnal" (l. 13).

In "He" the narrator has tested the city streets and concluded that the heart of all he sees is lifeless:

> I saw at last a fearful truth which no one had ever dared to breathe before—the unwhisperable secret of secrets—the fact that this city of stone and stridor is not a sentient perpetuation of Old New York as London is of Old London and Paris of Old Paris, but that it is in fact quite dead. (*CF* 1.507)

Likewise, in "The Cats" the city is poisoned and dying in verses 1–3, and everything man-made is decaying in verses 5–6. In contrast to "He," however, the city is not completely dead; it is being reclaimed by nature and is the nocturnal playground of the cats.

Both "He" and "The Cats" contain visions of the future of New York. In "He" the future city has even higher buildings, bridges, and "impious pyramids flung savagely to the moon" (*CF* 1.514–15), creating something of the vista cats are populating in the poem (see l. 17). In "He" we also see "devil-lights burning" (*CF* 1.514–15), which echo the "death lights that glow" in the poem (l. 3). However, the author's visions of the future of the city vary. In the future of "The Cats," humans are absent and the city has been returned to nature. In "He" there appears to be technological advancement accompanied by cultural change, and the city is still populated by people (*CF* 1.515). This contrast is demonstrated using imagery associated with the streets, as the people in "He" have created "an unhallowed ocean of bitumen" (*CF* 1.515) while the cats play on "weed-cumber'd streets" (l. 18).

In conclusion, "The Cats" is an interesting poem because of its evocative portrayal of cats taking over a city at night, the environmental concerns it expresses, and its regular sound patterns. The poem also connects with two short stories written about New York in 1925, "The Horror at Red Hook" and "He." It adds to the body of Lovecraft's work in 1925, allowing us to argue that this was a productive period despite any issues documented in his personal life.

Works Cited

Baudelaire, Charles. "Le Chat," *Charles Baudelaire's Fleurs du mal / Flowers of Evil*, Fleursdumal.org is a Supervert production, accessed 21 March 2017 at fleursdumal.org/poem/132

Harvey, Gail, ed. *Poems of Creatures Large and Small*. New York: Avenel Books, 1991.

Hefner, A. G. "Lilith." *Encyclopedia Mythica*, accessed online on 9 February 2017 at www.pantheon.org/articles/l/lilith.html

Loucks, Donovan K. "Lovecraft's Fiction (Chronological Order)." *The H. P. Lovecraft Archive*, accessed 20 March 2017 at www.hplovecraft.com/writings/fiction/chrono.aspx

———. "Lovecraft's Poetry." *The H. P. Lovecraft Archive*, accessed 20 March 2017 at www.hplovecraft.com/writings/poetry/

New York City Department of Environmental Protection. *New York City's Wastewater Treatment System*. PDF Flyer accessed 5 March 2017 at www.nyc.gov/html/dep/pdf/wwsystem.pdf

Perdue, David. "Dickens's London." *David Perdue's Dickens Page*, accessed 5 March 2017 at charlesdickenspage.com/dickens_london.html

Lovecraft's Consolation

Matthew Beach

Consider a weird premise. It arises in part from witnessing the incredible fandom Lovecraft has inspired and the widespread joy people find in these tales grounded in a philosophy of the meaninglessness of human life within the cosmos. That the weird tale (as practiced by Lovecraft) could inspire something akin to joy seems strange, especially given that in his own analysis Lovecraft saw fit to defend weird fiction against the charge of not serving an uplifting purpose. In "Supernatural Horror in Literature" (1927), Lovecraft observes: "Against it [the weird tale] are discharged all the shafts of a materialistic sophistication which clings to frequently felt emotions and external events, and of a naively inspired idealism which deprecates the aesthetic motive and calls for a didactic literature to 'uplift' the reader toward a suitable degree of smirking optimism" (25). For Lovecraft, it is not the purpose of the weird tale to reassure readers about the conditions and future of human existence so that they may face it with a knowing if not arrogant grin. Quite the opposite.[1]

The premise, then, is that Lovecraft is an optimist; more specifically, that his work represents a weird form of philosophical optimism that carries with it a bizarre consolation if not joy. In addition to the numerous places in both his fiction and nonfiction where Lovecraft lambasts "smirking optimism," this is such a weird premise because of nearly a century of readings that tell us

---

1. As shall become clear below, HPL's critique of "smirking optimism" hinges on its uncritical faith in the known universe as well as an assured future. It is, I argue, a rejection of a particular form of optimism but not optimism in its entirety. For a more sustained exploration of HPL's view of optimism, see Beach, "Lovecraft's Optimism."

his tales are representative of philosophical pessimism. This is the image we have of Lovecraft. If you look up "pessimism" on Wikipedia, Lovecraft is cited as a literary example, alongside the likes of Beckett, Borges, and Baudelaire. Of course, Wikipedia is not the most reliable of sources, but it does index the cultural image of Lovecraft that has evolved over time. In more scholarly venues, Lovecraft's pessimism has been noted by critics such as S. T. Joshi, W. Scott Poole, Eugene Thacker, Thomas Ligotti, and many others, despite Lovecraft's own admission that he is not a pessimist but an indifferentist.

Certainly, there is a strong element of pessimism in Lovecraft's stories and worldview. But much of the criticism has stopped there rather than asking if there is more to Lovecraft's philosophy than pessimism alone. Because from what I've seen, there is something in his stories that in some way inspires something joyful, something optimistic, in us, and extends to us a weirdly consoling hand. Thus we are confronted with a question: how could such a seemingly pessimistic view of our place in the world be so beloved by so many people? What have his tales touched that they could inspire such devotion, despite what they seem to mean philosophically and existentially? And what is it about these weird stories that seems so strangely comforting?

As I have suggested elsewhere, there is more to Lovecraft's work and philosophy than his oft-noted pessimism or indifference regarding humanity's place in the cosmos. I argue that Lovecraft's theory of cosmological time advances a particular form of optimism, albeit one that looks quite weird to us. Drawing on the philosophical tradition, I suggest a rethinking of optimism through the work of Lovecraft as a theory of time that "interprets it as full rather than empty of possibilities. A theory of or orientation toward time as devoid of potential would therefore be the meaning of pessimism in this context" (162). What makes Lovecraft's optimism so strange is his insistence on the *impersonality* of the possibilities of time. In other words, his optimism is "weird" because it is grounded in a cosmological theory of time rather than the hopes and desires of the subject. Despite the seemingly bleak perspective this often paints of humanity's future, I ultimately argue Lovecraft's insistence on acknowledging the infinite possibilities of time (and space) is a form of weird optimism. More importantly, and further complicating the view of Lovecraft as a pessimist, his correspondence reveals that Lovecraft understood his cosmic philosophy of time as offering consolation if not a strange form of hope to those struggling with what he called the "local" problems of human existence.

As Eugene Thacker argues, Lovecraft's (and horror's) point of origin is "the world-without-us" (9). The genre represents an attempt to think through the "subtraction of the human from the world" or the impersonal, non-human dimensions of the world. Following Thacker, we could say Lovecraft bases his temporal perspective on the world-without-us rather than the subject, and therein lies both the horror and the potential of his optimism. For though Lovecraft's optimism is grounded in a theory of the world-without-us, the subject enters into an intimate and horrifying relation to this world in his fiction. The tension between these two poles of the individual and the cosmic form the crux of Lovecraft's weird fiction. His tales explore the horror and awe produced by the tension between the cosmic and the most "local" of human contexts—the body. Lovecraft's optimism therefore appears to involve a paradox, since it entails the subject's intimate involvement in the world-without-us, or what happens when the world-without-us clashes with what Thacker calls the "world-for-us." Lovecraft's weird optimism resides at precisely this point where the personal comes into tension (and even threatens to collapse into) the impersonal.

This intertwining of the personal and the impersonal, of the body in time and cosmic time, at the heart of Lovecraft's weird optimism meets even more intimately in what is arguably his greatest achievement: his personal correspondence. Of special interest here is a specific genre of letter that appears with relative frequency among (and within) Lovecraft's voluminous correspondence, the consolation letter. In brief, the consolation letter as a genre operates as an offering of sympathy to someone (the reader) experiencing suffering, pain, or loss. This sympathy is often offered not only through consoling words (of affection or advice) but primarily by forging an identification between the writer and the reader. The author of the consolation letter narrates his own pain or losses and thereby identifies his experiences with those of the reader. The consolation letter is thus a genre that shares and relieves pain through descriptive narrative. It also serves as an occasion for meditating on pain and its place in human life. In addition to (or by way of) sympathizing with the reader's suffering, the consolation letter attempts to draw the reader out of the isolation of their pain and back to the (social) world.

These letters therefore show a more personal and intimate side to Lovecraft's philosophy and, more generally, to Lovecraft himself. In his hands, the consolation letter often operates as an occasion to elaborate his views on the place of human suffering and life within cosmic time. In his correspondence, Lovecraft often spoke of cosmic time to those struggling with the very human problems of distress, pain, illness, and loss. His elaboration of his philosophy of cosmic time in the context of a consolation letter is revealing. It shows that he conceived of the same intersection between the cosmic and the local that drives his fiction as productive of more complex relations than just horror. It seems odd at first that Lovecraft would reference the very cosmic time he believes renders human suffering "insignificant" in these moments, but it is clear from his letters that he understands his philosophy as offering real consolation. His correspondence reveals Lovecraft applying his theories of cosmic time as a form of personal consolation and extending his sympathetic identification to those suffering.

Lovecraft explained his particular method of consolation in an 11 March 1936 letter to R. H. Barlow after one of their mutual acquaintances had a death in her social circle:

> Despite my upheaved programme I at once started a letter of what I thought to be the most consoling and useful sort—with sympathetic remarks (and citations of others who have bravely pulled out of similar bereavements) gradually giving place to cheerful discussion of general and impersonal topics in which long time-stretches (thus placing local and individual sorrows at the small end of the telescope) are concerned—answering a letter received early in February. History was the main theme—the dominant topic being Roman Britain and its long decline. . . . That, I find, is the kind of stuff a bereaved person likes to get from the outside world—sincere sympathy not rubbed in, and a selection

of general topics attuned to his interests and quietly reminding him that there is a world which has always gone on and which still goes on despite personal losses. I used this tone—apparently with good results—to Klarkash-Ton last September when his mother died. (O *Fortunate Floridian* 321)

The main contours of Lovecraft's approach to the consolation letter largely conform to the outline of the genre provided above. He offers sympathetic remarks and narrative examples of others who survived similar forms of bereavement as well as a cheerful discussion of the general topics that interest the specific reader. Lovecraft's observation that this type of discourse "from the outside world" is welcome registers that he understands how pain and loss can isolate the individual. He notes the expression of sympathy must be "sincere" and "not rubbed in," which implies that for Lovecraft the emotional component of the consolation letter should be heartfelt but brief. The purpose of the letter in Lovecraft's view is to bring the reader back to himself and the world, both through a treatment of topics the reader cares about and "quiet reminders" that "there is a world which has always gone on and which still goes on." As Lovecraft also notes in this letter, he used this approach before with "good results" in a letter to Klarkash-Ton (Clark Ashton Smith),[2] and it details the form of the consolation letters Lovecraft penned throughout his life.

The unique feature that distinguishes Lovecraft's consolation letters from the genre formula is the way he invariably brings his theories of cosmic time to bear on the question of pain and consolation. There is a hint of this already in the letter above, specifically when he refers to his discussion of history or "long time-stretches" in the consolation letter. For Lovecraft, the discussion of time is an effective tool of consolation because it places "local and individual sorrows at the small end of the telescope." This "telescoping" of "local and individual sorrows" (and indeed all human

---

2. This particular letter, composed sometime in September 1935, does not appear to survive. It was not included in the bulk of letters Smith provided to Arkham House following its request for HPL's letters after his death. Smith either did not keep the letter, lost it, or (most likely) did not wish to share it. The complete (surviving) HPL–Smith correspondence is available in *Dawnward Spire, Lonely Hill* (2017).

affairs) is precisely how Lovecraft's weird form of consolation operates. As a tool, the telescope aids in shifting perspective from the near to the far—or, conversely, in bringing things far away up close. To help relieve pain, make it more endurable, or simply put it in perspective, Lovecraft contextualizes the reader's local suffering within a larger framework of time. Here it is the context of "Roman history and its long decline," but even more frequently in these letters it is the framework of cosmic time (within which Lovecraft would consider Roman history "local"). The purpose of both is to draw the reader's attention to the infinite span of time and space, which colors how we read the seemingly stereotypical advice in this letter that life "goes on." For Lovecraft, life and human history goes on . . . from a local standpoint, though within the context of cosmic time it is but a brief moment "bound from a common nothingness toward another common nothingness." It is a chilling thought, but Lovecraft deploys it as a source of consolation rather than horror in his letters in order to "telescope" the pain felt by his reader during a period of suffering.

The technique Lovecraft calls "telescoping" in his letters is familiar to us: it is also the technique of his weird fiction. What is curious, then, is that Lovecraft applies the same technique he uses in his fiction to produce horror to provide consolation in his letters. What is it about the change in genre from fiction to (consolation) letter that allows this cosmic perspective to console rather than to horrify, at least for Lovecraft?

The best way to answer this is to look more closely at Lovecraft's elaboration of this weirdly consoling theme in his letters, particularly as it develops through an extended correspondence with one particular recipient: Helen Sully.[3] Sully does not figure very largely in Lovecraft scholarship; most mentions of her occur only in passing. Speaking of Lovecraft's correspondence with Sully, Joshi argues that "it becomes readily apparent that Sully was a high-strung, hypersensitive woman who was experiencing a series of disappointments (among them unfortunate love affairs) and was

---

3. HPL came into contact with Sully through their mutual friend, Clark Ashton Smith. Sully visited HPL in Providence in 1933, and later spent time with HPL's circle of friends in New York City (Frank Belknap Long, Donald Wandrei, etc.). The two kept in contact until HPL's death.

looking for Lovecraft to lend her some fortitude and encouragement" (*IAP* 935). He also notes that this correspondence has generated some controversy; it sparked a debate over whether Lovecraft suffered from depression because of the darker portrait of the author it often revealed. Lovecraft frequently discussed his bouts of melancholia and thoughts of suicide with Sully in these letters. Joshi concludes that the contextual evidence suggests that Lovecraft did not suffer from depression and "the passages in his letters to her cannot be taken straightforwardly" (936).

Yet we might take this a step farther and ask: why did Lovecraft choose to reveal these intimate details to Sully, and for what purpose? Joshi does observe that Lovecraft's "tactics" in these letters "was two-pronged: first, suggest that 'happiness' as such was a relatively little-realised goal among human beings; and second, suggest that he was in a far worse position than herself, so that if *he* could be tolerably contented, so much more should she be" (935). Yet perhaps we can also make a connection between Lovecraft's admission of melancholic thoughts and his "tactics" in these letters. Lovecraft wishes to console Sully, and he does so by drawing on an old sentimental technique: he forges a sympathetic identification between himself and his reader. I have felt this way too, he tells Sully, and I have survived it. So can you. This quick dismissal of Sully and protection of Lovecraft's genteel masculine image is part of a notable gender bias in Lovecraft scholarship that treats the women in his life—either his family members, wife, or correspondents—as negligible at best and as victimizers or distractions at worst.[4]

More than any of his other correspondents, Lovecraft's correspondence with Sully predominantly takes the form of the consolation letter. In the late winter of 1935, Sully confided to Lovecraft her excessive concern with people's opinion of her. From March to December of that year, Lovecraft wrote Sully a series of letters intended to console and advise her as well as cheer her up. Lovecraft's method of offering consolation, here and elsewhere, is to reframe the life of individual human beings within the larger context of time and space: "The people on Mars will never know that any human race exists—the people on Neptune can never know

---

4. W. Scott Poole's recent research into the role of women (and sexuality) in HPL's life has gone far to correct this misconception, but it is only the beginning.

that the Earth exists—the people on the planets of Alpha Centauri can never know that the solar planets exist—the people of trans-galactic systems can never know that the sun exists" (404).[5] As Lovecraft understands it, this reframing of Sully's concern for the opinions of others (predominately those in her social circle) within the larger context of "trans-galactic systems" underscores the absurdity of dwelling on the judgments of others.[6] After positioning Sully's concerns within the infinitely larger context of cosmic space, Lovecraft concludes by expanding out from Sully's individual life to the infinite span of cosmic time: "A few trillion years hence there will be no consciousness in existence that can know of the former existence of such a thing as a human race. The universe will be just as it would have been had no Earth existed" (404). This "telescoping" of Sully's concerns is definitely a strange method of offering consolation, but it is inspired by Lovecraft's optimism about the infinite potentials of cosmic time and space. He clarifies that he is not counseling a form of detachment or cynicism when interacting with others: "It is certainly not necessary to be a misanthrope" (404). Rather, he instructs her "not to expect too much" of other people and "to enjoy each [person] for his own specialty" while also filling her life with "non-human objects of beauty" and "significance" (404). Though this may read like a form of philosophical pessimism ("others will disappoint you; best not to expect much"), Lovecraft's consolation in these letters to Sully is best interpreted as the practical application of his cosmic optimism. He repositions human life and concerns within a cosmic context while allowing for (or at least not disallowing) the possibility of pleasure, surprise, and even hope.

In his consolation letters to Sully, Lovecraft discusses the pos-

---

5. All letters to Helen Sully are quoted from *Letters to Wilfred B. Talman and Helen V. and Genevieve Sully*. Page numbers are cited parenthetically in the text.
6. It should go without saying that HPL is not suggesting there are indeed "people" on Mars, Neptune, Alpha Centauri, etc. The tone of this passage is indicative of the humor HPL sprinkles into his letters with Sully, also in an effort to cheer her mood. For example, HPL ends the section of the letter discussing cosmic time with a blend of humor and his typical self-deprecating tone: "With which typical flourish Grandpa concludes an equally characteristic ream of sententious senile meandering" (6).

sibility and role of hope within his cosmic philosophy. He carefully clarifies that his consoling advice is distinct from traditional models of optimism that offer a blithe perspective on the future—that is, on hope. In a 15 August 1935 letter, Lovecraft tells Sully his advice is *"not irresponsible and platitudinous optimism"* (427; italics in original). Lovecraft separates his optimism from "irresponsible" forms because he integrates rather than ignores the harsh realities of human existence within cosmic time and space. He also defends his cosmic philosophy against the charge of pessimism in a 23 September 1935 letter to Sully: "I am not a *pessimist*, but merely a realistic *indifferentist*" (435; italics in original). Lovecraft's description of himself as a "realistic indifferentist" does not indicate that he is indifferent to human life and endeavors; rather, it registers his assertion that the cosmos is indifferent to particular human lives and endeavors, whatever they may be. For Lovecraft, this perspective is consoling because it means the cosmos does not intentionally intervene in the lives of human beings for good or ill: "It is just as childishly romantic to postulate an actively hostile & malignant cosmos . . . as to postulate a friendly, 'just', & beneficent one. The truth is that the cosmos is blind & unconscious—not giving a hang about any of its denizens, nor even knowing that they exist" (435). And though the cosmos may be indifferent to its "denizens," for Lovecraft this does not mean all human existence is for naught: "It [the cosmos] doesn't try to pain them any more than it tries to help or please them—& if any of them can manage to have a good time somehow, in spite of the chaotic jumble of conditions & emotions around & within them, that's quite all right with the universal powers that be" (435). Nor does the universe's indifference to human affairs rule out the practical benefits of an informed hope or optimism: "It would seem to be the part of good sense to harbour great hopes in a sort of light, indefinite way—extracting from them whatever bracing power their imaginative associations may possess, but keeping also in mind the ineluctable natural laws & probabilities which actually prevail" (435). Lovecraft does caution Sully to avoid unrealistic hopes that ignore the conditions "which actually prevail," an extreme form of optimism he aligns with the flights of fancy characteristic of Romanticism: "Naturally such a course is for many difficult, but almost anyone can probably ... approach it in a degree sufficient to remove at least some of the pains & shocks of unrestrained romanticism. In any case it is worth trying" (435).

As his advice to Sully begins to indicate, Lovecraft's philosophy of weird optimism entails a form of pragmatism in daily life. United with his primarily aesthetic outlook on life, his weird optimism leads to a utilitarian pragmatism that seeks to maximize (artistic and intellectual) pleasure while minimizing (physical and emotional) pain. As he advises Sully in the August 15, 1935 letter: "The highest consistent and practicable goal of mankind is simply an absence of *acute and unendurable suffering*—a sensible compromise with an indifferent cosmos which was never built for mankind and in which mankind is only a microscopic, negligible, and temporary accident" (428; italics in original). As Lovecraft suggests here, the highest goal of mankind is to minimize humanity's suffering during the "negligible" period it inhabits the earth—a sentiment that in large part informed his political conversion to socialism in the 1930s. For Lovecraft once humanity acknowledges it inhabits an "indifferent cosmos" that was "never built for mankind," the rational consequence is to maximize pleasure and minimize all forms of pain during the brief and "temporary" period of life. For Lovecraft dwelling on the cosmically insignificant span of human life only leads to a brooding distraction at best or melancholy at worst, both of which increase (emotional) pain and detract from possible pleasures.

Though he often admits in his letters to suffering from periods of melancholy himself, his theories of cosmic time entail a more optimistic and pragmatic approach to humanity's insignificance. As he writes Sully in a 4 December 1935 letter, "So the voice of sound reason would seem to be saying, 'cheer up!' There aren't any phenomena in the cosmos really worth being mournful or depressed about" (451). Once again he advises her to adopt a more pragmatic approach to living that makes use of the brief time allotted to humanity within cosmic time: "What ... is of any real use or significance except planning for a sensible future? And how can anybody plan sensibly except by ditching all myth-born sentimentalities; studying the scientific mechanics of human thought, feeling, and behaviour; and steering a realistic course based on phenomena as they are rather than as one would like them to be" (451). For Lovecraft, negative effects such as melancholy have to be moved through to open up the pragmatic potential for a "sensible future." Much of his consolation amounts to offering pragmatic advice on how to alleviate pain and suffering so his reader can resume a "realistic course" of action in a cosmos devoid of absolute values. As he tells Sully in the same letter, "The only criteria of conduct, thought, and feeling which one can logically envisage are purely *relative* and *proximate* ones, utilitarian and aesthetic in their nature. Human impulses and behaviour are simply *what they are*—wholly outside any *absolute* realm of approval or disapproval" (444; italics in original). Reminding his reader about the insignificance and ephemerality of mankind within cosmic time functions not as an occasion for melancholy but rather as a reminder to make pragmatic use of what limited time is available.

In addition to elaborating his theory of cosmic time and the pragmatic hope it implies, Lovecraft also comments in these letters on human loss and death. Sully had expressed a feeling of "oppression at the thought of inevitable human losses," and Lovecraft responds in a 28–29 June 1934 letter with the advice that Sully should attempt to cultivate "an increased sense of *objectivity* and a heightened realisation of the true proportions of the universe and of the insignificance of mankind and all its affairs therein" (366; italics in original). While once again this does not appear consoling to someone feeling oppressed by the transience of time, Lovecraft offers this remark to frame his more pragmatic advice to Sully to accept and prepare for the inevitability of loss in life: "There is no reason why anyone *should* be sure of retaining all the landmarks—either human or non-human—to which one has grown used and of which one has grown fond; so that the realistic analyst accustomed himself from the very first to the idea of tantalising impermanence in every department of life" (366). Acknowledging Sully's sense that life is defined by loss, Lovecraft notes: "Parents and friends die; beloved houses and landscapes become hopelessly altered or destroyed; social milieux and other environmental supports decay and become metamorphosed; and one's self grows old, exiled from the beauty, vividness, and adventurous expectancy of youth" (366).

While agreeing with Sully that these are "the basic and inescapable conditions of life," Lovecraft suggests that "*because* they are basic and inescapable we can build certain palliatives or defences against them. Knowing that nothing and nobody is certain of lasting, we can wisely refrain from pinning too much of our hold on life to any one object—human or otherwise" (366; italics in original). For Lovecraft, accepting that loss is inescapable within (cosmic) time helps prepare one for its inevitable occurrence and softens the pain of loss when it does occur. Though he is advising a form of pragmatic detachment that refrains from investing too much in people and places, Lovecraft stresses to Sully that he is not saying that "we need to abandon all kindliness and affection toward individuals" (366). Rather, "we ought to remember how transient and infinitesimal all individuals are, and to avoid making our entire sense of equilibrium and contentment dependent upon the life and proximity of a few definite persons" (366). For Lovecraft, time heals all wounds. Not because it places distance between the bereaved and what they lost, but because time constantly reminds us to adjust ourselves to the reality that all things are "transient and infinitesimal."

Once again, Lovecraft's consolation operates through a telescoping of human affairs within cosmic time that leads to a pragmatic course of action. What is most remarkable about this letter, though, are his peculiar comments on human existence and nonexistence within the frame of cosmic time. He first tells Sully that "[m]emory and objectivity join hands in making existence a little more tolerable," by which he means that preparing for and remembering loss helps alleviate the sense of oppression at human impermanence (366). He then goes on:

> When we bring ourselves to realize that *time* is only one element in an infinitely complex cosmos, we tend to protest less when something that *is* becomes something that *has been*. The difference between 'is-ness' and 'has been-ness' tends to vanish—we feel that the mere quality of duration does not amount to so much after all. Why should a thing be 'immortal' in time, when the basic fact of its *having existed* is virtually equivalent so far as the larger universe is concerned. (366–67)

This is a curious and perplexing statement. At first it seems Lovecraft is saying the universe does not care if a particular entity (human or otherwise) existed or not, an opinion he often voices in his correspondence. Yet given the context it appears he is suggesting something more complex. Lovecraft argues that "having existed" is "equivalent" to a form of immortality in time "as far as the universe is concerned." How so? There is a further clue in his proceeding words to Sully, where he tells her the difference between a living and a deceased friend is "not as vast as one might imagine" since "[b]oth exist as images in the mind" (367). While he admits there are differences and that the "change is unfortunate," the persistence of the lost object's image in the mind and in memory amounts to a form of immortality (367).

Framed by his comments to Sully on the retention of the lost in memory, the above passage appears to be suggesting that the universe itself retains some form of "memory" of the entities that have existed and perished within it. What this "immortality in time" amounts to, or where this memory resides, is less certain. What is clear is that Lovecraft seems to be arguing that having existed amounts to a kind of (materialistic) immortality within the context of cosmic time—something was rather than was not in time, and that is good enough. The argument is once again based on his telescopic perspective on time. Within the context of time in an "infinitely complex cosmos," the distinction "between 'is-ness' and 'has been-ness' tends to vanish." By this Lovecraft means that within infinite time the span of a human being's life is so miniscule it vanishes. Hence the comment that "duration does not amount to so much after all." From the perspective of "the universe," then, all that is left is whether something existed or not rather than how long it existed or whether it continues to exist. How this existence then equates to a form of immortality within cosmic time remains opaque.

At this point, it must be asked: just how consoling is Lovecraft's consolation? His technique of evoking the telescopic effect of time to alleviate the sting of suffering reads as alternately effective (in terms of the potential perspective it provides) and, well, weird. Shifting the reader's focus to the fluctuations of cosmic time risks coming off as unsympathetic to the reader's (local) pain and even increasing the reader's suffering by rendering it meaningless from a cosmic perspective. Of course, as he indicated in his letter to Barlow, Lovecraft did not see it that way. For him, the impersonality of cosmic time represents a relief to the intense personality of human pain and suffering. And there is indication his correspondents agreed with him. Sully often sought recourse for her suffering in her correspondence with Lovecraft, so her continual solicitation of his advice serves as indirect evidence of its consolatory effect (at least for her). Certainly, it is quite possible that his lengthy discussions of cosmic time in these letters have a self-serving function and that the only one consoled by this advice is Lovecraft himself. Nevertheless, there does appear to be a weird consoling power in the perspective provided by contextualizing human suffering in the grander scheme of the cosmos. What makes his consolation effective is how this telescopic view adjusts the reader's perspective of the interrelations between time and pain or suffering. This is a technique often employed in the consolation genre (i.e., "The world goes on"), though not to the weird extent that Lovecraft develops it. Whether or not this weird consolation is effective in general remains an open question; this form of consolation is particular to Lovecraft and was crafted specifically for a circle of devoted friends.

The issue remains how the same technique Lovecraft uses to evoke horror in his fiction can serve a consolatory effect in his correspondence. He offers up to his grieving or suffering correspondents the same knowledge that drives the narrators in his stories mad—the insignificance of the human race within the "black seas of infinity" ("The Call of Cthulhu," *CF* 2.21). The answer resides precisely in the different function and manner of address between the two genres. Whereas Lovecraft's tales are meant to evoke a mood for an imagined audience, his letters are written for a specific reader already entrenched in an intense affective experience. Lovecraft's technique of drawing the personal into relation with the impersonal, or the local into relation to the cosmic, therefore functions in a more intimate and direct fashion in these letters than in his tales. As Lovecraft often noted in his correspondence, his fiction is not concerned with individuals but with "phenomena." His letters, though, provide insight into how he perceived the potential range of responses to an actual individual's encounter with the impersonality of time. For Lovecraft this encounter held the potential to console as well as to horrify, and it is this former possibility that he fleshes out in his correspondence when he writes to those in pain. In his consolation letters, he also has to work to break down or at least alleviate a mood over time rather than building one up. As we have seen, he does so by offering pragmatic advice on how to turn back to "the outside world," as he calls it in his letter to Barlow, mixed with disquisitions on his weird optimism regarding the infinity of cosmic time.

In a sense, then, though they operate according to the same technique, Lovecraft's consolation letters represent an inversion of the form of his weird fiction: his tales focus on phenomena rather than individuals to build up an intense mood of horror over time, while his letters break down an intense mood for a specific individual. Both do so by focusing on the phenomena of cosmic time and space, with the difference that in the consolation letter these impersonal phenomena are drawn into more intimate relation with the personal. The versatility of Lovecraft's weird optimism in performing both of these textual functions is surprising at first, but becomes less so when we remember his theory of time as containing the potential for both terror and awe, pain and pleasure, madness and curiosity—in short, for horror and consolation.

Lovecraft's philosophy operates (and consoles) by holding open the potentials of time rather than filling them with supposed (consoling) certainties. It does not offer predictions or traditional forms of hope. As he declares to another correspondent, Fritz Leiber Jr., in a letter dated 18 November 1936, "So far as future history is concerned, I'm damned if I know what lies ahead" (*Letters to C. L. Moore and Others* 280). All that is certain for Lovecraft is uncertainty and what it entails—a program of pragmatic action, a refusal to hide behind supposed certainties, and, as he tells Sully, a guarded, realistic, weird optimism. Lovecraft's correspondence therefore offers an insightful elaboration of the theories of cosmic time developed within his fiction. His consolation letters help clarify that his philosophy does not solely represent a form of cosmic pessimism, nor does it necessitate a more "local" (human) stance of pessimism or resignation. Rather, his cosmic philosophy, grounded in the unpredictable potentials of time, is best understood as offering the consolations of a weird form of optimism.

Works Cited

Beach, Matthew. "Lovecraft's Optimism." In *Lovecraftian Proceedings 2*, ed. Dennis P. Quinn. New York: Hippocampus Press, 2017. 160–75.

Joshi, S. T. *I Am Providence: The Life and Times of H. P. Lovecraft.* New York: Hippocampus Press, 2010. 2 vols.

———. *The Weird Tale.* Austin: University of Texas Press, 1990.

Ligotti, Thomas. *The Conspiracy against the Human Race: A Contrivance of Horror.* New York: Hippocampus Press, 2010.

Lovecraft, H. P. *The Annotated Supernatural Horror in Literature.* Ed. S. T. Joshi. New York: Hippocampus Press, 2nd ed. 2012.

———. *Dawnward Spire, Lonely Hill: The Letters of H. P. Lovecraft and Clark Ashton Smith.* Ed. David E. Schultz and S. T. Joshi. New York: Hippocampus Press, 2017.

———. *Letters to C. L. Moore and Others.* Ed. David E. Schultz and S. T. Joshi. New York: Hippocampus Press, 2017.

———. *Letters to Wilfred B. Talman and Helen V. and Genevieve Sully.* Ed. David E. Schultz and S. T. Joshi. New York: Hippocampus Press, 2019.

———. *O Fortunate Floridian: H. P. Lovecraft's Letters to R. H. Barlow.* Ed. S. T. Joshi and David E. Schultz. Tampa, FL: University of Tampa Press, 2009.

Poole, W. Scott. *In the Mountains of Madness: The Live and Extraordinary Afterlife of H. P. Lovecraft.* Berkeley, CA: Soft Skull Press, 2016.

Thacker, Eugene. *In The Dust of This Planet: Horror of Philosophy, Volume 1.* Winchester, UK: Zero Books, 2011.

"The Inability of the Human Mind": Lovecraft, Zunshine, and Theory of Mind

Dylan Henderson

No one intimately familiar with H. P. Lovecraft's life and work can read Lisa Zunshine's *Why We Read Fiction: Theory of Mind and the Novel* without thinking, at least once, about Lovecraft, for his fiction, whether short or long, complicates almost every claim that Zunshine makes about reading. In *Why We Read Fiction*, Zunshine contends that readers enjoy novels because the form playfully challenges their "Theory of Mind," their ability to interpret seemingly ambiguous actions and behaviors and, in the process, second-guess what others are thinking and feeling: "I can say that I personally read fiction because it offers a pleasurable and intensive workout for my Theory of Mind. And, if you have indeed read this study of mine from cover to cover . . . I suspect that this is why you read fiction, too" (160).

According to Zunshine, novels present readers with a complex social situation that, like a ball of yarn, must be slowly and thoughtfully unraveled. Doing so "engages, teases, and pushes to its tentative limits our mind-reading capacity" (4) in a way that readers find both stimulating and satisfying. It also allows them to "try on different mental states" and tempts them with "intimate access to the thoughts, intentions, and feelings of other people in our social environment" (25). To support this thesis, Zunshine points to the experience of autistic individuals, who often exhibit "a lack of interest in fiction and storytelling" (8), claiming that, because their Theory of Mind is impaired, they perceive the complex and ambiguous social situations depicted in fiction as either baffling or meaningless. And yet, as intriguing as Zunshine's thesis is, it leaves those familiar with the life and work of H. P. Lovecraft with unanswered questions. Most importantly, how does Theory of Mind explain the popularity of an author who, demonstrating an impaired Theory of Mind in his personal life, minimized it as much as possible in his own fiction?

Of course, to retroactively diagnose Lovecraft, a man who has been dead for more than eighty years, with autism would be unethical, but even a cursory analysis of his behavior reveals that, at the very least, his Theory of Mind, his ability to gauge the internal states of other people, was limited. As a child, he exhibited all the "key symptoms" Zunshine associates with autistic children, including a "profound impairment of social and communicative development and the 'lack of the usual flexibility, imagination, and pretence'" (8). Perennially serious and uninterested in childish play, Lovecraft devoted his childhood to cognitive pursuits: reading eighteenth-century literature, studying chemistry and astronomy, and composing stories, poems, and essays. Children his own age "puzzled" him:

> You will notice that I have made no reference to childish friends & playmates—I had none! The children I knew disliked me, & I disliked them. I was used to adult company & conversation, & despite the fact that I felt shamefully dull beside my elders, I had nothing in common with the infant train. Their romping & shouting puzzled me. (*Letters to Rheinhart Kleiner* 35)

Lovecraft, in other words, found the activities of his peers not just unappealing but inexplicable. His peers, in turn, probably found him both awkward and a little strange. Clara Hess, for instance, who was one of Lovecraft's neighbors when they were young, describes how one evening several children in the neighborhood "assembled to watch him from a distance" as he peered through his telescope (Joshi and Schultz 166). Hess assumed at the time that he was lonely, but when she approached him and prompted him to talk about his hobby, Lovecraft interpreted her interest, not as an invitation to participate in the neighborhood's social life, but as an inquiry into astronomy and responded accordingly, providing a technical response that drove Hess back to her friends. As abbreviated as this exchange was, it reinforces our perception of young Lovecraft as both unusually precocious and socially limited, unable, it seems, to understand how other children interact with one another.

Of course, in these accounts both Hess and Lovecraft may have exaggerated: indeed, they almost certainly did. At school, Lovecraft had several "childish friends & playmates," including the two Munroe brothers; a gang of boys "whose members ranged from nine & fourteen years in age" with whom he organized the Providence Detective Agency (*Letters to Alfred Galpin* 19); and Harold W. Munro, who wrote a brief memoir of their time together at Hope Street High School. Even so, the picture that emerges from these disparate accounts is one of a gifted but awkward child, a boy who, though he did not and could not make friends easily, could still be charming, inventive, and even fun when accompanied by those appreciative of his powerful yet playful intellect.

As Lovecraft grew older, transitioning slowly from adolescent to adult, he remained unable to understand others, to accurately gauge what they were thinking and feeling. More importantly, he seemed to feel little desire to do so. True, he experienced a sort of social renaissance while in high school, where he met several congenial acquaintances, but after he failed to earn a diploma, he retreated into a private inner world for several years. His friendship with Munro, for instance, lapsed: "After Hope Street days, I never talked with Lovecraft but saw him several times. Very much an introvert, he darted about like a sleuth, hunched over, always with books or papers clutched under his arm, peering straight ahead, recognizing nobody" (Joshi and Schultz 163). At the time, Munro must have been baffled by his former friend's sudden reclusiveness, but Lovecraft, it seems, paid no attention to Munro at all; for not only did he not talk to him on these occasions, he did not even seem to recognize him.

And yet, judging from the enthusiasm with which Lovecraft participated in the amateur journalism movement and the sheer number of friends he acquired later in life, he was neither shy nor misanthropic. If he struggled socially, which he evidently did before attending Slater Avenue—and after leaving Hope Street—it was because he remained unaware of the impression he made on other people. Even when interacting with his spouse, whose Jewish ancestry he refused to acknowledge, insisting that she was now "*Mrs. H. P. Lovecraft of 598 Angell Street*" (Joshi and Schultz 126;

italics in original), Lovecraft seemed unable to judge how other people might respond to his words. As a child, he could not fathom why other children behaved as they did, nor could he, when grown, understand other adults.

In 1921, at the age of thirty, Lovecraft would write one of his most quoted conclusions: "I know always that I am an outsider; a stranger in this century and among those who are still men" (CF 1.272). In one form or another, that same sentiment, that feeling of being a perpetual stranger, appears in almost every one of Lovecraft's stories, from "The Shadow over Innsmouth," in which a traveler finds himself trapped and alone in a city inhabited by half-human monstrosities, to "The Whisperer in Darkness," in which an aged recluse finds his isolated home besieged by extraterrestrials. More examples, should they be needed, of this inability to relate to others can be found in Lovecraft's letters. Indeed, it forms a leitmotif in his life, reappearing, for instance, in the surprisingly and unnecessarily acrimonious debate he initiated in the pages of the *Argosy* in 1913 and in his often strained relationship with fellow writer Robert E. Howard. Presented with so much evidence, Gary and Jennifer Myers have argued in their book *Lovecraft's Syndrome* that, though unorthodox, a posthumous diagnosis is possible.

Lovecraft's impaired Theory of Mind, which, in adulthood, metastasized into a total lack of interest in the inner lives of ordinary people, would result in a novel that, according to Zunshine, has no reason to exist, for whenever possible it frustrates, rather than stimulates, the reader's Theory of Mind. Lovecraft's longest work of fiction, *The Case of Charles Dexter Ward*, does not contain a single scene that stimulates the reader's Theory of Mind or "pushes to its tentative limits our mind-reading capacity." Unlike contemporary writers, who are urged to "show, not tell," Lovecraft eschews mimesis, the depiction of action and dialogue as if it were occurring in real time, in favor of diegesis. As a result, *The Case of Charles Dexter Ward* consists almost entirely of a series of summaries, dialogue being particularly rare. When characters do interact, Lovecraft describes the interaction from a distance, his lens, so to speak, never zooming in close enough to observe subtleties like body language or facial expressions.

Consider, for instance, the following exchange between Dr.

Marinus Bicknell Willett and Charles Dexter Ward's father, in which the doctor informs the elder Ward that, though the authorities believe that his son has escaped, in reality Willett has killed the man masquerading as his son: "Ward's father was told at once over the telephone, but he seemed more saddened than surprised. By the time Dr. Waite called in person, Dr. Willett had been talking with him, and both disavowed any knowledge or complicity in the escape" (CF 2.217). Note how Lovecraft summarizes the actual conversation, the exchange between Willett and Ward's father, as succinctly as possible, condensing what might otherwise be a chapter-length discussion into a single sentence and depriving the reader of any opportunity to engage his Theory of Mind. Lovecraft even explains, in four words ("more saddened than surprised"), his character's emotional reaction, in the process simplifying the interaction even more.

This pattern, in which Lovecraft summarizes an important exchange and then informs the reader of the emotions and motivations involved, reappears throughout the novel. Crucial scenes, to which most authors would devote a full chapter, are condensed into a few sentences. When Willett, for instance, who at this point does not know that Ward has been murdered and replaced by Joseph Curwen, interviews the impostor, Lovecraft summarizes the entire exchange, in the process denying the characters the opportunity to speak for themselves:

> Ward, however, would not be quizzed long in this vein. Modern and personal topics he waved aside quite summarily, whilst regarding antique affairs he soon shewed the plainest boredom. What he wished clearly enough was only to satisfy his visitor enough to make him depart without the intention of returning. (CF 2.313)

As condensed as this scene is, it contains not only the gist of the conversation, in which Curwen (identified here as "Ward") refuses to discuss "modern and personal topics," but an explanation of the emotions ("boredom") and the motivations (a wish "to make him depart") in play.

Quoted dialogue is not, however, entirely absent from *The Case of Charles Dexter Ward*, but Lovecraft employs it, not to engage the reader's Theory of Mind, but to further the plot. As a result, dialogue exists primarily in the form of monologues and letters. Near the end of the novel, for instance, Lovecraft quotes from Willett, who says that "I can answer no questions, but I will say that there are different kinds of magic. I have made a great purgation, and those in this house will sleep the better for it" (*CF* 2.359). There is, however, no exchange. Readers never learn how Ward's father responded to this remarkable statement, nor do they learn anything more about either the speaker or the setting. The dialogue occurs in a vacuum, and it tells readers little or nothing about the characters involved. Indeed, what little dialogue exists often gives readers a false impression of the characters involved, an impression, that is, that Lovecraft almost certainly did not mean to convey. Many readers, for instance, including myself, will deduce from Willett's boastful claim that he is, in scholar S. T. Joshi's words, "pompous and self-important" (*IAP* 669), in the process imagining a hero very different from the one Lovecraft probably intended.

For Lovecraft, dialogue is nothing more than a rhetorical device, a means of emphasizing a particular point. As for the characters and their emotions, thoughts, and behaviors, they matter not at all. Characters exist because the plot requires their existence, but in terms of complexity they are among the simplest in adult literature. Curwen, for instance, is evil, Ward naïve, and his parents loving. The characters are more complex than that, of course, but not by much. Lovecraft, as he himself recognized, struggled with characterization in part because he found everyday people uninteresting. "The crucial thing is my lack of interest in ordinary life. No one ever wrote a story yet without some real emotional drive behind it—and I have not that drive [. . .]. Individuals and their fortunes within natural law move me very little" (*SL* 5.18–19). By incorporating letters into the text, Lovecraft plays to his strengths, for they allow him to bypass interactions that would expose the flimsiness of his characters. When Willett, for instance, decides that he must kill Curwen, whom Ward's father still believes to be his son, he writes the elder Ward a letter that Lovecraft quotes in full. This one letter, which informs Ward's father that he will never see his son again, allows Lovecraft to convert an emotionally charged scene, one that would have called for complex characters and interactions that would have challenged a reader's Theory of Mind, into a few straightforward paragraphs. Lovecraft even explains the elder Ward's reaction, stating that the "half-dazed parent" found "something calming about the doctor's letter in spite of the despair it seemed to promise and the fresh mysteries it seemed to evoke" (CF 2.361).

It is true, however, that some of Lovecraft's shorter works contain more complex characterization than *The Case of Charles Dexter Ward* does. Indeed, at times Lovecraft reveals a remarkable ability to paint memorable portraits of individuals. One recalls Delapore of "The Rats in the Walls," whose nurses his son, a "maimed invalid" (CF 1.377), for two years before the boy dies, or Robert Olmstead of "The Shadow over Innsmouth," who learns to revel in the monstrous transformation he once fought, or Nathaniel Wingate Peaslee of "The Shadow out of Time," who is abandoned by all but his youngest son. And yet, note how Lovecraft creates these characters. Instead of providing his readers with lengthy scenes in which multiple characters interact with one another, instead of offering puzzles, in other words, that diligent readers must decode in order to truly understand each character's inner nature, Lovecraft employs a straightforward approach, one that requires no Theory of Mind whatsoever. With a few rapid brush strokes in the form of descriptive sentences, he adds background and depth to his creations. In "The Shadow over Innsmouth," for instance, Lovecraft summarizes Olmstead's growing acceptance of his hybridity in a single paragraph:

> So far I have not shot myself as my uncle Douglas did. I bought an automatic and almost took the step, but certain dreams deterred me. The tense extremes of horror are lessening, and I feel queerly drawn toward the unknown sea-deeps instead of fearing them. I hear and do strange things in sleep, and awake with a kind of exaltation instead of terror. . . . Stupendous and unheard-of splendours await me below, and I shall seek them soon. *Iä-R'lyeh! Cthulhu fhtagn! Iä! Iä!* No, I shall not shoot myself—I cannot be made to shoot myself! (CF 3.230)

Instead of requiring readers to use their Theory of Mind to imagine what Olmstead is thinking and feeling, Lovecraft simply informs his readers of everything they need to know. Indeed, this one paragraph contains Olmstead's entire transformation: it begins with him contemplating shooting himself and ends with him insisting that he "cannot be made" to shoot himself. Having read Zunshine's argument, one might assume that readers would feel cheated by Lovecraft's direct approach, but the poetic, almost jeweled quality of the writing itself prevents Lovecraft's work from ever seeming plain or straightforward.

If Lovecraft eliminates, whenever possible, opportunities for readers to engage their Theory of Mind, why is his fiction so popular? Perhaps, one might argue, short stories, which are primarily what Lovecraft wrote, do not need to challenge a reader's Theory of Mind as much as novels do. And yet, *The Case of Charles Dexter Ward* is a 51,500-word novella, and according to an online poll conducted by the *H. P. Lovecraft Archive*, visitors to the website rank it higher than all but three of Lovecraft's tales ("Visitors' Favorite Stories"). Though Zunshine does not consider the possibility, it may be that, by downplaying Theory of Mind, Lovecraft's work actually appeals *more* to certain readers. Clark Ashton Smith, for instance, who admired and, in some ways, imitated Lovecraft's work, considered weird fiction's otherworldly focus an asset, a welcome change from the realism then in vogue. When his mentor George Sterling urged him to abandon the cosmic in favor of the earthly, Smith condemned the very Modernists Zunshine praises, dismissing their work as neurotic and small-minded: "I [. . .] refuse to submit to the arid, earth-bound spirit of the time; and I think there is sure to be a romantic revival sooner or later— a revolt against mechanization and over-socialization, etc. [. . .] Neither the ethics or the aesthetic of the ant-hill have any attraction for me" (264).

Lovecraft himself felt much the same way. In his essay "Supernatural Horror in Literature," he criticizes Sheridan Le Fanu, Wilkie Collins, Robert Louis Stevenson, and other nineteenth-century practitioners of horror, for focusing on "events rather than atmospheric details," which are, to the horror genre, far more important: "Because of its 'human element' [this school of writers] commands a wider audience than does the sheer artistic nightmare. If not quite so potent as the latter, it is because a diluted product can never achieve the intensity of a concentrated essence" (48). Zunshine never acknowledges that some readers find the rich and detailed characterization she admires a nuisance, an unwelcome intrusion that distracts from the story itself. Indeed, it may be that more readers would side with Lovecraft than with Zunshine, who exalts writers, specifically Ernest Hemingway, Virginia Woolf, Henry James, and Vladimir Nabokov, whom many readers—not all of whom are autistic—consider either tedious or bewildering. More would, I suspect, agree with Lovecraft's estimation of Henry James, a writer he calls "too diffuse, too unctuously urbane, and too much addicted to subtleties of speech to realise fully all the wild and devastating horror in his situations" (*Annotated Supernatural Horror* 68), than with Zunshine's.

The advantages gained by downplaying Theory of Mind are not insignificant. By doing so, Lovecraft attracts those who, like Smith, seek an imaginative escape from a sometimes oppressive humanism. Lovecraft's preference for diegesis over mimesis, which is one of the ways he discourages Theory of Mind, also shapes his writing style, resulting in remarkably dense prose. As discussed above, in *The Case of Charles Dexter Ward* Lovecraft often condenses what could be lengthy scenes into a few brief sentences. Doing so allows him to dramatically increase the pace. As a result, many of his works seem far longer than they really are. Tales like "The Shunned House," a 10,700-word story that meticulously reconstructs the history of a two-hundred-year-old haunted house, seem more like novels, or history textbooks, than short stories. And yet, though the plots involved are as complex as those found in far longer novels, even Lovecraft's lengthiest works, novellas like *At the Mountains of Madness* and *The Case of Charles Dexter Ward*, conform to Edgar Allan Poe's Unity of Effect. The concentration, coupled with purification, that Lovecraft achieves in his fiction would not be possible if he, like most other contemporary authors, described scenes as if they were occurring in real time. Dialogue, in particular, would disrupt the atmosphere that Lovecraft considered crucial to a successful weird tale, and twentieth-century speech patterns would wreak havoc on his distinctive, deliberately archaic prose. Of course, Lovecraft does include some dialogue. In *The Case of Charles Dexter Ward;* for instance, the story concludes with a conversation between Willett and Curwen, the only back-and-forth exchange in the entire novella. It is all the more powerful for its rarity.

As her title indicates, Zunshine bases her book *Why We Read Fiction* on an assumption: that we do read fiction. Many do not, and it may be that the approach she favors, the one exemplified by Virginia Woolf and Henry James, is partly to blame. Reacting to the very style Zunshine praises, Lovecraft approached writing fiction from a different perspective, one that deliberately deemphasizes characters, their inner states, and their interactions with one another, and the lasting popularity of his work would seem not only to challenge but to undermine Zunshine's thesis. The simplest explanation may be that most readers, when placed on a spectrum, have more in common with the autistic than they do with literary critics. In any case, many readers, myself included, would agree with Lovecraft that "life has never interested me so much as the escape from life" (*Letters to J. Vernon Shea . . .* 30).

Works Cited

Joshi, S. T. *I Am Providence: The Life and Times of H. P. Lovecraft.* New York: Hippocampus Press, 2010. 2 vols.

Joshi, S. T., and David E. Schultz, ed. *Ave atque Vale: Reminiscences of H. P. Lovecraft.* West Warwick, RI: Necronomicon Press, 2018.

Lovecraft, H. P. *The Annotated Supernatural Horror in Literature.* Ed. S. T. Joshi. New York: Hippocampus Press, rev. ed. 2012.

———. *Letters to Alfred Galpin.* Ed. S. T. Joshi and David E. Schultz. New York: Hippocampus Press, 2003.

———. *Letters to J. Vernon Shea, Carl F. Strauch, and Lee McBride White.* Ed. S. T. Joshi and David E. Schultz. New York: Hippocampus Press, 2016.

———. *Letters to Rheinhart Kleiner.* Ed. S. T. Joshi and David E. Schultz. New York: Hippocampus Press, 2005.

Myers, Gary, and Jennifer McIlwee Myers. *Lovecraft's Syndrome: An Asperger's Appraisal of the Writer's Life.* CreateSpace Independent Publishing, 2015.

Smith, Clark Ashton, and George Sterling. *The Shadow of the Unattained: The Letters of George Sterling and Clark Ashton Smith.*

Ed. David E. Schultz and S. T. Joshi. New York: Hippocampus Press, 2005.

"Visitors' Favorite Stories." *The H. P. Lovecraft Archive*, 27 October 2011, hplovecraft.com/writings/favorites.aspx. Accessed 26 October 2018.

Zunshine, Lisa. *Why We Read Fiction: Theory of Mind and the Novel.* Columbus: Ohio State University Press, 2006.

Briefly Noted

H. P. Lovecraft and his work are about to increase exponentially in popularity as a result of two major media ventures that will be released in the coming months. The cult director Richard Stanley, best known as the director of the science fiction film *Hardware* (1990), has just completed work on a film version of "The Colour out of Space," starring Nicholas Cage. (Regrettably, Stanley appears to be using the American spelling of "colour" in the title of his film.) The screenplay was written by Scarlett Amaris. The African-American director Jordan Peele, who gained celebrity with the grim film *Get Out* (2017), has completed an adaption of Matt Ruff's novel *Lovecraft Country* (2016) as an eight-part miniseries for HBO. On a considerably lesser scale, S. T. Joshi is involved in as many as five forthcoming documentaries on Lovecraft: two in French (by Gilles Menegaldo and Martine Chifflot), one from Canada (by Qais Pasha), one by a Japanese TV program (*Dark Side Mystery*, on the NKH public television channel), and one by a French TV program (for the European cultural TV channel ARTE). In addition, Cadabra Records has just released Joshi's *Selections from "H. P. Lovecraft: A Short Biography"* as an LP.

H. P. Lovecraft's "Sunset"

H. P. Lovecraft and S. T. Joshi

Musical adaptations of the works of H. P. Lovecraft are still relatively rare. We are all familiar with the two poems, "Mirage" and "The Elder Pharos" (from *Fungi from Yuggoth*), set to music by Harold S. Farnese (1885–1945). These adaptations are for solo voice (soprano) and piano. Farnese later proposed to Lovecraft the rather grotesque idea of writing the libretto to an opera, initially titled *Yurregarth and Yannimaid* (later *Fen River*), based on elements from his evolving pseudomythology; but this project evidently came to nothing. After Lovecraft's death, Farnese composed an "Elegy for H. P. Lovecraft" (1937), as did Alfred Galpin ("Lament for H.P.L."). Both of these pieces are for solo piano, but of course they do not qualify as "adaptations" of Lovecraft's work.

The first item published by the specialty firm Fedogan & Bremer was a reading of the thirty-six sonnets of *Fungi from Yuggoth*, with musical accompaniment by Mike Olson; but his score was manifestly intended as background music rather than a self-standing composition. The CD appeared in 1987 and has recently been re-released with additional material.

I myself, aside from my work on Lovecraft over the decades, have been involved in the realm of classical music since I was eight years old, when I first began to play the violin. As outlined in my memoir, *What Is Anything?* (2018), during my years in high school I played the violin (also briefly the viola), sang in choirs (as a tenor), arranged music (including a re-orchestration of Bach's *Brandenburg Concerto No. 6*), and composed music. This music was entirely instrumental and mostly for strings, as those were the instruments whose range and resonance I knew best.

But I largely gave up musical composition (and, for that matter, violin playing) during my college years at Brown. I realised that the full-fledged pursuit of music and literature would be difficult to manage simultaneously, so I chose the latter. But my musical interests never waned, even if for decades I became simply an appreciator.

Shortly after I moved to Seattle in 2001, I joined the Northwest Chorale, one of many community choirs in the city. Its director, Lynn Hall, was a superb musician and had an uncanny ability to get the most out of his amateur group. We performed such major works as Handel's *Messiah*, *Requiems* by Mozart, Brahms, Duruflé, and the contemporary British composer John Rutter, Bach's *B Minor Mass*, and many shorter works.

My work in the choir led me to consider writing brief compositions specifically for it. I had always admired Lovecraft's poem "Sunset" (first published in the *Tryout*, December 1917) as a short and moving paean to the aesthetic and spiritual beauties of the natural world, so I undertook to set it to music for four part *a cappella* (unaccompanied) choir in early 2018.

I was under the impression that this was the first work for choir based on a specific Lovecraft work; but only recently have I discovered that the composer Jonathan Adams (whose composition, "The Ancient Track," for solo voice and piano and based on the Lovecraft poem, appears in the *Lovecraft Annual* No. 2 [2010]), had beaten me to the punch—with an adaptation of "Sunset"! His version, while quite moving, strikes me as more hymn-like than mine, and Adams does not engage in the (perhaps naïve) word-painting—derived from Handel, Vivaldi, and Mozart—that appears in my version.[1]

My piece received its world premiere performance on May 11, 2019, at the Northwest Chorale's spring concert, held at the First Free Methodist Church in Seattle.[2]

---

1. All the works mentioned here—Mike Olson's music for *Fungi from Yuggoth*; the compositions by Farnese and Galpin; and Adams's "The Ancient Track" and "Sunset"—can now be found on the expanded *Fungi from Yuggoth* set (2 CDs) issued by Fedogan & Bremer in 2015.

2. The performance, recorded by Greg Lowney, can be heard at www.youtube.com/watch?v=Hy8sLLmj9RA&feature=youtu.be

The Pathos in the Mythos

Ann McCarthy

In *H. P. Lovecraft: Against the World, Against Life,* Michel Houellebecq posits meaninglessness as a central Lovecraft theme, claiming that Lovecraft "destroys his characters, invoking only the dismemberment of marionettes" (32). This reading is borne out somewhat in the popular conception of Lovecraft. That is to say, everybody knows Cthulhu, but no one is talking about Albert N. Wilmarth. Well, I am here to talk about Albert N. Wilmarth and some others. Their lives contain fascination and suffering. Discussing Charles Robert Maturin's *Melmoth the Wanderer* in "Supernatural Horror in Literature," Lovecraft praises "the white heat of sympathetic passion on the writer's part which makes the book a true document of aesthetic self-expression" (40). My goal in this paper is, via close reading, to locate this passion as it manifests itself in different ways in *The Case of Charles Dexter Ward*, "The Whisperer in Darkness," "The Rats in the Walls," and Victor LaValle's *The Ballad of Black Tom*, a recent retelling of "The Horror at Red Hook." The characters' relationships with history and one another, their rich feeling, need not be diminished by any perceived futility in relation to the larger universe.

Dr. Willett's description of Charles Dexter Ward's early academic pursuits and rambles invoke the youngster's budding genius and love for scholarship, the city of Providence, and its institutions of learning and historical archives:

> His walks were always adventures in antiquity. ... The boy used to stroll past the long lines of the pre-Revolutionary homes with their great central chimneys and classic portals. On the eastern side they were set high over basements with railed double flights of stone steps, and the young Charles could picture them as they were when the street was new, and red heels and periwigs

set off the painted pediments whose signs of wear were now becoming so visible. (*CF* 2.221)

This deep imaginative engagement with his surroundings brings Ward joy. There is an artistic bent in his historicism. "He would pause to drink in the bewildering beauty of the old town as it rises on its eastward bluff, decked with its two Georgian spires . . . He liked most to reach this point in the late afternoon, when the slanted sunlight touches the Market House and the ancient hill roofs and belfries with gold, and throws magic around the dreaming wharves" (*CF* 2.224). This flight of absolutely gorgeous, appreciation-suffused writing is not something a reader coming to Lovecraft via Houellebecq would expect.

Ward's devotion to historical research sets him apart from his peers. "His social activities were few; and his hours were spent mainly at home, in rambling walks . . . and in pursuit of antiquarian and genealogical data at the City Hall, the State House, the Public Library, the Athenaeum, the Historical Society, the John Carter Brown and John Hay libraries of Brown University, and the newly opened Shepley Library in Benefit Street" (*CF* 2.221). This long, specific list of civic institutions imbues Ward's scholarship with a doggedness, a relentless, thorough, admirable seeking. His initial antiquarian interest had extended from local history and genealogy to "colonial architecture, furniture and craftsmanship." As his researches focus in on Joseph Curwen, he abandons study of the "antiquities he loved so keenly" (*CF* 2.221).

As something sinister invades his ethos, the nature of Ward's studies changes, but they remain passionate and admirable:

> During October Ward began visiting the libraries again, but no longer for the antiquarian matter of his former days. Witchcraft and magic, occultism and daemonology, were what he sought now; and when Providence sources proved unfruitful he would take the train for Boston and tap the wealth of the great library in Copley Square, the Widener Library at Harvard, or the Zion Research Library in Brookline, where certain rare works on Biblical subjects are available. (*CF* 2.278)

He continues "haunting all the sources of vital statistics in Providence." (*CF* 2.278).

Ward's goal is preservation and restoration of Providence history, heretofore hidden because of its ugliness. "His romancing about Curwen doubly excited him" because information about Curwen has been "concealed" and is in danger of being forgotten, of utter "deletion" (*CF* 2.226). His research takes him so far and wide and into nooks and corners and garrets, such a romantic dream of the academic: "old letters, diaries and sheaves of unpublished memoirs in cobwebbed Providence garrets and elsewhere yielded may illuminating passages" (*CF* 2.226). This is the goal: illumination. We call labor undertaken without financial compensation "labor of love." The information he uncovers forms the basis of Willett's narrative of Curwen's life, and is in itself a great scholarly achievement: "Joseph Curwen was revealed by the rambling legends embodied in what Ward had heard and unearthed" (*CF* 2.227). Illumination, then, and revelation.

This nobility and passion in pursuit of knowledge for its own sake are thrown into relief by the contrasting nature of Ward's evil ancestor's pursuit and use of local history and magical knowledge. Joseph Curwen uses talks with dead people to generate kompromat on the living, that he may use as leverage in business and personal dealings, amassing wealth and power and legitimacy in the town. Only "direct talks with the long dead may have furnished the data" (*CF* 2.236).

"The Whisperer in Darkness" stages another drama of passionate research. Albert Wilmarth introduces himself to us as "Then, as now, a professor of literature . . . and an enthusiastic amateur student of New England folklore" (*CF* 2.468). Notable here is his enthusiasm and the uncompensated nature of his labor in lore. Also notable is the "then, as now." His experience in the weird did not drive him mad, kill him, or even turn him off his interests. In *The Secret Life of Puppets*, Victoria Nelson writes that all Lovecraft's work ends with the protagonist "either mad or engulfed in and metamorphozing into an alien creature himself" (105). Not so our friend Wilmarth.

Albert Wilmarth's friendship with Henry Akeley begins when Akeley reads Wilmarth's letters to the editor in the *Brattleboro Reformer*, in which Wilmarth rejects supernatural explanations of the phenomenon of weird inhuman bodies floating in the river after a major flood. Akeley writes, "Now my object in writing you is not to start an argument, but to give you information which I think a man of your tastes will find deeply interesting. This is private" (CF 2.477). "I will tell you about this later if you do not dismiss me at once as a madman" (CF 2.477). A "recluse" reaches out (CF 2.474)! What a relief for him to have found a kindred scholar spirit in the newspaper.

S. T. Joshi tells us in the notes that: "The name, and certain facets of [Henry Akeley] ... derive from a reclusive painter named Bert G. Akley, living in a cabin outside of Brattleboro, who Lovecraft met ... in 1928." Joshi quotes Lovecraft's postcard describing Akley as a "rustic genius" and praising his painting and general autodidactedness, but notes: "through it all he retains the primitiveness of the agrestic, and lives in unbelievable heaps and piles of disorder" (*Call of Cthulhu* 404). Compare this to Wilmarth's description of Akeley, which has a moment of condescension but, in general, much more a sense of parity: "From the first I saw he was he was a man of character, education, and intelligence, albeit a recluse with very little worldly sophistication" (CF 2.474).

The epistolary collaboration that follows is intense:

> During late May and early June, I was in constant correspondence with Akeley; though once in a while a letter would be lost, so that we would have to ... perform ... laborious copying. We were trying to compare notes in matter of obscure mythological scholarship and arrive at a clearer correlation of the Vermont horrors with the general body of primitive world legend. (CF 2.484)

Their collaboration is warm, generative, exciting, and a triumph of shared eccentricity. "For one thing, we virtually decided that these morbidities and the hellish Himalayan *Mi-Go* were one and the same order of incarnated nightmare. There were also absorbing zoölogical conjectures" (CF 2.484). "My own zeal for the unknown flared up to meet his, and I felt myself touched by the contagion of the morbid barrier-breaking" (CF 2.505).

Also, concern for each other's safety marks their relationship. When Wilmarth reads the letter describing the Mi-Go's nocturnal assault attempts on the farmhouse, his "attitude toward the matter was by this time quickly slipping from a scientific to an alarmedly personal one. I was afraid for Akeley in his remote, lonely farmhouse.... I spoke of visiting [him] in spite of his wishes, and helping him explain the situation to the proper authorities" (*CF* 2. 493). Wilmarth sensitively describes the penmanship in Akeley's late letters as "pitifully tremulous" and "shaky" (*CF* 2.492, 494). When he finally visits the farmhouse and beholds what he thinks is Akeley, both pain and admiration are palpable: "But as I looked my resignation was mixed with sadness and anxiety; for certainly, this face was that of a very sick man. I [. . .] realised how terribly the strain of his frightful experiences must have told on him. Was it not enough to break any human being—even a younger man than this intrepid delver into the forbidden?" (*CF* 2.516). (It is of little consequence that Wilmarth is actually encountering one of the fungi from Yuggoth disguised as Akeley.)

I will be talking more about *The Ballad of Black Tom* later, but a quick digression: a great way that the father/son relationship is conveyed in that work is through the sharing of a meal. This holds throughout human culture. The repast Wilmarth partakes of at the farmhouse is one of the saddest meals ever. Wilmarth eats alone. "Throughout the lunch I thought of Akeley sitting silently in the great chair in the darkened next room. Once I went in to beg him to share the repast, but he whispered that he could eat nothing" (*CF* 2.520). The food is good, and "a Thermos-bottle beside a cup and saucer testified that hot coffee had not been forgotten" (*CF* 2.519). Coffee is a drink full of meaning; when the Arab world introduced coffee and coffeehouse culture to Western Europe, it helped to inspire the European Enlightenment. It was a drink for scholars to share. But Wilmarth dumps out the coffee after one spoonful because of its weird, acrid taste. Though Wilmarth doesn't make the leap, the reader can see that the coffee has been drugged.

Now we will move onto another meal: Delapore feasting on Norrys. But, I argue, it is a meal inspired by fatherly love and antiwar sentiment. Delapore's son Alfred writes home from the war in 1917. He is stationed near their ancestral home, Exham Priory, and writes to his father with "interesting ancestral legends" (*CF* 1.376). Based on the research in his son's letters, Delapore buys the priory:

> I bought Exham Priory in 1918, but was almost immediately distracted from my plans of restoration by the return of my son as a maimed invalid. During the two years that he lived I thought of nothing but his care, having even placed my business under the direction of partners. In 1921, as I found myself bereaved and aimless ... I resolved to divert my remaining years with my new possession. (CF 1.377)

Delapore leaves America to divert himself from the pain of his son's death.

Victoria Nelson describes Delapore's monologue over Norrys's corpse as a psychotic break, a descent all the way out of human language. She begins her quotation of it, however, right after a sentence that is key to my understanding of the cannibalism as a feast of love: "Why shouldn't ... a De La Poer eat forbidden things? ... the war ate my boy, damn them all" (CF 1.396). Only by leaving out that key line can Nelson sustain her argument that Lovecraft's stories "offer no identification with suffering" (134).

While it is a retelling of "The Horror at Red Hook," Victor LaValle's *The Ballad of Black Tom* echoes the plot of "The Rats in the Walls" in that Charles Thomas Tester's embrace of the ancient gods is a reaction to the racist murder by Officer Malone of Tester's father Otis. The love between the characters is far more developed and fleshed out than such feelings are in Lovecraft. LaValle establishes a movingly intense father-son relationship with economy of style, crystallizing it all in a dinner suffused with protective concern and mutual feeling. Otis Tester is only in his early forties, but years of laboring have left him in constant pain and with limited mobility. LaValle writes, "It took time to convince Otis to step out. Otis never left the apartment, hardly left his bedroom. He'd become like a dog gone into the dark so he could die alone, but Tommy had different plans. Or maybe he needed his father too much to let him go easily" (28). Hearing that Tommy is going into the employment of a creepy white man, Otis gifts him with a straight razor, and with the story of having had to rely on that razor when he travelled north years earlier. LaValle writes:

> Tommy looked from the razor to his father. All his life he'd known his dad and mom as pillars that solidly, stolidly, held up

the roof of Tommy's world. Reliable, supportive, but not particularly remarkable people. To think of Otis now, suddenly, as a teenage boy who'd defended himself with this weapon...That past became yet another world, a new dimension, of which Tommy had just become aware. Again, the pinch, the pain, of such revelation. (34)

Otis says: "you don't want to walk into that white man's house unarmed or unaware. Anything goes bad, you get out, and you get back to me." He repeats the refrain a few sentences later: "I don't care if you've got to spill blood to do it, but you get out of the house at the end of that job and you get back to me" (35). Tom Tester doesn't use the razor until after his father's death, when he mutilates Officer Malone to whom he whispers, "I'll take Cthulhu over you devils any day" (143). It is a line as powerful and intense as "The war ate my boy."

Finally, I would like to argue that the essay "Supernatural Horror in Literature" is itself an act of love. On the subject of this essay, Nelson writes, "Lovecraft sketched the development of the Gothic in the kind of careful detail that shows his high awareness both of the tradition and of his own place in it" (103). It has ten chapters, but three are on the Gothic. His project, rather, is to trace out something particular and new, starting in the canon and moving out into the present: the weird. In November 1925, Lovecraft writes reports that "W. Paul Cook wants an article from me on the element of terror and weirdness in literature' for his new magazine, the *Recluse*" (Joshi 608). Joshi points out that the specific nature of the study was left to Lovecraft, who decided to do an exhaustive historical survey, employing scholarly work as psychological self-defense. In a 1925 letter, Lovecraft reports: "This course of reading & writing I am going through for the Cook article is excellent mental discipline, & a fine gesture of demarcation betwixt my aimless, lost existence of the past year or two & the resumed ... hermitage amidst which I hope to grind out some tales worth writing" (quoted in Joshi 615). Joshi posits that Lovecraft's "greatest achievement" in the essay "was to designate Machen, Dunsany, Blackwood and M. R. James as the four 'modern masters' of the weird tale" (613). So, in his essay, which he kept working on even after publication, Lovecraft gave us a tradition, a tradition especially for "minds of the requisite sensitiveness." He writes, "It is a narrow though essential branch of human expression, and will chiefly appeal as always to a limited audience with keen special sensibilities" (96).

And here we are, so many scores of years later, we of "keen special sensibilities," his weird progeny, brought together in shared love of literature and bizarrerie.

Works Cited

Houellebecq, Michel. *H. P. Lovecraft: Against the World, Against Life.* Tr. Dorna Khazeni. San Francisco: Believer Books, 2005.

Joshi, S. T. *I Am Providence: The Life and Times of H. P. Lovecraft.* New York: Hippocampus Press, 2010. 2 vols.

LaValle, Victor. *The Ballad of Black Tom.* New York: Tor, 2016.

Lovecraft, H. P. *The Annotated Supernatural Horror in Literature.* Ed. S. T. Joshi. New York: Hippocampus Press, 2nd ed. 2012.

———. *The Call of Cthulhu and Other Weird Stories.* Ed. S. T. Joshi. New York: Penguin, 1999.

Nelson, Victoria. *The Secret Life of Puppets.* Cambridge, MA: Harvard University Press, 2001.

Briefly Noted

S. T. Joshi's biography *I Am Providence: The Life and Times of H. P. Lovecraft* appeared in March 2019 in a two-volume French translation supervised by Christophe Thill, with ten translators working with him. The book, published by ActuSF, was widely discussed in the French media, especially when Joshi himself traveled to France in May to give a succession of interviews in the course of his attendance of a major convention, Les Imaginales, in the town of Épinal. A German translation by Frank Rossnagel is in progress: the first volume appeared in 2017 and the second volume should be out soon. An Italian translation by Pietro Guarriello is in progress.

"Now Will You Be Good?": Lovecraft, Teetotalism, and Philosophy

Jan B. W. Pedersen

> It is an aesthetic matter with me. I think drink is ugly, & therefore I have nothing to do with it.—H. P. Lovecraft, Letter to Zealia Brown Reed Bishop, 13 February 1928 (*Spirit of Revision* 104–5)

Introduction

Lovecraft's teetotalism[1] is well known among Lovecraftians, but the lengths to which he went to incorporate his views and how he sought to influence the people around him via his various writing remain relatively unexplored. This essay focuses on Lovecraft's teetotalism and opens with a brief sketch of the historical background from which his dry outlook emerged. It continues by providing evidence for Lovecraft's advocacy of abstinence and Prohibition from a variety of sources, including biographical material, philosophical essays, letters, poetry, and fiction, with a view to showing how he communicated his dry philosophy and how it softened as he advanced into middle age. The essay ends by arguing that although there can be no doubt that Lovecraft was a teetotaler par excellence, his later softened position is more balanced and rooted partly in the realization of his own idiosyncrasy and anachronism.

---

1. Ironically, HPL has in recent years inspired certain alcoholic beverage companies to produce a wide range of eldritch-sounding drinks. The Narragansett Beer Company's *Lovecraft series* comprises seven exquisite beers and has in collaboration with The Sons of Liberty Spirit Company also created Lovecraft Hopped Whiskey. The Lovecraft Brewing Company, whose range of products encompass beers such as *Innsmouth Porter, Dreamlands ESB,* and *Mother Hydra Old Ale,* also draws inspiration from HPL.

Against a Drunken Background: England

Lovecraft was an Anglophile, and his teetotalism is connected to his beloved English heritage ("Anglo-Saxondom," *CE* 5. 32–33). In seventeenth-century England drunkenness was generally perceived as a benign and laughable condition. However, by the eighteenth century, and particularly with the advent of the Gin-Craze in the 1720s, the face of drunkenness changed.[2] New laws intended to boost the economy permitted everyone to produce gin from English cereals, and thus stills mushroomed in various parts of the country. As one might expect, the consumption of gin among the population skyrocketed as a result; according to historian Iain Gately, by 1723 "every man, woman, and child in London knocked back more than a pint of gin per head per week" (181).[3] The effect on the population was dire, particularly in the city of London, where squalid and decayed living conditions already made life difficult for many.

In time the government eventually noticed that overconsumption of gin among the population was not a force for good, and through five different Acts passed in 1729, 1736, 1743, 1747, and 1751, the authorities sought to bring matters under control.

In the years leading up to the Act of 1751 English painter, social critic, and editorial cartoonist William Hogarth got involved in the fight against gin, and he famously produced two engravings, *Gin Lane* (Figure 1) and *Beer Street* (Figure 2), with the intention of showing the madness of gin-induced dipsomania by contrasting it with the happy state of being of the "healthy" beer drinker.

Gin Lane is particularly disturbing because amidst the chaotic scenery that includes an impaled child, a child being fed gin, and a hanged man, we find "Lady Gin" sitting on a staircase with her

---

2. It is possible that gin, a clear, juniper-flavored spirit distilled from grain and malt, was invented in seventeenth-century Holland. Etymologically speaking, this makes sense because the word "gin" derives from the older "genever" or "jenever," referring to juniper in the Dutch language.

3. The alcohol per volume (APV) of gin ranges between 37.5% and 50%, and in eighteenth-century England it was usually served by the dram or drachma, which measures ⅛ of an ounce. The high AVP of gin and the inexpensiveness of its production contributed to its popularity. To put it bluntly, it was an easy and inexpensive way of getting drunk fast.

clothing in disarray exhibiting foul leg ulcers.[4] Furthermore, she is in a seemingly happy and careless daze, letting her child plunge to its death over the nearby railing. The link to the terrible consequences of overconsumption of gin is clear and is further amplified upon noticing that the child of Lady Gin will meet its end at the front door of a basement gin store named "Gin Royale" that advertises its intoxicating beverages with the catchphrase: "Drunk for a Penny/Dead Drunk for Two Pence/Clean Straw for Nothing."

Both engravings originally came with accompanying verses, so that no one could be mistaken about their individual messages. *Gin Lane* opens with the negative line "Gin, cursed Fiend, with Fury fraught," and Beer Street with the positive "Beer, happy Produce of our Isle."

The Gin-Craze eventually faded away, but this singular episode in English history owes its end not only to governmental acts and the dramatic engravings of a skilled artist. New ideas flourished in political philosophy addressing how society molds people, and they likewise contributed to the effect. Romantic philosopher Jean-Jacques Rousseau's *The Social Contract* is important in this regard, as it opens with the now famous line: "Man is born free but he is everywhere in chains" (49). If we view the gin-craze personified by the gin-soaked hussy depicted in Hogarth's *Gin Street* through Rousseau's spectacles, it becomes clear that the drunken citizens of London may not solely be responsible for their fate. Their unfortunate situation could at least in part have been brought about by unfavorable social structures in eighteenth-century England. No doubt times were hard and particularly so for women, who were viewed as subordinate to men and who had little access to education and suffered from unfair laws that favored men in matters concerning money and inheritance.

---

4. The leg ulcers could be the result of syphilis, a venereal disease that could well have been introduced into Europe by sailors accompanying Christopher Columbus on his voyages to the New World. If the sores indeed are syphilitic leg ulcers, it points to the promiscuity of Lady Gin and the possibility of her being a prostitute, which adds to the overall uneasiness of the engraving.

Figure 1: William Hogarth, *Gin Lane* (1751). The engraving together with the accompanying verses is meant to shock and conveys human degradation to an extreme degree.

Figure 2: William Hogarth, Beer Street (1751). The engraving is a celebration of English industriousness and serves as an approval of having a pint of beer (or more) post work hours. Beer Street comes in two versions. The first, which is depicted here features a blacksmith lifting a Frenchman with one hand. The 1957 version replaced the Frenchman with a lump of meat and added a pavior and a maid.

Overconsumption of alcohol remained a problem in England after the Gin-Craze, but as we move into the nineteenth century the problematic custom was addressed from a different angle. Thomas Trotter, M.D., and late physician to His Majesty's fleet under the command of Admiral Earl Howe, K.G.,[5] alerted people to the dangers of alcohol from a medical perspective. Printed in London in 1804, Trotter's *An Essay, Medical, Philosophical, and Chemical on Drunkenness and Its Effect on the Human Body* leaves few in doubt that alcohol is a bad thing. He sets the tone from the beginning on the title page with a quotation from Shakespeare's *Othello*, "O! thou invisible spirit of wine, if thou hast no name to be known by, let us call thee—devil" (2.3.280–82), and goes on to spell out not only the negative impact alcohol has on the human body, but also how it wreaks havoc on the mind. In italics Trotter writes: *"The habit of drunkenness is a disease of the mind"* (172).

The nineteenth century also saw the birth of teetotalism in England. The neologism refers to the total abstinence from alcoholic beverages, but how this rather peculiar word came about is unclear. A popular notion is that the term was coined quite unintentionally in 1833. The *Charleston Observer* notes:

> *Teetotalers.*—The origin of this convenient word, (as convenient almost, although not so general in its application as *loafer,*) is, we imagine, known but too few who use it. It originated, as we learn from the Landmark, with a man named Turner, a member of the Preston Temperance Society, who, having an impediment of speech, in addressing a meeting remarked, that partial abstinence from intoxicating liquors would not do; they must insist upon tee-tee-(stammering) tee total abstinence. Hence total abstainers have been called *teetotalers*.

If the *Charleston Observer* is correct, the curious word "teetotaler" was born from the stuttering of Richard Turner[6]—a member of the Preston Temperance Society founded in Preston, England, in 1833 by local newspaper owner, industrialist, and politician Joseph Livesey. This singular society organized various meetings to pro-

---

5. K.G. refers to Knight of the Order of the Garter, which is an order of chivalry founded by King Edward III in 1348.
6. According to historian Iain Gately, Turner's first name is Richard (273).

mote its course and attract new members, and in 1834 it founded the first temperance magazine, the *Preston Temperance Advocate*, which ran until 1837.

Bacchus in America

That the populace of America also came face to face with the joys and sorrows of alcohol is not surprising, because many of the early European settlers were jovial drinkers.

After the American Revolution (1775–83), whiskey became the national drink in America. It was a cheap and "safe" drink, since the alcohol eradicated germs, and by the 1820s the average white American male downed about half a pint of whiskey per day (Rorabaugh 7).[7] However, the "Whiskey-craze" did not go unnoticed, and medical doctors such as Benjamin Rush eventually began to speak out about the dark side of alcohol, including the build-up of tolerance and the need for an increased intake over time if the desired euphoric state of mind were to be achieved.

Already in 1784 Rush published *An Inquiry into the Effects of Spirituous Liquors*, and by 1850 the book had reach massive popularity and sold a staggering 170,000 copies (Rorabaugh 7). Rush argued not only that was alcohol dangerous to human health, but that American democracy would suffer and ultimately break down if voters were nothing but drunken bacchants. Unemployment, crime, poverty, family violence, starvation, gambling, and prostitution were, in Rush's view, associated with drunkenness and altogether it made for bad voters (Rorabaugh 9).

Rush was not the only physician battling against the consumption of alcohol in America. In 1812 the Massachusetts Society for the Suppression of Intemperance (MSSI), comprised of members of the Congregational clergy connected to the Andover Seminary, Boston business leaders, and a number of physicians, was founded. The society campaigned against the overconsumption of whiskey and represented a classical approach to temperance, meaning that temperance is about moderation and is something to be sought between two extremes: too little and too much. To understand this better, it is prudent to evoke the ancient Greek philosopher

---

7. The APV of whiskey was at the time about 50%.

Aristotle, who if he were alive today would argue that the raison d'être of the MSSI was to spread the idea that drinking alcohol is easy, but to drink with the right person(s) and to the right degree and at the right time and for the right purpose and in the right way—that is not within everybody's power and is not easy and thus praiseworthy (Aristotle, *Nicomachean Ethics* 2.60.2).

However, among those involved in the fight against drunkenness this attitude toward temperance was soon to give way to a more radical take on the matter. The American Temperance Society (ATS), founded in 1826 in Boston, together with religious groups including the Quakers, the Methodists, and the Baptists were soon to denounce the "classical" call for temperance issued by MSSI and required members to take *the teetotal pledge* and keep away from all forms of alcohol (Rorabaugh 11–13). With time this particular approach to temperance gained influence, and by 1842 the first law aimed at limiting the sale of alcohol in saloons had been put in place.

Between 1840 and 1850 more than two million whiskey-drinking Irishmen and beer-loving Germans immigrated to America, supplying as it were fresh support for the cult of Bacchus.[8] However, many an evangelical lobbied successfully for statewide prohibition, which was put into effect between 1851 and 1855 in the six states of New England, New York, Michigan, Indiana, Iowa, and Delaware (Rorabaugh 21). None of these laws lasted beyond 1865, the year the American Civil War ended, but nonetheless a "dry" movement had taken root and was gaining popularity. The movement turned into a cultural force with the advent of the Independent Order of Good Templars (IOGT) in 1851. Standing in opposition to alcohol-drinking Freemasons, this lodge counted post-1865 seven million women and men as members (Rorabaugh 20).

The following period, ending with the Eighteenth Amendment

---

8. The cult of Bacchus was an orgiastic cult, originally meant for women only, that expanded in Italy approximately 200 years B.C.E. Dionysus, the Greek God of wine and ecstasy, whom the Romans labelled Bacchus, was the focal point of the cult. For the purpose of this article I assume that a modern follower of Bacchus is a person who does not shy away from enjoyment and revelry involving drunkenness.

to the United States Constitution, passed in 1919 and going into effect in 1920, which saw a national ban on the production, importation, transportation, and sale of alcoholic beverages, represents a "war" of attitudes. It was a clash between teetotalism and liberty.

A figure important to the general temperance movement is its foremost orator, John Bartholomew Gough (1817–1886; Figure 3).[9] His crusade against alcohol was felt considerably in both England and America, and in 1880, ten years before Lovecraft was born, he published *Sunlight and Shadow*, a book containing many a dramatic proclamation, including that beer is the most animalizing of drinks and a beverage that dulls the intellect, clouds the moral sense, and "feeds the sensual and beastly nature" in us (364).

Figure 3: John Bartholomew Gough (1817–1886)

---

9. Gough died while lecturing and is buried at Hope Cemetery in Worchester, Massachusetts.

Although Prohibition produced positive effects among the population, including a dramatic decline in cases of cirrhosis of the liver and the number of arrests due to drunkenness (MacCoun and Reuter 161), it lost its appeal over time. One problem was that the law by and large was draconian in nature and violators faced heavy fines, imprisonment, and confiscation of property. Additionally, it took an army of government agents, also known as G-men, with intrusive powers to enforce the amendment, and it gave birth to new kinds of criminals including bootleggers,[10] moonshiners,[11] and rum-runners.[12]

Championed by Franklin D. Roosevelt, the Twenty-First amendment to the American constitution put an end to Prohibition in 1933, but the repeal did not signal a total victory of "wet" over "dry." Individual teetotalers as well as dry communities dedicated to Prohibition lived on and exist in America even today, and thus it can be said that the war of attitudes never really ended.

In Vino Veritas: The Early Lovecraft (1890–1925)

Lovecraft was exposed to this war of attitudes quite early in life. At the age of five or six, he supposedly read Gough's *Sunlight and Shadow*, of which the Phillips family had a copy in the family library (*SL* 1.35). Whether he picked it up by his own initiative or from the recommendation of a family member is uncertain, but one can speculate that because his beloved grandfather Whipple Van Buren Phillips spent time in the temperance town of Delavan, Illinois, in the 1850s (Joshi, *IAP* 6), it is quite possible that Lovecraft was introduced to Gough's book by his grandfather.

That grandfather Phillips influenced the young Lovecraft on

---

10. Bootleggers were smugglers who during Prohibition continued to sell alcohol. The term originates in the time of King George III, when smugglers hid goods in their voluminous sea-boots to avoid the attention of the king's guard.

11. Moonshiners produced low-quality alcohol in secret during the Prohibition period. The term is akin to the English term *moonraker*, which refers to mid-sixteenth-century smugglers in Wiltshire, a county in southwest England.

12. Rum-runners were international bootleggers who during Prohibition traded in alcohol mainly between the Caribbean islands and America. One of the more famous rum-runners is William S, McCoy, who smuggled Scotch (whiskey from Scotland) into Georgia on board his schooner *Henry L. Marshall* registered under the British flag.

matters of alcohol could explain why Lovecraft, in a letter of 13 February 1928, proclaims that wine had been banished in his family for three generations (*The Spirit of Revision* 104–5). This is a remarkable statement and if it is true, how could Lovecraft possibly have such knowledge of his family, unless a thoughtful family member such as Whipple Van Buren Phillips related it to him?[13]

That Lovecraft took issue with the consumption of alcohol is evident from a number of his early philosophical writings. To add weight to this claim, let us begin by looking at Lovecraft's own amateur magazine, the *Conservative*, which ran for thirteen issues between 1915 and 1923. In the first issue he has an editorial stating: "The Conservative will ever be found an enthusiastic champion of total abstinence and prohibition" ("Editorial," *CE* 1.51). It is hard to imagine a clearer statement linking the *Conservative* with teetotalism without the actual use of the word. The piece concludes with Lovecraft reminding his fellow conservatives that "he who strives against the Hydra-monster Rum, strives most to conserve his fellow man" (*CE* 1.51). "Hydra-monster Rum" is a negative moniker for rum, and it seems safe to say that Lovecraft uses this phrase as a generic reference to what he perceived as one of the many scourges of alcohol.

The editorial is followed in subsequent issues by a series of essays or heated opinion pieces rallying against alcohol, starting with "Liquor and Its Friends," appearing in the *Conservative* for October 1915. Here Lovecraft protests against the reinstatement of the presence of liquor at American state dinners by the new secretary of state, Robert Lansing, who took over from William Jennings Bryan. Bryan, a religious fundamentalist, pacifist, and supporter of Prohibition, managed to abolish wine from tables of the state and thus in Lovecraft's view gave "the American people a high governmental example of decency" ("Liquor and Its Friends," *CE* 5.16). Nevertheless, Bryan resigned from his post after the torpe-

---

13. Although it might be that alcohol had not been a part of the Lovecraft family for three generations, one source speaks of HPL being intoxicated by alcohol at least once in his life. The story goes that HPL attended a party where his drink was supposedly spiked by a roommate of Samuel Loveman named Pat McGrath, with the result that HPL became talkative, smiling, laughing, and gesticulating. (Loveman 211).

doing of the ocean liner *Lusitania* by a German U-boat in May 1915.[14] Lovecraft finishes the essay by making clear that those who are not on his side in matters of alcohol disregard natural law and moral rectitude and will contribute to the downfall of civilization (*CE* 5.16–17).

"More *Chain Lightning*"[15] appeared in the *United Official Quarterly* for October 1915 and celebrates Andrew Francis Lockhart, an amateur journalist and editor of the journal *Chain Lightning*, who had successfully campaigned for the closing of licensed saloons in the city of Milbank, South Dakota. Central to the piece is Lovecraft's pro-prohibitionist argument stating:

> As to the "personal liberty", "rights of man", and other popular phrases similarly misused, there are few indeed who can fail to perceive that the "liberty" and "right" of a man voluntary to transform himself to a beast, and in the end to degrade himself and his descendants permanently in the scale of evolution, is equivalent to his "liberty" and "right" to rob and murder at will. If the law may justly suppress theft and homicide, it may certainly with equal justice suppress the manufacture, sale and consumption of that liquid evil which incites most of the world's theft and homicide. As to "moderate" drinking, we might on similar ethics condone "moderate larceny" or "moderate manslaughter". Human nature admits of no exact middle course in drinking. He who usually drinks "a little", will always on occasion drink "a little too much", wherefore the only sane course is absolutely total abstinence. (*CE* 5.18–19)

Lovecraft's argument is overly dramatic and much too extreme. Admittedly, alcohol influences a person's cognitive functions and sometimes quite negatively, but to enjoy a drink of one's own free volition does not usually result in endless bacchanal,[16] and to equate moderate drinking with moderate larceny or moderate manslaughter in order to persuade the reader of the beauty of tee-

---

14. For more information on how the sinking of the *Lusitania* inspired HPL and in particular his short story "The Temple" (1920), see Reilly.
15. Chain lightning is a slang word for raw whiskey.
16. For more information on HPL's aversion toward ecstasy, revelry, and the cultist rites associated with Bacchus, see Quinn.

totalism is more telling of Lovecraft's disgust for alcohol than it bears witness to good argumentation.

"A Remarkable Document" appeared in the *Conservative* for July 1917 and is less pompous than Lovecraft's previous writing on the demon rum. It praises the temperance advocate Booth Tarkington, who instead of relying on lofty idealism, approached temperance and Prohibition from a scientific angle. At this point a beginning sophistication of Lovecraft's attitude toward alcohol is emerging, and we also get a hint of his boredom with the ordinary, which comes to light in his 1917 poem "Fact and Fancy"[17] and later becomes an important theme in his wonder stories.[18] Lovecraft writes:

> No one can deny that life in conventionally civilised communities is dull and monotonous to the point of loathsomeness; and if this basic ennui be so potent a factor in the desire for liquor, then we cannot expect to banish the evil till we have found some means of brightening the gloom which causes it. (CE 5.26)

Lovecraft in this essay puts on the spectacles of Rousseau and connects with the "victims of alcohol" by recognizing that they have a common enemy; namely the dullness of everyday life. Lovecraft speculates that in order to do away with the plague of liquor one has to take care of ennui first, and this practical if not Romantic approach is new.

"The Recognition of Temperance" is the last philosophical essay evidencing Lovecraft's views on matters of alcohol that I will focus on here. Published in the *Little Budget of Knowledge and Nonsense* for April 1917, this short piece celebrates the notion that science has caught up with the drinkers and that Prohibition is spreading steadily in Europe and America based on the recognition of "alcohol as foe of national efficiency and prosperity" (CE 5.284). The wording of the essay is sober and relatively bereft of the drama Lovecraft evoked in "Liquor and Its Friends," as the

---

17. For more information on "Fact and Fancy" and how it relates to HPL's Romanticism, see Pedersen, "Howard Phillips Lovecraft: Romantic on the Nightside."

18. For more information of HPL's relationship with wonder, see Pedersen, "On Lovecraft's Lifelong Relationship with Wonder."

emphasis is on the transformation of the temperance movement, its shift away from evangelism and moralizing and its embrace of science and government. However, it also delivers a criticism of the supposed cultivated upper-middle-class cosmopolitan whose wine cellar still celebrates the essential evil. "The presence of liquor on the sideboards of a certain type of 'solid citizen' is as distressing as it is incongruous," Lovecraft writes (CE 5.284). The essay ends on a positive note, stating that alcohol, the "mother of ruin and death," is now exposed for what it is, and that the "social prestige of wine" must be destroyed through "lofty example and polite ridicule" (CE 5.285).

Young Lovecraft's formidable aversion toward alcohol is made quite clear from reading his early poetry. In "The Power of Wine: A Satire" (1914) he writes:

> Unhappy man above the beasts was plac'd;
> Stript of his joys, and with mere Reason grac'd:
> Sweet Wine alone his pleasures can restore;
> Let him but quaff, and he's a beast once more! (AT 212–13)

The satirical element of the poem is obvious as Lovecraft portrays the unfortunate predicament of human beings. Unlike the other beasts of nature, human beings are endowed with the ability to have reasons for action, but rational deliberation often entails awareness of complexities, not forgetting doubt, and thus trouble and unhappiness enter human life. Owing to alcohol's ability to dull the faculties, the restoration of happiness is found in the consumption of wine, which effectively levels the consumer of alcohol with the non-rational beasts on the *scala naturae*.[19]

By paying attention to the somewhat spiteful wording of the poem it becomes clear that its conceptions are parallel in tone and suggestion with those of John Bartholomew Gough, who acrimoniously promoted the idea that alcoholic beverages dulls the intel-

---

19. *Scalae naturae* is the Latin term for "ladder of being,'" a hierarchical structure derived from the writings of the ancient Greek philosophers, particularly Aristotle, who organizes life in accordance with level of perfection. Human beings are the most perfect, followed by animals, plants, and minerals at the bottom of the scale. Christian scholars in the medieval period added God and angelic beings above human beings.

lect and calls forth the beast in us.

The young Lovecraft was quite aware that his teetotalism was not merely a personal idiosyncrasy and that he was part of a potentially revolutionary movement aiming to straighten a wayward nation. He did not shy away from taking leadership, of which the first stanza of "Temperance Song" (1916) stands in support:

> We are a band of brothers
> We fight the demon Rum,
> With all our strength until at length
> A better time shall come.
>
> (Chorus)
>
> Hurrah Hurrah! for Temperance, Hurrah!
> 'Tis sweet to think that deadly drink
> Some day no more shall mar! (*AT* 397–98)

For Lovecraft to use the phrase "band of brothers," originating in the famous St. Crispin's Day speech from Shakespeare's *Henry V*, indicates an attempt to call up epic feelings in his fellow teetotalers—feelings signalling that by rallying together and walking that extra mile in the name of teetotalism, victory over the demon rum would be within reach.

Going forward to the year 1919, Lovecraft displays his poetic splendor once more by producing two satirical poems hailing the downfall of Bacchus in America and the success of the temperance movement. The short "On Prohibition," claiming "the Demon Rum is dying" (*AT* 243), is one of them, and "Monody on the Late King Alcohol," where Lovecraft has the Maenads—the maniacal dancing worshippers of Dionysus from Greek mythology—exclaim "*Alcohol is dead*" (*AT* 243), is the other.

The year 1919 signals a turning point for Lovecraft, because from this time onwards no poetry of his is concerned with temperance and Prohibition. However, things are different when it comes to fiction, beginning with the macabre tale "The Tomb." Written in June 1917 and later published in the March 1922 issue of the *Vagrant*, "The Tomb" tells the story of the eccentric and alienated Jervas Dudley, who finds an old tomb in a wooded hollow close to home, harboring the remains of the Hyde family.

Figure 4: The Necronomicon: Tomb by Les Edwards. Courtesy of Les Edwards www.lesedwards.com

The story is important because it contains a rather morose "memento mori/carpe diem"[20]–orientated drinking song,[21] of which the first two stanzas read:

> Come hither, my lads, with your tankards of ale,
> And drink to the present before it shall fail;
> Pile each on your platter a mountain of beef,
> For 'tis eating and drinking that bring us relief:
>   So fill up your glass,
>   For life will soon pass;
> When you're dead ye'll ne'er drink to your king or your lass!
>
> Anacreon had a red nose, so they say;
> But what's a red nose if ye're happy and gay?
> Gad split me! I'd rather be red whilst I'm here,

---

20. *Memento mori* is Latin for "remember that you will die." The origin of the phase is uncertain, and philosophical deliberations on human mortality go back as far as antiquity, as Plato voices it in the *Phaedo* (64a4). The aphorism *carpe diem* ("seize the day") originates in the writing of the Roman poet Horace (*Odes* 1.11.8).

21. For more information on what inspired HPL to write the peculiar "Drinking Song," see Fulwiler and Murray.

> Than white as a lily—and dead half a year!
>   So Betty, my miss,
>   Come give me a kiss;
> In hell there's no innkeeper's daughter like this! (*CF* 1.46)

The drinking song reveals one of the unsettling problems with human existence—namely, that each one of us lives on borrowed time—but it also teaches us how to deal with this singular problem. The song promotes a hedonistic philosophy; but where the first stanza hails the somewhat Ecclesiastical idiom "eat, drink and be merry,"[22] the second, with its celebration of Betty, adds a sexual dimension to the supposed wisdom of Solomon, transmuting it into a more Dashwoodian outlook rooted in the motto "do what thou wilt."[23] At first glance this might seem an over-interpretation, but the extent of Dudley's drunken revelry at the Hyde family's mansion later in the story indicates otherwise. Here Dudley confesses to the reader: "Amidst a wild and reckless throng I was the wildest and most abandoned. Gay blasphemy poured in torrents from my lips, and in my shocking sallies I heeded no law of God, Man, or Nature" (*CF* 1.49). What happens to Dudley in this Hellfire-Club-ish setting is the very animaliza-

---

22. Shaped as a response to the question of how to live, the part of the Old Testament labelled Ecclesiastes, or in Hebrew Qohelet, meaning teacher or preacher, contains philosophical idioms such as "eat, drink and be merry" (8:15). The author of the Ecclesiastes is unknown, but scholars have thought it to be the legendary, wise, and incredibly wealthy King Solomon. Solomon was king of Israel supposedly around 970 to 931 B.C.E., and according to legend he possessed a magic ring called the Seal of Solomon that enabled him to command demons or Jinn. Other responses to the question of how to live exist in the philosophical literature. The Ancient Greek philosopher Aristotle, for example, suggests that we should live a "eudaimonic life" and distance ourselves from the life of pleasure (*Nicomachean Ethics*). For the Roman stoic philosopher Seneca life was to be owned; it was to be about accomplishment and not to be wasted on "wine and lust" (*On the Shortness of Life*, in *Moral Essays* 1.3, 8.1).

23. Sir Francis Dashwood or simply Lord Dashwood is known for establishing exclusive clubs in Britain in the eighteenth century. The clubs labelled Hellfire Clubs lived by the motto: "Fais ce que tu voudraseat," or "Do as thou wilt," and were basically places where rich and powerful people could engage in "immoral behaviour" and revelry in accordance with that of the ancient cult of Bacchus. For more information see Ashe.

tion Gough warns about in his book *Sunlight and Shadow*, and what Lovecraft wished to convey with his use of the word "beast" in the poem "The Power of Wine." Dudley is a bacchanal supreme, and his drunken revelry leads to an eroticized state utterly repugnant to Lovecraft, who believed "eroticism belongs to a lower order of instincts, and is an animal rather than nobly human quality" (*SL* 1.106).

Two years after writing "The Tomb" Lovecraft produced the short story "Old Bugs" (1919). Published in *The Shuttered Room and Other Pieces* in 1959, its purpose was to dissuade Alfred Galpin, a friend of Lovecraft's, from sampling alcohol before it became prohibited. We know this because in his "Memories of a Friendship" Galpin writes: "On the occasion of Prohibition I sallied forth to find out what the stuff was like before it was banned, told him of the results, and received in admonition a farcically diverting skit in which he indulged to the utmost his passion for slang" (Galpin 197).

The farcically diverting skit that Galpin is referring to is indeed "Old Bugs." Set in the 1950s, the story is centered on Sheehan's Pool Room, the acknowledged nexus of Chicago's subterranean traffic in liquor and narcotics. The titular character Old Bugs, who is no other than the future Alfred Galpin himself, is brought to an unbearable low point by "evil habits, dating from a first drink taken years before in woodland seclusion" (*CF* 1.91). In an introductory note to the first publication of "Old Bugs," Galpin states that in the end of the story Lovecraft had addressed him and asked "*Now will you be good?!*" adding a further authoritative rhetorical punch to an otherwise emotional tour de force (Galpin 193).

The short story "Sweet Ermengarde; or, The Heart of a Country Girl," originally written between 1919 and 1921 under the pseudonym of Percy Simple and published in 1943 in *Beyond the Wall of Sleep*, likewise testifies to Lovecraft's continuing preoccupation with alcohol. The first paragraph of "Chapter I: A Simple Rustic Maid" reads:

> Ermengarde Stubbs was the beauteous blonde daughter of Hiram Stubbs, a poor but honest farmer-bootlegger of Hogton, Vt. Her name was originally Ethyl Ermengarde, but her father persuaded her to drop the praenomen after the passage of the 18th Amendment, averring that it made him thirsty by reminding

him of ethyl alcohol, C_2H_5OH. His own products contained mostly methyl or wood alcohol, CH_3OH. (CF 1.221)

Besides bearing witness to Lovecraft's comical acumen and affection for chemistry, the paragraph hints at the ruinous lineage of sweet Ermengarde. The idea is that her connection to the honest bootlegger Hiram Stubbs is corruptive due to his intercourse with alcohol and has a role in her selfish and most manipulative behavior at the end of the story.

The final work from Lovecraft's earlier writing that incorporates a warning against alcohol is "The Quest of Iranon." Written in 1921 and published in the *Galleon* in 1935, this dreamland story centers on Iranon, a yellow-haired youthful singer who claims he is a prince hailing from Aira, a city of unheard-of beauty. Iranon is a wanderer and his preferences contrast those of the dromedarymen in the story, who in their drunken and ribald antics mirror the exploits of the Hyde families and their guests in "The Tomb."

During his quest, Iranon teams up with the boy Romnod, a fellow seeker of beauty and song, and together they travel to Oonai, the city of lutes and dancing, where they dwell until Romnod dies as an old, dream-deprived alcoholic. Iranon, a teetotaller and thus untouched by the ruinous powers of wine, remains young and finally leaves Oonai to continue his quest for Aira; he ultimately fails only because Aira is a utopia—a place that does not exist.

The emphasis on the harmful effects of wine is clear enough in this little Dunsanian masterpiece, but unlike in Lovecraft's earlier writing, the atmosphere the dreamer of Providence builds around the drunken is one of sadness. Alcohol in Lovecraft's view deprives human beings of the finer and more sensitive qualities upon which the dreamer and poet depend.

In Aqua Sanitas: The Later Lovecraft (1925–37)

On 3 March 1924, Lovecraft married Sonia Greene whom he had met at an amateur journalist convention three years earlier; he then moved in with her in her apartment in Brooklyn, New York. Things were fine at first, but when Sonia lost her business and Lovecraft found himself unemployable financial trouble quickly turned life sour for the newlyweds. Sonia and Lovecraft eventually separated and in April 1926 he moved back to Providence.

The year 1926 signals a turning point in Lovecraft's authorship, because during that summer he produced his signature work of fiction, "The Call of Cthulhu." Published in *Weird Tales* in 1928, the novelette deals in part with the infamous Cthulhu cult, whose members share many of the characteristics attributed to the intoxicated maenad or bacchant of ancient times. The nameless rites and bloodthirstiness of the degenerate cult of Esquimaux that Professor William Channing Webb speaks of at the American Archaeological Society's annual convention in St. Louis testifies to this. Inspector Legrasse's tale of the murdering Louisiana swamp worshippers, whose animal fury and orgiastic license elevated them to daemoniac heights, is likewise indicative. Perhaps the strongest support in favor of the Cthulhu cultists' commonality with the cult of Bacchus is the description of what will happen once great Cthulhu emerges from his tomb to revive his subjects. By then humankind would be

> free and wild and beyond good and evil, with laws and morals thrown aside and all men shouting and killing and revelling in joy. Then the liberated Old Ones would teach them new ways to shout and kill and revel and enjoy themselves, and all the earth would flame with a holocaust of ecstasy and freedom. (CF 2.40)

It is clear that the world will end in utter orgiastic madness. The bacchanal of all time equals the end of all things civil as humankind by then has surrendered to headlong hedonism and elevated individual pleasure to the point of ultimate value.

Lovecraft's use of the phrase "beyond good and evil" signals a turning away from a traditional order, and he clearly borrowed the phrase from the German philosopher Friedrich Nietzsche (1844–1900). Nietzsche, who like Lovecraft detested alcohol,[24] is the author of *Beyond Good and Evil*, in which he criticizes dogmatism and traditional philosophers, and promotes a new philosophy

---

24. Nietzsche's aversion toward alcohol is evident when reading his *Twilight of the Idols*, where he holds that the "The German people has deliberately made itself stupid, for nearly a millennium: nowhere have the two great European narcotics, alcohol and Christianity, been abused more dissolutely" (*Afgudernes ragnarok* 65).

based on free spirits whom he describes as "investigators to the point of cruelty, with uninhibited fingers for the unfathomable, with teeth and stomachs for the most indigestible" (*Beyond Good and Evil* §44). This well describes the Cthulhu cultist, and both cultist and free spirit can rightfully be labelled Dionysian. However, to be a Nietzschean free spirit is not the same as being a revelling Cthulhu cultist. The Dionysian aspect of Nietzsche's philosophy emphasizes creativity and a "yes" to life, contrasting with that of "Apollo worshipping" philosophers like Socrates, who effectively said "no" to life and annihilated himself by drinking hemlock when sentenced to death by the city of Athens. Nietzsche's free spirit involves looking for greatness, autonomy, and individuality. It is the business of creating new values while rebelling against the traditional ascetic ones. This is precisely what the Cthulhu cultist is doing, but the cultist is not free to create new values. A Cthulhu cultist is at best liberated from old values, but remains enthralled by hedonism dictated partly by the Old Ones. If truly free she would be able to do something else other than shout, kill, and revel in joy, but that is simply not the case. Armed with the teachings of the Old Ones, the cultist takes hedonism to a level indistinguishable from sadism, where civilization is impossible—and that is anti-Nietzschean.

In the immediate aftermath of writing "The Call of Cthulhu" Lovecraft sought to forge a connection between his works set in the dreamlands and what was later to be known as the Cthulhu Mythos, and again alcohol was used as a plot device.

In the short story "Pickman's model" (1926) we meet the hard-boiled but unbalanced narrator Thurber, who struggles to convey to his friend Eliot the secrets of reality he has uncovered during his aesthetic exploits with the New England painter Richard Upton Pickman. During the colloquy, Thurber reaches out for alcohol three times in order to calm his nerves, but then—in a display of Aristotelian moderation—calls for coffee, because as he puts it: "We've had enough of the other stuff but I for one need something" (*CF* 2.71). The idea that alcohol can have a positive effect hints at a change in Lovecraft's attitude. This new outlook presents itself again in 1928, when Lovecraft learned that publisher Farnsworth Wright, who suffered from Parkinson's disease, on occasion drank too much. In a display of sympathy, Lovecraft contemplated sending him a case of "synthetic bootleg brilliancy," i.e. alcohol (de Camp 305).

That alcohol can be a force of good is also echoed in the 1927 novelette *The Case of Charles Dexter Ward*, where Lovecraft lets Doctor Willett regain consciousness with the aid of brandy after his horrifying experiences in the catacombs beneath Joseph Curwen's bungalow (CF 2.348).

Alcohol, as well as the ghoulish Pickman, plays a role in the wondrous dreamland novella *The Dream-Quest of Unknown Kadath*. Written in late 1926 and early 1927, it centers on Lovecraft's alter ego and dreamer extraordinaire Randolph Carter, who enters the Dreamlands on a quest to reach Kadath, the elusive dwelling place of the gods. During his quest Carter consults the zoogs, who share with him their moon-wine, which Carter wickedly makes use of later in the story when he questions the patriarch Atal in the Temple of the Elder Ones in Ulthar. Atal, being somewhat close-mouthed, soon falls victim to Carter's moon-wine, and robbed of his reserve he "babbled freely of forbidden things" (CF 2.106), thus propelling Carter onwards toward Ngranek on the isle of Oriab.

However, at this point Lovecraft is back to his old teetotaller self, and the "dry" philosopher of Providence is quick to punish Carter for his wickedness and liaison with alcohol. In Dylath-Leen Carter tries his moon-wine trick yet again, but this time on a sinfully smirking merchant who remains unaffected. In a sinister act of quid pro quo, the merchant offers Carter a taste of his own wine, and Carter soon loses consciousness despite his exercise of temperance. He later wakes up surrounded by sardonic merchants on the deck of a ship flying with unusual swiftness of the coast of the Southern Sea.

As we move into the last decade of Lovecraft's life it is evident that he has lost his faith in Prohibition. "In 1919 I was a whole-hearted prohibitionist, but in 1928 I am more or less neutral," Lovecraft writes in a letter to Zealia Bishop (*Spirit of Revision* 104–5). The reason for this change of attitude is grounded in the fact that despite the constitutional ban, alcohol was relatively easy to get hold of in 1928 and the social improvement Lovecraft previously thought outlawing alcohol would bring simply did not occur.

This widespread practice of bootlegging and the seemingly unquenchable thirst for alcohol among Americans found its way into Lovecraft's novel *The Case of Charles Dexter Ward*. The novel takes place in Rhode Island during the time of Prohibition, and bootleggers make an entry in chapter 3, where Sergt. Riley of the Second Station flags bootleggers as the likely culprits to acts of vandalism, including hole digging in and around the North Burial Ground (*CF* 2.290). The everyday nature of crime related to alcohol is emphasized again later in the novel, when a number of "hi-jackers" on a quest for liquor shipments are shocked when uncovering human remains and not alcohol inside coffins bound for wizard Curwen's bungalow (*CF* 2.303–4).

That Lovecraft was aware that spirits such as whiskey were easy to get hold of even in the lowliest of places during the time of Prohibition is evident when reading "The Shadow over Innsmouth" (1931). Here Lovecraft allows the narrator to purchase an easily obtainable but expensive quart bottle of whiskey in the rear of a dingy variety-store in Innsmouth. In an echo of the methods of Randolph Carter, the purpose of this action is to get hold of the "magic" that will loosen the tongue of the traumatized drunkard Zadok Allen and move the plot forward toward its dramatic conclusion.

Summary

Taking all into consideration, there can be no doubt that Lovecraft was a dramatic teetotaller. This is evident from his early writing, where his bombastic views in favor of total abstinence and Prohibition are akin to those of both Joseph Livesey and John Bartholomew Gough.

The later Lovecraft is somewhat more nuanced because the negative consequences of Prohibition became hard for him to ignore, since he was concerned not merely with personal gentlemanly behavior and civility but also society as a healthy orderly whole. If Prohibition did not work as a force of good, then he was quite ready to abandon it in his later years. Having said that, Lovecraft did not change his mind on alcohol itself and his utter disgust for it never diminished. To him it was an aesthetic matter and drinking was simply ugly to him (*Spirit of Revision* 104–5).

However, evidence that Lovecraft changed his mind with regard to the presence of alcohol in society can be found in a 1932 letter addressed to fantasy writer Robert E. Howard, who famously created Conan the Barbarian and Solomon Kane and who enjoyed his beer immensely (Finn 93–94). Here Lovecraft states that he can sympathize with those who are inclined to "grant the hard-pressed classes the surcease to drink as a compensation for their burdens and helplessness" (*SL* 4.57–58). In doing so Lovecraft displays a keen awareness of the sufferings of others in a society far from perfect; however, supplying alcoholic beverages to the downtrodden was not Lovecraft's preferred method of helping out those in need. He continues:

> The more drink-sodden they get, the worse their biological stock becomes, and the less chance they have of getting out of their rut either by individual success or by conceded political action toward a more equitable social order. [...] It would be wiser to study means for the reduction of general misery through the controlled allocation of labouring opportunities, the granting of old-age pensions and unemployment incurrence, and the gradual undermining of excess-profit motive, instead of condoning the woes of the helpless by giving them poison to make them forget about it. (*SL* 4.58)

The first part of the citation makes it clear that although Lovecraft cares about the well-being of his fellow citizens he still entertains the idea that alcohol is corruptive. Alcohol might bring relief momentarily, but in the long run the bad effects of drinking far outweigh the good. The latter part of the citation is indicative of Lovecraft's growing engagement with political philosophy and his inclination toward socialism, which he thought a possible remedy for bettering society.

In some senses Lovecraft became a more balanced or temperate teetotaller in his later years. The forceful outbursts against the demon rum and his glorification of Prohibition diminished; this is naturally linked to the negative consequences of Prohibition, which caught Lovecraft by surprise. However, the fact that Prohibition did not have the desired effect was not the only influencing factor. A growing awareness of his personal idiosyncrasy and anachronism also had a part to play. By 1928 Lovecraft thought of himself as old-fashioned, and his only point of contact with members of the younger generation was through an abstract philosophical or scientific lens. He was keenly aware that his tastes and habits were those of conservative country-gentry of centuries past and thus outmoded (*Spirit of Revision* 104–5).

To wrap things up, it seems fair to say that Lovecraft's teetotalism plays a significant part in his life story, philosophy, and literary work. It is an indicator of what he feared the most namely the beast within. He feared our animal appetites, and the idea that alcohol functions as a catalyst for bad behavior kept him dry, fueled his amateur journalism, propelled his poetry and his use of "hard likker" as a baneful trope in his fiction. *Nunc est bibendum!*

Works Cited

Aristotle. *The Nicomachean Ethics*, Tr. H. Rackham. Loeb Classical Library. Cambridge, MA: Harvard University Press, 2003.

Ashe, Geoffrey. *The Hell-Fire Clubs: A History of Anti-Morality*. Stroud, UK: Sutton Publishing, 2005.

Charleston Observer. 10, No. 44 (29 October 1836): 174, columns 4–5.

de Camp, L. Sprague. *Lovecraft: A Biography*. Garden City, NY: Doubleday, 1975.

Finn, Mark. *Blood and Thunder: The Life and Art of Robert E. Howard*. Austin, TX: MonkeyBrain Books, 2006

Fulwiler, William. "'The Tomb' and 'Dagon': A Double Dissection." *Crypt of Cthulhu* No. 38 (Eastertide 1986): 8–14.

Galpin, Alfred. "Memories of a Friendship." In *Ave atque Vale: Reminiscences of H. P. Lovecraft*, ed. S. T. Joshi and David E. Schultz. West Warwick, RI: Necronomicon Press, 2018. 196–205.

Gately, Iain. *Drink: A Cultural History of Alcohol*. New York: Gotham Books, 2018.

Gough, John Bartholomew. *Sunlight and Shadow; or, Learnings from My Life-Work*. London: Hodder & Stoughton, 1880.

Horace. *Odes and Epodes*. Edited and translated by Niall Rudd. Loeb Classical Library. Cambridge, MA: Harvard University Press, 2004.

Joshi, S. T. *I Am Providence: The Life and Times of H. P. Lovecraft*. New York: Hippocampus Press, 2010. 2 vols.

———, and David E. Schultz. *An H. P. Lovecraft Encyclopedia*.

2001. New York: Hippocampus Press, 2004.

Lovecraft, H. P. *The Spirit of Revision: Lovecraft's Letters to Zealia Brown Reed Bishop*. Ed. Sean Branney and Andrew Leman. Glendale, CA: H. P. Lovecraft Historical Society, 2015.

———, and Divers Hands. *The Shuttered Room and Other Pieces*. Sauk City, WI: Arkham House, 1959.

Loveman, Samuel. "Lovecraft as a Conversationalist." In *Ave atque Vale: Reminiscences of H. P. Lovecraft*, ed. S. T. Joshi and David E. Schultz. West Warwick, RI: Necronomicon Press, 2018. 240–42.

MacCoun, Robert J., and Peter Reuter. *Drug War Heresies: Learning from Other Vices, Times, and Places*. Cambridge: Cambridge University Press, 2001.

Murray, Will. "A Probable Source for the Drinking Song from 'The Tomb.'" *Lovecraft Studies* No. 15 (Fall 1987): 77–80.

Nietzsche, Friedrich. *Afgudernes ragnarok*. Tr. Jens Erik Kristensen and Lars-Henrik Schmidt. Copenhagen: Gyldendal, 1999.

———. *Beyond Good and Evil*. Tr. Walter Kaufmann. New York: Vintage, 1989.

Okrent, Daniel. *Last Call: The Rise and Fall of Prohibition*. New York: Scribner, 2010.

Pedersen, Jan B. W. "On Lovecraft's Lifelong Relationship with Wonder." *Lovecraft Annual* No 11 (2017): 23–36.

———. "Howard Phillips Lovecraft: Romantic on the Nightside." *Lovecraft Annual* No. 12 (2018): 165–73.

Quinn, Dennis. "Endless Bacchanal: Rome, Livy, and Lovecraft's Cthulhu Cult." *Lovecraft Annual* No. 5 (2011): 189–215.

Reilly, Geza A. G. "'All Things Are Noble Which Serve the German State': Nationalism in Lovecraft's 'The Temple.'" *Lovecraft Annual* No. 12 (2017): 92–100.

Rorabaugh, W. J. *Prohibition: A Concise History*. New York: Oxford University Press, 2018.

Rousseau, Jean-Jacques. *The Social Contract*. Harmondsworth: Penguin, 1968.

Seneca. *Moral Essays*. Volume II. Tr. John W. Basore. Loeb Classical Library. Cambridge, MA: Harvard University Press, 1933.

Trotter, Thomas. *An Essay, Medical, Philosophical, and Chemical on Drunkenness and Its Effect on the Human Body*, London: Printed for T. N. Longman, and O. Rees, 1804.

Lovecraft's Open Boat

Michael D. Miller

The title of this essay refers to Stephen Crane's immortal short story "The Open Boat," yet, as I have discovered over the years in teaching this story, its significance seems to be waning while H. P. Lovecraft's stories are waxing among new readers, and the significance of this is worth inquiry. For literature scholars this development adds more credence to the notion that supernatural or non-mimetic literature possesses something revelatory about the human experience, and also that the cherished "realism" of elite scholars may not have the timeless appeal these scholars maintain. For Lovecraft and devotees of the cosmic this perhaps confirms what we already know; confrontation with alienation of the universe is a theme that will never lose its ability to resonate. Lovecraft's celebrated couplet in "The Call of Cthulhu" (quoted from the *Necronomicon* of the mad Arab Abdul Alhazred) may have double meanings indeed:

> That is not dead which can eternal lie,
> And with strange aeons even death may die. (CF 2.40)

The sentiment can be applied not just to Lovecraft's cosmic entities, but to the corpus of his work (and other literate works of cosmicism). The core theme of realism—nature's indifference to mankind—often falls short of the great theme of the weird tradition: man's insignificant role in the universe.

Our first consideration is how opposed Crane's version of "nature's indifference to mankind" is to Lovecraft's "cosmic insignificance," if at all. In "The Open Boat" we have four survivors (captain, cook, correspondent, and oiler) from the sinking of the steamer *Commodore*. They are lost at sea, driven on endlessly by an uncaring ocean. If this boat was lost in the gulfs of space in a

Lovecraft story we might be facing the same philosophical predicament if we imagine the earth as the open boat. For the uninitiated, "The Open Boat" is a story based on Crane's actual life experiences after the steamship *Commodore* was wrecked on New Year's Day 1897. Crane had written a newspaper article reporting on the disaster before writing the short story. In the later version, just as in the true-life event, three of the four men survive to tell the tale, Crane in both cases being the aforementioned correspondent. Beyond Crane's ability to make readers feel for these men and their humanity, there is an outstanding control of figurative language merged with stylistic journalistic reporting. In one sense this is interesting given that Lovecraft's career initially started in journalism (albeit amateur), so the narrative of "reporting" is part of his literary makeup; but Lovecraft was also clear about how realism should work in fictional weird narrative: "Only the human scenes and characters must have human qualities. *These* must be handled with unsparing *realism*, (*not* catch-penny *romanticism*) but when we cross the line to the boundless and hideous unknown ... we must remember to leave our humanity and terrestrialism at the threshold" (*SL* 2.150; emphases in original). The thematic denouement of these writers is of course at far distant places in the broad spectrum of literature. To Crane this denouement leaves the survivors (and readers) as interpreters of the nature's indifference to man; to Lovecraft, we become interpreters of something more alienating and disturbing.

Crane's story is broken into seven sections (perhaps a reference to the seven mad gods who rule the sea) where, in each case, indifference and insignificance incrementally consume the men of the open boat. While the correspondent (and Crane) refer to this as "nature," it is not a leap at all to suggest what they are beginning to understand (or interpret) is actually cosmicism. In section I, our first instance of this is when the captain "buried in that profound dejection and indifference which comes, temporarily at least, to even the bravest and most enduring when, willy nilly, the firm fails, the army loses, the ship goes down" (Charters 329). This realization that life is not fair or just, and human beings are not important or as significant as we believe is the first encounter with what we might call "Cranian realism." However, on a larger scale this experience is also alienation from meaning at all when observed from the point of view of Lovecraft's cosmicism, as S. T. Joshi makes clear: "the notion of *cosmicism*, or the suggestion of the vast gulfs of space and time and the resultant inconsequence of the human species" (in Lovecraft, *Call of Cthulhu* xv). Compare the contemplative moment of the captain's brush with meaninglessness to one of Lovecraft's first great cosmic utterances from the opening of "Facts concerning the Late Arthur Jermyn and His Family":

> Life is a hideous thing, and from the background behind what we know of it peer daemoniacal hints of truth which make it sometimes a thousandfold more hideous. Science, already oppressive with its shocking revelations, will perhaps be the ultimate exterminator of our human species—if separate species we be—for its reserve of unguessed horrors could never be borne by mortal brains if loosed upon the world. (*CF* 1.171)

The characters of Arthur Jermyn and the captain have both had meaning and significance torn from them in their utter unimportance in the grand scheme of things, but the Lovecraft passage goes much further into the nature of the revelation. While the immediate reference in the Lovecraft story is to the origin and family line of the protagonist—"if separate species we be"—the passage makes clear that it is *science* that is the genesis of the epiphany, not a chance encounter with the "grave-edge."[1] Science also might be the ultimate exterminator of Crane's once (and perhaps still) captivating story. As we have mastered many (but not all) of the elements nature has thrown at us, this situation may not be as resonate as those tied to the consequences of science that occur around us daily. The revelations of science between 1897 and 1920 (the date of "Arthur Jermyn") are testament to this philosophical development.

While Darwin was already in play for most realists, as was mechanistic materialism (prior to Einstein's theory of relativity) for Lovecraft, the year 1900 alone bore a remarkable number of scientific breakthroughs that may have paved the way for the sci-

---

1. A kenning used by Crane in the story for death.

entific/philosophical based literature of Lovecraft (and others) to outlast the realists. Moses Gomberg identified the first organic radical, Hugo de Vries published his results of the Mendelian Inheritance,[2] Ernst Zermelo discovered Russell's Paradox,[3] Barnum Brown found the skeleton of Tyrannosaurus rex, Max Planck stated his quantum theory hypothesis, and Freud published *The Interpretation of Dreams*. All these were perhaps scrutinizing what role humans may have in the universe. Following on in section II of "The Open Boat," when the men in the dingy encounter a flannel of gulls, we get another blast of the nature (Cranian)/cosmic (Lovecraftian) philosophy of indifference. "The bids sat comfortably in groups, and they were envied by some in the dingy, for the wrath of the sea was no more to them than it was to a covey of prairie chickens a thousand miles inland. Often they came very close and stared at the men with black bead-like eyes. At these times they were uncanny and sinister in their unblinking scrutiny" (Charters 331). Consider how Lovecraft imparts this scrutiny from a scientific perspective, looking at us from his famous "Call of Cthulhu": "The sciences, each straining in its own direction, have hitherto harmed us little, but some day the piecing together of dissociated knowledge will open up such terrifying vistas of reality, and our frightful position therein, that we shall go mad from the revelation of flee from the deadly light into the peace and safety of a new dark age" (*CF* 2.22). But a key phrase in the next paragraph is extremely important: "That glimpse, like all dread glimpses of truth, flashed out from an accidental piecing together of separated things" (*CF* 2.22). As Crane's story moves forward to find some meaning from his revelations of nature, Lovecraft has inserted the role of randomness into the mix that renders any purposeful interpretation of mankind's place in nature (and the cosmos) obsolete.

With a mild break in section III, Crane hits the reader in section IV with one of the first profound outcries of the correspondent: "If I am going to be drowned—if I am going to be drowned—if I am going to be drowned, why in the name of the seven mad

---

2. Biological inheritance that follows the laws of Gregor Mendel.
3. Bertrand Russell's discovery of the contradictions of naïve set theory.

gods who rule the sea, was I allowed to come thus far and contemplate sand and trees? Was I brought here merely to have my nose dragged away as I was about to nibble the sacred cheese of life?" (Charters 335). Lovecraft, ever so ahead of his predecessors and contemporaries, had no fear in providing the answer, a resounding yes. This is carried through in such passages in essays as:

> By my thirteenth birthday I was thoroughly impressed with man's impermanence and insignificance, and by my seventeenth, about which time I did some particularly detailed writing on the subject, I had formed in all essential particulars my present pessimistic cosmic views. The futility of all existence began to impress and oppress me, and my references to human progress, formerly hopeful, began to decline in enthusiasm. ("A Confession of Unfaith," *CE* 5.147)

Notable here is "impress and oppress," for Lovecraft was not defeated by his revelations. Imaginative escape perhaps provides the purpose of temporary balm: the "most persistent wishes being to achieve, momentarily, the illusion of some strange violation of the galling limitations of time, space, and natural law which forever imprisons us and frustrate our curiosity about the infinite cosmic spaces beyond the radius of our sight and analysis" ("Notes on Writing Weird Fiction," *CE* 2.176). It should be noted that both Crane and Lovecraft reject religion as providing any viable answers, and this and other instances of similarity between them may invite further study. In short, Crane, "awed by his parents' fervent adherence to their beliefs, . . . watched them live according to endlessly interpreted religious dogma. He put his own faith, equally passionate, in reality, in his intense desire to be instructed by what he saw as a fierce and godless universe" (Phillips ix). Lovecraft's was less passionate: "In theory I am an *agnostic*, but pending the appearance of rational evidence I must be classed, practically and provisionally, as an *atheist*. The chance of theism's truth being to my mind so microcosmically small, I would be a pedant and a hypocrite to call myself anything else" (*SL* 4.57).

Readers that reach section VI encounter the obvious theme of the story and perhaps of Crane's literary output, but it could also be seen as the first glimpse or encounter with the cosmic, had

Crane with the realist parlance of the times been focusing on the heavens.

> When it occurs to a man that nature does not regard him as important, and that she feels she would not maim the universe by disposing him, he at first wishes to throw bricks at the temple, and he hates deeply the fact that there are no bricks and no temples. Any visible expression of nature would surely be pelleted with his jeers. . . . A high cold star on a winter's night is the word he feels that she says to him. (Charters 341)

One need simply replace "nature" in this passage with "the universe" and we have arrived at the event horizon of Lovecraftian cosmicism.

In VII, the final section of the story, Crane either slips or admittedly acknowledges cosmicism as the "unconcern of the universe" and may already be Lovecraftian; however, that is only half of the meaning. What of the interpretation of this realization? That is where "unconcern" or "indifference" do fall into opposition for Crane and Lovecraft (and perhaps for "realists" and "cosmicists"):

> It is, perhaps, plausible that a man in this situation, impressed with the unconcern of the universe, should see the innumerable flaws of his life and have them taste wickedly in his mind and wish for another chance. A distinction between right and wrong seems absurdly clear to him, then, in this new ignorance of the grave-edge, and he understands that if he were given another opportunity he would mend his conduct and his words, and be better and brighter during an introduction, or at tea. (Charters 343)

This is the delusion of the earth-gazer in a Lovecraftian universe, where both the optimist and the pessimist are rendered insignificant. The unconcern of the universe for Lovecraft manifests itself this way: "Now *all* my tales are based on the fundamental premise that common human laws and interests and emotions have no validity or significance in the vast cosmos-at-large" (*SL* 2.150; my emphasis). Crane's vision still seeks out the potential for meaning, as Ann Charters theorizes "about the puniness of humankind in the face of an indifferent nature and about the consequent value of solidarity and compassion that arise from an awareness of our common fate" (63). These are the interpreters Crane would like us to be, which is, in its simplicity, an optimistic view. Lovecraft's is "go mad or seek a new dark age," but let us not mistake him for a simple pessimist (as has been done by many scholars). Lovecraft makes quite clear that, "contrary to what you may assume, I am *not a pessimist* but an *indifferentist*—that is, I don't make the mistake of thinking that the resultant forces surrounding and governing organic life will have any connexion with the wishes or tastes of any part of that organic-life process" (cited in Joshi, *IAP* 771). Learning (or interpreting) that we are all in this together is not enough for "both [pessimists and optimists] envisage the aims of mankind as unified, and as having a direct relationship (either of frustration or fulfilment) to the inevitable flow of terrestrial motivation and events" (771).

H. P. Lovecraft was well aware of the impact and pull of science on the longevity of not only weird fiction, but all literate fiction: "The time has come when the normal revolt against time, space, and matter must assume a form not overtly incompatible with what is known of reality—when it must be gratified by images forming *supplements* rather than *contradictions* of the visible and the measurable universe. And what, if not a form of *non-supernatural cosmic art*, is to pacify this sense of revolt—as well as gratify the cognate sense of curiosity?" (*SL* 3.295–96). Lovecraft's move from "earth-centered" works like Crane's to "universe-centered" is not just a literary move, but a move we will have to take and are taking each day, year, decade, century, and eon, as we move through the void. What is the message? All together in insignificance. Universal indifference. We have great works that marvel at the defiance and that is about all. Crane would celebrate our mutual fate as a new hope and purpose free of religious dogma, but Lovecraft was light years ahead, and knew instead, our gift for imagination provides the only succor:

> I still find existence enough of a compensation to atone for its dominantly burthensome quality. These reasons are stronger linked with architecture, scenery, and lighting and atmospheric effects, and take the form of vague impressions of adventurous expectancy coupled with elusive memory—impressions that certain vistas, particularly those associated with sunsets, are avenues of

approach to spheres of conditions of wholly undefined delights and freedoms which I have known in the past and have a slender possibility of knowing again in the future. Just what those delights and freedoms are, or even what they approximately resemble, I could not concretely imagine to save my life; save that they seem to concern some ethereal quality of indefinite expansion and mobility, and of a heightened perception which shall make all forms and combinations of beauty simultaneously visible to me, and realizable to me (Cited in Joshi, *IAP* 934)

The brotherhood of man cannot hold . . . only the imagination can. Looking away through starlight and the distant shore of the great galactic void, the silence of blinking stars reveals that we are not interpreters, only outsiders, on an insignificant speck, in an accelerating and expanding universe.

Works Cited

Charters, Ann, ed. *The Story and Its Writer*. 7th ed. New York: Bedford/St. Martin's, 2007.

Crane, Stephen. "The Open Boat." In Charters 328–46.

Joshi, S. T. *I Am Providence: The Life and Times of H. P. Lovecraft*. New York: Hippocampus Press, 2010. 2 vols.

Lovecraft, H. P. *The Call of Cthulhu and Other Weird Stories*. Ed. S. T. Joshi. New York: Penguin, 1999.

Phillips, Jane Anne. "Introduction." In *Maggie: A Girl of the Streets and Other Short Fiction* by Stephen Crane. New York: Bantam, 1986.

Lovecraft Seeks the Garden of Eratosthenes

Horace A. Smith

Sixteen-year-old H. P. Lovecraft chose a title for his article in the 14 September 1906, issue of the *Pawtuxet Valley Gleaner* that was likely to attract notice: "Is There Life on the Moon?" Its conclusion makes strange reading for the modern student of astronomy, aware of the desolate and apparently lifeless nature of the lunar surface: "Now all the evidence is very convincing, and in all probability is correct, so we must consider our satellite to be a body which, although not containing any high or animal life, is yet not wholly dead" (*CE* 3.26–27). The evidence to which Lovecraft alluded was that obtained by one whom Lovecraft called the "greatest living selenographer," Harvard professor William Henry Pickering (1858–1938). There is, however, more behind this article than is at first apparent. Not mentioned in the account are the young Lovecraft's own efforts to don the mantle of observational astronomer and verify for himself Pickering's startling discoveries.

Following his even earlier interest in chemistry, Lovecraft was in 1902 swept by enthusiasm for astronomy. It was an enthusiasm that would be tempered as he aged but which would never leave him. His early ambition to become an astronomer, his weekly and monthly astronomical articles for newspapers, and the influence of astronomy upon his fiction figure in biographical and critical studies. Of the former, one need only mention S. T. Joshi's *I Am Providence: The Life and Times of H. P. Lovecraft*, in which the young Lovecraft's involvement with astronomy takes up significant portions of Chapters 4 and 5. Of tighter focus, and bridging both the biographical and the critical, is T. R. Livesey's "Dispatches from the Providence Observatory: Astronomical Motifs and Sources in the Writings of H. P. Lovecraft." Livesey discusses at length Lovecraft's (sometimes imperfect) knowledge of astronomy, how he acquired that knowledge, and how his scientific background influenced his writing. My discussion is more limited, focusing on the teenage Lovecraft's attempts by his own observations to prove or disprove Pickering's contention that the moon is an abode of life.

William H. Pickering joined the staff of the Harvard College Observatory in 1887, an institution that his older brother Edward Charles Pickering had already directed for a decade. The elder brother is remembered as a pioneer of modern astrophysics, whose work in stellar spectroscopy, photometry, and photography during his long directorship paved the way for twentieth-century developments in the field. William (whom we shall just call Pickering, unless there is a chance of confusion with Edward) is regarded as one of astronomy's eccentrics. He receives credit for his early work in photography, for his photographic discovery of Phoebe, the ninth moon of Saturn, in 1899, and for a number of innovative ideas. Despite these laudable contributions, his career had a too-imaginative side that damaged his reputation. His extensive studies of our own moon drew him to conclusions that were dismissed as nonsense by most professional astronomers of his day. Sheehan and Dobbins in *Epic Moon: A History of Lunar Exploration in the Age of the Telescope* somewhat uncharitably title the chapter on Pickering's work "The Madman of Mandeville"—Mandeville, Jamaica, being the location of Pickering's final observatory.

Astronomers scrutinized the moon through telescopes of increasing capability as the nineteenth century progressed, attempting to settle what were still open questions as that century dawned: was the moon a changing and living world or a changeless and dead one? A consensus emerged that the moon was an airless, lifeless, and largely immutable place.

Taking up the study of the moon in earnest during the 1890s, Pickering soon rejected that consensus. Alterations in the appearance of certain lunar features, he announced, were not mere plays of light and shadow. The moon, he believed, had a tenuous atmosphere, permitting the deposition and evaporation of hoarfrost. More astonishing was Pickering's contention that the moon harbored plants, or even, as he suggested later in his life, hordes of small animals, perhaps insects, that could be seen migrating en masse across the floors of particular craters. Life on the moon had adapted to its strange conditions, Pickering proposed, so that cycles of lunar life were ruled not by the annual motion around the sun but by the monthly sequence of lunar phases. In reaching these unorthodox conclusions, Pickering relied mainly upon visual observations, believing with some justice that the eye at the eyepiece could detect finer details than could the photographic emulsions of the time. He made his views known early enough for his vision of lunar life to have influenced H. G. Wells when he wrote *The First Men in the Moon*, published in 1901 (Dobbins and Baum 105–9; Sheehan and Dobbins 255). Among the craters Pickering believed held life was Eratosthenes. In the 1920s, when he published a map of Eratosthenes, Pickering was inspired to name areas after flowers—Azalea, Aster, Dahlia, and Violet, among others—turning the crater in name into the garden of the moon that he believed it actually was (Pickering, "Eratosthenes No. 4" 69).

The reception of Pickering's ideas was not to his liking. While other astronomers agreed that craters seem to change during the course of the monthly lunar cycle, few interpreted what they saw along his lines. Most professional astronomers placed Pickering's lu-

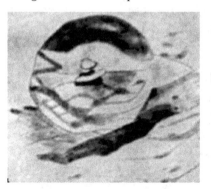 

The crater Eratosthenes, as sketched by Pickering in 1901, rotated to be more easily compared with Lovecraft's drawings (Pickering, "The Canals of the Moon" 190). An image taken by Lunar Orbiter 4 is shown for comparison (Lunar Orbiter Photo Gallery, LPL Institute). Lovecraft's resolution of detail in Eratosthenes is obviously very poor compared to either of these images. Pickering's drawing is not bad, but his interpretation was wildly imaginative.

nar vegetation in the same disreputable category as his contemporary Percival Lowell's artificial Martian canals (a subject in which Pickering was also very interested). Even his brother Edward was reluctant to accept William's interpretations of what he saw. He advised caution in private letters to his younger sibling, but in vain, and these and other differences led to strained relations (Plotkin 103; Sheehan 172–73). In a 12 September 1912 letter to Edward, William wrote:

> Whatever reputation as an astronomer I lost when I published my former observations, will be nothing to the destruction produced when these [new results] get into print, & especially the drawings. I have seen everything practically except the selenites themselves running round with spades to turn off the water into other channels! (Jones and Boyd 373)

William was being facetious, since even he did not advocate the existence of shovel-toting inhabitants of the moon, but he clearly knew what most astronomers thought of his ideas.

In February 1903, Lovecraft was delighted to purchase his first new book on astronomy, Princeton professor Charles Augustus Young's *Lessons in Astronomy* (Joshi 80). When Lovecraft turned to its section on the moon, he would have found that Young described a moon devoid of air and water, without "satisfactory evidence" of ongoing volcanic activity, and without "conspicuous changes." In other words, *Lessons in Astronomy* presented Lovecraft with the consensus picture of a dead and immutable moon. Young only briefly mentioned Pickering's belief in perceptible lunar changes, and he made no mention of Pickering's belief in life on the moon (Young 105–28).

Nonetheless, it was the contentious question of life and change on the moon that quickly attracted Lovecraft's attention when, barely a teenager, he trained his own telescope on our nearest celestial neighbor. It is not certain how Lovecraft first learned of Pickering's ideas, but there are likely places. Lovecraft must have encountered Young's mention of Pickering when he read his prized *Lessons in Astronomy*, but that mention is brief and not too enlightening by itself. Pickering had published results of his lunar studies in 1895 in the *Annals of the Harvard College Observatory*, a publication aimed at professional astronomers. However, as

Livesey has noted, Pickering's displeasure at the reception of his ideas by the professional astronomical community led him, as the twentieth century began, to publish in magazines where his work would be seen by amateur astronomers and the general public. Among these was *Popular Astronomy*, a publication little mentioned by Lovecraft but which Livesey (12) has persuasively argued was read by him. Nonetheless, it is perhaps likely, as Livesey (11) suggests, that Lovecraft first became aware of the details of Pickering's ideas through a pair of articles that Pickering wrote for the widely circulated *Century Magazine*.

The first of Pickering's *Century* articles, "Is the Moon a Dead Planet?," appeared in the May 1902 issue. The sequel, titled "The Canals in the Moon," appeared in June. The focus of the second article was Eratosthenes. Pickering presented drawings and photographs of the crater, calling attention to the way it changed in appearance through the course of the lunar day. As the crater warmed in the sun after the long and cold lunar night, vegetation darkened areas on its floor, or so Pickering informed his readers. Vegetation on the moon! Life on the moon! What young amateur astronomer's enthusiasm would not be whetted by such a hypothesis? Lovecraft's certainly was. Could he, too, see the markings that revealed that life existed a quarter of a million miles away?

After more than a century, what resources remain for tracing Lovecraft's interest in Pickering's ideas? There are such of his letters as address the subject of astronomy, but they are seldom detailed and look back on his early observing days from a remove of years or decades. Better are the weekly and monthly articles on astronomical topics which Lovecraft contributed to newspapers between the years 1906 and 1918 (available in *CE* 3). Those, however, are meant for a general audience, and, while they disclose his interests and are likely to have been shaped by Lovecraft's own observations, they rarely describe them. Most important are the juvenile scientific periodicals that Lovecraft published between 1903 and 1909, at the very time when Lovecraft's enthusiasm was taking him to the telescope.

The nature of these numerous but modest publications is described by Joshi in Chapter 4 of *I Am Providence*. In fact, the term "publication" is generous in their connection. They consist of hand-drawn and, later, hectographed magazines, each just a few pages in size. His readers surely included family and friends, but we do not have any lists of subscribers. Several of these publications have astronomical content, with titles such as the *Scientific Gazette, Astronomy, Annals of the Providence Observatory*, and the *Rhode Island Journal of Astronomy*. It is the last that is most important to this discussion, for within its pages Lovecraft recounted his astronomical observations. Sixty-nine issues of this magazine (referred to here as the *Journal*) survive within the Lovecraft Collection of the John Hay Library of Brown University (MS Lovecraft, Box 15, and online through the Brown University Digital Repository). I digress to add that I often found these brief publications a delight to read, peppered as they are with Lovecraft's versions (and perhaps sometimes parodies) of journalistic formulas and advertisements of the early 1900s.

While the survival of Lovecraft's juvenile periodicals enables this discussion, we must regret the loss of other documents. Some issues of his publications, including some of the *Journal*, appear to be lost (Joshi in *CE* 3.351). Moreover, surviving issues of the *Journal* frequently include drawings of astronomical objects as Lovecraft saw them. Those drawings must have been copied from originals made at the telescope. However, any original records Lovecraft made at the eyepiece now appear to be lost, though he must have kept them for a time, since the *Journal* occasionally incorporated observations made well before the issue date.

In 1909, after ending the *Journal* and his other periodicals, Lovecraft began a private notebook of astronomical observations. Unfortunately, all that is publicly available of this notebook is a small portion transcribed by David H. Keller and originally published in *Lovecraft Collector* No. 3 (now available in *CE* 3.332–34). Presumably because of his difficulty in reading Lovecraft's handwriting, Keller's transcription of the notebook contains a number of errors. To mention just one example, Lovecraft's 3-inch telescope is described as being a "Bardore," whereas it was actually manufactured by the well-known French firm of Bardou and Sons. From this very incomplete transcription, we cannot tell to what degree Lovecraft's early interest in observing the moon continued in 1909 and subsequent years.

As we get our first glimpses of Lovecraft the observational astronomer in the pages of the *Journal,* we find him exploring the moon and planets with what is, by the standards of today's amateur astronomy, a rather modest telescope, purchased in July 1903, from the mail-order firm of Kirtland Brothers & Company for $16.50 (Joshi 81). This refracting telescope had an objective lens 2¼ inches in diameter and was set upon an altazimuth tripod mounting, purchased from Reuben L. Allen, a local supplier of optical instruments, for $8. It came with a terrestrial eyepiece magnifying 45 times and an astronomical eyepiece providing a power of 100. In 1905, issues of the *Journal* mention a power of 135, that being about as high a power as a telescope of 2¼ inches aperture can usefully employ, implying that a third eyepiece or perhaps a Barlow lens had been acquired at some point.

The *Journal* debuted 2 August 1903, and in the first issues the reader sees Lovecraft immediately jumping into a research project. It does not, however, involve the moon. Instead, it is the determination of the then-unknown rotation period of cloud-shrouded Venus. It was a hopeless project, as Lovecraft would eventually realize. Nonetheless, the fact that he attempted it demonstrates that, even as a novice observer, he strove to be not only a sightseer but also an investigator.

Lovecraft recalled his early nights as an amateur astronomer in a letter to Alfred Galpin of 21 August 1918:

> My observations (for I purchased a telescope early in 1903) were confined mostly to the moon and the planet Venus. You will ask, why the latter, since its markings are doubtful even in the largest instruments? I answer—this very MYSTERY was what attracted me. In boyish egotism I fancied I might light upon something with my poor little 2¼-inch telescope which had eluded the users of the 40-inch Yerkes telescope!! And to tell the truth, I think the moon interested me more than anything else—the very nearest object. I used to sit night after night absorbing the minutest details of the lunar surface, till today I can tell you of every peak and crater as though they were the topographical features of my own neighbourhood. I was highly angry at Nature for withholding from my gaze the other side of our satellite! (*Letters to Alfred Galpin* 27)

The first weeks of the *Journal* show Lovecraft becoming familiar with observing and with the appearance of common celestial objects in his small telescope. His targets encompassed more than the moon and Venus, and are just such objects as we would expect a new observer, guided by amateur astronomy manuals of the day, to study. Drawings of modest fidelity appear in the *Journal* depicting ringed Saturn, Borrelli's comet, a crescent Venus, Jupiter with its Red Spot, sunspots, and the moon. A healthy dose of basic astronomical information is also served to Lovecraft's readers, whoever they might have been. At this time Lovecraft seems to have rarely let a clear night pass without attempting some observing, though his observations were made chiefly in the evening rather than the predawn hours. As he noted, "even astronomers are loath to arise early" (*Journal*, 11 October 1903). The light pollution that brightens the skies and dampens the spirits of today's urban amateurs would have been much less in the Providence of 1903, but in any case Lovecraft focused his attention on bright objects that could be easily found and seen to advantage with his modest telescope. The modern amateur's annoyance with cloudy weather soon finds its counterpart in the *Journal*'s pages. As Lovecraft's letter to Galpin noted, the moon saw particular attention. We find Lovecraft gradually acquainting himself with the moon's major craters, following its mountain ranges, and making his own maps of the lunar seas.

It is after Lovecraft has gained some experience as an observer, in the *Journal* for 6 December 1903, that drawings of Eratosthenes first appear. "On the 1st some strange markings were visible in the crater Eratosthenes at the end of the [lunar] Apennines they resembled the canals of Mars. Also a shading on the SE. side extending opposite to the shadows, proving it's [*sic*] independence. It was seen again on the 4th. On the 5th one of the canals reached *over* the E. wall and other markings were visible. Their nature is unknown." Lovecraft used the term canal for dark narrow features on the moon, as had Pickering, and he explicitly referenced Pickering's second *Century* article.

These observations provide the first evidence that Lovecraft had undertaken a special observational study of Eratosthenes. Undeterred by the small size of his telescope, Lovecraft sought to see the markings that Pickering had ascribed to life. In the same *Journal* issue, he compared his own drawings of Eratosthenes to the much more detailed drawings published by Pickering, who of course used much larger telescopes. Lovecraft wrote that "it is safe to say that there is something changeable about the crater Eratosthenes. It would bear careful study with large instruments." When Lovecraft presented observations of Venus in the first issues of the *Journal*, it was clear that he aimed to determine the rotation period of that planet. In contrast, he disclosed far less about his motivation when he began to discuss Eratosthenes. No recapitulation of Pickering's hypotheses appeared at this time in the *Journal*, and it was left to his readers, if they had not read the *Century* articles, to puzzle over why Eratosthenes was significant.

Small drawings of Eratosthenes followed in the 13 December 1903, issue, but perhaps by then Lovecraft was having second thoughts about what he had seen, for he only noted that "Eratosthenes is very complicated." His 1903 observations of Eratosthenes were summarized in the *Annals of the Providence Observatory*, Volume I, issued in 1904, which added no new information.

It is worth interrupting the story at this point to remind the reader why seeing genuine features within Eratosthenes was a daunting task for Lovecraft. Eratosthenes is a relatively large crater, about 59 kilometers in diameter. Its walls and central mountains cast long and easily seen shadows soon after sunrise and again two weeks later as sunset approaches. However, as the sun climbs above Eratosthenes, the crater walls become less conspicuous in the telescope and various lighter and darker spots, lines, and patches gradually appear and grow more pronounced in and around the crater floor. As the sun once more sinks toward the horizon, the spots and patches become less visible until they are lost in shadow.

To Pickering, the evolution of these features during the course of a single lunar day could only be explained by the presence of something like vegetation. Any changes in spot development from one lunar cycle to another would only enhance that probability, for shadows and fixed rocky terrain would look much the same at the same phase, month after month, but perhaps not so frost or vegetation. In seeking to confirm Pickering's observations, Lovecraft had to study the crater carefully, looking for changes in Eratosthenes from one night to the next and also from month to month.

Lovecraft quickly discovered that many of the features drawn by Pickering were beyond the reach of his small instrument. While Pickering sketched a complex web of spots and lines, Lovecraft could see only a few dark, linear features. Of course, he was limited to a magnification of 100 or 135, whereas Pickering used powers of several hundred, reaching as high as 795 when he observed with the Harvard 13-inch telescope at Arequipa, Peru. Moreover, even were his telescope optics excellent, and the air through which he gazed perfectly steady, a telescope of only 2¼ inches aperture would have trouble seeing features smaller than about 2 or 3 seconds of arc in angular size, little better than a tenth the apparent angular diameter of Eratosthenes,

Thus, in his search for changes, a direct comparison of his own drawings of Eratosthenes with those of Pickering was out of the question. Instead, Lovecraft had to intercompare his own drawings of the crater, taking into account differences in lunar phase and observing circumstances. Those features that he did detect tested the limits of his telescope. It was no simple task for him to see markings in Eratosthenes, to sketch those markings on multiple nights, and then confidently to establish the reality of any differences among his drawings. Experience and practiced judgment would be necessary to separate the real from the imagined, and the ordinary from the extraordinary, as Lovecraft again and again turned his telescope toward the moon.

Lovecraft's initial study of Eratosthenes continued into the winter of 1904, with observations reported in January. Either his aversion to cold weather was not pronounced in his youth, or his desire to observe overcame any discomfort (a point also raised by Livesey 78–79). At this time, he dithered as to the reality of the features he saw. In the *Journal* for 31 January 1904, he noted that he had observed Eratosthenes twice but that "the reality of the markings will be answered to-morrow night if clear." Alas, there ensued a long break in the publication of the *Journal*. In an undated note, Lovecraft later wrote that "After Jan. 31, 1904 a long skip in the publication of the R. I. Journal occurs, marked by temporary attempts (not preserved) to recommence it. The resumption was really begun Ap 16 '05 after which it was hectographed every week. In September it was made fortnightly but it was issued irregularly."

The cause of the interruption is not stated. 1904 was not, however, an easy year for Lovecraft. His grandfather, Whipple Phillips, died that March, leading to the traumatic removal of Lovecraft and his mother from the house he regarded as an ancestral home. Still, I wonder what happened that next night, which would have been well before his grandfather's passing. Perhaps it was cloudy.

When at last the *Journal* resumes, it is quickly apparent that Eratosthenes had not been forgotten. A day after the publication of the first issue of the resumed *Journal*, on 17 April 1905, Lovecraft rushed out an "Extra" edition. The headline exclaimed:

> MORE CHANGES ON ERATOSTHENES
> Crater Proven Variable Tonight at 8^h30^m
> Has not changed before since May 28, 1904.

The extra edition bears the time 9:00, indicating that this discovery was proclaimed only half an hour after it was made. Lovecraft noted that "On Decr. 1, 1903, the work of observing the crater was taken up here, with successful results until May 28, 1904, after which no change could be found." The conclusion that Eratosthenes was invariable after May 28 was, according to Lovecraft, reported in the *Journal*, but that issue must have been one of the aborted restarts that is now missing. However, whatever his earlier doubts, Lovecraft was now sure that he had observed genuine features in Eratosthenes and that those features had changed in a manner that could not be attributed to shifting shadows, and he was excited about that. The extra included a box containing the exhortation: "NOTICE / Would the local owners of telescopes over 2 in. aperture please notify us what Eratosthenes appears to be in their instruments / SYSTEMATIC OBSERVERS." Following "Systematic Observers," the last line in the John Hay Library copy ends with what appears to be "PAI," which runs off the page before the word is finished. Could Lovecraft have been so enthused as to have meant to pay such observers? Below that box is another: "WANTED Amateur drawings of Eratosthenes." The discussion of Eratosthenes continues on the next page, noting that

"Eratosthenes was first brought to general notice by an article in the 'Century' written by Prof. W. Pickering of Harvard." One may infer from this extra that Lovecraft believed that some copies of the *Journal* would fall under the eyes of those who not only had astronomical interests but who possessed telescopes as large as or larger than his own. Lovecraft vowed to resume regular observations of Eratosthenes, which had apparently lapsed. Subscribers who wished to decorate with a Lovecraft original could take advantage of the offer: "FOR SALE Drawings of the variable crater ERATOSTHENES Reasonable rates Apply Office."

Surprisingly, no observations of Eratosthenes appear in following issues, though in several Lovecraft complained of poor observing conditions. Nor do we discover whether anyone answered his call for observations. The *Journal* for 23 April 1905 did mention Pickering's 1903 book on the moon, which expanded upon his *Century* articles and provided a photographic atlas of the moon. However, Lovecraft only discussed Pickering's depictions of the

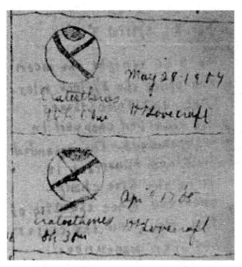
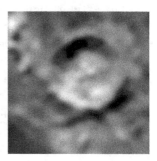

Two of Lovecraft's drawings of Eratosthenes from the 17 April 1905 extra (H. P. Lovecraft Collection, John Hay Library, Brown University Digital Repository). For comparison, I include a recent low-resolution image of Eratosthenes taken before full moon. From it, one can perhaps see how Lovecraft imagined linear features when viewing with his small telescope.

"faces in the moon" visible to the naked eye, not his controversial findings. Not until the *Journal* for 3 September 1905 does Lovecraft return to the question of lunar life. When he does it is with a serial titled "Is There Life on the Moon?," which runs over three issues of the *Journal*. That series is not based upon Lovecraft's own observations, but instead describes Pickering's results. The verdict of the series is nonetheless a strong one:

> Now all the evidence is very positive and convincing, the only way to "get around" it being to tell the observers that they either lie or are mistaken, but neither of these is possible with a man of Prof. Pickering's skill, experience, and integrity, so, except for chronic skeptics there remains little more to be said than that there is life on the moon.

At the time, Lovecraft apparently did not place himself in the category of chronic skeptic, but he may have counted himself among the unnamed other observers. It was the first time that Lovecraft presented the gist of Pickering's hypotheses to his *Journal* readers.

Why is there no further mention of his own result, touted in headlines in the 17 April extra? Had he lost confidence in his observations? Had someone he respected passed him a word of caution? The question of the Ladd Observatory and its astronomers comes to mind at this point.

In writing to Rheinhart Kleiner in a letter dated 16 November 1916, Lovecraft stated:

> The late Prof. Upton of Brown, a friend of the family, gave me the freedom of the college observatory, & I came & went there at will on my bicycle. Ladd Observatory tops a considerable eminence about a mile from the house. I used to walk up Doyle Avenue hill with my wheel, but when returning would have a glorious coast down it. So constant were my observations, that my neck became much affected by the strain of peering at a difficult angle. It gave me much pain, & resulted in a permanent curvature perceptible today to a close observer. (*Letters to Rheinhart Kleiner* 74)

Did Lovecraft disclose his study of Eratosthenes to his acquaintances at Ladd Observatory? Did he attempt to use their much larger telescope to study the crater? Neither the director of the observatory, Winslow Upton, nor the second astronomer on the staff, Frederick Slocum, specialized in lunar and planetary observations. However, they were professional astronomers with much more knowledge and experience than Lovecraft. Did they see his *Journal* issues and did he rush to them with his 17 April extra?

We can only hazard doubtful answers to these questions. The letter to Kleiner at first glance implies that Lovecraft was free to use the Ladd Observatory's 12-inch telescope, but more thought renders that unlikely. It would be one thing to give the teenage Lovecraft free access to the observatory library and quite another to allow him to use its major instrument at will. In the *Journal* Lovecraft makes only two, possibly three, mentions of observing through the Ladd Observatory telescope. The *Journal* for 27 September 1903 reported that the transit of a Jovian moon was seen at the Ladd Observatory on the 21st, but it is not specified that it was Lovecraft who saw it. He might not have been the observer on that occasion, but little more than a month later the *Journal* for 1 November 1903 recounted Lovecraft's visit to the Ladd Observatory on October 31. He certainly looked through its telescope on that occasion, observing the moon, Jupiter, and Saturn, and even criticizing the telescope's chromatic aberration. Two and a half years later he observed the sun, Mercury, and Venus through the Ladd Observatory telescope on 21 March 1906, according to the April 1906 *Journal*. However, other than these few instances, whenever Lovecraft reported telescopic observations in the *Journal*, they appear to be those made with his own telescope.

In a letter to Duane W. Rimel dated 29 March 1934, Lovecraft reminisced: "I suppose I pestered the people at the observatory half to death, but they were very kind about it" (*Letters to F. Lee Baldwin* ... 157). In that letter Lovecraft recalled seeing the observatory equipment in action, reading endlessly in the observatory library, and being supplied with lecture slides made there, but he made no claim to extensive use of the 12-inch telescope. A letter to Jonquil Leiber, dated 29 November 1936, also indicates only intermittent use of the telescope: "As a boy I used to haunt the Ladd Observatory of Brown University—looking through the 12-inch refractor now & then, reading the books in the library, &

probably making an unmitigated nuisance of myself through my incessant questioning of everybody present" (*Letters to C. L. Moore and Others* 178).

Surely, if Lovecraft had been able to direct a telescope much larger than his own, he would have turned it toward Eratosthenes, whatever he thought of the telescope's chromatic aberration. Nowhere in the *Journal* does he mention such observations. Nor does he reveal whether he ever told the Ladd Observatory staff of his Eratosthenes project, though it would seem a likely subject for his "incessant questioning." Had he done so, he might have been disappointed in their response. At the least, they might have directed Lovecraft to the eminent observer Edward Emerson Barnard's very critical review of Pickering's book on the moon, recently published in the *Astrophysical Journal*. In 1905, Lovecraft still harbored ambitions for a career in astronomy, and a word of caution from Professor Upton might have seemed a significant rebuke. That, however, is speculation, for no such criticism is mentioned in the *Journal*. In any case, any astronomy-induced curvature to his neck was probably the result of his many nights with his own telescope, rather than with the Ladd Observatory instrument.

There is evidence that, by the spring of 1906, the more experienced Lovecraft was becoming a critic of his early astronomical observations. In the April 1906 *Journal*, he dismissed his 1903 and 1905 observations of markings on Venus as probably imaginary. Caution recurs in the August 1906 *Journal*, in which Lovecraft noted that, although the cusps of the moon appeared prolonged in his telescope on June 28 (possibly indicative of a lunar atmosphere), this "was probably imagination."

On 14 September 1906, Lovecraft acquired the 3-inch Bardou telescope that he would keep for the rest of his life. In the October issue of the *Journal* that announced the acquisition, Lovecraft showed himself dissatisfied with his older telescope, noting that "2¼ inches is much too small an aperture for our work" and that views of the moon in the 3-inch telescope were "superb." He went on to state that the shadings of Venus that he had seen with his 2¼-inch instrument could not be verified with the 3-inch Bardou telescope, something which may have further shaken his confidence in his observations of changes in Eratosthenes. No observations of Eratosthenes with the Bardou telescope would ever be reported, although Pickering himself would later declare that a 3-inch telescope was sufficient to see the major features within that crater (Pickering, "Eratosthenes No. 1" 579).

At this point we must pause to consider two Lovecraft documents whose places in our story are not completely clear. The first is a somewhat puzzling short essay by Lovecraft titled "My Opinion As to the Lunar Canals" (*CE* 3.15). As we have already noted, these lunar canals are not the water-filled bodies that the word usually brings to mind. Lovecraft proposed that the canals are dark natural features of the moon analogous to the bright lunar rays that surround some craters. Surprisingly, he went on to write: "As to Prof. Pickering's theory—i.e.—That they are streaks of vegetation, I have but to say that any intelligent astronomer would consider it unworthy of notice, as our satellite is wanting in both water and atmosphere, the two essentials for life either animal or vegetable." Joshi (82) states that this note is dated 1903, but that the date is not in Lovecraft's handwriting.

If the 1903 date is correct, it would make the essay one of Lovecraft's first astronomical writings, and it would confirm a very early awareness of Pickering's work. A 1903 date for the note is actually supported by its strong rejection of Pickering's ideas. Lovecraft's writings during the years following 1903 would in contrast be either supportive of Pickering or, at worst, neutral. Accepting a date of 1903 does require, however, that Lovecraft quickly raised his opinion of Pickering. Clearly, Lovecraft had heard of Pickering by the time he wrote the note, but perhaps he had not yet fully digested Pickering's *Century* articles, in which Pickering argued that, even if the moon had no liquid surface water, it did have a thin atmosphere. As late as the 27 September 1903 *Journal*, Lovecraft stated flatly that "the moon has no atmosphere," contrary to Pickering's contention. By the time of his observations in December 1903, Lovecraft appears to be more open to Pickering's views. Thus, a date between the winter and the autumn of 1903 is plausible.

The second item's place in this story is uncertain, not because it has no date but because it bears two dates. It is an essay optimistically titled "The Moon: A Brief account of all that is known concerning our satellite, 7th edition." The essay carries two dates, first stating that it was written on 26 November 1903, but then noting that it was revised on 24 July 1906 (*CE* 3.17–20). Parts of this essay are incorporated into Lovecraft's article in the *Pawtuxet Valley Gleaner* for 19 October 1906 (*CE* 3.32–35) and in an unfinished serialization begun in the August 1906 *Journal*. The essay includes a brief account of Pickering's conception of a moon with atmosphere, hoarfrost, volcanism, and simple vegetation, noting that "this question will be more fully described in another volume." It concludes with the statement: "The writer confidently believes that there is no pursuit more interesting than the study of the moon, and all are urged to devote themselves to this branch of knowledge for in the history of the world some of the most recondite facts have been brought to light by the efforts of an amateur."

If the conclusion was written on 26 November 1903, it shows a Lovecraft already primed to begin his observational study of Eratosthenes the following month. On the other hand, if the wording has been changed at a later date, perhaps as late as July 1906, then there may be hindsight imbedded in the words. Considering that Lovecraft was at work on Eratosthenes at the start of December 1903, it seems likely to me that the 1903 first edition of the document already included both mention of Pickering and the encouragement for amateurs to pursue selenography.

Lovecraft experienced a partial breakdown in late 1905 continuing into 1906, and this may have contributed to the abrupt cessation of his research efforts (Joshi 100–101). His collapse in 1908 has been attributed at least in part to his realization that his weakness in mathematics meant that he would never become a professional astronomer (Joshi 127–28). Lovecraft's observational study of Eratosthenes of course required no mathematics.

There is no denying that at the time of his 1905 *Journal* extra, Lovecraft was convinced that, like Pickering, he had seen genuine changes in Eratosthenes—changes that could not be attributed to the varying reflections of sunlight from a fixed and rocky terrain. However, the changes he reported pushed to the limit his ability to see details on the moon. Through experience Lovecraft gradually became more aware of the problems that bedevil all lunar observers: nights of poor definition, tricks of changing light, and the limitations of telescopes. By 1906, with or without advice from the Ladd Observatory astronomers, he had become a more severe judge of his own observations. Lovecraft never repudiated his observations of changes in Eratosthenes, as he did his detections of markings on Venus, but he stopped mentioning them. After 1905, questions regarding lunar life would hang on Pickering's observations, not his own.

A serial titled "Will Man Ever Reach the Moon?" in the April–July 1906 *Journal* (and the similar article in the *Pawtuxet Valley Gleaner* for 12 October of that year) noted only that, were such a trip possible, Professor Pickering's discoveries might be verified. Nevertheless, the 14 September 1906 article in the *Pawtuxet Valley Gleaner* quoted at the start of this paper, "Is There Life on the Moon?," tells us that his flirtation with Pickering's theories was not entirely over. Livesey (19) has also plausibly suggested that Lovecraft is the unidentified writer whose identically titled article came to the attention of the editor of *Popular Astronomy* early in 1906.

As 1906 advanced, and as Lovecraft began his contributions to the *Pawtuxet Valley Gleaner* and the *Providence Tribune*, the *Journal* began to take on the more impersonal tone of his newspaper work. It was, however, approaching its end. Regular publication of the *Journal* ceased with the January 1907 issue, though attempts at resumption were made in April of that year and early in 1909. Just before it ended, Lovecraft provided us with a fine drawing of what appears to be his astronomical equipment on the cover of the December 1906 issue.

Pickering and lunar vegetation do not often figure in Lovecraft's writings after 1906. I am not aware that Pickering is mentioned in his letters, though I have by no means made an exhaustive search of his many epistles. It seems likely that Lovecraft, so skeptical about the supernatural, likewise developed a greater skepticism regarding Pickering's lunar vegetation. Exactly when that happened is unclear. The last mention of Pickering's hypotheses by Lovecraft of which I am aware does, however, adopt a neutral tone. In an article published on 6 March 1915 in the *Ashville Gazette-News* (CE 3.287–90) titled "The Earth and Its Moon,"[1] he wrote: "The Moon is generally considered to be a dead

---

1. Livesey (13) has suggested that Pickering's March 1915 *Popular Astronomy* arti-

world; a body without air, water, life, or volcanic activity. Prof. W. H. Pickering, however, has lately concluded from his observations that slight traces of atmosphere, hoar-frost, and vegetation of a low type, as well as feeble remnants of volcanic force, are to be found upon our satellite." The article continued: "The conjectures of the earlier astronomers concerning 'the inhabitants of the moon' seem now quite amusing." Lovecraft's amusement was not explicitly directed at Pickering but toward earlier and more extreme adherents of lunar life, such as Franz von Paula Gruithuisen (1774–1852), who thought that he had detected signs of lunar inhabitants and their cities (Sheehan and Dobson 75–94). Still, Lovecraft's tone had become arguably more reserved and no clear support was given to Pickering's conclusions.

Pickering himself remained true to his ideas. He continued to contemplate the moon and Mars from his Jamaican home until the end of his life in 1938, fine-tuning his ideas concerning life on both worlds and encouraging amateurs to examine for themselves the garden of Eratosthenes. A crater on the moon is named Pickering after both William and his brother Edward.

In a 1919 letter to Rheinhart Kleiner, Lovecraft stated that "I should describe mine own nature as tripartite, my interests consisting of three parallel and dissociated groups—(a) Love of the strange and fantastic. (b) Love of the abstract truth and of scientific logick. (c) Love of the ancient and the permanent" (*Letters to Rheinhart* 184). Lovecraft's astronomical investigations are clearly linked to the second of these and raise the question of whether some kind of scientific career might have been possible for him. In this connection, Livesey (76–78) questions whether Lovecraft had the perspective to be a good scientist. He suggests that Lovecraft placed too much weight on his sometimes outdated science books, to the point that they became a part of his identity. New discoveries that overthrew the ideas in his books therefore threatened that identity and might be resisted—obviously not the frame of mind wanted in a scientific researcher. Livesey calls attention to Lovecraft's early failure to embrace relativity as an example of this resistance.

---

cle, "Meteorology of the Moon," may have been published early enough to have inspired HPL's return to the subject.

In the astronomical observations discussed here, the young Lovecraft was not dealing with anything as transformative as the replacement of Newtonian physics by relativity. A new value for the rotation period of Venus would not change Lovecraft's developing worldview, no matter what number was found. Life on the moon is a weightier subject, and Lovecraft probably hoped to confirm Pickering's results. In the end, however, he appears to have restrained his enthusiasm and backed off from claiming that his own observations proved Pickering right. Lovecraft's observational projects can be criticized as naïve, but they show a basic appreciation of evidence-based science. Although we do not see any flashes of fledgling genius (he was just in his teens, after all), there is nothing in these first investigations to suggest that Lovecraft, under different circumstances, could not have become a solid scientist. Whether the science could have been astronomy is a different question. Livesey (76–78) points out that, even could he have mastered his mathematical shortcomings, Lovecraft's sensitivity to cold as an adult, as well as the increasing dependence of astronomy upon the tedious analysis of photographic plates, might have moved him toward other fields.

Pickering's hypotheses also touch on the strange and the fantastic, so we might ask whether Lovecraft's youthful search for life on the moon influenced his fiction. I would say that there is nothing as specifically influenced as was H. G. Wells's account of lunar conditions in *The First Men in the Moon*. Livesey has already noted that Lovecraft's knowledge of astronomy colors his fiction in many places, but these cannot be directly tied to his interest in Eratosthenes or Pickering. Lovecraft's juvenile stories, written around the time of his observations, do not appear to draw upon Pickering's ideas, though there was apparently a now-lost tale based upon astronomer Peter Andreas Hansen's proposal that there could be an atmosphere and life on the far side of an ellipsoidal moon (Joshi 87). There are frequent references to the moon in Lovecraft's later stories (see Livesey 82–83), but nothing that closely resembles Pickering's vision of lunar life. A loose connection can perhaps be made with the creatures and plants that dwell on the moon in *The Dream-Quest of Unknown Kadath*, but that fictional moon bears little resemblance to the one posited by Pickering. Nor do the ill-fated inhabitants of Ib, who are said to have come from the moon in "The Doom that Came to Sarnath," appear to have arrived from Pickering's moon. Some of Lovecraft's alien creatures do have an element of the vegetable about them. The Fungi from Yuggoth, the vegetable entities of Mercury in "The Shadow out of Time," and the Elder Things in *At the Mountains of Madness* come to mind, but it would be a stretch to connect them with Pickering's lunar plant life. The narrator in *At the Mountains of Madness* in fact goes so far as to refer to "the sterile disc of the moon" (*CF* 3.131), though the context allows an ironic reading. Nor does it appear that any of Lovecraft's fictional scientists is modeled upon Pickering, although some of them do make discoveries that set them apart from their more conventional peers.

I venture a few final comments about Lovecraft as a young astronomer. Aside from any unspecified help he may have received from the Ladd Observatory staff, Lovecraft seems to have learned observational astronomy on his own, through reading and doing. In his studies of Eratosthenes and Venus, he attempted to see detail that, to be generous, challenged the capabilities of his small telescope. He would eventually learn to doubt observations made at the limits of visibility, but it took him three years to develop his acumen in that regard. Not until 1932 would the Providence amateur astronomy association, The Skyscrapers, be organized. Lovecraft attended a meeting in 1936, shortly before his death, and left impressed (*Letters to James F. Morton* 392). Had such an organization existed thirty years earlier, it might have provided valuable advice for the beginning observer, and for better or worse have steered Lovecraft along different paths.

Works Cited

Barnard, Edward Emerson. Review of W. H. Pickering's *The Moon*. *Astrophysical Journal* 20 (1904): 359–64.

Dobbins, Thomas, and Baum, Richard. "Observing a Fictional Moon." *Sky and Telescope* 95, No. 6 (1998): 105–9.

Jones, Bessie Zaban, and Boyd, Lyle Gifford. *The Harvard College Observatory: The First Four Directorships*. Cambridge, MA: Harvard University Press, 1971.

Joshi, S. T. *I Am Providence: The Life and Times of H. P. Lovecraft.* New York: Hippocampus Press, 2010. 2 vols.

Livesey, T. R. "Dispatches from the Providence Observatory: Astronomical Motifs and Sources in the Writings of H. P. Lovecraft." *Lovecraft Annual* No. 2 (2008): 3–87.

Lovecraft, H. P. *Letters to Alfred Galpin.* Ed. S. T. Joshi and David E. Schultz. New York: Hippocampus Press, 2003.

———. *Letters to C. L. Moore and Others.* Ed. David E. Schultz and S. T. Joshi. New York: Hippocampus Press, 2017.

———. *Letters to F. Lee Baldwin, Duane W. Rimel, and Nils Frome.* Ed. David E. Schultz and S. T. Joshi. New York: Hippocampus Press, 2016.

———. *Letters to James F. Morton.* Ed. David E. Schultz and S. T. Joshi. New York: Hippocampus Press, 2011.

———. *Letters to Rheinhart Kleiner.* Ed. S. T. Joshi and David E. Schultz. New York: Hippocampus Press, 2005.

Pickering, William. H. "The Canals in the Moon." *Century Magazine* 64 (1902): 189–95.

———. "Eratosthenes No. 1." *Popular Astronomy* 27 (1919): 579–83.

———. "Eratosthenes No. 4." *Popular Astronomy* 32 (1924): 69–78.

———. "Is the Moon a Dead Planet?" *Century Magazine* 64 (1902): 90–99.

———. "Meteorology of the Moon." *Popular Astronomy* 23 (1915): 129–40.

———. *The Moon.* New York: Doubleday, Page, 1903.

———. "Visual Observations of the Moon and Planets." *Annals of the Harvard College Observatory* 32 (1895): 116–17.

Plotkin, Howard. "William H. Pickering at Jamaica: The Founding of Woodlawn and Studies of Mars." *Journal for the History of Astronomy* 24 (1992): 101–22.

Sheehan, William P. *Planets and Perception.* Tucson: University of Arizona Press, 1988.

———, and Thomas A. Dobson. *Epic Moon: A History of Lunar Exploration in the Age of the Telescope.* Richmond, VA: Willmann-Bell, 2001.

Young, Charles Augustus. *Lessons in Astronomy: Including Uranography.* Boston: Ginn & Co., 1903.

Diabolists and Decadents: H. P. Lovecraft as Purveyor, Indulger, and Appraiser of Puritan Horror Fiction Psychohistory

Scott Meyer

> The deepest form of fascination, that of the artist, derives its strength from being both horror and the possibility of conceiving horror.
> —André Malraux, Preface for Faulkner's *Sanctuary*

Introduction

Like Jonathan Edwards before him, Howard Phillips Lovecraft is a hugely influential "American original" (Guran). His works inspired an essential canon of horror writers and storytellers including Stephen King, Alan Moore, Guillermo del Toro, Neil Gaiman, John Carpenter, and many more. His stories have been adapted into countless formats including video games, comic books, TV series, and movies. Like the Puritans, Lovecraft's legacy and influence survived years of often hostile criticism yet remains intriguingly popular today. The *Wall Street Journal* has called him an author who matters now more than ever (Callia).

His popularity can be attributed in part to his uncanny ability to channel the old New England environment and ethic that has been described as a Lovecraftian "regionalism" (Talbot). I contend that this regionalism is in fact a "Puritan regionalism" that instigated him to appropriate and employ philosophic and expressionistic tactics that made portions of his writings such as "The Picture in the House" an outpouring of an imaginative Puritan psychohistory. This particular New England regionalism is as much about the imaginative outworking of the Puritan mind as it is about a regionally situated locale and soil. In the case of H. P. Lovecraft, I will analyze when and how he appropriates from the Puritans and from the myths surrounding them, including those he contributes to or invents (especially as it relates to the eminent Cotton Mather in particular), and how he was unable—or perhaps unwilling—to escape Puritan regionalism in his artful storytelling.

The New England Aristocratic Gentleman

Lovecraft is known as "the Old Gentleman," which is an acknowledgment of his devotion to the inseparable notions of aristocracy, race, nobility, and class in his life and writings (Clere). He took great pride in his family's New England lineage, claiming to trace his bloodline back to the arrival of George Phillips to Massachusetts in 1630 (Joshi, "Howard Phillips Lovecraft"). His tales are very frequently guided by "the gentleman narrator," who lent certain cultured sensibilities to the direction and tone of the tale. His writing often hinged on the tension of order and natural arrangements hanging by a thread, and on the notion that humankind's encroaching on the culture and space of the Old Ones (the ancient alien race of unspeakable monsters who settled and cultivated New England long before the Indians or Puritans) is an unsettling disruption to a caste system that ultimately cannot be done.

To say that Lovecraft was a man of his times is an understatement and deflection. He was more a man out of time, living firmly in a romanticized past and fantasizing about a dangerous future. Much like the Puritans in their jeremiads, Lovecraft praised a social order and hierarchical system that was slowly fading. This tendency toward the insistence on existing in a rigid class-based society where respect and rights are parceled out by rank and birth is itself a tie to the Puritan conceptions of hierarchy (Bushman 1, 147, 267). It was in this ingrained similarity to the views of the social structure of the Puritans that Lovecraft gave his stories their own invaluable order and attitudes, which provided the most obscene and horrifying breakdowns and tragedies later in the narrative. The perspective and voice of his stories reflected a vision of his gentleman narrator who speaks with an expectation of class and social hierarchy resplendent with vestiges of Puritan regionalism. Understanding the background of the narrator, we can move on to the influences, sources, and depictions of Puritan regionalism in his works and thought.

Horror on the Brain: Group Neuroticism in the Puritan Morbid Imagination

The formative years of the Puritan era were fraught with peril and risk, including Indian attacks, disease, and other sundry threats (Marsden 11–17). This shared experiences created in the Puritan divines and colonial populace something of a group neurosis that included a paranoia and expanded imagination as an essential part of the early colonial survival mechanism. Psychologist and author André Tridon likened the surviving Puritan ethic to a neurosis of the mind (252). Lovecraft himself commented that in the Puritans there was to be found "a profound study in group-neuroticism; for certainly no one can deny the existence of a profoundly morbid streak in the Puritan imagination" (*SL* 3.174–75).

This group neuroticism at that time manifested itself in a multitude of ways at different times, including but not limited to witchcraft obsession, visions from God, a morbid introspection during the conversion process, and a vivid escapist eschatology of predetermined future glory. It is within this lineage of historic regional neuroses that Lovecraft lived his life and conducted his work. His special attraction to the history, heredity, and hierarchy in the imagination of New England made his collision with tradition that much more impactful and intriguing. This is how Lovecraft situated himself in an especially effective manner to appreciate and appropriate Puritan imagery and imagination in his works.

Lovecraft as an Extension of the Puritan Imagination

One of the ways that he extended this Puritan regionalism was in his energetic commitment to precise descriptive wordiness, which brings to mind the pen of Jonathan Edwards himself. Both placed a great deal of emphasis in bringing the audience a serious step closer to the thing described via precise but creative prose. A brief typical example of such prose is in the story "The Lurking Fear." The gentleman narrator has a suspicion that he is about to discover something terrible and states: "I felt the strangling tendrils of a cancerous horror whose roots reached into illimitable pasts and fathomless abysms of the night that broods beyond time" (*CF* 1.361).

Lovecraft often wrote with a big "biblical" style much like many of the Puritan divines. When giving advice to aspiring writers in his work "Literary Composition" (1920), Lovecraft directed them to read the King James Bible for inspiration, complete with a pseudo-sectarian anti-Catholic dig that would have very much pleased the Puritans:

> An excellent habit to cultivate is the analytical study of the King James Bible. For simple yet rich and forceful English, this masterly production is hard to equal; and even though its Saxon vocabulary and poetic rhythm be unsuited to general composition, it is an invaluable model for writers on quaint or imaginative themes. Lord Dunsany, perhaps the greatest living prose artist, derived nearly all of his stylistic tendencies from the Scriptures; and the contemporary critic Boyd points out very acutely the loss sustained by most Catholic Irish writers through their unfamiliarity with the historic volume and its traditions. (*CE* 2.41)

In both his headspace and style, Lovecraft approached his work while firmly placed in Puritan regionalism, and from this place he spewed forth every horrible tale he had to tell.

Another way in which the style and perspective of Lovecraft was rooted firmly in Puritan regionalism was in the ways in which he was unorthodoxly influenced by Puritan Calvinism by way of his interpretation of the theological premise into a secularized, fatalistic, nihilistic determinism. Simply put, in his stories there was no outrunning or outgunning the Ancient Ones (the monsters of old evil) of New England. Destruction was a foregone conclusion, and all that a shattered human narrator can do is to attempt to find sensible logic in the terror of inevitable despair. Famed fantasy writer and horror icon Neil Gaiman puts it this way:

> The interesting thing is in Lovecraft, people don't do the wrong thing in the way that you normally do in horror fiction. In horror fiction, you do the wrong thing: you go into the shop and you buy that cat-headed object you probably shouldn't, or whatever, and

everything goes bad. In Lovecraft, you simply get a room in a wrong place, move to the wrong town, read the wrong story. You're just screwed.

Much like the thinking of the Puritans in America, the people and communities in Lovecraft's stories were thought to be guided, sometimes rewarded, but more often punished, by forces far more powerful than themselves. Lovecraft was able to effectively tap into the helplessness that comes from an obsession with a seemingly capricious fate. Horror author Thomas Ligotti states it this way: "Although Lovecraft did have his earthbound illusions, at the end of the day he existed in a no man's land of nihilism and disillusionment. As a fiction writer, he will ever be a contemporary of each new generation of mortals" (Ligotti 205). In this model of free will bending to stronger forces, Lovecraft continued to operate from a familiar spot within his Puritan regionalism by a tacit intersection with the providence of fate (God) so intrinsic to Calvinist Puritan doctrine.

Lovecraft as Heir to Nathaniel Hawthorne's Puritan Fictionalizing

Lovecraft admired Nathaniel Hawthorne from a young age and would grow to see many parallels in his work and imagery. Hawthorne's *The House of Seven Gables* most likely served as an inspiration for "The Picture in the House" (Joshi and Schultz 107), which will be analyzed in the upcoming section. Lovecraft called it "New England's greatest contribution to weird literature" (*Annotated Supernatural Horror in Literature* 64). He noted that the house in the story itself was "typifying as it does the dark Puritan age of concealed horror and witch-whispers," which is a theme that Lovecraft would run with through much of his work.

A fascinating appraisal and comparison of Hawthorne comes from Lovecraft himself in his 1927 work "Supernatural Horror in Literature," referenced above. Lovecraft describes Hawthorne as "a gentle soul cramped by the Puritanism of early New England; shadowed and wistful, and grieved at an unmoral universe which everywhere transcends the conventional patterns thought by our forefathers to represent divine and immutable law" (61). This was high praise and an insightful analysis of Hawthorne, emphasizing old-school Puritan regionalism and the themes of utilizing historic presumed values and spaces to tell effective stories.

Lovecraft was also indebted to Hawthorne in his desire and ability to effectively ground the stories in the literal Puritan regionalism of the given environment. American Gothic writers so often turned to the ancient haunted lands of Europe to tell their tales, yet Hawthorne paved the way for Lovecraft by situating his stories in one of the youngest countries on earth while still creating a creepy, "old" atmosphere (Osborne). Lovecraft was influenced by Hawthorne in making our young country seem not at all innocent and in fact even more horrific and threatening than the old country that the Puritans came from.

In both Hawthorne and Lovecraft we see some common themes, including an ability to appreciate and utilize Puritan regionalism as a strong rhetorical device in telling tales of American horror. Donald R. Burleson concludes that:

> If Hawthorne could have read Lovecraft, he would have found a world of familiar images, themes and concepts there, but would have seen them cosmically transmuted. To Hawthorne, things on the stable side of reality were "shrouded in a blackness, ten times black." For Lovecraft, whose dark visions spanned the abysses between the galaxies, ten times black would not have been nearly black enough. (44)

Lovecraft and the Puritans

In briefly appraising Lovecraft's interest in and appreciation of the Puritans in his letters we find some enlightening references that will help us to understand his lens when writing "The Picture in the House." Lovecraft shows a florid burst of macabre appreciation for the artfulness of the Puritans, even going so far as to call them "marvellous" (*SL* 1.275). Reading the lengthy quotation below, one can see just how influenced Lovecraft was by the narrative mission and artistic swaths with which they painted the walls of their errand into the wilderness:

> Puritanism? I am by no means dispos'd to condemn it utterly in the pageant of the world, for it is not life an art, and art a selec-

tion? The Puritans unconsciously sought to do a supremely artistic thing—to mould all life into a dark poem; a macabre tapestry with quaint arabesques and patterns from the plains of antique Palaestina . . . antique Palaestina with her bearded prophets, many gated walls, and flattened domes. The fatuous floundering of the ape and the Neanderthaler they rejected—this and the graceful forms into which that floundering had aimlessly blunder'd—and in place of slovenly Nature set up a life in Gothick design, with formal arches and precise traceries, austere spires and three interesting little gargoyles with solemn grimaces, call'd the father, the son, and the holy ghost. On shifting humanity they imposed a refreshing technique, and an aimless and futile cosmos supply'd artificial values which had real authority because they were not true. Verily, the Puritans were the only really effective diabolists and decadents the world has known; because they hated life and scorned the platitude that it is worth living. Can you imagine anything more magnificent than the wholesale slaughter of the Indians—a very epick—by our New-England ancestors in the name of the lamb? But all aside from that—these Puritans were truly marvellous. They did not invent, but substantially developed the colonial doorway; and incidentally created a simple standard of life and conduct which is, apart from some extravagant and inessential details and a few aesthetic and intellectual fallacies, in all truth the most healthy and practical way of securing happiness and tranquillity which we have had since the early days of Republican Rome. (*SL* 1.275)

In his personal life and upbringing he didn't always appreciate the Puritan legacy of Rhode Island in quite the same way. In a letter to Maurice W. Moe, Lovecraft defines the doctrines he was forced to endure as a child in the First Baptist Church of Providence as "Puritanical" and states that he felt no connection to their "simple faith" (*SL* 1.10). He did, however, share both the Americana of his native land and the idealized identification of the Puritans as Britons sharing in all the assumed historical and contemporary rights and privileges of the "Colonial Tory," as he calls himself in another letter (*SL* 1.72).

Lovecraft defends his choice to live a mild and chaste life as "not from a standpoint of Puritan morality" (*SL* 1.229) but from that of the gentleman artist. The irony here is the unacknowledged debt that Lovecraft owes the Puritans for this stance, as it was something inculcated partly through the regional ethic of New England at that time just as the Bohemians he references are in part a result of the cultural attitudes tied to certain times, peoples, and geographies. When not mentioning the Puritans by name, Lovecraft shows his Puritan New England heritage when discussing the nature of humanity. Here in his letters Lovecraft describes humankind's state in language that is distinctly Puritan, bringing to mind the Westminster Confession of Faith section 6:4–6 and Bible verses such as Jeremiah 17:9 and Psalm 51:5 on the total depravity of humankind, to all of which the Puritans by and large would have wholeheartedly subscribed.

We end our analysis of Puritan references in Lovecraft's letters by recounting a stunning—if cheekily hyperbolic—defense of the Puritans and the puritan art of life. There is no reason to assume that he is not genuine in his feelings here, though the impetus may be more in correcting the "shallow asses" who attack the low-hanging fruit of fundamentalism without having an artist's eye for the undeniable contributions that the Puritans made on New England, America, and the world, especially as it relates to morbidity, narrative, philosophy, and other areas near and dear to Lovecraft's dark heart.

> And as for Puritan inhibitions—I admire them more every day. They are attempts to make of life a work of art—to fashion a pattern of beauty in the hog-wallow that is animal existence—and they spring out of that divine hatred of life which marks the deepest and most sensitive soul. I am so tired of shallow asses rant against Puritanism that I think that I shall become a Puritan. (*SL* 1.315)

In understanding the tone, context, subtext, and attendant issues that Lovecraft was often balancing and indulging in while writing his personal correspondence, it is important to note the potentiality that he was treating the Puritans with a healthy dose of flippant parody as an argumentative ploy between friends. Whether serious or "trolling," his comments about the Puritans in his letters were both astute and certainly true in the context of the New England Puritan regionalism in the works of both parties that this paper is examining.

Lovecraft had a particular fascination with Cotton Mather, seen both then and now as the dreaded gargoyle of New England. Most commonly known for his writings concerting the Salem witch trials, though in actuality the most prominent American figure of his time, Cotton Mather would have summed up to Lovecraft the morbid fundamentalist old-world religiosity to which Lovecraft was introducing an narrative alternative.

It is important to note exactly how Lovecraft references Cotton Mather in his work. Mather's seminal work *Magnalia Christi Americana* (or *The Story of Christ in America*) is a pseudo-hagiography that recounts the legendary narratives of the Puritan forefathers settling New England for the Protestant faith. It is a narrative of formation replete with journal notes, diary entries, tales of native peoples, beasts of the woods, and of course the God of New Jerusalem himself, the original Old One. This book resonated with Lovecraft so much that he saw fit to reference it no less than four times in his work, including "The Picture in the House," "The Unnamable," "Pickman's Model," and *The Case of Charles Dexter Ward*.

Mather's work on witchcraft, *Wonders of the Invisible World*, was referenced in *The Case of Charles Dexter Ward*. Space constraints prevent a complete analysis of the ways in which Mather's books were utilized in the works of Lovecraft, but it is sufficient to say that Lovecraft was very familiar with the chief Puritan Cotton Mather and his most influential works, including the occasions for which they were written. Lovecraft plays off of these works by enveloping them into his own New England regionalism where they continued to play a part in the ongoing horror narrative in that unique part of the world.

Sourcing the Puritans in Lovecraftian Fiction

Like Hawthorne, Lovecraft had to "discover a usable American past that suited his necessity for archaicism" (Shreffler 19). He found this both in the New England environmental landscape and in the myths and histories surrounding the Puritan people who trod that ground years before Lovecraft did. We should note that like so many critics and authors before and since, Lovecraft did not necessarily understand the actual historical Puritans properly or accurately. His study of Puritanism had yet to be informed by scholars such as Perry Miller, Robert Middlekauff, Harry Stout, and Edmund Morgan, who did so much to enable historians and students to view the Puritans without the dour stench that had been placed on them before. As we have seen, Lovecraft saw the Puritans as being "the only really effective diabolists and decadents the world has known; because they hated life and scorned the platitude that it is worth living." This of course is a very ironic thing to be said by one of the most famous pessimistic misanthropes in all literature and is perhaps an example of his projecting the roots of his Puritan regionalism.

It is this idea that the Puritans buried deep their worst sins that informed his approach to works such as "The Picture in The House." Lovecraft stated that "An abnormal Puritan psychology led to all kinds of repression, furtiveness, & grotesque hidden crime, while the long winters & backwoods isolation fostered monstrous secrets which never came to light" (*SL* 3.423). It is from these recesses of Puritan myths and assumptions that Lovecraft informs and highlights this frightening story of a Puritan gone sour.

One of Lovecraft's pieces most pregnant with Puritan regionalism is indeed the short story "The Picture in the House." Peter Cannon refers to it as a "rooted in authentic Puritan psychohistory" (38). The story involves our narrator—a young gentleman genealogist—making his way back into his ancestral New England towns to discover more about his lineage. In doing so he is struck with fear and wonder in taking in the very old houses that dot the New England woods:

> Searchers after horror haunt strange, far places. For them are the catacombs of Ptolemais, and the carven mausolea of the nightmare countries. They climb to the moonlit towers of ruined Rhine castles, and falter down black cobwebbed steps beneath the scattered stones of forgotten cities in Asia. The haunted wood and the desolate mountain are their shrines, and they linger around the sinister monoliths on uninhabited islands. But the true epicure of the terrible, to whom a new thrill of unutterable ghastliness is the chief end and justification of existence, esteem most of all the ancient, lonely farmhouses of backwoods New England; for

there the dark elements of strength, solitude, grotesqueness, and ignorance combine to form the perfection of the hideous. (*CF* 1.206)

Musing on these old ancestral homes, the narrator comments on the Puritans who colonized these New England woods:

> In such houses have dwelt generations of strange people, whose like the world has never seen. Seized with a gloomy and fanatical belief which exiled them from their kind, their ancestors sought the wilderness for freedom. There the scions of a conquering race indeed flourished free from the restrictions of their fellows, but cowered in an appalling slavery to the dismal phantasms of their own minds. Divorced from the enlightenment of civilization, the strength of these Puritans turned into singular channels; and in their isolation, morbid self-repression, and struggle for life with relentless Nature, there came to them dark furtive traits from the prehistoric depths of their cold Northern heritage. By necessity practical and by philosophy stern, these folk were not beautiful in their sins. Erring as all mortals must, they were forced by their rigid code to seek concealment above all else; so that they came to use less and less taste in what they concealed. (*CF* 1.207)

As the gentleman narrator gets caught in a bad storm, he spies one of these near-derelict New England homes and proceeds to let himself in after nobody comes to answer the door.

Once inside he notices the humble antiquity of the room, commenting that "I could not discover a single article of definitely post-revolutionary date" (*CF* 1.209). The items inside the house plainly situate this setting within Lovecraft's Puritan regionalism. As his uneasy fear begins to settle in around him, the narrator notices an eighteenth-century Bible, a copy of *The Pilgrim's Progress* from the same time period, a book concerning missions and adventures in the African continent, and "the rotting bulk of Cotton Mather's 'Magnalia Christi Americana'" (*CF* 1.211). It is worth noting that Lovecraft owned a first edition of the *Magnalia Christi Americana* and was presumably very familiar with this work.

As the narrator is curious and frightened by the pictures in the book concerning Africa depicting a tribal cannibalization scene, a hunkering old Puritan lumbers down the stairs. Lovecraft describes him in this way:

> The appearance of this man, and the instinctive fear he inspired, prepared me for something like enmity; so that I almost shuddered through surprise and a sense of uncanny incongruity when he motioned me to a chair and addressed me in a thin, weak voice full of fawning respect and ingratiating hospitality. His speech was very curious, an extreme form of Yankee dialect I had thought long extinct; and I studied it closely as he sat down opposite me for conversation. (*CF* 1.212)

The narrator's notice of the old-fashioned Yankee dialect is a nod toward Lovecraft's conception of the ancient isolated Puritan being more likely to be able to have seen or intermingled with the Ancient Ones: suffice to say that this old Puritan represents the elder trails of humanity on this continent and thus a closer rub with the old evil forces and their corrupting instincts at work here for so long especially in New England.

The story continues with the narrator and the Puritan studying the African book while cagily chatting in the study. We then slowly find out through a soft dripping of blood through the ceiling and a haunting eeriness in the Puritan's demeanor that he had in fact given in to the Puritan fear of "going native" (Rowlandson) and became a cannibal himself due to the corrupting influence of the book and its graphic, bloody pictures of foreign people, strange lands, and bloody occult practices. (In this we have an instance of xenophobia not uncommon to both the Puritans and to Lovecraft himself.) The Puritan then begins to turn on our narrator while giving a bone-chilling talk about eating flesh, when lightning from the storm destroys the house and our narrator seemingly survives to flee to safety and tell his tale.

Conclusion

Lovecraft represents a compelling and terrifying use of Puritan regionalism in storytelling. He was able to appropriate and reference a movement and mission that was in his bones and beneath his feet without being in his head or heart. In utilizing some of the hallmarks of the Puritan imagination he shows the reader that he in fact is not that far away from the ethic and environment that is ancient America: the wooded New England countryside. He manages to add horror and compelling romance to a region and people already weighed down with so much interest, misperceptions, and misremembrances.

Philosophers Gérard Legrand and Robert Benayoun said it poignantly: "Lovecraft's grandeur resides in nothing less than the creation of a personal mythology which ridicules 'modern history'" (16). In embracing Puritan regionalism Lovecraft left a mark that helped to define a genre once belonging to Hawthorne and now enjoyed by so many through the expansion and solidification of the Lovecraftian New England more deeply into both the pop culture psyche and the history of literature.

Works Cited

Boerem, R. "Lovecraft and the Tradition of the Gentleman Narrator." In *An Epicure in the Terrible: A Centennial Anthology of Essays in Honor of H. P. Lovecraft*, ed. David E. Schultz and S. T. Joshi. New York: Hippocampus Press, 2011. 269–85.

Burleson, Donald R. "Hawthorne's Influence on Lovecraft." In *Lovecraft and Influence: His Predecessors and Successors*, ed. Robert H. Waugh. Lanham, MD: Scarecrow Press. 2013.

Bushman, Richard L. *From Puritan to Yankee: Character and the Social Order in Connecticut, 1690–1765*. Cambridge, MA: Harvard University Press, 1967.

Callia, Michael. "Here's Why H. P. Lovecraft Matters More Than Ever." Wall Street Journal (13 October 2014). blogs.wsj.com/speakeasy/2014/10/13/heres-why-h-p-lovecraft-matters-more-than-ever/ Accessed 13 March 2017.

Cannon, Peter. *H. P. Lovecraft*. Boston: Twayne, 1989.

Clere, Bert. "H. P. Lovecraft's New Deal." *Ethos Review* (11 January 2016). www.ethosreview.org/intellectual-spaces/lovecraft/ Accessed March 13, 2017.

Gaiman, Neil. In *The Eldritch Influence: The Life, Vision and Phenomenon of H. P. Lovecraft*. Directed by Shawn R. Owens. Hermetic Productions, 2003.

Guran, Paula. "Joyce Carol Oates: The Gothic Queen." Interview. Dark Echo Online. September 1999. www.darkecho.com/darkecho/horroronline/oates.html Accessed 11 March 2017.

Joshi, S. T. "Howard Phillips Lovecraft: The Life of a Gentleman of Providence." In *H. P. Lovecraft Centennial Guidebook: A Hand-*

book on the 100th Birthday of the Great Horror Writer, ed. Jon B. Cooke. Pawtucket, RI: Montilla Publications, 1990. www.hplovecraft.com/life/biograph.aspx Accessed 15 March 2017.

———, and David E. Schultz. *An H. P. Lovecraft Encyclopedia*. Westport, CT: Greenwood Press, 2001.

Legrand, Gérard, and Robert Benayoun. "H. P. Lovecraft and the Black Moon." *Cultural Correspondence* Nos. 10–11 (Fall 1979): 16.

Ligotti, Thomas. *The Conspiracy against the Human Race: A Contrivance of Horror*. New York: Hippocampus Press. 2010.

Lovecraft, H. P. *The Annotated Supernatural Horror in Literature*. Ed. S. T. Joshi. New York: Hippocampus Press, 2nd ed. 2012.

Marsden, George M. *Jonathan Edwards: A Life*. New Haven, CT: Yale University Press, 2003.

Osborne, Michael. "Men without Enough Past: Exploring Hawthorne's Influence on H. P. Lovecraft." University of Houston at Clear Lake Online Resource. 25 October 2016. www.coursesite.uhcl.edu/HSH/whitec/LITR/5431rom/models/2016/rpr16rp1Osborne.htm Accessed 14 March 2017.

Rowlandson, Mary. *A Narrative of the Captivity and Restoration of Mrs. Mary Rowlandson*. Extracts in *The Norton Anthology of American Literature: Beginnings to 1820*, ed. Nina Baym. Vol. A. New York: Norton, 2012. 257–88.

Shreffler, Phillip A. *The H. P. Lovecraft Companion*. Westport, CT: Greenwood Press, 1977.

Talbot, Nick. "All about Alienation: Alan Moore on Lovecraft and Providence." Interview. TheQuietus.com. 31 August 2014. www.thequietus.com/articles/16129-alan-moore-providence-cthulhu-philosophy-language-lovecraft. Accessed 11 March 2017.

Triton, André. *Psychoanalysis and Behavior*. New York: Alfred A. Knopf. 1920.

Aquaman and Lovecraft: An Unlikely Mating

Duncan Norris

There is a well-known Internet meme that depicts the DC Comics character Aquaman triumphantly rising atop the ocean on the head of a controlled Cthulhu, commonly captioned with "I'm useless they said. I have stupid powers they said," or "Who's useless now?" The image had enough social currency that in 2016 Quantum Mechanix created a licensed figurine version of the image for the world's largest comic and pop culture festival, Comic-Con International: San Diego.

This is unusual in that it is a rather positive depiction of Aquaman, albeit tinged with a certain dry mockery. For decades this character has suffered the indignity, if such a phrase can be said of a fictional entity, of being an ongoing joke in pop culture for the supposed inadequacy of his powers. This ridicule comes most especially in connection with his portrayal on television in the cartoon series *Super Friends* (1973–86) riding an oversized seahorse and with an uninspiring costume. Adding to this derision is that Aquaman's actually not inconsiderable powers have been in the process hyperbolically reduced to that of commanding fish.

The very concept of an Aquaman film became a running gag inside the Hollywood-based show *Entourage* concerning the character of Vince, who played Aquaman in a fictional blockbuster movie (Lawrence) while the adult-orientated cartoon and figurine-based shows *Family Guy* (S07E04) and *Robot Chicken* (S01E08), among a host of others, portray him particularly darkly as pathetically inept, especially out of water. This parody has gone to such lengths that any joke relying on the idea "Aquaman is useless" is now considered overdone to the point of cliché (Bradley).

The comicality of the Aquaman/Cthulhu meme thus lies in juxtaposing the supposed impotence of Aquaman versus the omnipotence of dread Cthulhu, whom Aquaman now has enthralled as he is a master of all the creatures of the sea. Like many memes, it is primarily designed to be humorous and doesn't hold up to any sort of serious scrutiny. Aside from the ridiculous question of how any mortal mind would fare against the Ruler of R'lyeh, the more basic truth is that Cthulhu is not—August Derleth's assertions of symbolic elementalism to the contrary—a water creature (Joshi 643–44). It is merely imprisoned underwater in the corpse-city of R'lyeh until the stars are right. Yet given that both Aquaman and Cthulhu dwell in former land cities sunken under the ocean, and communicate telepathically with lesser beings, there is at least a strand of natural association between the heroic Justice League member and the eponymous creature of Lovecraft's Cthulhu Mythos. This dangling thread was certainly picked up upon by director James Wan in his 2018 film *Aquaman*, and it is worthwhile to examine the results and see the effect Lovecraft and his writings have in popular culture so long after his death in relative obscurity in 1937.

Aquaman as a film was a noted success. At the time of its release it was the second highest-rated movie with audiences from the filmic DC Extended Universe (DCEU), and the only one of two such films to have a Rotten Tomatoes Fresh Rating (a rather low bar of only above an aggregated 60%) from critics (Rotten Tomatoes, *Aquaman*). It was, by a significant margin, the most financially successful film in the DCEU, making over $1.147 billion at the worldwide box office and finishing in fifth place overall for the year (Box Office Mojo, *Aquaman*). This is considerably more than the $821 million earned by the next biggest installment in the franchise, *Wonder Woman*, which placed tenth in 2017 and was the only DCEU film that passed *Aquaman* in both audiences and critical ratings as of the time of release (Rotten Tomatoes, *Wonder Woman*).

The plot of *Aquaman* is the typically paradoxical blend of the simplistic and convoluted that characterizes the modern blockbuster comic book film. Arthur Curry, a.k.a. Aquaman, is the son of lighthouse keeper Thomas Curry and the princess Atlanna of

Atlantis, the latter meeting and falling in love with the former when rescued by him. This heritage gives Arthur both superpowers and the right to rule Atlantis. Yet Arthur has turned his back on his underwater kingdom after the Atlanteans forced his mother to return there and ritually sacrificed her to The Trench, another underwater kingdom presided over by monstrous fishmen, for the liaison that resulted in his birth.

Arthur's half-brother Orm thus rules Atlantis and is manipulating the other underwater kingdoms, using a surface pirate named David Kane, into joining under his leadership to declare him Ocean Master so he can invade the surface world. Forced to action by Orm's plan, Arthur undertakes an expedition to Atlantis, accompanied by Princess Mera of the underwater Kingdom of Xebel, and meets with his old tutor Vulko. He advises Arthur to seek a lost artifact, the Trident of Atlan, and use it to claim the throne from his brother. Captured, Aquaman is goaded into challenging Orm in ritual combat, loses, and is rescued by Mera. They travel to a lost Atlantean kingdom in the Sahara Desert and learn how to track down the missing Trident from the information there. Meanwhile Orm arms Kane with Atlantean technology, which Kane alters to become Black Manta in order to gain revenge on Aquaman for allowing the death of Kane's father earlier in the film. Black Manta attacks Aquaman and Mera in Sicily as they discover the nautical heading needed for travel from the information retrieved in the desert, but the pair escape.

Finding their desired location is in The Trench, Aquaman and Mera are attacked by the monstrous inhabitants that dwell therein but escape via a wormhole to a hidden inner-earth sea. Here they discover Atlanna alive, and Aquaman convinces the guardian of the Trident, the Karathen, to let him take possession of it. They all head off to join the battle between the Atlanteans and allies against the Kingdom of the Brine. Naturally, Aquaman now defeats Orm in combat and takes the throne, ending the war.

Altogether it is rather standard fare for a comic book movie, and it is important not to ascribe Lovecraftian influence simply because a work uses some of his broad tropes or has superficial similarities. An interesting case in point is *Bird Box*, another 2018 movie created by and for the movie and television streaming platform Netflix. This film was hailed as a noted success, with 45 million accounts alleged to have watched it in the first seven days of release (Charara), although its Rotten Tomatoes ratings hover around 60% for both audience and critics (Rotten Tomatoes, *Bird Box*). *Bird Box* had a brief flare of pop cultural notoriety after people started injuring themselves undertaking the so-called Bird Box Challenge, which consisted of attempting to do daily tasks whilst blindfolded à la the characters in the film.

Bird Box is commonly described as Lovecraftian, and not without reason. In the film's unique post-apocalyptic scenario, Earth has been overrun by some entities that drive almost all who see them to madness, followed immediately by suicide, with the exception of the already mentally ill, who become a cult that wishes everyone to see the entities. The film focuses, mixing flashbacks and real-time actions, on the journey of Malorie Hayes and her two children as they attempt to head to an alleged haven whose location is being broadcast on the radio. This must be achieved while blindfolded to avoid sight of the malevolent entities. The film certainly has a Lovecraftian feel, with its unexplained entities, uncaring and unstoppable horrors, and evil, undefined cultists. The only images of the entities, which are associated with unexplained winds not unlike the flying polyps of "The Shadow out of Time," ever seen by the audience are a few briefly glimpsed drawings laid out on a table by a cult member who has infiltrated the main character's safe house. These stark charcoal depictions, which are implied but never clearly stated to be the creatures, are manifestly influenced by interpretations of Lovecraft's created entities, including one that is a patent homage image of Cthulhu. None of this seems accidental, and it is to be expected given the film's pedigree. It is based on the debut novel of the same name by Josh Malerman, who openly admits the influence of Lovecraft on it but at a remove. In an interview question to this effect he stated: "*The Mist* by Stephen King was more or less my introduction to that Lovecraftian 'overlapping of dimensions.' I like Lovecraft, but don't know if I know him well enough to consider him a 'favorite'" (Spiegelman). This admission aside, Malerman's connection to the Lovecraftian milieu was sufficient to include his story "A Fiddlehead Party on Carpenter's Farm" in the Lovecraftian anthology *Shadows over Main Street* (2016).

In the same interview cited above, Malerman also names *Creepshow* (1982) and *Evil Dead* (1981) as among his five favourite scary movies. Both are notable for their indirect influence from Lovecraft without being overly Lovecraftian or channeling the deeper ideas underpinning cosmic horror. Malerman specifically states that a reason for placing *Creepshow* on the list is "because it brought E.C. Comics to life." This connection of comics, and E.C. Comics in particular, to Lovecraft will be explored in a later section. Further cementing the connection of the film *Bird Box* to Lovecraft is screenwriter Eric Heisserer, who has a noted Lovecraftian influence in many of his previous films (Norris 114). But what prevents *Bird Box* from reaching the truest and highest realms of Lovecraftian and cosmic horror is the nature of the unseen entities. They whisper in human voices (near the end of the film Malorie hears the voices as that of her dead lover, another former survivor whose house was their initial refuge) and seem to be manifestations in the form of, or in connection to, the human dead. One character even says "Mom?" upon being exposed to sight of the entities. Such anthropocentric ideas are at odds with the indifferent unimportance of humanity so starkly portrayed in Lovecraft's best works. This doesn't invalidate the Lovecraftian feel much of the film generates, but equally highlights the differences, influences, alterations, and interpretations that occur when translating the ideas of Lovecraft into the medium of film, and the very specific tendency toward anthropocentrism necessary to generate a greater mass market appeal.

Aquaman, however, is a film that wears its inspirations openly, and in surprising ways. The first clue is in its initial setting. In the opening scene the Curry Lighthouse is given a location graphic proclaiming it to be in Amnesty Bay, Maine. While (contrary to the assertions of some in fandom or those seeking to arrogate some of Lovecraft's glamour unto themselves) not all New England locales are innately Lovecraftian, and the setting is reasonably faithful to the comics wherein the location of Amnesty Bay is Massachusetts, this does lead the aware viewer to wonder at the choice in connection with a sentient being from the oceans washing ashore there. However, doubts about such musing are soon dispelled. In two separate camera shots over the coffee table in the Lighthouse the alert viewer sees a paperback edition of *The Dunwich Horror*, first slightly cut off and then in a shot panning up with the spine clearly legible and in the center of frame. Thus, the Lovecraftian connection is transformed from the realm of speculative to definitive.

It is important at this juncture to take a moment to examine some of the background of director James Wan, and after this an examination of a trio of tweets he made in connection with Lovecraft and the production of *Aquaman*. Wan is ethnically Chinese from Malaysia but grew up in Australia after moving there at the age of seven and identifies nationally as Australian. This Australian identity is particularly important to his Hollywood career. His first feature film, co-created with fellow Australian Leigh Whannell,[1] was the extremely successful horror film *Saw* (2004), which has gone on to numerous sequels and more significantly added a new iconic figure in the character of Jigsaw to the horror movie pantheon. The main setting device of the original *Saw* film, with the protagonists trapped in a room with legs secured via metal cuffs and with access to saws only capable of cutting tissue and bone, being forced to choose between mutilation or death inside a specific time limit, is clearly influenced by the end of the iconic Australian film *Mad Max* (1979). This film literally ends with the protagonist, played by Mel Gibson in his first starring role, giving exactly such a choice to the final remaining villain. Thus, Wan is one to wear his influences openly, but equally being altered to his own, often darker, interpretations.

Equally, Wan is not above injecting allusions and filmic references for their own sake. For example, early in the film Thomas Curry, played by celebrated New Zealand actor Temuera Morrison, makes a slight jest about how he was going to cook Atlanna some eggs when he discovers her eating his goldfish. At face value this is simply a minor quip to deal with a potentially uncomfortable situation, which is internally consistent to the film and the character. However, it also a meta-reference instantly recognizable to anyone from New Zealand (and to a lesser extent Australia,

---

1. Who incidentally has a cameo in *Aquaman*.

which has deep cultural and historic ties to its neighbor; significantly, New Zealanders make up the second largest country of origin outside of Australia in the Australian population) (*2016 Census: Multicultural*) to Morrison's previous role as Jake the Muss in the seminal film *Once Were Warriors* (1994). Morrison's line in that film about cooking eggs has, in the arcane way certain moments long survive their creation, become deeply embedded in the cultural landscape of New Zealand. This is so much a part of the public consciousness there that the New Zealand government had Morrison reference it in internal tourism advertisements, while Morrison himself chose to appear in a video for the Women's Refugee 2016 Annual Appeal because of his connection with the character and the infamous line. In *Once Were Warriors* Jake's wife Beth's refusal to cook eggs for Jake's friends results in his brutally attacking her, a depiction of domestic violence that is shocking in its graphic realism. Thus Wan, in choosing to have Morrison as Thomas Curry offer to cook a lady some eggs, subconsciously signals at a deep level to the knowing audience that he is a good person.

In another minor reference the evil doll Annabelle, from *The Conjuring* (2013) and the *Annabelle* series of horror films starting in 2014—Wan was director of the former and the producer of the latter—can be seen briefly in a background shot. Wan clearly enjoys making such allusions and is able, as demonstrated with Thomas's eggs line, to use them to add depth and meaning to scenes as well as amusing but insubstantial references such as Annabelle.

To this end Wan issued a tweet on 4 June 2015, the day he was formally announced as the director of *Aquaman*: "'For ocean is more ancient than the mountains, and freighted with the memories and the dreams of time.'—H. P. Lovecraft" (hashtag #worldcreation). The quotation comes from the conclusion of the third paragraph of "The White Ship." Thus from the very beginning Wan clearly had Lovecraft in mind in his vision for *Aquaman*. (Purists would note that Wan does fail to capitalize "Time" as Lovecraft did in the original, but this really is quibbling, especially as Twitter is not a medium noted for its niceties of grammar.) The chosen quotation is also, relatively speaking, somewhat obscure in the Lovecraftian canon, a 1919 story commonly placed in the category of Dream Cycle stories. It is, to use the pop culture vernacular, somewhat of a deeper cut than might be expected given the more common appropriation of quotations from the *Necronomicon* or move obvious ocean-related tales such as "Dagon," "The Call of Cthulhu," or "The Shadow over Innsmouth." "The White Ship" is perfectly apt thematically and connects well in the main body of the tale with its ideas of fantastic adventure, exotic locales, and strange journeys, all of which abound in the *Aquaman* film. It is also worth noting that "The White Ship" culminates tragically with a wreck upon the shore of a lighthouse ending the adventure, while *Aquaman* starts with a wrecked person cast up upon the same unique building, which becomes a tragedy in time.

Two other tweets by Wan are neither as straightforward nor as complimentary. On 18 December 2018 he was responding to an online article by movie critic Keith Phipps with the rather lurid title "*Aquaman* Owes a Lot to H. P. Lovecraft. It's Also His Worst Nightmare,' with the even more clickbait subheadline "The racist author influenced the DC movie—and would have hated it." The article, as might be reasonably inferred, is rather unflattering to the Old Gent but even it openly admits, "Lovecraft's influence is all over *Aquaman*." To give the piece its due, Phipps mostly adheres to facts and offers more nuance than might have been expected. Concerning Lovecraft's racism he states that "Lovecraft, in other words, just had a habit of saying the quiet part out loud." Yet several glaring repeated exceptions to this nuance occur in which Lovecraft's opinion on something created eighty-one years after his death is somehow definitively stated in the body of the piece as it is in the headlines.

Wan's response concerning Lovecraft's racism was as follows: "I wrestled with this. How much was I willing to lean into this talented xenophobe. I realized I couldn't make an AQM movie without acknowledging his influences on me. So I decided, 'f*ck it, I'm gonna own it.' Have one of my characters quote his work. Which one? . . . Black Manta." He then stated: "For all the reasons you pointed out in your article, AQUAMAN would've been the ultimate horror movie/story for Lovecraft. And I'm OK with that" (Cavanaugh).

So, as is often the case in modern times, Lovecraft's undisputed racism and xenophobia have unfortunately become a central issue in assessing the merit of his work. This monograph does not intend to wade further into this quagmire. Rather, as the topic at hand is the connection between Lovecraft and *Aquaman*, a few salient points concerning Wan's tweets should suffice. The idea posited by Phipps, and carried on in part by Wan, that Lovecraft would have hated *Aquaman* solely for its positive portrayal of mixed race is rather absurd. It likely stems from a false and pernicious perception, promulgated by those with a strong agenda to do so, that Lovecraft spent basically all his time writing stories and being racist.[2] Race certainly was an issue of import to Lovecraft. It is mentioned reasonably frequently in his letters, but it is dwarfed in discussions of other interests, topics, and passions such as antiquarian pursuits, travel, scientific developments, history, or literature, to name but a few. Lovecraft had a great love from childhood of Greek myth and legend, and these commonly invoke mixed-race children of mortals and other beings, of which Aquaman would certain qualify. It is easy to forget, in corporations' modern arrogation to themselves of pre-existing ideas, names, and characters with an eye on copyrightable intellectual property for marketing and merchandise, that Atlantis is a Greek mythological concept wholly invented and initially promulgated by Plato as a meditation on government in his *Dialogues*. It thus seems disingenuous to ascribe to Lovecraft hatred of a film built around mythological ideas and archetypes that he is known to have enjoyed. It is as ridiculous, and as without foundation, as stating Lovecraft would have loved the film because the villainous antagonist Black Manta was portrayed by Yahya Abdul-Mateen II, an American person of colour!

Putting aside reductive arguments about the various opinions of others about what the opinion of someone else might have been, it is worth examining the more tangible connections between *Aquaman* and Lovecraft as presented in the final film. The aforementioned copy of *The Dunwich Horror* is interesting in both

---

2. Perhaps the nadir of such thinking is Donna Haraway's sublimely surreal description of Cthulhu as a "misogynist racial-nightmare monster" in *Environmental Humanities* 6 (2015): 160.

its straightforwardness and subversion. This is one of Lovecraft's better-known stories and its more traditional good-versus-evil monster hunt, which takes up the second half of the tale, makes it more readily accessible than much of Lovecraft's more esoteric and less traditionally formulated works. Much for that same reason it is also divisively viewed in the Lovecraft community, beloved for example by Robert M. Price ("What Roodmas Horror") yet held in low esteem by S. T. Joshi (716). The story been filmed twice under its own title,[3] and referenced in numerous other films such as Lucio Fulci's 1980 *City of the Living Dead* (a.k.a. *The Gates of Hell*). Yet most germane to its inclusion in *Aquaman* is the subversion of the themes of the tale. Arthur Curry is, like Wilbur Whateley and his brother, a child of mixed human and inhuman heritage, yet this miscegenation creates in Arthur a great and worthy hero in the most classical of paradigms. Given the concerns Wan expressed about Lovecraft's xenophobia and his deliberate attempts in the film to propagate against such ideas, *The Dunwich Horror* is well chosen for its juxtaposition in Aquaman's home.

One of the more visually striking elements of *Aquaman* is the creature design of the inhabitants of the Kingdom of the Trench. These beautifully rendered humanoid fish monsters, created by computer-generated imagery (CGI), are both effectively hideous and frightening. In physical aspect they could easily be taken as a visualization of some of the Deep Ones as described in "The Shadow over Innsmouth" and even more so as understood in the post-Lovecraft interpretations of these beings. The audience gets an extended scene of these creatures as they attack the vessel Arthur and Mera are traveling on as they locate The Trench. The overwhelmed heroes must then swim down through a swarm of the monsters, keeping them at bay only with flares. In these moments *Aquaman* ventures directly into an unambiguous horror film, the genre for which Wan is perhaps best known and in which he (pardon the pun) made his bones.

This creature design of the beings from The Trench comes directly, at times almost in shot-for-panel reproduction, from the

---

3. Both versions feature Dean Stockwell.

start of the *New 52 Aquaman* run of comics by Geoff Johns, Ivan Reis, and Joe Prado. The 2011 *New 52* series was designed by DC Comics as a reboot/reimagining/relaunch of all its superhero comics with new first issues, and this connection should come as no surprise as Geoff Johns is also one of the credited "Story by" authors on the *Aquaman* film as a well as an executive producer. Lovecraft has long been an influence in comics, from loose adaptations in 1950s issues of EC Comics' *The Haunt of Fear, Tales from the Crypt,* and *The Vault of Horror* to the emergence of Arkham Asylum as the repository for the Dark Knight's villains in *Batman* #258 (October 1974). This trend has continued in various forms to the present day, with heavy Lovecraftian influence in titles such as *Hellboy* (to which Geoff Johns has contributed as an author, and which series itself has spawned three live-action films) and endless direct adaptations, reimaginings, and Cthulhu Mythos works such as *Fall of Cthulhu, Neonomicon, The Chronicles of Dr. Herbert West,* and *Only the End of the World Again,* to name but a few of the more widely available title.

The monster guarding the Trident of Atlan, the Karathen, is likewise connected to Lovecraft at a remove. The patent resemblance of the name to the mythical Kraken is not a coincidence, and the Tennyson poem "The Kraken" has long being posited by Robert M. Price, following on from Philip A. Shreffler, as a major influence upon "The Call of Cthulhu" (Price, "The Other Name of Azathoth"). As a massive entity of colossal destructive potential dwelling in a ruined city at the bottom of the ocean, who communicates via telepathy and has numerous tentacles, the Karathen might appear at first glance to be an ersatz Cthulhu. She even declares of eating Arthur, "I haven't feasted in aeons and I am famished," even though the bones of other she has eaten are clearly visible and a lesser timespan has passed since the fall of Atlantis. This is likely in homage to Great Cthulhu's infamous hunger upon awakening "after vigintillions of years" (*CF* 2.53), the word aeons getting six separate mentions in "The Call of Cthulhu" alone, including the famous couplet from the *Necronomicon*. Yet while clearly riffing on the tropes of Cthulhu, the Karathen is again somewhat of a subversion. Telepathically voiced by no less an unthreatening and beloved figure as Mary Poppins actress Julie Andrews,[4] she is rational, communicative, and moral. As she decides on Arthur's worthiness to claim the Trident, it is his humbleness that convinces her as much as anything, and she ultimately even chooses to accompany him into battle and acclaims him in dramatic fashion after he claims his title of king.

A less obvious Lovecraft connection is the location of a lost outpost of Atlantean civilization in the Sahara Desert, The Kingdom of the Deserters. This basic idea of Atlantean survivals was a far from infrequent trope in the pulps of Lovecraft's day, and even promulgated as truth in the modern assertions of so-called alternative historians, although the locale is often shifted to a great actual civilization such as in Egypt. In fictional examples Robert E. Howard had the imagined African city of Negari in the Solomon Kane tale "The Moon of Skulls" as a decadent descendant of Atlantis. However, the Lovecraft/Sahara connection is an explicit and demonstrable one. In "The Last Test," a revision tale for Adolphe de Castro, Lovecraft gives us some of the origins of the villain Surama. This dubious person is brought back from "the vaults with your devilish Atlantean secrets" by the misguided Clarendon "after a long stay in Northern Africa, during which he had studied certain odd intermittent fevers among the mysterious Saharan Tuaregs, whose descent from the primal race of lost Atlantis is an old archaeological rumour" (CF 4.63). Later it is made even more unambiguous, with Clarendon declaring: "You ought to hear Surama! I tell you, things were known to the priests of Atlantis that would have you drop dead of fright if you heard a hint of them" (CF 4.91). All this highly pulp flavor is purely Lovecraftian invention. The previous published version of the story, as "A Sacrifice to Science" in *In the Confessional and the Following* (1893), contains none of these elements.

Yet the greatest Lovecraftian connections to *Aquaman* are thematically and literally linked with his ideas of the forces of the depths rising to wipe out humanity. "Dagon" famously states at the near conclusion of the tales the narrator's fears: "I dream of a day when they may rise above the billows to drag down in their

---

4. Interestingly, Julie Andrews turned down a cameo role in *Mary Poppins Returns*, which debuted in direct competition with *Aquaman*. *Returns* was an underperforming success at the box office making $349 million on a $130 million budget.

reeking talons the remnants of puny, war-exhausted mankind—of a day when the land shall sink, and the dark ocean floor shall ascend amidst universal pandemonium" (CF 1.58). Such ideas dovetail well with Orm's ambitions in *Aquaman*, and at one point he launches a warning pseudo-attack on the land by returning millions of tons of garbage dumped into the seas upon the shores of major cities. It is worth remembering that in the DCEU that *Aquaman* is explicitly stated by internal references to events in other films to inhabit, Earth has suffered two catastrophic invasions by aliens in recent times, in *Man of Steel* (2013) and *Justice League* (2017), respectively. These attacks were only repelled by the aid of super-powered beings, and humanity is far from harmonious and not united politically, socially, or militarily. *Justice League* in particular has as a plot point the demoralization of humanity in general after the death of Superman in *Batman vs. Superman: Dawn of Justice* (2016).

As Wan stated in his tweet quoted earlier, Lovecraft gets a direct transcription on to the screen in the form of a villain dialogue. Black Manta, in his first full appearance in his newly made costume, confronts and attacks Aquaman immediately after the latter discovers the heading necessary to find the missing Trident. Literally heralded by an explosion, Black Manta lands triumphantly and exclaims, in a voice distorted by his new suit,[5] "Loathsomeness waits and dreams in the deep, and decay spreads over the tottering cities of men." The alert Lovecraft aficionado will recognize these words as coming from the conclusion of "The Call of Cthulhu," and the connection with *Aquaman's* overarching plot are obvious. Yet this is a particularly apposite tribute for two reasons. Inside the *Aquaman* narrative it is a suitably bombastic, megalomaniacal-sounding line and appears appropriate enough to the character who utters it, thus not causing the casual viewer to be removed from Coleridge's willing suspension of disbelief within the fictional reality created inside the film. Its deeper resonance for those familiar with the seminal Lovecraft work whence it derives also fits with a thematic idea of the hidden perils of the deep ocean, represented by Black Manta and his Atlantean technology

---

5. So distorted in fact that the present author didn't actually fully comprehend what was said until undertaking repeated viewings.

in this act and foreshadowing the hideous nightmare creatures of The Trench, and the subversion of the Karathen, in the next two action scenes. Wan characteristically chose his homage well.

Overall, while it would be a mislabeling to characterize *Aquaman* as a particularly Lovecraftian film, there is a certainly a direct and indirect degree of Lovecraft's influence weaving its way both in the genesis of the film and in some of its more direct final elements. "The Shadow over Innsmouth" also looms large over Amnesty Bay and deep into The Trench, and the resonance of Lovecraft continues to reverberate through the cultural zeitgeist in new and surprising ways.

Works Cited

Aquaman Cthulhu Q Fig Max. *Qmxonline*, qmxonline.com/products/aquaman-cthulhu-q-fig-max

Australian Bureau of Statistics. "2016 Census: Multicultural." www.abs.gov.au/ausstats/abs@.nsf/lookup/Media%20Release3.

"Baby Not on Board." *Family Guy*. Fox, 2 November 2008.

Box Office Mojo. *Aquaman*. www.boxofficemojo.com/movies/?id=dcfilm0617.htm

Bradley, Laura. "A Brief History of Pop Culture Dumping on Aquaman. The Man. The Myth. The Eternal Punchline." *Vanity Fair*. www.vanityfair.com/hollywood/2018/12/aquaman-jokes-family-guy-big-bang-theory-south-park

Cavanaugh, Patrick. "Aquaman Director Comments on Film's H. P. Lovecraft Influence." comicbook.com/dc/2018/12/19/aquaman-h-p-lovecraft-james-wan-comments-influence/

Charara, Sophie. "Netflix Reveals 45 Million Accounts Watched Bird Box in Opening Week." *Forbes*. www.forbes.com/sites/sophiecharara/2018/12/31/netflix-bird-box-views-45-million/#2a67c6791037

"The Deep End." *Robot Chicken*. Adult Swim, 4 October 2005.

Danziger, Gustav Adolphe. *In the Confessional and the Following*. San Francisco: Western Authors Publishing Association, 1893.

Joshi, S. T. *I Am Providence: The Life and Times of H. P. Lovecraft*. New York: Hippocampus Press, 2010. 2 vols.

Kendall, G. "How The Animated Justice League Erased Super Friends' Aquaman." CBR.com. https://www.cbr.com/how-animated-justice-league-saved-aquaman/

Lawrence, Derek. "Revisiting the Original Aquaman Movie with Entourage Creator Doug Ellin." *Entertainment Weekly*. ew.com/tv/2018/12/17/aquaman-entourage-doug-ellin/

Mad Max. George Miller, director. Roadshow Films, 1979.

Melrose, Kevin. "Geoff Johns to Write New Aquaman Series." CBR.com. www.cbr.com/geoff-johns-to-write-new-aquaman-series/

Norris, Duncan. "Lovecraft and Arrival: The Quiet Apocalypse." *Lovecraft Annual* No. 11 (2017): 110–17.

Once Were Warriors. Lee Tamahori, director. Fine Line Features, 1994.

Phipps, Keith. "Aquaman Owes a Lot to H. P. Lovecraft. It's Also His Worst Nightmare." slate.com/culture/2018/12/aquaman-movie-hp-lovecraft-racism-miscegenation.html

Pulliam-Moore, Charles. "Entourages Version of the Aquaman Movie Was Surprisingly on Point." *Gizmodo*. www.gizmodo.com.au/2018/09/entourages-version-of-the-aquaman-movie-hype-was-surprisingly-on-point/

Price, Robert M. "What Roodmas Horror." In *The Dunwich Cycle: Where the Old Gods Wait*, ed. Robert E. Price. Oakland, CA: Chaosium, 1995. ix–xii.

———. "The Other Name of Azathoth." In *The Cthulhu Cycle: Thirteen Tentacles of Terror*, ed. Robert M. Price. Oakland, CA: Chaosium, 1996. vii–xvi.

Rotten Tomatoes. *Aquaman*. www.rottentomatoes.com/m/aquaman_2018

———. *Bird Box*. www.rottentomatoes.com/m/bird_box

———. *Wonder Woman*. www.rottentomatoes.com/m/wonder_woman_2017

Spiegelman, Ian. "Author Josh Malerman Is More Stoker Than Lovecraft." *USA Today*. www.usatoday.com/story/life/books/2014/06/13/why-bird-box-author-josh-malerman-is-more-stoker-than-lovecraft/10379935/

How to Read Lovecraft

A Column by Steven J. Mariconda

Number 3: Play and the Eternal Youth

In previous installments of "How to Read Lovecraft," we looked at the young Lovecraft's penchant for scenario-based play, his tendency to theatricality, and his fondness for the performative. When he turned to literary creation, he perpetuated a similar posture in his written work—creating a "frame" that included a setting, the objects within that setting (i.e., props), and certain explicit and implicit rules or boundaries—and then undertook to formulate the adventures that took place within those boundaries. We also noted that the Cthulhu Mythos itself may be seen as an extension of Lovecraft's childhood paracosm, a complex and deeply felt imaginative universe. In this installment I will examine Lovecraft's psychology and how it underpins his sense of playfulness in art.

At the present critical moment, it is unfashionable to consider the author outside the text, and to pull in biographical information to support the explication of the work. My own position is that the most appropriate manner in which to approach Lovecraft is to focus on the text itself, and only on the text. I am a believer in close reading, and have found a great deal of insight in studying Lovecraft using this approach.

However, the critical needle between pure formalism and historical-biographical criticism tends to oscillate. It can also be helpful to elucidate Lovecraft in light of his personal experiences. He is among the most biographical of writers. This seems an odd claim to make, given that he is a writer of weird fiction. But he was so much in his own fiction that it is practically impossible to extricate the man from the work. Not only is there literal biography (that is to say, specific details from the actual material life of Lovecraft) in the fiction; the author's intellectual-emotional life is documented there even more vividly than it is documented in his many letters. In many ways, his work can be considered his own intellectual imaginative biography. This is where he lived life—in the imagination.

With this caveat I would now like to examine a facet of Lovecraft's personality that is at the root of his playful artistic posture. In the next installment I will look specifically at the fictional texts for hints of Lovecraft's playfulness.

Readers of Lovecraft's letters will recognize an unusual trait of the author, in that he constantly harkens back to his childhood, specifically between 1893 and 1908. Lovecraft was a remarkably precocious youth and seemed to be fully aware and fully formed as a personality by the age of four. He had what amounted to an eidetic memory going back to that age. As a toddler, he appeared to have many of the imaginative-emotional characteristics that he would carry with him throughout his life. He reiterates this over and over in the letters.

Specifically, in a series of letters to J. Vernon Shea, Lovecraft notes that his personality (more properly, his persona) was largely in place by the age of three or four, and that by the age of seventeen or eighteen he had basically become fully himself intellectually and imaginatively. Lovecraft was born old, one might say. He had cemented his interests in classical mythology, astronomy and the sciences, the weird, and New England history and culture. These were the imaginative materials that he worked as an adult.

In certain letters, particularly to Maurice W. Moe, Lovecraft casts his mind back to periods around the turn of the century and creates word-pictures of the cultural milieu at that moment. These reminiscences take the form of long paragraphs with phrases separated by ellipses. They present a kind of a kaleidoscopic or imagistic view of that particular historical moment in time. They are remarkably detailed and almost uncanny in their prescience.

> Good old '06! Not a bad year, but getting too near modernity to have the fullest charm. That's the year I first broke into print—monthly astronomy articles etc. Also, the year I got my present telescope. Providence Journal moving into its new building . . . . . little old open cars (converted horse-cars!) still on a few of the local lines, but a legislative act passed requiring vestibules on the closed cars . . . . . had a fine new grey suit and ruin'd it the first day

I wore it, in a spill from my bike on Irving Ave. hill in September ..... but after all, only the trousers got the worst of it, and the tailor did a marvellous job on the right knee. Damn the slipping handlebars that caused it! ..... Oh, yes, and '06 was the year I tried out an acetylene bike lamp instead of my old oil one ..... Hope St. High School ..... back in September despite the breakdown which took me out the preceding spring ..... pleasant new physics-teacher—Brown student named H. W. Congdon ..... wonder where he is now? ..... getting interested in chemistry—my old specialty of '99—again—new laboratory down cellar in 598 Angell like the old one at 454 ..... fitting up a summerhouse and landskip garden in the vacant lot next the house ..... San Francisco earthquake ..... theatre (New Park) opened with nothing but biograph pictures, hitherto us'd only to chase late lingerers out of Keith's—illustrated songs— "When the Whippoorwill Sings, Marguerite" ..... "When the Mocking-Bird is Singing in the Wildwood" ..... "A Picnic for Two" ..... "She Waits by the Deep Blue Sea" ..... "If the Man in the Moon was a Coon" ..... "The Moon Has His Eyes on You" ..... Belasco's "Darling of the Gods" gets around to the local stock company ..... wonder what's become of the guy that play'd the hero? ..... Sayonara! Sayonara! ..... his name was William Ingersoll, and he was no youth even then ..... Another theatre with nothing but Biograph films ..... the Scenic—made over from the old Westminster Unitarian Church in Mathewson St., and gawd damn the vandal who took down the marvellous Ionick portico—Providence's closest approach to the Parthenon—to make way for that cursed foyer with the cheap electric sign! This dump has an Orchestra—not merely a piano like the New Park. Leader is a fat little fiddler named Charley Miller ..... wonder if he's alive now? New illustrated song howled by a duet—"Aren't You Coming Back to Old New Hampshire, Molly?"[1]

These memories seem to have more emotional charge for Lovecraft than do the circumstances of his present day. There is a vitality about these passages that is quite remarkable and bespeaks a direct connection to a deeper consciousness.

I am proposing here that the adult Lovecraft, by virtue of heredi-

---

1. Lovecraft to Maurice W. Moe, 29 July 29 1929; p. 190.

tary sensitivity but most forcefully the environment of his childhood, was under the sway of a Puer/Senex complex. Puer and Senex are from the Latin for "child" and "old man." Puer and Senex are what Carl Gustav Jung called archetypes—the archaic, primordial images present in the collective unconscious and common to the psychic makeup of all human beings. They are inherited potentials that are actualized when they enter consciousness as images, or manifest in behavior on interaction with the outside world (Stevens 77). The contradictory tendencies of Puer and Senex are ultimately interdependent, forming two faces of a single psychological complex, each a shadow side of the other.

The playful nature of Lovecraft flows from the dominance of the Puer Aeternus, or "eternal child." According to the prominent Jungian Marie-Louise von Franz, "The man who is identified with the archetype of the Puer Aeternus remains too long in adolescent psychology; that is, all those characteristics that are normal in the us at 17 or 18 are continued until later life, coupled in most cases with to create a dependence on the mother" (1).

One immediately recognizes Lovecraft in this description. Von Franz continues:

> Great difficulties [are] experienced in adaptation to the social situation. In some cases, there is a kind of a social individualism: being something special, one has no need to adapt, for that would be impossible for such a hidden genius, and so on. In addition, an arrogant attitude arises towards other people, due to both an inferiority complex and false feelings of superiority. . . . The one situation dreaded throughout by such a type of man is to be bound to anything whatsoever. (von Franz 2)

Readers of Lovecraft's biography will be familiar with his similar foibles, as well as his disinclination to be pinned down to a career or marriage. Most importantly for our purpose, the Puer Aeternus puts the conscious creative mind in close touch with the collective unconscious—subject to archetypal representations, and inclined to play:

> The childhood life is the fantasy life, the artists life. He believes that this childhood life is the true life, and all the rest is empty persona running after money, making a prestige impression on other

people, having lost one's true nature, so to speak. That is how he sees adult life, for he has not found a bridge by which he could take over what we call the true life into adult life. (van Franz 12–13)

American psychologist James Hillman echoes these concepts: "The Puer Aeternus displays an aesthetic point of view: the world is beautiful images or is a vast scenario. Life becomes literature, and adventure of intellect or science, or of religion or action, but always a weighted and their psychological" (Hillman 49).

Hillman points out another aspect of the Puer Aeternus archetype that seems to reinforce the notion that it dominated Lovecraft's psychological makeup. The Puer Aeternus has a special relation in form with the Senex archetype. They are, if you will, "a two-headed archetype, or a *Janus-gestalt*" (Hillman 35).

> Senex is the archetypal image for the wise old man, or solitary sage. . . . His temperament is cold and distant, he views the world from outside. Is concerned with structure and abstraction makes him the principle of order, whether through time, or hierarchy, or exact science and system. . . . His intellectual qualities include the inspired genius of the brooding melancholic, creativity through contemplation, deliberation in the exact sciences and mathematics. (Hillman 38–40)

Representations of the Senex include Father, Elder, Mentor, and Wise Old Man. The Senex archetype makes the individual seem wise beyond his years, ambitious for recognition by seniors, and intolerant of his own [chronological] youthfulness Hillman 45).

Readers of the letters will immediately note the congruence of the Senex with another aspect of Lovecraft personality that is eccentric, and that has often been remarked upon. Beginning in his twenties, Lovecraft considered himself an old man and adopted this as a persona. He would refer to his elderly aunts as "my darling daughters" and his colleagues as "my grandsons."[2] He had numerous protégés much younger than he and took great delight in

---

2. HPL actually signs himself "Theobaldus Senex" in several letters to James F. Morton, Edward Cole, Wilfred Talman, and Maurice W. Moe; see for example HPL to Moe, Oct. 30 1731 [i.e., 1931]; *Letters to Maurice W. Moe and Others*, ed. David E. Schultz and S. T. Joshi (New York, Hippocampus Press, 2018), p. 276.

mentoring them and promoting them to others as his adoptive grandchildren. The extent to which Lovecraft did this at times seems almost pathological, raising question about what his motives were. In some circles this behavior has created speculation that Lovecraft was either a homosexual or a latent homosexual. (The most famous example is when he adopted thirteen-year-old Robert Barlow as a "protégé" after the young man sent him a fan letter. Lovecraft was thirty-three and Barlow was sixteen when the former went to Florida and stayed with him in a cabin on a lake island for most of six weeks. He repeated the trip the following summer with the same modus operandi. This behavior is baffling and even borderline disturbing—but becomes perfectly comprehensible in the Puer/Senex schema.)

I think Lovecraft's notion that he fundamentally remained the youth of the early 1900s on the one hand, and that he was the grandfather of his young protégés on the other, is perfectly accommodated by applying the concepts of Jung. The twinned archetype of the Puer/Senex represents a single coin with two sides. On the one side the Puer is the eternal youth. On the other side the Senex is the wise old man. It is clear on reflection that this characterizes Lovecraft self-image.

For our purpose of examining Lovecraft's playfulness, let us consider the concept of the Puer Aeternus in greater detail. The Puer Aeternus, as noted, is the eternal youth and is associated with creativity and in particular with playfulness. This is where it ties in with our thesis. At a very young age Lovecraft established a way of being, psychologically and imaginatively, where he created a world for himself and found in that world a kind of a happiness, a way to live in the face of the many unfortunate incidents of his youth.

We need not rehearse in detail the serious difficulties Lovecraft faced in his first eighteen years. Firstly, his father had a violent breakdown due to the effects of incipient syphilis and was confined in a mental institution less than a mile from his home. This happened when Lovecraft was three years old. I find it very likely that the curious and hyperaware Lovecraft, although perhaps not familiar with the specifics of this terrible situation, was mindful of whispered conversations and a negative affect in the household, and that he acquired a deep sense of alienation and shame as a result. He knew something was deeply wrong, and perhaps suspected that it had something to do with him. He possibly had a sense of guilt and fear around the circumstances, as no doubt conversations had to be conducted in the home regarding the handling of his father's affairs and the unstable state of his father's health. His father was conscious during the five years prior to his death and was regularly consumed by fits of violence.

Subsequent to this, there were several deaths in the household; and ultimately the Lovecraft family benefactor Whipple Phillips died of a stroke, apparently in the home. At that point to the household had to be dissolved, and Lovecraft was moved from a large Victorian mansion to a duplex home only three squares away. He had an incredible sense of loss about this, and it marked him permanently.[3] Concurrently his mother was becoming mentally unstable and apparently progressing to schizophrenia.

However, for our focus we need to look at how Lovecraft found a way to be a child, how he found a way to exist in the world during this difficult developmental period. He did not socialize well, but found solace in several things. First of all, in the form of the imagination—reading the *Arabian Nights,* Grimm's fairy tales, ancient mythology, and similar fare. Secondly, by creating a kind of a world for himself. We have seen in an earlier installment how he enjoyed setting up dioramas on a tabletop, and playing out long threads of plot over weeks at a time. Similarly, he set up an outdoor play area, like a life-size diorama, which he called New Anvik after a village in a boy's book. He here manipulated imagined trains and buildings and acted out different scenarios of detective and war and so forth in the setting. When he moved to his new residence the age of fourteen, he re-created this play area and the vacant lot next to his home. He was playing like

---

3. The strength of HPL's childhood persona and the depth with which he identified with his environment reflected by a comment to Shea in a later letter in which he recounts the loss of his home: "I felt that I had lost my entire adjustment to the cosmos—for what indeed was HPL without the remembered rooms & hallways & hangings & staircases & statuary & paintings . . . & yard & walks & cherry-trees & fountain & ivy-grown arch & stable & gardens & all the rest? How could an old man of 14 (& I surely felt that way!) readjust his existence to a skimpy flat & new household programme & inferior outdoor setting in which almost nothing familiar remained?" (4 February 1934; *Letters to J. Vernon Shea* 221).

this until the age of eighteen, when he realized he was getting too old and he had to turn the setup over to another boy.

Von Franz puts it this way in the context of the Puer Aeternus: "The essence of play is that it has no visible meaning and is not useful. I think that nobody can really develop the inferior [psychological] function before having first created a ... Sacred Grove, a hidden place where he can play" (103).

In terms of writing, we need to go back to Lovecraft juvenilia to see how writing became an imaginative haven for him and became a kind of locus (or figurative "Sacred Grove") in which he could play. It was not just his writing of the material, but also his humble attempts to publish it to his small circle of family members. A friend of Lovecraft recalled:

> As a boy, not yet nine years old, he had published *The Scientific Gazette*, a weekly periodical devoted to chemistry, which was written in pencil and issued in editions of four carbon copies. This appeared from March, 1899, to February, 1904. A second venture, *The Rhode Island Journal of Astronomy*, began as a weekly in 1903 and ended as a monthly in 1907. It was printed in hand-lettering, duplicated on the hectograph and issued in lots of twenty-five copies. (Kleiner 51)

Lovecraft would then distribute these copies to his relatives, and apparently would even mail copies to certain relatives who were not to located in Providence. Thus, at a very early age, he had an imaginative platform and posture. And he wrote from the beginning primarily as a means to amuse himself and as a means to play.

These early periodicals are the work of a child, but show Lovecraft projecting his consciousness into a space where he can be both serious and humorous, and where it was completely up to him how the tone and tenor would mix. Ostensibly, he played it straight with very formal titles like the *Rhode Island Journal of Astronomy*. And much of the content was intended to be straightforward and scientific. However, within the space there were areas for play. He would often insert inside jokes that would only be relevant to members of the family. He also would run advertisements for his other activities both real and imagined. And in these advertisements he had room to come up with other whimsies and inside jokes.

It is important to emphasize the *sheer volume* of output that the boy Lovecraft created with his publications over the period of, say, 1898 to 1908. He had a total of three publications that had long runs. These were scientific: the *Rhode Island Journal of Astronomy, Astronomy* (a.k.a. *The Monthly Almanack*), and the *Scientific Gazette*. At times he issued these periodicals *daily*. Sometimes the dailies extended through a sequence of consecutive days into months at a stretch. Not only would he run at least one of these periodicals as a daily, on any given day he might be writing and publishing one or even two of the others *in parallel*. Interspersed with this incredible output were many point-in-time efforts that included "booklets" of poetry, fiction, and essays on other topics.[4]

He therefore learned how to stay occupied and engaged, in a rather strangely adaptive way. As von Franz says regarding the Puer Aeternus:

> If you are inventive enough, you can always avoid boredom if you know how to put yourself into reality. One puts one's spontaneous fantasy into reality, and then boredom is gone forever. Then life can be agreeable or disagreeable, exciting or not, but it is certainly not boring anymore. So boredom is a symptom of life being dammed up—that one does not know how to get what one has within oneself into reality. If one knows how to play, boredom goes. (62)

Lovecraft was writing for an audience that included primarily himself. He found a way to amuse himself and he found a way to take his lived experience and reflect in the manuscripts he was creating. It would appear that it mattered to him little whether anyone else actually read these periodicals, or whether they commented on them or understood either the serious content or the inside jokes that were included.

The adult Lovecraft believed the fundamentals of his personality were fully in place during this period. At the age of forty-six, he wrote to James F. Morton: "Hell, I was an old-timer thirty years ago! I printed papers by hand in pencil in 1899 & probably before—& I began hectographing the *Rhode-Island Journal of Astronomy* early in 1905" (*Letters to James F. Morton* 381).

Many other statements in Lovecraft's letters confirm that he was psychologically in the grip of the Puer archetype: To J. Vernon

---

4. A good survey of the timing and extent of the juvenilia is in Joshi and Schultz 132–35.

Shea, he makes some of his most explicit and startling statements in this direction:

> Fundamentally, I have never changed. At 3½ I was listening avidly to fairy-tales & witch-stories, feeling a strange awe & kinship with the old houses on the hill, dragging my mother around to queer street vistas, exulting in old farmhouses & ancient landscapes & spectral wooded ravines . . . . . & I'll be damned if my basic interests & major pursuits are a bit different now! . . . It is as if my fascination with the idea of time had had some effect on my personality, so that *all the years I have lived or shall ever live are as a single point in my consciousness.* (*Letters to J. Vernon Shea* 192–93)

Later he continues even more emphatically:

> I am perhaps the only living being to retain the feelings & images of the lost boys' world of 1900. The others who knew it in its physical day have become other persons with minds filled with other images & perspectives—& the modern boys who could duplicate its psychology live in a world so different that their imagination cannot bridge the gap. But I remain—one who was a boy in 1900, & to whom the long years have brought no lotos-blooms of oblivion & no prisms of altered mood & vision. (*Letters to J. Vernon Shea* 194)

Finally, we come to the matter of how Lovecraft's inherent sense of playfulness, borne in part from the Puer Aeternus, manifested itself in his mature fiction. Not much critical work has been done in this area, but as usual S. T. Joshi is in the vanguard. Joshi establishes that Lovecraft did not favor the use of overt humor in the weird tale. It is true that Lovecraft rarely created an atmosphere of whimsy in his narratives by intent. (The exceptions are some of the Dunsanian tales.) But Joshi finds a significant amount of humor in the tales in three distinct forms—puns, in-jokes, and satire. Joshi notes that puns are more prevalent in those tales which Lovecraft did not write for immediate publication—that is, tales he wrote solely for his own amusement. In particular, he cites *The Case of Charles Dexter Ward* and *The Dream Quest of Unknown Kadath* (309). Both were written in 1927, after Lovecraft reverted to his youthful "Puer Aeternus" mode upon his return to Providence from New York.

When Joshi comes to the point of discussing what the purpose of Lovecraft's humor, he identifies multiple motives. Puns, he says, indicate Lovecraft fascination with language, while in-jokes are consistent with Lovecraft's concepts of uncommercial and amateur writing (again, writing solely for his own amusement). Joshi states that "Lovecraft never consciously intended his tales to appeal to a wide audience, and employing these in-jokes he was wilfully restricting still further the number of those who could fully understand his tales." Then he zeroes in on the most important point for our forthcoming examination of Lovecraft's tales: "In many cases the in-jokes could be comprehended only by his very closest associates, and *in not a few cases it is likely that they could be comprehended only by Lovecraft himself*" (319; emphasis added). In the next installment, I posit that *"in not a few cases"* can be strengthened to *"in almost all cases"* Lovecraft was playing in a way he only could appreciate.

Works Cited

Hillman, James. *Senex and Puer.* James Hillman Uniform Edition, Volume 3. Washington, DC: Spring Publications, 2005.

Joshi, S. T. "Humor and Satire in Lovecraft." In *Lovecraft and a World in Transition: Collected Essays on H. P. Lovecraft.* New York: Hippocampus Press, 2014. 308–21.

———, and David E. Schultz. *An H. P. Lovecraft Encyclopedia.* Westport CT: Greenwood Publishing Group, 2001.

Kleiner, Rheinhart. "Howard Phillips Lovecraft." 1936. In H. P. Lovecraft, *Letters to Rheinhart Kleiner.* New York: Hippocampus Press, 2005. 251–55.

Lovecraft, H. P. *Juvenilia, 1895–1905.* Ed. S. T. Joshi. West Warwick RI: Necronomicon Press, 1984.

———. *Letters to J. Vernon Shea, Carl F. Strauch, and Lee McBride White.* Ed. S. T. Joshi and David E. Schultz. New York: Hippocampus Press, 2018.

———. *Letters to Maurice W. Moe and Others.* Ed. David E. Schultz and S. T. Joshi. New York: Hippocampus Press, 2018.

Stevens, Anthony. "The Archetypes." In *The Handbook of Jungian Psychology: Theory, Practice and Applications,* ed. Renos K. Papadopoulos. Abington, UK: Routledge, 2012. 74–93.

Von Franz, Marie-Luise. *Puer Aeternus.* Boston, MA: Sigo Press, 1981.

Reviews

S. T. JOSHI AND DAVID E. SCHULTZ, eds. *Ave atque Value: Reminiscences of H. P. Lovecraft.* West Warwick RI: Necronomicon Press, 2018. 502 pp. $49.95 hc [o.p.], $29.95 tpb. Reviewed by Kenneth W. Faig, Jr.

The title of this collection derives from the title of the article that Edward H. Cole published about his late friend H. P. Lovecraft in his amateur journal, the *Olympian* (Autumn 1940). In fact, Cole's memoir (which appends an exclamation point to its title) leads off the present collection. Cole was not the only memoirist to reference classical antiquity in his tribute; fellow amateur journalist Ernest A. Edkins published "O Artemidorus, Farewell!" in his *Causerie* in 1937, referencing a second-century C.E. writer who left an extant work on the interpretation of dreams.

I must confess that fifty-five years ago, as a beginning student of Latin, I pondered over why one might wish to say "Hail and Farewell" all in one phrase—it seemed liked saying hello and goodbye all at once. However, that modern font of wisdom Wikipedia informs me that the phrase comes from Poem 101 of Catullus, wherein he addresses his dead brother: "Atque in perpetuum frater ave atque vale."

The loss of Howard Phillips Lovecraft in the late winter of 1937 came as a surprise to all but a few of his wide circle of friends and correspondents. Almost immediately, these friends and correspondents began to offer tributes to their departed colleague—some very brief, others consequential. Sometimes, of course, brief, straightforward recollections prove the best. Writing in his memoir "Caverns Measureless to Man" of his first tribute to Lovecraft published in *Weird Tales* in 1937, Kenneth Sterling stated: "I see no reason to change a word."

The first of Lovecraft's friends to compose a substantial memoir of the late author was W. Paul Cook, who self-published his *In*

Memoriam: Howard Phillips Lovecraft—Recollections, Appreciations, Estimates in 1941. Cook's memoir—probably most famous for Mrs. Winslow Church's recollection of the young Lovecraft's having endeavored to set a fire exactly one foot by one foot—was reprinted for wider circulation in the Arkham House omnibus *Beyond the Wall of Sleep* as early as 1943. However, Lovecraft's earliest true biographer was probably Winfield Townley Scott, whose essay "His Own Most Fantastic Creation: Howard Phillips Lovecraft" was printed in Arkham House's volume of Lovecraft miscellany, *Marginalia*, in 1944. Other friends followed Cook in penning substantial memoirs of Lovecraft—perhaps most notably Frank Belknap Long in *Howard Phillips Lovecraft: Dreamer on the Night Side* (Arkham House, 1975). Others have followed Scott as biographers of Lovecraft, most notably L. Sprague de Camp in *Lovecraft: A Biography* (Doubleday, 1975) and S. T. Joshi in *H. P. Lovecraft: A Life* (Necronomicon Press, 1996). An expanded two-volume edition of the latter work was published as *I Am Providence: The Life and Times of H. P. Lovecraft* (Hippocampus Press, 2010).

Peter Cannon edited an earlier collection of memoirs of Lovecraft, *Lovecraft Remembered* (Arkham House, 1998), still available from the original publisher at this writing (2018). Cannon organized his collection of memoirs according to his identifications of the writers—neighbors, amateurs, Kalems, ladies, professionals, fans, and critics. Cannon prefaced each grouping of memoirs with a short essay. Joshi and Schultz cover much of the same ground as Cannon, although they have adopted a different method of organization and a different set of admission criteria. First and foremost, they have insisted upon a biographical focus—therefore, none of the articles included in Cannon's "Critics" section have been admitted to *Ave atque Vale*. Secondly, they have insisted that the memoir-writer have had a personal connection with Lovecraft—if not an in-person acquaintance, at least an acquaintance by correspondence. So, by way of example, Winfield Townley Scott virtually wrote his own exclusion verdict for his memoir "His Own Most Fantastic Creation":[1]

---

1. Joshi and Schultz have admitted to their collection a remarkable letter written to Scott by HPL's erstwhile neighbor Clara Hess. Miss Hess first met HPL's mother in the home of Whipple Phillips's cousin Theodore W. Phillips at 612

I did not know Lovecraft; I doubt if I ever saw him—for persons who only saw him remember him perfectly well all these years afterward. There was that memorable oddity. For ten years I lived a few blocks from him, yet I recall no knowledge of his existence until, posthumously, the news began to seep back from Sauk City, Wisconsin. (*Lovecraft Remembered* 8)

Secondly, rather than trying to adhere to Cannon's groupings, Joshi and Schultz have grouped their memoirs in rough chronological order, beginning with overviews and then covering in order childhood and early adulthood (1890–1922), early professional career (1923–30), and later years (1931–37), before concluding with sections of brief (prose) tributes and poetic tributes. Of course, no classification system is infallible, and some of the memoirs collected by Joshi and Schultz do cross over the assigned chronological groupings. However, their method of organization does facilitate a reading from the chronological perspective ordinarily adopted by a biographer.

In the overview section of *Ave atque Vale*, the memoirs by W. Paul Cook and Sonia Davis are certainly the stand-outs. Joshi and Schultz follow the Necronomicon Press text for Davis's principal memoir, based on the original manuscript. To some extent, Mrs. Davis wrote her memoir as a rebuttal to Cook's memoir, particularly as to the alleged penury of Lovecraft's life following their separation at the end of 1924 and the circumstances surrounding his return to Providence in 1926. The whole truth of Lovecraft's finances will probably never be known, and S. T. Joshi's fact-based account in *I Am Providence* is probably our best guide. That Sonia paid most or all of Lovecraft's rent and some of his other living expenses during his residence at 169 Clinton Street in Brooklyn would not surprise me. The extent to which this regime still applied following Lovecraft's return to Providence seems more doubtful. Sonia would surely have discontinued her financial support after Lovecraft informed her (falsely) that they had been divorced in the spring of 1929. In fact, Lovecraft never signed and filed the divorce decree, so that he was considered to be a married

---

Angell Street. She notes that Susie's eccentricity increased with age and includes a poignant vignette of a confused Mrs. Lovecraft's embarrassing her on the Butler Avenue streetcar.

man when his 1912 will was filed for probate by his executor Albert A. Baker in 1937.

All in all, Joshi and Schultz have added about a dozen memoirs not found in Cannon—most of them short. One notable item in both books is Will Murray's interview with Harry Kern Brobst, which first appeared in *Lovecraft Studies* (Fall 1990).[2] Lovecraft's close relationship with Brobst, who worked as a psychiatric nurse in Providence during most of the period 1932–37, provides an example of his ability to form friendships outside his circle of amateur journalists and weird fiction aficionados. Brobst depicts Lovecraft's narrow living circumstances in his room at 10 Barnes Street: his coat hung on a peg outside his room, his room dusty and his bed linen dirty, the only nourishment evident being some cheese. Lovecraft probably had no running water in his room and relied upon the bathroom and kitchen down the hallway. His room did have tiny alcoves that he used for his bed and for the oil-fueled heater he used both for cooking and for supplementary heating. Whether he had a small closet or relied upon an armoire to store his suits and other clothing is unknown to me. Perhaps his humble circumstances at 10 Barnes Street help to explain why Lovecraft shied away from meeting Providence literary columnists Bertrand K. Hart and Winfield Townley Scott. Embarrassment about his marital problems may also have contributed to his preference for keeping a low profile in his native city. Brobst caught two glimpses of Lovecraft's elder aunt Mrs. Clark, who lived upstairs at 10 Barnes Street, when he called in Lovecraft's absence, but Lovecraft never introduced her to his friend because of her invalidism. Mrs. Clark died on 3 July 1932.

Particularly striking is Brobst's account of his visit to Lovecraft at Jane Brown Memorial Hospital on 14 March 1937, the day before Lovecraft died.[3] With the assistance of a nurse, Lovecraft was

---

2. The interview appears in abridged form in the "Fans" section of *Lovecraft Remembered* (pp. 385–95) under the title "Autumn in Providence: Harry K. Brobst on Lovecraft," with Murray's original questions replaced by explanatory text. The interview is published in *Ave atque Vale* as it originally appeared in *Lovecraft Studies*.

3. In *I Am Providence* (2008), Joshi dates the Brobsts' visit to HPL at Jane Brown Memorial Hospital to 13 March 1937, not 14 March. Mrs. Gamwell doubtless continued to visit her nephew daily. Joshi dates HPL's stomach tap to the day before his death.

using a urinal when Brobst first entered his room, and requested that his friend leave until he was finished with this necessity. That Lovecraft was still urinating less than twenty-four hours before his death bespeaks the vitality that was still left in the man. I wonder if he died the following morning at 7:15 A.M. with a loud death rattle. Such a death is often characteristic of a life cut tragically short. The day before he died, Lovecraft spoke to his friend Brobst of his terrible pain; Brobst was able to elicit a faint smile only when he reminded Lovecraft of the ancient philosophers who faced death with stoic calm.

The memoirs by early friends and neighbors gathered by Joshi and Schultz do emphasize Lovecraft's oddity as a young man. Harold W. Munro wrote of the neighborhood girls who were scared of Lovecraft, while Brobst told of a former classmate who recalled the terrible nervous tics that eventually forced Lovecraft's withdrawal from high school. Joshi and Schultz have admitted to their compilation L. Sprague de Camp's account of his 1975 interview with the aged Rev. John T. Dunn, Lovecraft's erstwhile companion in the Providence Amateur Press Club (1914–16). (I wonder whether de Camp's tape-recorded interview with Dunn on 20–21 May 1975, survives in the archive of his works in the Harry Ransom Center at the University of Texas at Austin.[4] The full interview might reveal additional details of interest.) Dunn recalled Lovecraft's formal speech and stilted manner and how some of the club members made fun of him out of his presence. Even Rheinhart Kleiner recalled Lovecraft's "extreme formality of manner" as a young man. Overall, the Providence Amateur Press Club was a fairly long-lived group, and lady members Caroline Miller and Eugenie Kern were also still living when de Camp interviewed Dunn. It would have been interesting to have a feminine recollection of the early Lovecraft, although it is possible that Miller and Kern, late in their lives, would not have remembered him.[5] Of the females associated with the club, only Sarah "Sadie"

---

4. The Howard Gotblieb Archival Research Center at Boston University also contains a collection of de Camp's works.

5. This despite Winfield Townley Scott's dictum that everyone who ever met HPL in person recalled him. When L. Sprague de Camp hosted a dinner for the Providence Lovecraftians at the Minden Hotel in 1975, the waiter unexpectedly

Henry—the sister of member William A. Henry and eleven years Lovecraft's senior—was interested enough in him to make a teasing telephone call to his home to ask for a date.[6] Of the females who early encountered Lovecraft, both Sarah Henry and Eugenie Kern remained single for their entire lifetimes.

Winifred Virginia Jackson and Sonia Haft Greene—the female amateur journalists whose names are most often linked with Lovecraft—were also considerably older than he. Myrta Alice (Little) Davies (1888–1967) may have been the only close contemporary of Lovecraft whose name has been linked romantically with his. As for Lovecraft as lover, we have only Sonia Davis's testimony that her husband was "adequately excellent" in that department. When angry, she told him that he loved cats more than human beings. Of course, speculation over Lovecraft's oddity in his earlier years is likely to continue. Todd R. Livesey's remarkable essay "A Consanguineous Union: Incest Imagery in Lovecraft," arguing that Lovecraft may have been sexually abused by his mother, published only in part in the EOD amateur press association, deserves wider circulation. Winfield Townley Scott quoted psychiatrist F. J. Farnell (who later lived in Lovecraft's erstwhile home at 598 Angell Street) regarding a "psycho-sexual contact" between mother and son (*Lovecraft Remembered* 16).

The memoirs collected by Joshi and Schultz differ in consequentiality and sophistication. Some friends of Lovecraft wrote most eloquently as critics, rather than memoirists. Certainly, Fritz Leiber's critical essays "A Literary Copernicus" (*Something about Cats*, 1949) and "Through Hyperspace with Brown Jenkin" (*The Dark Brotherhood*, 1966) far outshine anything he wrote by way of biographical tribute or memoir. However, the specialist in Lovecraft's biography will find much to glean in the memoirs collected by Joshi and Schultz. I will cite only a few examples.

1. Sonia Davis writes of two fifty-pound scrapbooks—probably

---

told those present that he used to see HPL on the street all the time.
6. HPL replied that he would have to ask his mother for permission, and never got back to Miss Henry. Much as Susie Lovecraft might have been concerned about the contemporary young working-class women who belonged to the Providence Amateur Press Club, imagine her horror at a thirty-five-year-old working woman's appearing on her doorstep at 598 Angell Street for a date with her twenty-four-year-old son.

an exaggeration as regards weight—kept by her husband for cuttings of his newspaper astronomy columns, perhaps including even the lost *Pawtuxet Valley Gleaner* columns of 1907–08. These scrapbooks have apparently not survived unless they remain in private hands.

2. Early amateur colleague Andrew Francis Lockhart—who like John T. Dunn was imprisoned for resisting the draft—writes of Lovecraft's potential claim of British citizenship on account of the paternal grandfather (George Lovecraft [1815–1895]), who never became a naturalized U.S. citizen and never renounced his British citizenship. Lockhart also states that the hectograph edition of the *Rhode Island Journal of Astronomy* was twenty-five copies, which leads me to wonder if there are still copies in private hands to delight the collector. Earlier in 2018, Necronomicon Press issued a facsimile edition of a previously unknown juvenile astronomical publication, *The Annual Report of the Science of Astronomy and Its Progress During 1903* (second edition, 1904). As for collectors, Sonia Davis writes that her husband's locks were kept after they were shorn (to the accompaniment of his mother's tears) at age six. Now there would be a find for the Lovecraft collector—a physical relic of the author himself!

3. De Camp and Joshi–Schultz both state that John T. Dunn belonged to the M.F. religious order—but the Missionaries of Faith were not established until 1992, long after he died. Perhaps de Camp misunderstood and should have written [O.]F.M.—Order of Friars Minor; i.e., Franciscans. Dunn spent most of his priestly career as a hospital chaplain in Portsmouth, Ohio, where de Camp interviewed him.

4. Paul Livingston Keil remembered only "another amateur journalist named Long" as an additional companion when he and Lovecraft and James F. Morton visited the Poe Cottage in Brooklyn in 1922. One wonders whether he barely remembered Long or disliked him.

5. To what extent was Lovecraft's March 1924 removal to Brooklyn a true "elopement"? He had announced his intention to relocate to New York in a letter to J. C. Henneberger dated as early as 2 February 1924. Muriel Eddy writes that Lovecraft visited her family the night before he left for New York and announced to them the gift of unneeded furniture, which arrived by express the very day of his removal. If these accounts are true, Lovecraft

had evidently announced to his aunts his decision to relocate permanently in New York before he left Providence. Apparently it was only his intended marriage to Sonia H. Greene that he kept secret from everyone except his partner.

6. George Kirk writes in his journal in October 1924 that HPL hanged himself after Sonia left and that "RK is in the tombs[7] for picking pockets." Both of these assertions, certainly the first, were fantasies meant only for Kirk's journal. More from the Kirk journal: in July 1926, he has dinner in Providence with HPL and a young bookseller interested in local history named Tycon. I believe Kirk has made a mistake for James A. Tyson (1901–1970), who founded his bookstore in Providence in 1923. So, in fact, Lovecraft knew each of the "big three" of Providence bookselling, including James A. Tyson, H. Douglass Dana, and Richard —— of what had become Dick's Bookshop on Richmond Street by the time I was in Providence in 1970–72. At one point, I had a copy of a newspaper obituary for Dick, but I have long since misplaced it. I also met Mary V. Dana, widow of H. Douglass Dana, who was still in business in their Old Corner Bookshop on Weybosset Street. Mrs. Dana, who has a short memoir of Lovecraft and Barlow in *Ave atque Vale*, was kind enough to let me browse in her upstairs workroom. She still had a few Lovecraft-related items to sell, including letters from Whipple V. Phillips to his grandson; but I purchased none of them.

7. Did Lovecraft visit Mystery Hill? H. Warner Munn claims vivid recollection of such a visit. But Munn is confused about other matters in his memoir, and may be confused about the claimed visit to Mystery Hill.

8. The usually reliable Harry K. Brobst conflates two streets when he writes of Guinea Gold branching off Benefit Street. Guinea and Gold were in fact two of the alleys or gangways between South Main and South Water Streets, which included others with names like Dime, Doubloon, and Silver. On the same page, the editors opine that Lovecraft and Brobst saw the so-called "Roger Williams root" at the Rhode Island School of Design Museum; in fact, I believe they saw it at the Rhode Island Historical Society Cabinet, then located on Waterman Street.

9. Amateur friend Ernest A. Edkins remarks of Lovecraft that

---

7. The Tombs was a municipal prison in New York City.

"his attitude toward the *risqué* was rather austere." Paul La Farge notwithstanding, I agree with Edkins and think that Lovecraft's only sexual experience (unless he was sexually abused by his mother) was probably with his wife. In his final letter to August Derleth, written in the summer of 1950, R. H. Barlow remarked that Lovecraft was the most asexual person he had ever encountered. He wrote to Derleth that Lovecraft's bias against sex—he allegedly called the sexual climax a "mere tickle"—hindered the development of his own sexuality. As an adult, Barlow was homosexual while Derleth was bisexual.

10. I have devoted much labor to Lovecraft's ancestry. However, Kenneth Sterling remarks succinctly: "Although Lovecraft was interested in genealogy, I don't think he took it seriously." I suspect that Wilfred B. Talman—next to James Morton perhaps the most ardent genealogist among Lovecraft's friends—would have agreed with Sterling. As a young man, Lovecraft was interested enough in his ancestry to copy crumbling family charts in 1905. He was happy to add new ancestors to his charts based on discoveries published by others, but was really not a researcher in his own right. I am not sure how Lovecraft would have reacted to changes in his genealogical charts necessitated by subsequent discoveries—e.g., losing Mary (Barrett) Dyer in his Casey line while gaining Ann (Marbury) Hutchinson in his Place line. I presume he would have been glad to welcome John Dryden and Nathaniel Hawthorne as remote relatives. As for the clergymen and landed squires he claimed in his direct paternal line, it appears they were actually mainly tenant farmers and weavers. Lovecraft probably laughed heartily when Frank Long showed him his cartoon depicting a group of dinosaurs as Lovecraft's ancestors. He probably would have valued such ancestors more highly than the Bible's Adam and Eve.

11. Clark Ashton Smith writes of Lovecraft's serving as "father-confessor to a young woman"—surely this was Helen V. Sully. In her own memoir, Sully recounts the famous episode of Lovecraft's frightening her during a late-night visit to St. John's Cemetery. Her description of the smile on Lovecraft's face in the wake of her fright is telling.

12. Not everyone cared for Lovecraft. Alfred Galpin quotes Hart Crane's disparaging remarks regarding "Sonia Greene's piping-voiced husband." Samuel Loveman also confirms that "neither

cared for the other." During his first decade in the amateur journalism hobby, Lovecraft engaged in many controversies—over pacifism, prohibition, the 1916 Irish rebellion, and other topics—but despite the harshness of the words exchanged, these disputes rarely ended in personal animosity. However, his strong belief that the focus of amateur journalism should be the literary education of its members rubbed some hobbyists, who mainly enjoyed it for its social aspects, the wrong way. Some members of the Columbus, Ohio "Woodbee" club felt that Lovecraft unduly favored his own friends when he served as the United's official editor in 1920–21. Anthony Moitoret and William Dowdell, then of Cleveland, shared the sentiments of some of the Woodbees. However, it was president Ida C. Haughton's allegation that Lovecraft mishandled the money in the official organ fund that infuriated Lovecraft. He wrote a poem, "Medusa: A Portrait," which depicted Haughton as a monster and drew an illustration of her (and other enemies in the amateur journalism hobby) hanging from a gibbet in his private correspondence. Lovecraft evinced no remorse when he learned that Mrs. Haughton had suffered fatal burns in a fire in 1933.

13. Although they both lived in New York City in 1924–26, Lovecraft never seems to have met his erstwhile foe Elsa Gidlow.[8] Gidlow had served as president of the rival United faction when Lovecraft was president of the so-called Hoffman–Daas faction in 1917–18. Lovecraft's amateur journalism foes scored a victory when they captured the offices in the Hoffman–Daas faction in the 1922 election. The National's executive judges offered him the consolation of their association's presidency when William Dowdell resigned later that year. While Lovecraft's party resumed control of the Hoffman–Daas United faction in the 1923 elections, the association never recovered and died a quiet death under Lovecraft's anointed successor, Edgar Davis, in 1925–26.

---

8. HPL objected mostly to what he considered to be Gidlow's literary and philosophical degeneracy. He reacted more instinctively to her colleague Roswell George Mills, who may have made indecent proposals to him in a letter that HPL shared with his correspondent Rheinhart Kleiner. HPL did instinctively dislike effeminacy in males and obesity in either sex. He disliked obesity in no one more than himself, and after he swelled to over 200 pounds during the initial months of his marriage, dieted himself down to 140, and maintained that weight for the rest of his life.

14. Who did what when in Lovecraft's life has always attracted notice. Rheinhart Kleiner lays claim to having introduced Lovecraft to his future wife on a harbor cruise at the National Amateur Press Association convention in Boston in 1921. On a lesser note, Wilfred B. Talman claims that as a student at Brown University in 1924 he introduced Lovecraft to the harbor-side diner Jacques' (a.k.a. Jake's), whose cheap and plentiful food the author came to love so well. Talman writes that Lovecraft got along especially well with the counterman Domingo at Jacques'. I wonder whether consulting a 1924 Providence directory might enable us to identify Domingo. In her memoir, Zealia Bishop recalls having lunch with Farnsworth Wright at Jacques' in Chicago—did Chicago also have a restaurant named Jacques' or was she confusing the location of her luncheon with Wright with Lovecraft's favorite diner? As far as I know, she never visited Lovecraft in Providence.

15. Talman also writes of having tea with Lovecraft and his wife Sonia at 10 Barnes Street. He states that the visit was "very unpleasant at times" and that Mrs. Lovecraft remarked that "cats are the only things H. really loves." It is possible that Sonia was more involved with her husband's life after he returned to Providence than most students of his life realize.

16. Among the who did what whens of Lovecraft's life is the issue of who attended his funeral services, which were held on Saturday, 18 March 1937, at Horace B. Knowles's Sons funeral home at 187 Benefit Street. De Camp (*Lovecraft: A Biography* 428) asserts that four persons were present: Annie Gamwell, Edna Lewis, Ethel Phillips Morrish, and Edward H. Cole. Joshi (*I Am Providence* 1009) writes that those present at the funeral home were Annie Gamwell, Edna Lewis, and Mr. & Mrs. Brobst. Brobst (325) emphatically asserts that he and his wife were present, although he erroneously recalls that the services took place at a Baptist church rather than a funeral home. Brobst asserts that Mrs. Gamwell declined his offer to accompany the small party to the burial at Swan Point Cemetery. Joshi asserts that Ethel Morrish and Edward H. Cole joined the funeral home party at the cemetery. Cole asserts that Annie Gamwell, a relative (presumably Ethel Morrish), and he were those present for Lovecraft's interment at Swan Point. Joshi states that Cliff and Muriel Eddy arrived late at the cemetery as the

hearse was leaving. So what is the truth of the matter? If the weather in Providence on March 18, 1937 was still wintry, Mrs. Gamwell may have excused some attendants at the wake from attending the interment. (Her friend Miss Lewis was only a few years younger than she.) If the funeral home gave a memorial book containing a "Those Who Called" page to Mrs. Gamwell, it is presumably still in private hands and its contents are unknown to me.

Another interesting question is whether any clergyman presided over the wake or the interment. Robie Phillips and her daughters had belonged to the First Baptist Church, so that if any clergyman was called upon, it makes sense that a Baptist might have been chosen. While he was himself an atheist, Lovecraft did choose to be married in an Episcopal church in New York City in 1924, probably in memory of his father's religious affiliation. Winfield Scott Lovecraft and Sarah Susan Phillips had been married in St. Paul's [Episcopal] Church on Tremont Street in Boston in 1889. Surviving correspondence reveals some of Mrs. Gamwell's feelings for her nephew; we have also her friend Marian Bonner's testimony for how deeply she felt for him. While one might wish that Edna Lewis (1868–1955) and Ethel Morrish (1888–1987) had been interviewed at length about Mrs. Gamwell and her nephew, perhaps they would have preferred to limit their testimony to something like the following: "Mrs. Gamwell was my dear friend/relative; Howard Lovecraft was her beloved nephew." Ordinary people have the privilege of taking their feelings with them to the grave. Mrs. Morrish (a first cousin once removed of Annie Gamwell) did live to attend the dedication of memorial stones for Lovecraft and his mother in the Phillips lot at Swan Point Cemetery in 1977. Dirk Mosig had led the campaign to fund the memorials.

17. Talman asserts that Lovecraft was no anti-Semite and Kenneth Sterling concurs, writing: "I never saw Lovecraft evidence in any way whatever a sign of racial or religious bigotry on a personal level." However, Samuel Loveman posthumously renounced his friendship with Lovecraft after he saw some of the things in Lovecraft's letters to Frank Long. Lovecraft's letters to his aunt Mrs. Clark contain even worse racial aspersions—for example, a speculation as to how much Mrs. Clark's maid-of-all-work Delilah Townsend (1870?–1944) might have fetched in the slave market.

Yet, as far as is known, Lovecraft was always polite to Mrs. Townsend, who had been in service with the Phillips family since the 1890s.[9] To his credit, Lovecraft never published his poem "On the Creation of Niggers," but to his demerit (despite his youth) he did write the poem and never saw fit to destroy the manuscript. As for the politics of the young man Lovecraft, Kleiner asserts that portraits of Robert E. Lee and Jefferson Davis adorned the walls of his study when he visited him in Providence in 1916. Kleiner attempted to hide his pipe, but Lovecraft's mother detected it, and stated her belief that smoking would be "soothing" for her son. Perhaps Winfield Scott Lovecraft had been a smoker.

18. Sonia Davis writes of her husband's love for the architectural drawings of George D. Laswell as published in the *Providence Journal*—of how her husband loved to seek out the places depicted after Laswell's sketches appeared in the newspaper. It may be worth noting that the Oxford Press of Providence published a collection of Laswell's *Corners and Characters of Rhode Island* in 1924.

19. The editors annotate Dorothy C. Walter's "Three Hours with H. P. Lovecraft" with the observation that their mutual friend may have been either Cook or Coates, but Walter herself writes that it was "Mr. Cook who had wanted us to meet." The title of this memoir seems somewhat inconsequential, but actually it is a delightful reminiscence, with hilarious accounts of Lovecraft's discovery that Walter's aunt was the bird lover who was urging the belling of Providence's cats in the newspaper, of Cook's desire to show Lovecraft the "real Vermont" after his experience of Brattleboro, and of Lovecraft's apology when he had to cancel an initial appointment because of the extreme cold. Walter's account of how she made bold to send Lovecraft an invitation to visit her absent their formal introduction is delightful.

The student of Lovecraft's life could go on and on with the fascinating sidelights provided by the memoirs assembled by Joshi and Schultz. *Ave atque Value* enjoys some advantages as a result of their able editorship. There is a thorough index compiled by Joshi.

---

9. Mrs. Townsend and her family lived for a time in the no-longer-extant colonial house at 6 Olney Street, which served as HPL's model for the town home of Joseph Curwen in *The Case of Charles Dexter Ward*. Mrs. Townsend is buried in Grace Church Cemetery in Providence.

Schultz has provided a bibliography that cites the original appearances of all the memoirs that he and his co-editor have collected. In addition, the editors have provided a section containing biographical sketches of virtually all the contributors. The editors have provided more than four hundred notes for the collected memoirs, and in general I believe they have provided exactly the right amount of annotation. In this day of Wikipedia and other online resources, there is really no need to annotate something like Boston's Old City Hall (45 School Street), which Lovecraft and Cook visited. Lovecraft would probably have abhorred its French Second Empire architecture. If someone wants to know that a Ruth's Chris steakhouse is among the current tenants, it's best to let him pursue his own researches. Lovecraft seems to have had a virtually unlimited capacity for ice cream, but I suspect that he might have found a steak at Ruth's Chris somewhat overwhelming.

The editors do helpfully provide corrections—most of them dates—when the memoirists' memories have gone astray. One error they don't catch is W. Paul Cook's assertion that Lovecraft survived William Clemence—actually, the reverse is true and Clemence died in 1938. He wrote of his intention to write a memoir of Lovecraft, but to my knowledge he never did pen such an account. Sonia Davis states that Commodore Abraham Whipple was her husband's ancestor, but in fact he was only a collateral relative (meaning that he and Lovecraft shared a common ancestor). In the note on page 119, the editors state that Lovecraft's uncle Edwin E. Phillips died in his sixties, but in fact he was fifty-four when he died in Providence City Hospital in November 1918. Little-mentioned uncle Edwin deserves the attention of a thorough researcher. I found out from a Providence businesswoman and Rotarian that Edwin was an early member of the Providence Rotary chapter.

As a bonus, the editors have provided poetical tributes to Lovecraft written by his friends August Derleth, Samuel Loveman, and Clark Ashton Smith soon after Lovecraft died. These poems are reproduced first in facsimile, and then in transcribed form. All three of the poetic tributes chosen by the editors for publication in *Ave atque Vale* reflect heartfelt emotions; however, there is no doubt that Clark Ashton Smith's tribute "To Howard Phillips Lovecraft" is the best of the three.

There is little need to compare and to contrast the Joshi-Schultz and Cannon editions of biographical memoirs of Lovecraft. The thoroughgoing Lovecraftian will need to have them both. However, as Arkham House has receded from activity as a publisher, it is good to have Joshi's and Schultz's *Ave atque Vale* widely available through Amazon.com and other vendors. The Joshi–Schultz compilation offers the advantages of a thorough index, copious annotations, bibliography, and biographical sketches of memoirists. For the thorough student of Lovecraft's life, there is no substitute for Joshi's two-volume biography *I Am Providence*,[10] but both *Ave atque Vale* and *Lovecraft Remembered* suggest that there is room for republication of shorter biographical surveys. Scott's "His Own Most Fantastic Creation" (1944), Derleth's *H.P.L.: A Memoir* (Ben Abramson, 1945), Long's *Howard Phillips Lovecraft: Dreamer on the Nightside* (Arkham House, 1975), and Shea's *In Search of Lovecraft* (Necronomicon Press, 1991)[11] would make a valuable omnibus volume of shorter biographical writings on Lovecraft. Joshi gathered many of the classic critical essays on Lovecraft in *H. P. Lovecraft: Four Decades of Criticism* (Ohio University Press, 1980), but a new, more readily available edition would help to add to the critical essays included there and in *Lovecraft Remembered*.

Is there an overall impression left from perusing the many varied memoirs that comprise *Ave atque Vale*? For me, it is the sense of *progression* in Lovecraft's life. There is little question that he was a sheltered and overprotected child who suffered under the dominion of a disturbed mother. Once and only once, he admitted to his wife how devastating his mother's influence had been. From this childhood emerged a rather narrow and pedantic young man who found no real place in adult life until he was recruited for the Hoffman–Daas faction of the United Amateur Press Association

---

10. In fact, there are multiple versions of Joshi's biography available. *I Am Providence* (Hippocampus Press, 2010) is more than half again the size of *H. P. Lovecraft: A Life* (Necronomicon Press, 1996). Joshi has also published a moderately abridged version of his original biography under the title *A Dreamer and a Visionary: H. P. Lovecraft and His Time* (Liverpool University Press, 2001) and a radically abridged version under the title *H. P. Lovecraft: A Short Biography* (Sarnath Press, 2018). While largely supplanted by Joshi's work, de Camp's *H. P. Lovecraft: A Biography* (1975) still offers its own unique perspectives.

11. Shea also published a shorter account of HPL titled "H. P. Lovecraft: The House and the Shadows" in the *Magazine of Fantasy and Science Fiction* (May 1966).

in 1914. From the fierce controversies of his early amateur years to the tangled politics that emerged between his United (1917–18) and his National (1922–23) presidencies, Lovecraft lived and learned. While the 1925 Brooklyn promenades of the Kalems in their Sunday finest, with canes, still seem rather juvenile, Lovecraft learned to navigate the social web with appropriate interactions. He gained the experience of a marriage, of a wife who could alternatively love and nourish him and accuse him of caring more for cats than for any human being. I agree with W. Paul Cook that the trials and tribulations of Lovecraft's years in New York City (1924–26) were a transformative experience for the author. By the time he resumed amateur activity by attending the National's 1930 Boston convention, he was more or less an elder statesman, but still he did yeoman's service on the critical bureau (1931–35; chairman, 1933–35) and as an executive judge (1935–36).[12]

Lovecraft invested a major portion of his time and energy to assist young writers and to help to develop talents like Derleth, Wandrei, Bloch, and Leiber. Years afterward, Derleth found the memories evoked by the intricate script of Lovecraft's letters haunting.[13] However, Lovecraft invested equal time with correspondents like the elderly poet Elizabeth Toldridge. Lovecraft had nearly one hundred active correspondents at the time of his death, and there were probably many in addition to Miss Toldridge for whom Lovecraft's letters were literally the light of their lives. His premature passing left a tremendous sense of loss that can be sensed in many of the memoirs left by his friends and correspondents. Lovecraft the atheist would not care to be the subject of a saint's life, but since criticism of Lovecraft as a racist and even as a sexual predator has become more and more strident, a sense of balance needs to be restored. He did progress from the young man who hung portraits of Robert E. Lee and Jefferson Davis in his study to the mature thinker who supported a moderate form of socialism and the recovery efforts of the Franklin Roosevelt administration.

---

12. It was HPL's second term as a National executive judge. He had previously served in this office in 1923–24.

13. See his poem "On Reading Old Letters: For H.P.L.," in *In Lovecraft's Shadow: The Cthulhu Mythos Stories of August Derleth*, ed. Joseph Wrzos (Sauk City, WI & Shelburne, ON: Mycroft & Moran, 1998), 341.

His personal interactions grew richer and more nuanced as his life progressed. Had he survived to middle age, the revelation of the horrors of the Holocaust in the wake of World War II might have cured him fully of any erstwhile prejudices he may have entertained against the Jews. Had he survived to be an old man, perhaps the struggles of the civil rights and the equal rights movements would have helped him modify his attitudes toward blacks and women and for that matter all minorities. As a young man, he had called the leaders of the American Revolution traitors. He did eventually learn to moderate his expressions of regret for the American Revolution and especially his expressions of disapproval of the American patriots. While retaining his Anglophilism, perhaps he would eventually have abandoned his disapproval of the political separation of Mother England and her colonies. The cancer that killed him prematurely deprived us of witnessing all these possibilities. The testimony of his friends in *Ave atque Vale* helps us to conceptualize the man he really was—a genius and an outstanding human being despite all his very human defects. If there is any aspect of Lovecraft's life that the memoirs in *Ave atque Vale* neglect, it is probably his thought and in particular his cosmic perspective. We must leave it to the critics of the past, the present, and the future to elucidate this important aspect of Lovecraft's life.

Finally, it is good to see the return of Necronomicon Press as a book publisher with the publication of *Ave atque Vale*. Necronomicon has issued this book both in hardcover (100-copy limited edition) and trade paperback format. The frontispiece is a photograph of Lovecraft dated 11 July 1931, presumably snapped (by Henry S. Whitehead?) in Dunedin, Florida, while Lovecraft was visiting there. I hope to see more new books from Necronomicon Press and more new collections of critical and biographical writing on H. P. Lovecraft in the future. The richness of Lovecraft scholarship available today is amazing compared with what was available when I first encountered Lovecraft's work in 1964. If future readers and scholars have an even greater richness of resources available when the bicentennial of Lovecraft's birth arrives in 2090, it will certainly be due, at least part, to the work of scholars such as Joshi and Schultz. *Ave atque Vale* comes highly recommended as a significant contribution toward achieving this goal.

CPSIA information can be obtained
at www.ICGtesting.com
Printed in the USA
BVHW081314080819
555374BV00005B/11/P